ANTUAN VANCE

THE CATALYST

BOOK ONE

 Smoking Rose
Publishing

Copyright © 2014 Antuan J. Vance
Published in 2015 by Smoking Rose Publishing

Printed in the United States of America

This book contains quotations exclusively from the King James Bible, which is public domain, and no other versions or translations of the Holy Bible.

ISBN: 0692406018
ISBN-13: 978-0692406014

www.AntuanVance.com

Cover art by Mykey Maker. http://www.mykeymadeit.com

To my phenomenal mother, who is a constant support in my life and has helped shape me into the person I am today, and Lisa Baldwin, who continues to be my most reliable and loving friend, thank you. You are my true and great gifts from God.

TABLE OF CONTENTS

ACKNOWLEDGMENTS

Special, humble thanks go to God the Father, Jehovah, Yahweh, Elohim, from whom my literary talent and best words came. Without Him, these pages and my mind would have been blank. I would have been overcome by laziness, distraction, and writer's block. Father, you are my inspiration, my everything.

A huge thank you to my brother, Mykey Maker, for the fantastic cover art. His talent pool is immense.

A special thank you to my church and all my church friends praying for me and the success of my book, even though they haven't read it.

I want to thank my talented friend Jackie Zantow for her moral support during the writing process. The time we spent together thwarting evil minions and bosses helped tremendously in easing the loneliness that comes with being me.

And of course, there is Anna Read, a friend and fellow aspiring novelist. I am truly grateful and blessed to have her honest criticisms, concerns, and thoughts on my manuscript. The truth refines and purifies.

To my small circle of friends and family: *You are fantastic, radiant, and full of potential. You are fearfully and wonderfully made. I love you. God bless you, wherever you may be.*

PROLOGUE

THE GOOD DOCTOR AND HIS BIRD sat at the top of an open stairwell. He suffered from three gunshot wounds: one in his right shoulder and two in his left thigh. Blood soaked his black "U2 Joshua Tree" T-shirt and blue jeans. A white poplin lab coat was wrapped around his hands.

Within those hands, he held the future of the world: a small crystalline sphere with five metallic rings, each ring connected to the next by a set of five circuits. In its center was a slowly swirling and pulsing green cloud. Its hum was soothing for the soul. He planted the sphere, which he called the catalyst, in a small, black pouch attached to the leg of his messenger bird, Sasha.

BAAM!! Eleven men with assault rifles blew themselves into the stairwell and stormed up the steps.

With the cavalry arriving, the good doctor whispered special instructions, wished Sasha well, and sent her on her way. She flew fast, if not erratically, into the night. She was heading west, first to the Blue Ridge Mountains, and then furthermore beyond the quarantined zones, north of the devastations, across the dead Mississippi and barren plains, to the Rockies.

In the remaining seconds before the boots reached the top level, the good doctor took out a metal flask full of milk and chugged as much of the contents as he could, which was all of it.

The men, soldiers of the North American Union, stormed the top of the stairwell in their red, white, and blues and surrounded the thirsty doctor. Their laser-sighted assault rifles were inches from his face. The commander in charge was named Collins. He had a muscular physique, long dark hair, a thick beard, and bright red battle scars on the right side of his face. The nostrils of his broad nose flared. He ordered all but one of the ten men to continue through the doorway to the rooftop and check for any sign of the catalyst, which they didn't find.

Collins hovered over the doctor. His face locked in a snarl, staring without blinking like a haunted portrait. After five minutes of searching, the soldiers delivered the bad news, with the exception of one, who said he saw a bird. It didn't register. Collins leaned in close to the doctor, his breath smelling of bad cheese, onions, and beer, and began what would be his shortest interrogation. "Where is the orb, Brown?"

"Really?" The good doctor, Brown, coughed and shook his head. "They say there are no dumb questions, but that takes the cake." Collins's eyes shot open. "I go through all of this and you think I'll just tell you where it is if you ask? It's gone. You hear me? It's gone. You're playing with technology you don't understand, but they do. They most definitely do, and they're using you. You're all puppets. You're going to kill us all with that device."

Collins didn't like being called dumb or being talked down to by a civilian scientist, let alone a filthy traitor saboteur. Being called a puppet? No, sir! Not in his house. Who's house? Collins's house. He leaned back, raised his right hand to his left shoulder, and applied a wide ranging backhanded slap to the doctor's face, making sure he put all his strength into it.

Brown's head bounced against the stairwell wall. Blood collected in his mouth. He spat and sagged.

Collins straightened Brown and leaned forward once more. "I can do this all day, Brown, but you've been shot and must be losing a lot of blood." He said *must be*, because oddly enough, he didn't see as much blood coming out of the man as he thought he should and that was suspicious. Yet, he let that go. "Don't you want to live to see your dog-ugly grandchildren through prison bars?"

"If you get your hands on the sphere, there will be no grandchildren for any of us," Brown argued.

"Lies!" Collins shot back. "We're saving our future children. That device is going to heal our planet and undo the damage of the Red."

"They're here, Collins," Brown insisted. "They're here in this facility. They've taken over your minds. All those changes Andrews, Cartwright, Zenji, and Prost made against my recommendations changed the device against us. It's going to change the world into something else. That's why I'm doing this." He pointed at himself. "Me! I'm the guy that brought the sphere here in the first place. I started this project and hired everyone. Even you. It's mine. It's always been mine. Don't you get that? Don't you understand? The world itself is dying. It was my responsibility to save it. And once you've activated that device, with their alterations, we're goners. There will be nothing left but them."

"Enough!" Collins screamed from the top of his lungs and stomped the stair he stood on. "No more lies. Tell me where the orb is or I will end you!"

Weak, but defiant, Brown raised his chin and stared into Collin's fierce brown eyes, "Then it ends here, with us, but the world will live on another day."

A gust of cold air blew through the door leading to the rooftop. Collins commanded, "Shut that door! Leave us alone and find that bird, if there ever was one." They followed his orders without hesitation or question. In a minute's pass, the two were alone.

Collins leaned close and said, "You have a tasty looking little daughter, Doctor. You're going to tell me where the device is or I'll find her. I'll get a good hold of her. Spoil her. Twist her tight little tits. Pass her around my men. We'll have her squealing like a little *pig whore*. Then, when I'm tired of her, I'll beat her to death."

"You're a dog, Collins," Brown said and spat blood onto the commander's face.

Collins recoiled and then swung his right fist as hard as he could into the left side of Brown's face, breaking his jaw and bursting his left eye socket. After doing such, Collins stomped Brown's chest and rained down a long series of vulgarities Brown chose to neither hear nor comprehend.

Of all the things to be grateful for, Brown was glad he had the ability to deactivate pain with a simple thought.

After a minute, Collins stopped and stared down at his victim. His nostrils flared and sweat beamed off his massive forehead.

Sagged against the stairwell wall, Brown thought of his daughter Abigail, his protégé Levi, and the wolf, Jared. Their journey would begin along the same path Sasha was taking beyond the western mountains. If activated without the orb, the device would destroy millions of lives, but those three would be safe. She would be safe.

He smiled and breathed out one hard, long breath,

which Collins thought was his last. Then, he willed himself into a hibernating state.

In his idle state, Brown listened to the harsh breath of his opponent, the orders he issued over his radio, and waited.

CHAPTER ONE
SAFE HAVEN

"FLICK," WAS THE SOUND OF THE LIGHT SWITCH and the room flooded with photons. Abbey could feel her consciousness rushing forward, her dream-state slipping away, and didn't want to believe what was happening. *No! Not now,* she thought. With all her mental might, Abbey struggled to hold on to the final moment. His strong arms had pulled her towards him. He was just about to kiss her.

"Wake up, honey. You have to wake, now," a deep, strong voice urged while shaking her left shoulder.

She pulled the pink blanket to her neck and blinked her light blue eyes to the familiar, wrinkled face of her father. "Ugh, I'm tired," she mumbled. It came out as *tiiiiiired* in a drawn out whine. She turned over and attempted to continue her slumber. "Let the rooster crow."

"I wish I could honey. I wish I could, but I can't, so get up."

"Awwwww," she whined and yawned. She pulled the blanket over her golden blond head. "I don't wanna," she continued, her words muffled under the blanket.

7

"God have mercy on our souls," he pleaded to the Lord under his breath before completely pulling the blanket off the bed, almost yanking her off too as he tossed it on the floor. "Abigail Lynn! This is an emergency situation. Get up, now!"

What the? Her eyes blasted open, disbelieving. She shot straight up, almost giving herself whiplash, and looked into the desperate man's eyes. As far back as she could remember—and though she hadn't put much thought into it, she had a flawless, photographic memory—the only emergency situation they'd ever had was when her grandmother died of radiation poisoning, a gift from the Red War. Even then, he never pulled a stunt like this. "What the heck, dad?" She pointed at the clock; her eyes were still adjusting to the light to see it clearly. "It's way too early o'clock in the morning. What's going on?"

Ignoring her question, which annoyed her, he went to her closet and pulled out her emergency backpack, supply satchel, and other accessories, which he stockpiled in her otherwise organized closet. He told her they should be prepared months in advance for the day he knew was soon coming, without giving any specifics as to what exactly was going to happen. "Tomorrow is just a matter a time", he'd said, as if that meant anything. He tossed the backpack and satchel on the bed and briefly ran to the window, peering into the cloud-filled, moonless darkness. "There's no time to explain it all, right now. I've already explained it in my notes, which are in your satchel. You'll have to listen to it on the way. Now, get dressed. Make it in layers, heavy for cold weather, and light for warmer weather, but not too heavy so it impairs travel on foot."

Dress in layers? Travel on foot? Abbey thought, shaking her head and refusing to be afraid. She remembered the horror stories he told her of the war. The mass destruction, death, and panic that swept the planet leaving billions dead, millions of sick people drifting for years before civilization finally collected itself. Looking at the backpack, satchel, and her father's erratic behavior, she raised her hands, palms forward, as if to slow someone's forward momentum or push them away. "Dad, what's going on? I need some information. You can't just barge in here, wake me up, and start, like, I don't know, flipping out without telling me what's going on. I'm an adult now, in, two days. I need to know what's going on."

Frustrated—at least, he looked frustrated—he turned from the window and checked his watch. Someone was late. He checked his phone. No messages. He put his right hand over his eyes and sighed. "Okay." He took a minute to compose his thoughts while eyeballing his watch. Every minute counted, and if he could pay for it, he'd willingly spend a drop of his blood for every minute he turned backward to give them more time. "The Red are back. Well, technically, they were never completely gone, just in hiding. The last few survivors of a dying race hemmed up in our corner of the world, waiting for us to get comfortable. They've taken over our research facility, and the restoration device, and are going to use it against us."

Abbey felt her heart briefly stop. A chill rose up her body.

"At six o'clock," her father pointed to the clock, "three hours and twenty-two minutes from now, every human being within a hundred mile radius of our research facility is going to die." He stopped. She could tell he was weighing her response, which was a mixture of terror, shock, and horror. Everyone she knew was about to die. "For now, you're going to a safe, secret bunker with Levi ninety miles northwest of here—"

As she commonly did, either without realization or care, Abbey interrupted. "Levi? What about you, dad? Aren't you coming with us? Won't you die here?"

"—in the Blue Ridge Mountains and the Quarantine Zone—"

She held up her hand again. "Wait, wait, wait, wait, wait. We're going into the Quarantine Zone to get *away* from trouble? It's death out there."

"He's going to keep you there," he continued, "and safe until it is okay to move again. Then, you're going to Montana—"

"Hold on! Montana? How are we supposed to get to Montana from the Blue Ridge Mountains? That means we'd cross the Devastation Zone, and, the Rogue Districts, and, the barren plains. How will we survive?"

"I have a facility there designed to support you two long-term, in the event the restoration now destruction device does as much damage as I expect it very well will."

She shook her head.

"After all these years, and despite my strong grasp of medical science, I am amazed that head of yours hasn't come unhinged," her father said.

Abbey pursed her lips. "You didn't answer my questions. Why aren't you coming?"

"Start getting dressed and I'll explain, okay? In layers. Underlings, tees, jeans, jacket, preferably something with a hood. Make sure you have plenty of pockets. You'll need a lot of pockets. You get the idea, right? Survival wear. Your best stuff. You won't be able to come back here."

"Wait. What?"

"Get dressed, Abbey!"

"Okay! Okay!" She rushed to her walk-in closet, partially closed the door so she could get dressed in privacy, and prospected her wardrobe, which was more than fair in size compared to most people this day and age. "But, you're coming with me, right?"

"No, honey, I'm not. Levi is. As you know, I have been working on the restoration device, the cradle as I call it, for years. I have a responsibility to finish what I started. I have a responsibility to stop them from killing everyone; and I'll try my best. However, it can't involve you and you won't be safe here. I suspect you won't be completely safe until you reach Montana."

Briefly, she stuck her head around her closet door. "But I'm going to see you again, right? You're coming to Montana, right?"

He smiled and said, "Yes, of course," but his eyes said otherwise. His eyes were solemn and dark. The hazel of his eyes had faded, as though death was so inevitable it had already taken claim of his body and sheer will alone allowed him to warn his daughter. His eyes said: This is it, kid. This is the last time you'll see your father. Soak it up. Take a picture; it'll last longer. And in that moment, standing there half-kept in her closet, Abbey recorded an image of the man she would always love and compare every man to: the strong, brown and silver-haired, oval-headed scientist in his long, white lab coat. Lukas Brown.

2

Fifteen long minutes later, Levi pulled up in his black sedan, hopped out of his car, and jogged to the front door. Abbey, who was crying, smiled and turned from the window. Outside of Christmases, and her dreams (Yes, her dreams, those were some steamy dreams), she hadn't seen Levi in the last three years. She announced his arrival to her father, who then returned with an angry, "It's about time."

He raced to the door to meet Levi while she checked

her room one more time for anything that was unforgettable and irreplaceable, which was everything. She wanted to take every single possession with her. If she could fit the walls in her bag, she would grab an axe and go to town on the foundation of this place. She loved her home. She loved her bed, pillows, blankets, dressers, and the Yoda lamp her father gave her ("Bright, your room is. Sleep, you must," her father would say any time the lamp was on after bedtime). She collected all of her mother's jewelry, a small supply of blushes, eyeliners, lipstick, tampons, and maxi-pads. Her father, perhaps the most intriguing and disturbing man on the planet, which wasn't necessarily a bad thing, insisted on covering every detail of her necessities and actually bought her a new jumbo pack of pads, tampons, and birth control. Yes, birth control. She wasn't even active, yet.

He asked a lot of questions. Were she and her boyfriend Jeremy—a relationship she thought she'd kept pretty discreet and off his radar—engaging in premarital sex? When was the last time she had her period? Did she have any tingling in the back of her neck? Were her eyes, at any point, growing sensitive? Was her vision in any way changing, either improving or declining? Did she detect any changes in her hearing? There had to have been twenty more questions from Doctor Dad, always the good doctor, she refused to recollect for her own sanity. She didn't intend on giving an answer to the first two questions, no matter how important he claimed they were or embarrassed she was being asked them. The rest were simple, if not confusing. Before he could ask more questions, her father looked at his watch and wondered where the heck—not hell, but heck, since her father never once swore around her—Levi was.

Levi's arrival was a relief. No more uncomfortable questions.

Those questions did raise a question she hadn't quite thought of in the twenty or so minutes she'd been awake. If she was leaving, and everyone would be dead in three hours, wouldn't that include her boyfriend, Jeremy, and her best friend, Violet?

The front door swung open after the first rap. It was followed by another, "It's about time." Levi, whose voice was deeper than she remembered, was full of apologies, mentioning something about a downed tree in the road. That didn't come off as an acceptable excuse to her father, who was short on time. They were all short on time.

Abbey peeked around the corner, into the hallway, to catch a glimpse of Levi. He grew a good five inches taller since the last time she'd seen him and was now three inches over her father. It also looked like he gained twenty or thirty pounds. She was never good at gaging weight, but from the size of his neck, arms, and chest, it was definitely all muscle. His russet brown skin-tone was slightly blushed.

His hazel eyes shifted from her father to her, he winked, and then looked back at her father. She blushed, because he caught her staring at him (Did he know she was staring at him? Perhaps he just thought she was eavesdropping on their conversation? Why wasn't she eavesdropping on their conversation?), and slipped back into her room as her father turned around to see what he was winking at.

"Is your eye okay?" her father asked. Levi responded with a yes before continuing on with the details of their plans. Plans she should have been listening to.

She willed herself to stop thinking of him—she had a boyfriend for Christ's sake—and to focus on what they were saying.

"Is she active, yet?" Levi asked. Her eyes shot wide

open, shocked. Was he asking if she was sexually active? No. There was no way he would ask such a thing, especially to her father. Did Abbey wonder if that was what he meant? Yes. What else would they be talking about?

"No," her father responded, "She's still dormant, besides the basics. I scanned her and it showed nothing. Even so, I still asked her some questions. You can tell from her eyes, though."

"Those bright, baby blues," Levi said with a smile.

"Yea. The C-I-C or catalyst will change that, assuming I don't get myself killed trying to get it out of their hands."

"If I came with you, we could stop this before it starts," Levi suggested.

"I told you," her father lectured. "There's only one way to stop it now. Protecting her and getting her to safety is your number one responsibility. You know how important, how special, she is. You handle your end and I'll handle mine."

"Even if it gets you killed?"

Abbey wanted to open her big mouth and yell, "Even if you get killed?" like an angry echo. Yet, somehow, she managed to keep her trap shut so she could hear his response.

"Yes, though I'm aiming for survival, even if it gets me killed. If the prospect of getting killed ever held me hesitant from doing what's necessary, they'd have won two decades ago in the Red War. I never know how things are going to end, or whether I'll walk out alive; all I know is that I have to finish what I started and you have to take my daughter to Montana. That's all that matters. Now, let's get out of here before we talk ourselves outside of our deadlines and the whole plan goes to heck."

14

The two walked to Abbey's room. She scuttled back to her bed on her tip toes and reached for her bags. As her father came through the door, she lifted her emergency backpack, full of first aid and outdoors survival essentials. It had to weigh a hundred pounds. She was sure of it. Knowing her father, a man that didn't know his own strength, it was probably two hundred pounds. She struggled to get it on her back; so her father rushed to her and took it from her.

"Abbey, Levi. Levi, Abbey. It's been a while. Yep. Nice to see you again. Yep, you too. Great. You two can get reacquainted in the car," her father said, mimicking a fake conversation between the two. He tossed the emergency backpack to Levi with little effort. Levi caught it one handed and swung it around his back.

Her mouth dropped open. *I know I'm not that weak!* She thought.

Levi grabbed her black and pink polka-dot luggage and tilted his head towards the door. She grabbed her brown leather satchel and followed him out of her room. She turned around one last time, wondering if her father was right when he said she wouldn't be back. She blinked back tears, said goodbye to her room, and then followed Levi to the front door. Her father followed them.

At the front door, Abbey stopped and looked at her father. As long as she could remember, he was always there. It was hard, very hard, for her to believe that she wouldn't see him again. Her heart ached. She felt tears swelling in her eyes again. She tried to fight them back but was no match for her emotions. She gave up the fight and let the tears run rapid down her face. Part of her was glad she hadn't put on makeup. Otherwise, she'd look like a clown.

Her father opened his arms. She fell into them and hugged him. There they stood for a minute, father and daughter, in one final embrace. He kissed her tear marked cheek, her forehead, and her blond-haired head. "The first time I saw you. I said to myself, 'Behold! The Father has given me a child, the last angel of a dying world.' In all my life, you are the most beautiful sight I have ever seen. You are my crowning achievement. I love you so much."

"I love you too, daddy," she sobbed. Tears poured down her face, her face buried in his shoulder.

"I love you, too," Levi called from the background. They all laughed.

Her father waved Levi over to them, "Get over here, quick." Levi came and joined in the hug. "I could be no prouder of a son from my own loins than I am of you."

Abbey broke the hug and yelled, "Eww! No dad, gross!" Then, she covered her ears and walked away.

Levi laughed. "Tell me how you really feel, you nasty old dog."

Her father backed away, a line of tears coming from his smiling face. "You've always been a good kid. I never had to fight you or struggle with teen angst. You know how to listen. You use your head. You're smart, honorable, brave, and strong. You have so much integrity, kid. You just don't know. I look at you, and I know, without a doubt, that your father would be so proud of the man you've become. It has been an honor raising you as my own. I wouldn't trust anyone else in the world to take care of my princess."

"You give me too much credit. I was a pain in the old meat sack and you know it, but thank you. You have been and are the best father a boy could hope for."

Her father, the good doctor Brown, who operated under another alias at the time, unofficially adopted Levi as his own son after his best friend, Jeremiah Jones, died in the war and Jeremiah's wife, Kennedy, died from radiation poisoning. Levi could have, would have, should have died weeks after her, but Brown intervened for his best friend's sake.

The two stared at each other, nodding, paying each other silent respects. It occurred to her that her father was not just saying goodbye to the young man he raised, but also to his best friend, Jeremiah, Levi's father, all over again.

They had their moment and then, without an added word, Levi walked to his car and her father into the house. Abbey stood there curious if she'd missed something, as if they'd spoken in a language she didn't understand, the language of men, or through a means she was not capable. Nevertheless, she said goodbye to her house and followed Levi to his sedan. He opened the passenger door for her, closed it when she was inside— the black leather interior was incredibly soft—and got into the driver's seat.

The sedan's engine growled like a threatening jungle cat and then they were on the move, onward to the mountains. At least, that's what Levi and her father thought. She, having realized she didn't want to say goodbye to anyone else, had other plans.

3

As the car drove away from the Brown Manor, and down the decadent streets of old Richmond, Levi reached for the computerized dashboard. His hand was slapped.

"Hey!" Levi complained and re-extended his hand towards the player. It was slapped, again. "What? Why are you hitting me?"

Abbey, lips pursed, held up a finger. "Wait. I have to ask you something."

"Hold on. Your dad said I am to play this as soon as

we got on the road." Again, he reached for the player. It was slapped, a third time. "Stop."

"Listen, first. I have to ask you something," she requested.

"Instead of saying you have to ask me something, just ask me," he reached for the player again and she slapped his hand a fourth time. "We have to listen to this. It's extremely important information, considering our current circumstances."

"Just stop trying to turn it on, Lee." It was rarely Levi from her. Since she was one, she called him Lee. For him, she was rarely Abbey, but Abigail. "I need your undivided attention," Abbey insisted.

This time, he kept both hands on the steering wheel; but he looked at her crossly. "Okay. Go on."

"We have to make a stop at my boyfriend's house and pick him up," Abbey said.

Considering Levi wasn't aware Abbey had a boyfriend (Was this news intentionally kept from him because he had feelings for the good doctor's daughter?), this news was a slap in the face. He recoiled and nearly veered off the road to the right. He overcompensated by veering to the left and then corrected himself and returned to the center of his lane.

"I'm sorry; did you say, 'stop and pick up your boyfriend' or are my audio receptors failing me?" Levi asked incredulously, mimicking his long-time friend, Artie, an android.

"Maybe I should drive," Abbey suggested with a frown on her face. She clamped on to the seat of her chair and braced herself for a collision.

Levi shook his head. "Nope. Not happening." *Not yet, anyway,* he thought.

"Well, then, drive straight. No point in going through all of this if I'm going to be killed in a reckless car crash."

There were a lot of ways he could have responded to that remark, he was sure, but Levi honestly couldn't think of any. His mind was still wrestling with the fact that she had a boyfriend. Abigail, his beloved Abigail, had a boyfriend. A boyfriend?

Of course, it made sense. She was a beautiful young woman with a cute butt and fair-sized chest for someone so thin. Unlike most people, she was completely healthy with no afflictions, bruising, rashes, acne, breathing complications, abnormal growths, mutations, or otherwise due to the radiation in the atmosphere and water. Unlike most people, medical enhancements protected her from the harmful effects of their current, post-Red War environment.

(In regards to those enhancements, she was completely oblivious; and her father did not want her to become aware until she absolutely needed to.)

"Lee."

Yep, she was flawless, like some Disney movie princess, with her pink, softly tanned skin, long golden blond hair, pixie-like facial features, and big brilliant blue eyes. Those eyes were magic blue, like some conjured up masterpieces of wizardry from Merlin himself, crystal balls of epic consequence.

"Lee?"

Of course, she would have a boyfriend. Any guy would be out of his mind if he didn't appreciate her perfect and delicate skin, the glossiness of her hair, or her sweet smell, even when she didn't wear perfume. Was it pheromones? It had to be pheromones. She smelled like a meadow full of alyssums and gardenia on some days and a fruity mixture of mango and coconut on others.

She was to die for. Men would line up against a wall and get shot down for a woman like her. Men would traverse across an endless desert for a glimpse of her beauty, a whiff of her hair, and to manage a kiss on her cheek. Oh, to kiss her lips might give a man a heart attack, put him in a coma, and have him wandering in the halls of the in-between of life and death, standing face to face with a door full of light that led to the afterlife. How could any man resist that soft, high, and queerly pleasant voice? She was perfection incarnate, no disrespect intended to our Lord and Savior Jesus Christ.

Abbey repeated his name three times, each time louder than the last. He drove, eyes on the road, mind in his thoughts. He held a glazed, glassy expression, which bore resemblance to a man under hypnosis. Eventually she screamed, "LEVI!"

That broke him out of his daze. Once more, he swerved and then recovered. It occurred to him that, had he driven this way two hours ago, he probably would have been pulled over by one of the street patrolmen. He shook his head and turned to her. "What?"

"What the heck, Lee?" Abbey complained. "Are you ignoring me? You're about to pass my boyfriend's street. Turn right at the next light." She pointed ahead, frowning.

"Your father gave me strict instructions to take you, and only you, to the mountains." It occurred to him, after saying that, that while her father, the good doctor, said to take her to the mountains, he did not exclude anyone else from joining them. He simply implied that Abigail was Levi's primary concern. To this thought, Levi frowned. "All the provisions and plans we made were for two people. You and me."

"I don't care, Lee. We're picking up Jeremy. He's my boyfriend. I can't just leave him here to die. And, my best friend lives right next to him. So, we're picking her up, too."

"No. No we're not."

"Yes!" Abbey insisted. "Yes we are."

"The rations, radiation shielding, tent, gear, even the travel schedule were all setup for two people. This car runs on blue energy, but it has range limits before it has to self-replicate. The added weight of more people will mean we'll have to stop more and it'll slow us down."

"What is blue electricity?" Abbey asked. "You're making stuff up so you don't have to pick them up and you're about to miss the turn! Why don't you want to help them?"

"It's not that, but—" Actually, it was partly that. He looked forward to spending time with her, alone, and traveling across the countryside, alone. It was supposed to be *their* time. She was supposed to laugh at his jokes. He had prepared several playlists. Now, he had to deal with a boyfriend *and* her best friend? She wasn't going to have any time with him. There would be no him and her. "We'll need more food. Where will they sleep? The tent isn't made for more than two full-sized adults." *And a wolf,* he thought, thinking of Jared, but did not say. "We can't just stop in the barren plains and check into a hotel."

"We'll figure something out," Abbey said. "We'll get food along the way. What we're not going to do is leave them here to die. It's not going to happen. My dad wouldn't want that."

"There's not enough time!" Levi exclaimed. "They're going to want, no, *need* an explanation. They'll have to pack. We're behind schedule as it is. If we stop, we might not make it at all. Then, we'll all die."

"I don't care." She unlocked her car door. "This isn't a negotiation, Lee. They're coming with us or I'm staying with them."

Levi locked her door. "That's crazy. You'll die. Why would you even consider that alternative?"

"I'd rather die than leave Jeremy here to die," Abbey replied. She unlocked and opened her door. The cement below her moved at an alarming speed.

Despite his instincts to slow down when the car door opened, Levi didn't. If he slowed down, it would make it easier for her to jump out. At their velocity, she wouldn't dare jump out of the car. At least, that's what he hoped.

"I'll jump!" Abbey threatened. "You turn this car around this instance or I'll jump, Lee!" She wore a stubborn but scared expression on her face.

She's bluffing. There's no way she'd jump out of a moving vehicle, he thought. *No way.*

Then again, there was only one way to find out whether she was bluffing or not. One outcome would result in her not jumping, but hating him. The other would result in temporary, but serious, scrapes, bruises, blood-loss, and broken bones. She wouldn't die; but she would experience tremendous pain and, again, hate him. Whether she jumped out or not, he'd still take her to the mountains. But the rest of their trip would be a complete nightmare.

She peered at the moving cement to her right and slowly stretched her right foot towards the outside of the vehicle.

"Are you crazy? You're going to rip off your leg!" Levi yelled. He lightly set on his brakes and drifted to the left lane to make a U-turn. "Son of a," he growled. "Bloody, darn it. You, freaking—" His muscular hands squeezed the steering wheel until his knuckles became white. "Fine!" He seethed at the steering wheel, refusing to look at her.

In his peripheral vision, Levi could see a look of satisfaction on Abbey's face—her lips pulled back and all of her teeth gleamed in the moonlit front compartment—as she closed the passenger door. This contorted expression of victory darkened her features. She looked sinister, wicked. He wanted nothing to do with this senseless, stubborn side of her.

A voice in the back of his mind told him she was going to give him trouble throughout the entire journey west to Montana, if they actually made it to the Blue Ridge Mountains in time. That voice also told him the three, her, her best friend, and Jeremy, would gang up on him and leave him wishing she'd jumped out of the car and rolled into a ditch.

At least he'd have Jared.

Loyal, dependable, Jared.

Levi made the left U-turn and drove to Jeremy's house. During which, he accepted the possibility that he might not be able to follow the good doctor's instructions.

4

Levi and Abbey arrived at Jeremy's house five minutes later. While they were on their way, she adjusted her hair in a way that looked identical to how it was prior to her adjustments. Levi suspected it was psychological. She also applied makeup. Her cheeks had a notable reddish hue that mimicked a perpetual blush. The lipstick was a slightly lighter pink than her lips normally were. Though he knew it was the female tradition, it was completely lost to him as to why a female as beautiful as Abbey would ever feel the need for cosmetic improvement. And he didn't understand why she felt the need to adjust her look at this moment, considering the urgency of their visit. This wasn't a date. They needed to get out of town an hour ago.

As they approached, Abbey pointed to a three story brick house—it stood alone, in the dark, illuminated only by the faint glow of the moon—and tried to unlock the door before the car came to a complete stop. She found the controls were non-responsive to her touch. She pushed and pulled, but the lock remained firm. Before she turned to him with narrow, accusing eyes, Levi knew what happened and what she was probably thinking. He was responsible. She was not aware of child safety locks. She was also not aware that there was another presence responsible for the activation of the child safety lock. As she opened her mouth, he shook his head.

"Listen, Abigail. We have two and a half hours to get to the mountains, unpack your stuff, and get situated before everything within a hundred mile radius dies or transforms. That includes going through checkpoint and a bathroom break. If they are coming with us, you need to get them out of there and in this car as soon as possible. I told your father I would get you to Montana. What I did not say was that we would both get killed before the journey even starts."

He wanted to, but couldn't tell her that, in two hours, a very special and important piece of technology would have flown across the sky and would meet them at the mountain entrance. If they were not there, it would leave without them.

Abbey rolled her eyes. "Yea, whatever; just let me out. You're wasting time."

Levi frowned. "I don't think you listened to a word I said."

"We're running out of time. Let me out of the car so I can get my boyfriend."

"Okay, but don't take your sweet time in there. If it takes too much time to convince him, it's not the end of the world," he paused, "except for him. Don't make it the end of the world for all of us."

She pointed at the door. "Unlock the door."

"Seriously, Abigail, time is of the essence," Levi

insisted.

"Lee! Unlock the door!" she yelled at him.

"Emma, please unlock the passenger door," Levi asked the car. Without a hitch, the door unlocked and opened on its own.

Her mouth dropped open. She pointed at the door. "Your car is voice activated?"

"Something like that," Levi mumbled.

"How did you get this?"

Without a moment's hesitation, Levi said, "I'm Batman."

She rolled her eyes and stomped into the darkness towards the unlit house.

"You can still close the door," Levi called after her. Though she heard him, she neither turned around nor acknowledged that she heard him. Instead, she trotted up the long, grassy walkway to the brick house.

The car door shut itself. The exterior lights shut off for power conservation.

"You're being hard on her, and a little out of your place. She has a boyfriend. Whether you like it or not, you have to acknowledge and respect that," the female voice with a British accent lectured from the car speakers.

Levi's grip on the steering wheel briefly tightened, and then, slowly loosened. He sighed and rested his hands in his lap. "I know that. I just, I didn't know about him, the boyfriend, until she told me. I don't know what he was thinking not telling me she has a boyfriend or that she might want to bring him along. I was completely sideswiped. You don't just send a man on a mission without all the details of the operation."

"Would you have agreed to this task had he told you?" Emma inquired. She mastered the tone of a teacher questioning a student.

This brought Levi to a pause. "Well, yes. Of course I would have agreed to it. I love her."

"You would have pursued this task with less enthusiasm, right? Perhaps you would have insisted on helping him at the facility."

"Yes, I suppose so," he admitted, hesitant to admit the basis of his motives for taking on his assignment.

"Then, you can understand, considering the circumstances of the situation, why he would refrain from including that information. Of course, you are a young man of honor and mettle, and would persist in your assignment whether it benefit you or not. He understood that. I suspect he kept this information from you to keep you from sacrificing yourself, the way your father did, and to preserve Abigail's privacy. Knowing she had a boyfriend, and the possibility that she wanted to bring him along, would have sparked the very emotions you have now. He needed you with a clear head and out of his and Pisces's way."

As Levi pondered that, he watched Abbey pound the front door. There were no taps, raps, or knocks. There was no rhythm or method to her madness. Alone, in the emptiness of the night, she was a flurry of double-fisted, panicked percussions. Following a full minute of battery, a porch light turned on over her head and the door opened. A tall, lean but muscular young man, Jeremy, stood in the entrance. A young brunette, wearing no more than a bra and panties, climbed out of the side window. After a brief conversation, Abbey entered the house. When the door of the brick house was shut, the brunette ran across the lawn holding a set of clothes in her hands. A line of thick thorn bushes, which ran from one end of the lawn to the road, separated Jeremy's home from a second. The brunette raced around the bushes, and in front of Levi's car, before sprinting across the neighboring lawn along the line of bushes.

"No, no, no, no, no!" Levi yelled inside of the car. He unbuckled his seatbelt, opened the car door, and rushed, low and crouched, after her under the cloak of darkness and behind the line of bushes that divided the two homes.

The young woman, panting and rushed, did not notice she was being pursued. She grabbed a ladder lying on the ground, planted it against her house, and climbed to the second story window. While she climbed, she dropped her small, violet tank top in the grass. She briefly looked at it, cursed under her breath, climbed one step down, and then continued to the top of the ladder. She forced the window open and slowly crawled inside. The window shut. The light in the room was turned on.

The ladder, an invitation for predators, remained unperturbed, but Levi chose to remain still for five minutes, just in case the young woman reminded herself of the dangers of a ladder outside her window. She never did. Parents across the world lament.

He fought any distracting thoughts of the half-naked young woman, and how frustrating the entire trip to Montana would be if Jeremy came along. He'd have to restrain himself from giving Jeremy a well-deserved beating. Perhaps he was dumping her at that very moment. If fortune favored them, perhaps she would come out of the house in tears, jump into the car, and demand they drove, immediately, as far from Jeremy's house as possible. That was his hope. It was wishful thinking. It was distracted thinking.

According to his training, in tense situations, it was best to keep a clear mind, assess the situation, formulate a practical plan for multiple outcomes, and then execute. Jeremy was cheating on Abbey with his neighbor. That was an opening he needed to capitalize on. But how?

How could he make it clear to her that her loyalty in Jeremy was misplaced? Her head could be thick. Fort Knox vault thick. He knew, right away, if he told her Jeremy was cheating on her with his neighbor, she wouldn't believe him. She was willing to jump out of a moving vehicle and face oncoming death for Jeremy. From his few psychology classes, he understood that human beings rarely, initially, accepted the truth. They protected themselves from information they didn't agree with. This was called denial. Humans needed, and would demand, evidence. If you provided them with evidence, they would refute the legitimacy, or interpretation, of that evidence. To overcome objection, and not have Abbey project her anger at him, instead of Jeremy, Levi knew he had to play it cool and be patient. He would collect evidence, provide it to her when the time was right, and if any future evidence presented itself, he would guide her to it, so she found it and came up with her own conclusions.

Levi reached in his pocket, pulled out his touch-screen tablet, and took a focused-flash picture of the ladder. He crossed through the thick, thorn-filled bushes, took a picture of the violet tank top, and then collected it. He took one last picture of her bedroom window, and then ran back to the car.

"That young woman was not Abigail," Emma said.

"No. She was not."

"You took pictures. Why?"

"I was collecting evidence and recording the scene," Levi said. He put the tank top in the glove compartment.

"There will be no need for evidence. When the time comes, the truth will be revealed. Besides, you have more important things to concern yourself with at the moment."

"Don't I? We still have to get through checkpoint. At

this rate, we won't get through before the good doctor finishes his side of the plan. They'll be on high alert. I just hope this identification card for Abigail works."

"And if it doesn't?"

Levi rubbed the left side of his face. "I hope you don't mind being shot at."

5

Abbey regretted everything that transpired in the car with Levi. The moment she walked away, she grieved. They used to have such a good relationship. She didn't want Jeremy to get in the way of that, but he had to. No matter what she felt for Levi, Jeremy was her boyfriend. Her father taught her to live up to her commitments. This was her doing just that.

When she got to the door, her stomach was in knots. Her chest hurt. There was an overwhelming dread. She felt something was wrong and knocking on the door would be the beginning of the end. Was she worried he'd say no? Maybe that was it. Perhaps she was concerned he'd think she was being stupid or crazy. Who knocks on your door a little after three o'clock in the morning and says "get packed in a hurry and let's drive to the mountains"? She'd have to explain everything about what her father said, and she didn't want to have to do that. No, that would cause trouble. Jeremy's father was military. If she told him, he'd tell his father, and his father would have a lot of questions for her father. Maybe that was the ill-feeling. Perhaps she was concerned for her father. Though, she didn't think that was it. There was something about this place, at this moment.

She knocked. There was no answer. She knocked longer. There still was no answer. She knew he was there. They spoke on the phone right before she went to sleep. They went to sleep together on the phone. His jeep was in the back. She saw it while walking towards the house. Why wasn't he answering? The ill-feeling in her stomach intensified. She beat the door. Pounded it. She kept pounding, because she didn't know what else to do. She yelled his name. Where was he?

Perhaps he was in a deep sleep, the kind where great dreams are made and no level of sound could break them.

Eventually, she stopped banging on the door. Her hand hurt. She hoped she hadn't bruised it. She'd never suffered bruising in her life, but her hand was on fire, and there was a first time for everything.

As she turned toward the car, the porch light came on and she heard a click. The door opened.

Without hesitation, Abbey went on the assault. "What the hell, Jeremy? What took you so long to answer the freaking door?"

"Abbey, it's three in the morning."

"Yea, but it didn't take someone beating the crap out of my house to wake *me* up, and it's never taken you that long before. Someone's in here with you, isn't there?"

Jeremy's mouth opened to a wide "O". Abbey translated that as shocked admittance. She pushed the door into him. "Let me in, Jeremy! Let me in, right now!"

He resisted, and found her to be alarmingly strong. "No one's here, Abbey. I was just sleeping. I was very tired."

"Then why won't you let me in?" she asked.

"Because it's my house, and I don't just let people barge in unannounced."

She pushed at the door again. "But I'm your girlfriend! I can come over whenever I want, and you're supposed to like it. That's what this is. If you don't want me around, then we can just end it right here."

"I-I don't, I don't want this to end," Jeremy

stammered. "Just, just calm down. Be reasonable."

"Let me in, Jeremy! Let me in, now, or end it right here."

To Levi's great dismay, Jeremy did not end it right there. He lowered his head, his shoulders slumped, and he stepped back from the door, allowing her to enter.

Abbey stepped into the house, eyes measuring the place for anything suspicious. Something was off. His behavior was off. Hell, the whole world today was off, or soon to be. She knew Jeremy wasn't being a hundred percent with her. She didn't know why. She wanted to press on the issue—lately, Jeremy was secretive and reserved—but time was of the essence. There just wasn't enough time to berate him over an issue that wouldn't matter if they were both dead. Then again, she did stick her foot out of a moving car for him. A *moving, freaking, car*. It didn't matter if Hell itself was spilling over into the world, and they were in its path. She wanted to know what was going on, *now*.

While closing the door behind her, Jeremy glanced at the door frame, turned halfway toward her, and then looked back at the door. The entire frame was cracked, almost splintered. The frame was made of very strong, thick oak. Had he not answered the door when he did, she may well have beaten through it. He looked at Abbey bewildered. He pointed at the door and opened his mouth to speak. "Did you?" He saw anger and fear in her eyes.

"Are you cheating on me, Jeremy? After sticking my neck out for you, are you cheating on me?"

"No, no. I'm—," he reached to grab her shoulders.

She backslapped his hand. "Don't touch me."

"I'm not cheating on you."

"Then what's all this about?" She pointed at the door. "This place gives me a bad feeling, and I can smell it. The sex. I can smell it on you. You've been up to some *funny business*."

Jeremy put both hands on his face and covered his eyes so he didn't have to look at her. There was a tattoo of an eye in a triangle on his right hand. "It's not, it's nothing. There's nothing, Abbey. There's, there's nothing." He uncovered his eyes and briefly glanced about his living room. "Why are you here, anyway? Don't you have classes in the morning?"

Her eyes narrowed. "No. I'm on spring break. Classes ended *last week*. Don't you even listen to me?"

He raised his hands. "Yes. Yes, I do. Okay, Abbey. I'm an idiot. I'm sorry. Just, just calm down and tell me why you're here."

Abbey stopped, looked around the living room, saw the couch, and walked to it. She slumped down and crossed her arms.

Jeremy sat beside her. "What is it?"

"You're going to think I'm crazy," she said.

Jeremy sat straight-faced, despite an urge to comment about her behavior. He knew she wasn't crazy. She was right on the money. And since he didn't want to exacerbate the issue, he wanted to focus on whatever was on her mind.

"It's a good thing I like crazy. Let's hear it."

Abbey breathed and rested her hands on her thighs. "Okay. I don't know how to say this lightly, but everyone in this city is about to die. At six o'clock, everyone is going to die."

He stared at her. They sat silent.

"And, why do you believe that?" Jeremy asked.

Taking in a deep breath, Abbey shared everything her father said, recalling the conversation in great detail, with the exception of his personal questions about her sex life, or lack thereof in her case. As she told her story, she weighed his reactions. He froze when she mentioned the Red and the research facility. When the story was over, his jaw tightened and he stood.

"I have to call my father," he said. He works at the research facility, in security. He'll know what's going on."

"No! My father doesn't even know I'm here. I'm supposed to be on my way already. If you call your dad, he'll talk to my dad. Or worse, he'll stop him from doing whatever it is he needs to do. I know he can stop it; but you can't intervene!"

"This is grave, Abbey," Jeremy said. "I don't know what's going on, or what your dad plans on doing, but I have to call my dad. He needs to know what's going on. I won't just leave him to die if he's really in danger."

Abbey recoiled from his words like a woman who stumbled upon a snake. She said the same thing to Levi, and the irony was a slap in the face. She stood and stomped to the door.

"I have to go," she said.

Jeremy pursued. "What? Why?"

"We're running out of time, and you're about to ruin everything," she said. "If you do, it'll be all my fault."

"Now just hold on a minute! What makes you think my dad would ruin things?"

"Because I know my dad," Abbey said. "He's a very calculated, resourceful man who would look for all other alternatives to prevent a disaster from happening. If your father was a reliable resource, he would have already utilized him. And, he had reservations, which I didn't mention, about me dating anyone in this city. Now, I see why."

"I can't just swallow this and go along with it," Jeremy argued. "If I were in danger, my dad would do something about it. So, I have to do the same."

"Well, here's a question for you: since my dad has

made it clear to me that we're in danger, why hasn't your father contacted you?"

Jeremy paused and frowned, caught off guard. "Well, maybe he doesn't know about the danger. He's the head of security. He doesn't handle the science or technical stuff. He's a military man. He just makes sure everyone in the building is safe."

"Right!" Abbey agreed. "And if the Red have taken over the research facility, that means that, being head of security, your father is either in on it, or working for them unaware of it. They have mind powers. You heard about it in class and on the news. They can hypnotize people and control their minds. What if your dad is one of them now? What if they're controlling his brain?"

It was easy to follow her logic, but Jeremy couldn't agree with it. "No. For all we know, they could be messing with your dad's brain too, so he can sabotage whatever restoration project they're working on."

"My dad was in the war," Abbey explained. "He was one of the scientists that created the neural inhibitor device. It prevented front line soldiers from being affected by Red mind powers and turning on each other. He has one of those devices inside his head, and mine."

"Well, what makes you think my dad doesn't have one of those inhibitor things?" Jeremy argued.

"After the war was over, people were interested in getting one in everyone. However, the politicians and public safety people were concerned about unknown long-term side effects—they didn't seem to care about that when it served them in the war—and bureaucracy got in the way. They said, 'The war is over; the threat is neutralized.' They said it was no longer necessary. So, they removed them from everyone who had them installed, except for my father. You know what I think, and what he thinks? The surviving Red influenced those politicians."

Jeremy needed to sit down. He looked for a chair and decided to return to the couch. Abbey followed and sat beside him.

"It's possible my dad could stop it," she assured. "I don't know everything. He doesn't like to tell me more than he feels I need to know. But I know we can't interrupt him or get anyone else involved. It's too dangerous."

"So, you just expect me to go along with your plan? Leave and not even call my dad."

Abbey rested her hand on Jeremy's hand and nodded. "Yes. Please. It's the only way. I really want you to come with me. Err, us. Levi's driving, as I mentioned. And maybe, Violet. She's usually up for anything."

Absently, Abbey looked at the clock and saw twenty minutes had passed. *Oh crap. Lee is probably going nuts outside,* she thought. The mere mentioning of Jeremy sent him on a tailspin to anger town, which caught her by surprise. Being men of faith, and science, her father and Levi were usually very logical, level-headed, and calm. Levi was exceptionally younger than her father and only two years her senior; so, she supposed it wasn't too much of a surprise that he still hadn't mastered his emotions. Still, there was something queer about his behavior. Was he concerned about the trip to Montana, upset she wouldn't listen to him or the message her dad left, or was there something else?

"Sure. I'll go with you. Let me just, collect my things," Jeremy said.

Excited, Abbey shot her fist in the air and cheered. "Yea! Okay. Let me run out and tell Levi before he craps a Chrysler. Don't take too long getting packed. It's life and death, and, as much as I'd like to believe Levi is fond of me, it wouldn't surprise me at this point if he drove

35

off without us. He was kind of crabby that I was bringing you and Vy along."

"What? Does he have a thing for you, or something against us?" Jeremy, the last person who should be suspicious of someone, frowned.

From his facial expression, Abbey suspected Jeremy felt threated, which, after the last twenty minutes, she enjoyed seeing. Considering the circumstances of the night, she decided it was in her best interest, and his best interest, to use that to her advantage.

She shrugged and said, "Yea, I don't know. He seemed kind of annoyed that I had a boyfriend. It wouldn't surprise me if he wanted me in his nice car, all by myself, all the way to Montana. He's a couple years older than me, same age as you, actually. I thought he had a college girlfriend in Washington State or something. I guess he doesn't. Hey, did you know he has a voice activated car? Have you seen one of those?"

Jeremy's lips trembled. She could only imagine how much emotional restraint it took to keep a straight face. This, she too enjoyed.

"No. No, I haven't," he said. "Well, you tell him I'm coming along, whether he likes it or not. No one's going to chaperone my girl across the country. I don't care what kind of car he has." He stood and rushed upstairs to his room. She could tell he was pouting.

"Don't take too long! You wouldn't want us to leave without you," she yelled after him. She smiled.

Boys acting like boys. That'll teach him. I wonder what he was doing before I got here, Abbey thought while inspecting the living room. For the first time, she noticed a window was ajar. She walked to the window and peered out. There was darkness, bushes, the brick house next door—*that's Violet's place,* she thought—and a pink sock on the ground, right outside the window. She used one hand to leverage the window. Then, she stretched herself to pick up the sock. It was too far away. She stretched even further and couldn't reach it. Finally, she climbed completely out of the window and grabbed it.

"Aha!" Abbey yelled. She stuffed the pink sock in her pocket, mumbled about him being the lowest of the lowest, and looked around for more evidence.

When there was none, she ran to Levi's car.

6

Looking out of the second story window, Jeremy watched as Abbey ran through the darkness to the car, and out of his line of sight. He picked up his phone and dialed.

"She's on her way to you," he said.

"What!?" the female voice responded, hysterical. "Why? Did you tell her? You said you wouldn't tell her."

"No, no, it's not about that," he reassured her. "I didn't tell her about us. It's about something else. Just, be cool. I thought I'd warn you before she got over there."

"Do you think she suspects something?" she asked.

"Well, about me, yes. It took me too long to answer the door. She said she could smell sex all over me." He paused. "You dropped something outside my window. What it is depends on whether she'll be knocking at your window or breaking in trying to kill you."

"That's not funny," she said. "I dropped my tank top outside of my window while climbing the ladder. If she sees that, she'll put two and two together and go ballistic."

"Daggit! Why did you leave it? Go pick it up before she gets over there," he commanded.

"No. I'm not going out there again. It's cold; and I'm already in bed. I just won't answer when she comes knocking. She'll either think I'm sound asleep or not here. You can't see me in the dark."

"No," he said. "You have to answer. If you don't, she'll probably just break your window like she almost broke my door down. Snag is strong. She cracked my door frame. It's solid oak. I don't even know how that's possible."

She shrugged, even though she knew he couldn't see it. "It's probably the radiation. I've heard it can break things down. Make them weaker, yadda-yadda. Why did she come over this late, anyway?"

"She's going to Montana, now, wants me to come with," he said, coolly. "She wants you to come, too. Said you'd be up for just about anything."

"Presumptuous snag. What did you tell her? Are you going?" she asked, hoping he said no.

There was a long pause.

"You said 'yes', didn't you?" she groaned.

"It's complicated. She'll explain it to you when she gets there. You're both off for break, anyway; so, just say yes and pack your shit."

"Who died and made you king, vop?" she shot back. "*She's* your girlfriend. You don't just order me around."

"Yea? You weren't saying that twenty minutes ago. If you don't want to come, don't, but I have a feeling you want to keep on getting what I've got coming."

"Someone's full of himself," she said.

"Like I said, you were full of me twenty minutes ago, and calling out my name like 'bingo'," he said with a smile. He mimicked her voice, "Oh, Jeremy! Oh, Jeremy! God, Jeremy!"

She laughed, "Shut up."

"Oh, Jeremy! You're so big. You feel so good," Jeremy continued.

"You just keep delivering the goods," she said.

Jeremy smiled, confident, "Oh, and I will. You can expect another big package. Overnight delivery."

She laughed again, then, grew quiet. "So, how do you expect to accomplish all of this while we're with Abbey in Montana?"

"She's bringing along some guy. I think his name is Levi. Said he was driving."

"Wait, what? Levi is coming? He's back?" she asked with a high-pitched voice.

Jeremy tensed and squeezed his phone. "Who the hell is this Levi guy, and why is everyone so goddamned happy to see him?"

"Oh, he's an old friend of Abbey's and mine. Her father raised him. He's kind of like her," she was going to say *hot*, but changed her mind, "older adopted brother, but more like a friend she's known forever. He's been in Washington, the state, not D.C., for almost four years, but he comes back on the holidays."

"Hmm, okay, and how do you know him?"

"Because, I've known Abbey since we were kids. I've practically lived at her place. I've seen him, spoken to him." *Smelled him, kissed him,* she thought. "We all went to the movies together. He was always studying, practicing kung fu, and stuff; but we pulled him out and made sure he actually did fun stuff."

"He knows kung fu?" Jeremy spat.

She laughed. "You're not feeling threatened, are you?"

"No. I was just making sure I heard you correctly," Jeremy said.

"Well, yes. You heard correctly."

There was a low tapping at her window.

"Hey, someone's knocking at my window," she said. "I'm guessing it's Abbey. Time to put on my tired face. See you soon."

Jeremy opened his mouth to respond, but heard a click. He closed his mouth and put down the phone. He knew he had to rush and get packed to go, but first he had to make one more phone call. He'd just toss all of his stuff in a book-bag and peel out. It wasn't as though her worries were legitimate. He'd be back in less than a week. A week tops.

He picked up the phone and dialed his dad. If anyone could clarify this before things went too far, if anyone could shut down this trip before that Levi guy stole away both of his girls, it would be him.

7

When Levi saw Abbey running to his car, his first thought was that she learned of the affair and would be anxious to leave. *Finally, we can go*, he thought. He started the car and remotely opened the door before she'd made it to the car. As she leaned in, he patted her seat and opened his mouth to say, "Sorry about your cheating boyfriend, let's get out of here." However, before he could get his words out, as usual, she beat him to it.

"Sorry I took so long," Abbey apologized. "We're leaving without Jeremy, but I have to grab Vy. You remember Violet, right?"

Violet, he thought. *How could I have forgotten Violet?*

"Of course, I remember her." Watching the clock, Levi squeezed the steering wheel. "But I said, 'be quick'. That was not quick. That was almost a half-hour. I can't even imagine how long it will take us to pick up Violet. We should have picked her up first. Where does she live?"

She shook her head, "Calm down before you break the steering wheel. Take a chill pill; she lives right next door."

"A chill pill? You've already taken almost half an hour

over a guy you were about to jump out of a car for; now, we're leaving him. Please don't waste any more of our precious time. Didn't your dad tell you that this is life and death? Are you so anxious to die for your 'friends'?"

"DAGGIT, LEVI!" She screamed and got out of the car. "Just shut up! I'll be right back!"

Abbey stormed away, around the bushes, towards the house with the ladder.

"No, you have *got* to be kidding me," Levi complained as he watched her. She followed the same path the half-naked girl traveled. Then, she climbed the ladder. "Oh piss on me! That was Violet?"

"Language, Levi!" Emma rebuked, "And control your temper. He who is wise holds his tongue and tempers his anger."

"Emma," Levi whined, trying not to sound like a child. "Her best friend *of six years* is having sex with her boyfriend; and she's risking *everything* for them." He slouched in the driver's seat and crossed his arms. "I can't take this. We have to go, now!"

"It is not for you to decide who lives or dies. She is doing right by her friends. Let her do what needs to be done. There is a lesson being learned here. Have patience."

"Yea, well, if this takes more than twenty minutes, patience might be the last lesson I ever learn."

8

Abbey, still fuming from her conflict with Levi, tapped on Violet's window. When she didn't get a response, she tapped quicker and harder for a stretch of five seconds. She stopped when she saw a dark form approach the window.

The window slid opened and out popped out a frazzled head of dark brown, blond, and violet hair. Heat poured out of the room like an exhaling breath.

"Okay, okay. You trying to break my window?" Violet asked.

The moment she saw Violet, Abbey had a feeling she couldn't place or understand. She saw something in Violet's eyes she hadn't seen before. Vibration. Her eyes vibrated. And she saw something behind those eyes, as though there was a force at work behind them. Who was that behind those eyes? What force? She saw the same whatever it was behind Jeremy's eyes. She had overlooked it. She didn't have a name for it, nor the time for it, but she wouldn't let it go unaddressed.

"What? Why are you looking at me like that?" Violet asked. "I know; I look like a wreck. I guess it's what you look like at three o'clock in the morning." She glared at Abbey. "What are you doing here, Abbey? How'd you get over here, anyway? Did your dad give you wheels?"

Abbey snorted. "No. Levi brought me. I'm here because—," she stopped and rubbed her shoulders. Until now, she hadn't noticed how cold it was outside. "Are you going to invite me in or should I just freeze my nips off?"

Violet slid the window all the way open and stepped back. Abbey climbed inside her room, which was dry, stuffy, and felt like eighty-eight degrees.

"Man, it's hot as Hell in here. You anemic or something? I feel like a kernel ready to pop. There's got to be a medium between out there and in here."

"Stop complaining," Violet snapped, before smiling. "Whiny snag."

"Yea yea," Abbey shook her head and smiled. "It's still hot, though. If someone escaped from Hell, and entered your bedroom, they'd ask you to crack open a window."

"Okay. I get it. Why are you here, and when did Levi

get back in town?"

Quickly, Abbey checked her tablet for the time, and then sat on Violet's bed. "We're running out of time, so I'll give you the abridged version."

As with Jeremy, Abbey explained to Violet everything her father told her. Nothing she said seemed to phase Violet, who always carried a nonchalant, apathetic, tough as nails attitude. Of course, Abbey knew it was a front, a cover, and that beneath it all, there was an abundance of emotion waiting to burst out. Sometimes it did and she cried for hours. Other times, she was steel. This was one of those steel moments. Life and death was whatever.

"So, are you coming?"

Violet blinked at Abbey.

"How is that even a question?" Violet asked and walked to her closet. "Of course, I'm coming. Why would I want to stay here and die? Let me just collect my things."

"Wow. That was easy. You just believed me," Abbey said, following Violet with her wide, pixie eyes.

Still controlled, nonchalant, Violet went through her closet, pulled shirts out and tossed them on the bed. She rushed to and from her drawers. "I know your dad and Levi. They're not your average day, run of the mill, conspiracy theory nut jobs. Your dad's a genius. Levi's, well, he's not necessarily a genius, but he's well off in the brains category. They don't just follow along with everyone else. They actually know things and make smart decisions. The right decisions. I have never known your father to do a thing wrong. Nor Levi. They always do the right thing." Instantly, she felt ashamed and blushed red. "Why wouldn't I believe them?"

What? Abbey thought. What was that feeling she was getting again? Something didn't feel right. "You still have a crush on Levi, don't you?"

"No," Violet said while stuffing her items in her suitcase. "Well, okay, kinda. Yes. I mean, he's hot. Who wouldn't?"

That was a thought Abbey didn't want to humor more than she already had. She glanced at the window and thought of Levi waiting out there with an attitude. What was his deal today? Was he that concerned they wouldn't make it in time? Was his anger his way of expressing fear?

"He's okay," Abbey said. "He's not Jeremy."

When she said that, Violet tripped over her own foot and toppled onto her suitcase. Her items sprawled onto the floor.

Abbey tried not to laugh, but she couldn't contain it. She leaned her head back and burst out a roaring laugh. She slapped her right knee and spilled tears.

Glancing at Abbey over her shoulder, Violet snarled and quickly reassembled what order she had in her suitcase. After a minute, she had things back where they were and left to collect her personal items from the bathroom.

When Violet came back to her room, she asked a question she knew would change Abbey's mood. "So, Jeremy's coming too, huh?"

Abbey frowned and relived her visit to Jeremy's home. She knew, though she didn't know how she knew, the precise amount of time she waited outside. The exact number of knocks she pounded on his door. All of these details came to her, but she did not share them. She only marveled, in afterthought, at the sharpness of her memory.

"He's cheating on me," Abbey finished. She pulled the pink sock out of her pocket and showed it to Violet. "I found this outside of his window."

At the sight of the sock, her sock, Violet's eyes widened. She knew Abbey found it, but somehow, seeing it scared her, made her flinch the way a criminal did when the investigating officer placed the murder weapon on the interrogation room table. She opened and closed her mouth three times before responding, "Really? Are you sure?"

Abbey shook the sock in front of her face. "This isn't an optical illusion, Vy. It's cold as ice out there. Unlike your room, which is still burning up—geez, seriously—his wasn't. And, he wouldn't let me in, at first. I think he was stalling while she jumped out of the side window. What I don't understand is: where did she go?"

Violet bit her top lip and shrugged. "Who knows? It's a big neighborhood."

That answer was the furthest from helpful, and Abbey knew Violet wouldn't be much help in solving that mystery, yet, she plodded along. "It's freezing out there. Whoever it was had to be cold, really cold. I probably just missed her. I wonder if Levi saw her."

At that thought, Violet's eyes widened in shock. She went red and looked out of the window. She remembered running past a parked car. A black sedan. The windows were tinted, and it was dark, so she couldn't see if anyone was inside. Yet, he had to be. Where else would he have been? He didn't follow Abbey to the house. He was waiting for her. Waiting for them, assuming Abbey didn't get a clue in the next couple of minutes and leave her behind.

Seeing this reaction, Abbey's eyes narrowed. *Now why would she react that way?* "What?"

Scrambling for an answer that wouldn't implicate her in the clear picture Abbey should have already drawn, Violet decided to respond to a question with a question. "Umm, Levi's still out there right?" she asked. "Won't he be pissed if we take too long? Shouldn't we get going?"

In unison, they looked at the clock on her wall. It was

three fifty-six.

"Crap," was all Abbey said before she hopped off Violet's bed and raced to the window. She saw Jeremy with a book bag on his back. He rolled a suitcase out of his front door. He locked the door and rolled his case to Levi's car. "How much more stuff you got to pack?"

"Umm, considering I'm never coming back to this hell hole, probably more than I can carry," Violet said. "You need to go?"

"Yeah," Abbey answered. "I just remembered I told Levi Jeremy's not coming, because I decided to leave him." Violet's eyebrows rose. "And Jeremy's carrying his stuff to Levi's car. Just, stop organizing like a dagged psychopath and toss your stuff in there. We have to go, now!"

The two scrambled to get the remainder of her stuff into a suitcase, including money from her safe, and climbed out of the window.

"You didn't mention your mom. Aren't you going to warn your mom?" Abbey said on their way down the ladder. She remembered Jeremy's hesitance to abandon his father. She hoped he hadn't called his father, but knew, if the situation was reversed, she would have called hers.

"She's passed out drunk with some guy from the bar, again," Violet said as her feet landed on the ground. Where was her tank top? "They just came in, drunk off their asses, ate the dinner I made—before I got to eat any of it, mind you—and went to screwing each other. Loud as hell, too. Banging the walls, swearing and screaming each other's names. I turned on my music loud as I could to drown them out. Then, she storms in, tits, bush and all out, and told me to shut up and get out. So I did. So I will. I'm not going to see that snag ever again. So what if she dies. She's dead to me. She died a long time ago."

Abbey didn't know how to respond. They kept on moving to the car.

Violet didn't look back.

She never would.

9

To pass the time, and not lose his mind, Levi closed his eyes and listened to the soothing melodies of the Miles Davis Quintet. His favorite song, 'It Never Entered My Mind', was first on his playlist, followed by 'Round Midnight', 'Bye Bye Blackbird', 'My Funny Valentine', and 'Someday My Prince Will Come', among many others in what was a box set. What made that collection his favorite—besides the beep-bops, high and low tempos, and the calm he found, even at his highest states of agitation—was that it was his father's. Like his godfather and mentor, Lukas Brown, his father, Jeremiah Jones, was a doctor. Sometimes, Levi would imagine his father wearing a long white lab coat, sitting in an office, eyes closed, leaned back in his chair, listening to the trumpet's melody while his mind went over the details of his patients' records. What medical mysteries did he uncover while listening to that collection? According to the good doctor, his father played it when he learned he was a father. That thought brought a smile to his face.

That smile disappeared when Levi saw Jeremy rolling a suitcase to his car. He stared, eyebrows almost furrowed to a unibrow "V", and tightened his grip on the steering wheel. "Didn't she say he wasn't coming? What happened to him not coming? He just cheated on Abigail. What's he doing rolling his stuff towards us?"

"Stay calm, Levi," Emma urged. "There's a rational explanation for everything. Perhaps he said he didn't want to come and then changed his mind. Or perhaps she invited him and then changed her mind."

Levi got out of the car. He was tense, hesitant, and uncertain of what to say to the guy that was not only dating the girl he loved, but cheating on her. He wanted to punch him in the face. No, not just punch. He wanted to grind his fist in Jeremy's face and mash it. However, he chose restraint and leaned on his car, waiting.

Whosoever is angry with his brother without a cause shall be in danger of the judgment, Levi thought to himself. *Is this about Abigail's honor, or my jealousy?*

He breathed.

Jeremy approached, dropped his bag, and stretched out his hand for a handshake. "You must be Levi," he said. "I'm Jeremy, Abbey's boyfriend."

Levi looked at Jeremy's hand, at him, and then the hand again. He didn't want to shake it, but he shook it with a tight grip. "Levi, son of Jeremiah, apprentice to the good doctor, and friend of Abigail. Lifelong friend."

They shook each other's hands and stared each other down. Their grips tightened on each other until Jeremy winced and released.

"Quite a grip you have," Jeremy said. *Must keep yourself pretty satisfied, thinking of my girl,* he thought with a sly smile.

"Thanks," Levi replied. *If you're a good little boy, this is the last time you'll ever feel it,* Levi thought with a sneer, instead of a smile.

Abbey and Violet rushed ahead, both with one of Violet's purple luggage bags in hand. "Nice to see you guys getting acquainted," Abbey said and nudged Violet along to the trunk. "Lee, you remember Vy."

"Of course, I do," Levi said, turning his eyes from Jeremy, his nemesis, to Violet, the co-conspirator.

Violet lit up at the sight of Levi. "Hey Lee, long time no see." As she waved a thin hand, her pale cheeks blushed. The acne and facial blemishes that once marred her face were all gone. With her pouty lips, pronounced cheek bones, and bright green eyes, narrowly hidden by her long multi-colored bangs, her beauty rivaled Abigail's. Then again, in his eyes, her beauty always rivaled Abigail's.

"Hey, Violet," Levi said, shocked by how stunning she was. He remembered the toned detail of her athletic body as she ran in bra and panties in front of his car, and her form-fitting black jeans, matching jacket, and green tank top was tight enough to offer a kind mental refresher.

Whosoever looketh on a woman to lust after her hath committed adultery with her already in his heart, Levi reminded himself.

He breathed again, deeper than before, shook the image of Violet undressed out of his head, and led Violet and Jeremy to his trunk and opened it. He pushed Abigail's bags to the back, put Violet's bags in, then Jeremy's luggage bag, which barely fit. He grumbled under his breath as he forced it in. "Your backpack isn't going to fit, Jeremy. You'll have to sit with it." He shut the trunk and sped to the driver's seat.

"Okay," Jeremy said and tossed it into the backseat.

"Everyone get in; we're already behind schedule," Levi said. He sat in the car and buckled his seatbelt.

Jeremy slid into the backseat. Violet was about to follow suit when Abbey stopped her. "I'd like to sit with Jeremy."

Violet opened her mouth to object, then, closed it. She thought, then, whispered, "I thought you were going to dump him. You don't want to sit up front with Levi? He's looking studly."

"No, I don't," Abbey said quickly, and harshly. She climbed in the backseat and slammed the door before Violet could respond. Violet sat in the front seat.

Levi, not too pleased with the seating arrangement, looked back at Jeremy and Abbey sitting together, albeit divided by a book bag, and scoffed, "Abbey, why are you in the back?"

Violet looked down. Her whole face turned red.

"Because it's my preferred seating, Lee," Abbey responded. "Aren't you in a rush? Get driving, mister."

"You have to listen to your father's recording," Levi argued. "He left explicit instructions that you listen to it when we got on the road. I made that very clear before we got here."

"Daggit, Levi!" Abbey shouted, earning a complaint from Jeremy as he put his hand to his ear. "Just drive the car! I'll listen to it when I listen to it."

"Watch your language, Abbey!" Levi growled, not knowing what else to say. He put the car in drive and slammed on the gas, shooting the car forward.

Thirty minutes later, on interstate sixty-four headed west towards Charlottesville and Waynesboro, Levi sat in the front, in his own mind, as was Violet. Abbey and Jeremy were in the back talking about his work and her school. After complaints from Abbey ("This old person music is boring," she whined) about the smooth jazz, which kept Levi in a calm mood, he flipped through his selections to 'On the Road, Playlist One'. It was a compilation of classic UK alternative rock bands, including The Beatles, U2, Coldplay, Muse, Keane, and Metric.

On the road, and generally in life, Levi found music was his escape, a way of clearing his mind. It was also a bonding agent for him, Abbey, and the good doctor in his youth. He always looked forward to Karaoke Tuesdays. The good doctor could carry a tune, especially when singing along to the man he claimed to be the greatest singer of all time, Bono. Abbey thought the Beatles were the bees' knees and knew the lyrics of every sing song they'd ever sang. When Violet came over, which was every other day, she found their selection limited, but was fixated on Coldplay. She said Chris Martin's voice was the place where dreams were born. It only seemed logical to start their trip with this playlists.

Violet sat slumped in her chair and watched the road, brooding over her mom, Abbey and Jeremy, and Levi's earlier words. A song came on. She recognized it, though she didn't know where or when.

"What's that song? I like it," Violet asked.

Levi broke his attention from the road, the time, and the cogs of their mission which were nearly out of whack if he didn't break the sound barrier pushing the car the furthest and fastest he could in less than an hour. He listened and forced a smile. "'Help Me, I'm Alive' by Metric. It's a great song. Have you heard of Metric?"

She shook her head and responded, "No, but I've heard this song before."

"I think Abbey sang it once during Karaoke Tuesday," Levi said. "I selected it during the battle round."

"Oh, yea."

There was silence for another two minutes.

"Listen, I hope you didn't take offense earlier when I asked Abigail to sit in the front seat. There is something really important she has to listen to. It explains everything that's going on and, other private stuff. It's too important to ignore. It's not that I didn't want to sit next to you or anything," Levi explained.

She shrugged and looked outside of the window, watched the trees go by, "It's whatever. You didn't want us to come, anyway."

Levi sighed. "I was wrong about that, too. I'm sorry."

"Can't say I haven't heard that one before," Violet mumbled.

"Hear me out," Levi said. It was a statement,

command, and request.

"It's not like I can do much else but hear you anyway," she said. "So, let's hear it. Why didn't you want us to come?"

Levi hesitated, and looked in his rearview mirror at Abbey and Jeremy, who were so engaged in their conversation ("My neighbor uses a line to dry her clothes. The wind must have carried it," he insisted), they were completely ignoring his.

"Okay," Levi started, "I expect Abigail told you about the Red returning."

"Yea," Violet said, eyes turning from the road. "I don't go on random cross country trips at three o'clock in the morning unless it's absolutely necessary."

Levi blinked. "Right. Okay, well, we, the good doctor and I, made an escape plan and no one else was included because we were short on time and didn't know who we could trust."

"So, you're saying I'm not trustworthy?"

"Are you trustworthy, Violet?"

He looked at her, met her eyes for too many seconds, and then looked back at the road. An unspoken message was transmitted in that look.

Violet tensed. He knew. Of course, he knew! He wouldn't say, but he knew. She grew anxious. Would he tell Abbey?

Levi continued, "The Red can read minds. If we just broadcast the return of the Red and tell people to flee, few, if any, would believe us. And the ramifications of the Red finding out we know before we're able to escape is grave. The police, the military, they no longer have chips in their heads. They can be read and controlled. A few orders and they can have us killed," Levi thought about that and smirked, "or at least try. Any influence reason or logic had in this country is gone. Little good remains. So, we're on our own, Abbey, her dad, and I. We're the only people the Red can't read and influence. So, we were the only ones in the escape plan."

"But, I'm her friend," Violet argued. "Yours as well. I've been so for six years! Doesn't that at least entitle me some consideration?"

"Take into mind that Abigail's father was under constant observation because he ran the program that would both restore the planet and obliterate them. You not having a cognitive encryption device makes you the perfect spy," he said, understanding half of what he said would probably sail right over her head. She didn't understand the functionality of the restoration device, nor the program he was describing. Did she know what a cognitive encryption device was?

"Spy?" she spit out. "I am not a spy."

"Not by choice," Levi clarified. "Imagine you're a highly intelligent, super-powerful telepath. Now, you cannot read three people, but you can read most everyone else. The most logical thing to do is to find someone they interact closely with and observe them through that person."

"Well, that makes sense, but I would know. Don't people know when someone's been in their mind?"

"Sometimes they do, sometimes they don't," Levi said. "Remember years ago when you were having those terrible headaches? You had them, on and off, for a good year. You went through a number of tests when your mother finally got around to taking you to the doctor."

"Yea," Violet said. "They didn't find anything wrong with me and, after a few weeks, the headaches stopped. Your memory is just as creepy as ever. How do you remember that?"

"The same reason they can't read my mind. My brain has been altered and improved by the same technology.

Your doctor didn't find the problem because he either overlooked it, misdiagnosed it, or was influenced not to address it. Her father, the good doctor, hacked the results of your MRI and noted significant, abnormal brain activity and growth in the region associated with telepathy. In other words, your mind was being probed and stimulated."

"What!?" Violet exclaimed, startling Abbey and Jeremy in the back and drawing their attention. "Why didn't he tell me or my mother?"

"You mean: why didn't he provide you with information he *illegally* acquired?" Levi shot back. "Hmm, probably because, if your mother found out, there would have been major blow back."

"So, to protect his own ass," Violet returned.

"His, mine, and Abigail's. You're talking about a single father trying to save the world and raise two kids."

She didn't respond. She wanted to, but she didn't have an answer, yet.

Levi continued, "To keep you and Abigail safe, sensitive information only passed between him and me. He didn't want to keep Abigail, the proverbial social butterfly, from having friends (as if he could try); so he kept things from her, and welcomed you with open arms, even though he knew they were looking in on us."

"That's why you kept to yourself and didn't have any friends?"

"You were my friend," Levi said. "Abigail is my friend. Her dad is my friend, mentor, and kind of my dad, too. I had acquaintances. I just didn't confide who and all I was to anyone outside of him, and Jared. We remained socially reclusive, but sometimes humored a façade of inclusiveness and normality."

"All of these what ifs, and maybes, and secrets, how can you live like that?" Violet shook her head. "How can you let us go on like that, with those things roaming in our heads?"

Levi reached out and touched her hand. "What were we supposed to do? Tell them to stop? I couldn't do anything. I was just a kid. The good doctor couldn't put an implant inside your head. They're illegal for Union citizens."

Violet frowned. Levi continued.

"What the history teachers didn't tell you is that the government rejected implants and any other attempts to hinder future Red telepathic influence. The politicians tied the psychological trauma of the most brutal and tragic war in Earth's history as side effects of the implants. All American citizens were ordered to have their implants removed after a couple staged murders. Fortunately, we're not Union citizens."

Violet sighed. "I keep forgetting you guys are Coalition citizens."

"Yep," Levi nodded. "The good doctor moved us to Seattle during the Coalition's formation."

"During its formation?" Violet did the math. "We were babies."

"You and Abbey were babies. I was a toddler. Get it right," Levi smiled. Violet rolled her eyes. "Those were the good ole days. Before people were trying to kill us and the good doctor changed his name to Lukas Brown."

"Wait a second!" Abbey yelled from the back seat, causing everyone else to start. "He never told me we were almost killed and he changed his name. He told me most of that story, but he didn't tell me he changed his name. What's his real name?"

Levi smiled, "Oh, Abigail, the things I could tell you if you actually followed instructions and listened to your father's recording."

"Lee, just, just shut up and tell me," Abbey rebutted.

"Can't do both, but I'll settle for the former," Levi said and rose the volume of the music. The Beatles were singing for help.

Violet shook her head at Levi. This was going to be an interesting trip.

CHAPTER TWO
EXIT STRATEGY

THE PSEUDONYMOUS GOOD DOCTOR, currently Lukas Brown, arrived at the military research facility, once an old power plant, a half hour after his daughter and protégé left his home. There were two security checkpoints to pass, each with two armed guards in the early hours, and three in the regular hours. He passed through, displaying his badge and pressing his fingerprint to the touchpads provided.

Once he passed through the checkpoints, he parked and checked his time piece. He knew his daughter well enough to know they were still in town. Levi was probably ringing his hands. She was a good kid; but she had a hard head. He was a responsible young man; but Lord save him from his temper. Lukas supposed it was alright to have a few failings, as long as it didn't stress your heart and send you to the death bed before your time. Levi would probably live another hundred years or so, assuming things went as planned and any of them made it out alive. It was all up to the Lord. If the Lord was willing, Lukas would do his best to serve and save the world God gave them.

There were two more security checkpoints: one at the building entryway and one ten doors straight ahead, leading to the restoration project's laboratory, tech center, and command center. The building was packed of early risers and late shifters. The lab coats filled and rushed through the halls. Armed guards stood like hungry gargoyles over them, waiting for the slightest sign of trouble so they could break from their statuesque states.

Most of the staff were to be there by four o'clock to prepare for the final stretch of the project. After seven years of research, building reconstruction, cradle assembly, tests, failures, and numerous safety and backup protocols, the project was finally at its last stage: commencement. After today, assuming the project went well, most of the scientists would be signing their end of project paperwork and moving on to similar projects scheduled in other parts of the world. The restoration project had the green light in the South American, Eurasian, and African continents. It was a world initiative all the survivors of the Red War hoped would save them from extinction. Little did they know, the extinction they intended to prevent would be accelerated by their own efforts.

Lukas thought somberly of their fates as he passed the enthusiastic faces and exchanged smiles, hellos, and nods. After his plan was fully in motion, those friendly faces would be contorted in fury and contempt for him. Some of them would die because of his actions. In the end, it was all on his head. If he stayed in Montana, the project would never have seen the light of day in Virginia. Because of him, everyone was in danger. If only he stayed vigilant in his search for the Red, when the search was still sanctioned by the government, they wouldn't have seized control of his project and turned the restoration device against humanity.

It was a pity this would end in violence; but Lukas wouldn't let his spirits sink. He had a plan; and it was already in play. He knew because the security officers were whispering amongst each other and pointing at their touch-screened walkie-talkies.

One week ago, Lukas planted an intricate computer virus in security's communications and operations systems. The virus was designed to cause a complete security blackout and lockdown. It took three days to implant the three-pronged virus he called 'the Trident'. The first prong disabled all communication to and from the research facility and any connected network. The second prong interfered with surveillance and intruder mechanisms. The third prong overrode all door locks. With all three installed, they remained dormant until each prong received one of its initiation triggers.

Lukas was a calculated chess player; and because he knew his daughter all too well, the first trigger (a call from Jeremy to his father, the head of security) would immediately impair inbound communications the moment the call was answered. He hastened his pace to the tech center, where the final power level tests were being performed on the catalyst, knowing that minutes after inbound communications went down all internal and outbound communications would go down. The walkie-talkies, linked through the internal dashboard, were a sign of that.

In the tech center were three lab assistants, two junior scientists, and two of the chief scientists of the project, Doctors Ryle Andrews and Francine Cartwright. The chief's duty was to oversee the interns, assistants, and junior scientists. Lukas's duty was to oversee the chiefs, unless the Congressional Science Committee wanted to overrule his judgments. When that happened, and it did a week ago, the chiefs had the distinct honor of taking control of his project. Recently, they changed the firing perimeters and radiation signatures of the restoration device. Fortunately, he held an advantage none of them could deny him, which kept them from completely removing him from the project once they got what they needed. The catalyst, a small and circuited crystalline sphere, the key component of the device, only responded to him.

Andrews, a short, heavy set man with a shiny bald patch at the center of his white-haired head, shuffled himself towards Lukas as he stepped through the doors. He came within inches of Lukas, scowling with a menacing stare.

"I hope you enjoyed your little trip, Brown, because your lack of presence puts us in a position when the dagged thing won't light up without you. The batteries are only at a twenty-five percent charge. We'll use ten or fifteen percent just to fire the thing," Andrews lectured. His breath smelled of mustard, tobacco, and rot.

Lukas stared blankly at Andrews. The inept man was a tool of his own destruction. It was like watching a man complain to his executioner that he didn't have enough bullets in his gun. He wanted the gun fully loaded, in his mouth, and steady when you pulled the trigger.

"Thank you. I did enjoy my trip, Doctor Andrews," Lukas said and shifted around Andrews.

Andrews stepped in his way and pointed his finger. "Did you not hear me? We have less than two hours before we have to fire that thing and you're not even going to acknowledge that you've gone off on some half-assed, late night errand with the fate of the world in your hands?"

"I left the fate of the world here, Andrews. That is why you're complaining, is it not? My errand involved seeing to my child. I was away from home for almost twelve hours," Lukas said and turned to Cartwright, who had her arms crossed and a blank expression on her face. She was thin, tall, and pallid, lifeless enough to resemble waxwork. Clusters of freckles speckled her face. Her long auburn hair was tied into a rushed ponytail. Her viridian eyes were still and locked on Lukas, examining him.

"It's kind of late to be checking on your daughter, Doctor," Andrews persisted. "I think you're up to something."

"Do you have a teenage daughter, Doctor Andrews? A teenage daughter with a secret boyfriend?"

Andrew's face went completely red. His hands balled into a fist. "What are you playing at? You know my children are all dead due to the radiation."

Lukas threw his hands up and shook his head. It was like arguing with a woman. Everything he said was going to be used against him.

Cartwright yawned.

"Are we boring you, Doctor?" Lukas asked, redirecting his attention at someone less excitable, more interesting, and attractive.

"Yes," she said. "It's been years of this, and you two haven't come to blows, yet. I'm beginning to think I'll never see Andrews lying flat on his back, bloodied at the nose." She showed the slightest signs of a smirk, and then it was gone. Cartwright was a respectable physician, and decent human being, but like any human, she had her dark moments.

The junior scientists stopped what they were doing to look at Cartwright, Andrews, and Lukas.

Andrews opened his mouth to protest, but Cartwright shook her head and said, "Communications just went down. That means no interdepartmental contact. No contact from the command center. We'll have to messenger everything until the system is back up. As per strict instructions from Perkins," Senator Perkins was head of the Congressional Science Committee and the self-appointed overseer of the project's outcome, "there are to be no delays. No matter what happens, we are to initialize. So, if you will be so kind as to stop pelting him with complaints that will neither stir his temper nor change the circumstances, Doctor Andrews, I believe Doctor Brown is due at the cradle assembly with our not so bright and shiny sphere. That way, we can get this show on the road."

Andrews opened his mouth to debate more; but Lukas was already moving towards the sphere. Before he was within arm's reach, there was an audible snap, like the striking of a match, and a dim green flame came to life in the center of the sphere, the catalyst. No matter how many times people saw it, they continually watched, frozen and jaw-slacked, at the spectacle as he picked it up and it came to full life in his hands. It shone with a blinding intensity and filled the room with green light. After it reached its peak, it settled down to a steady glow and hum. A green, luminous cloud swirled within.

"Always beautiful," Cartwright commented. Her lips were slightly parted. The glow gave her pale skin a green hue.

"Yes, you are," Lukas mumbled under his breath. He registered the smirk on her face, and knew she got the message.

Andrews walked towards the sphere, arrested by its light and hum, covetous. He reached out to touch it. It darkened. He frowned, slighted by a piece of technology, envious of Lukas's ability to excite it. If only he knew how this man commanded its obedience; perhaps, he himself could do the same. Hmm. Perhaps it wasn't something the doctor did or had in his possession. What if it was him, the individual? No, it had to be something on him. Technology didn't respond to people without word or touch. Yet, when he came near it, he uttered no words nor waved his hands in any particular fashion. It had to be on his person, then. And, whatever it was, he was going to take it.

Lukas placed the catalyst in a silver and glass carrying case. On his way out of the door, Andrews rushed forward.

"Since communications are down, one of us is going to have to stay close, just in case a message needs to be relayed," Andrews suggested at the door, holding it open.

Lukas stopped and turned around. He didn't want Andrews to follow him.

"Are you proposing you serve as my personal messenger?" Lukas asked in good humor, hoping Andrews's ego was stronger than his desire for the device he'd coveted since day one. "How modest of you." He glanced down the hallway at the security guards, still fumbling with their walkie-talkies and testing them. He needed to get moving.

Andrews was taken aback by the remark. "You egomaniac. I'm suggesting we both watch the device and one of us tends to the message if it is necessary. I'm not going to lower myself to your whim like you're the lord of the lab and I'm some intern. That ship has sailed. Who's to say you don't deliver the message and I stay with the sphere?"

"For the love of God, Andrews, it's oh three fifty. Are your panties already in a bunch? I hear they have a new starch spray for that. Makes'm stiff as cardboard, tough as nails," Prost said, approaching the door. He was average height with short dark hair. The women in the office swooned over his swimmer's build, tanned skin, and five o'clock shadow, which gave him a rugged handsomeness. He was young, with a fresh doctorate and well-connected parents. Lukas hired Prost because of his uncle's distinctive personality and abilities. He regretfully inherited more personality than abilities, Lukas discovered. In the lab, he was usually off topic and compensated by agreeing with the crowd. Did he have his own opinions? Yes. Some intelligent ones, but mostly *smart* ones. "Then again, baldy, maybe that's the problem. Something stiff is already up your—"

"Sam, please," Cartwright said. She stuck her head out of the door. "No more. As agitated as Andrews is, and as much as you love to stir things up, I'm surprised he hasn't had a heart attack, yet." She looked at Andrews. "Brown is fine on his own. He's always needed his space, and the last thing we need is you yelling at him down the hallway. Things are tense enough as it is with the clock counting down."

Andrews wagged his finger at Cartwright. "You hold on just a minute, Francis."

"Francine," she corrected, calmly.

"Last time I checked, you weren't the law of the lab, either," Andrews argued. "We're equals here, now. He doesn't get to boss me around, and neither do you."

"It's a democracy, of sorts, actually," Prost interjected. "We vote. That's what Perkins said last week, after he and Zenji introduced the new radiation signature and Brown pushed against it. Lost his wits about it, remember? So Perkins stepped in. Said, 'Brown operates as a supervisor, but the chiefs have voting authority to override at the discretion of the Congressional Science Committee.' Then, we voted for Zenji's changes."

"Voted? Yea, no. More like arm twisted by Perkins," Cartwright thought out loud. "In any event, he's already gone, sorry Andrews."

Andrews turned to see Lukas was gone.

"Speaking of voting," Prost said and raised his hand. "All in favor of Andrews not crying like a three-year-old girl who lost her favorite Binky doll?"

Andrews frowned.

Cartwright smiled.

2

The cradle assembly room was long, wide, and open like a concert hall. The walls, floors, and steps were stark white, with the exception of the two yellow guiding lines along the stairs and lower walkway. The floor sloped from the entryway downward at forty-five degrees. Lines of cables of metal tubing stretched along the lengthy flooring to the cradle assembly. The cradle was a nine foot wide, circular, glass disk with a complicated series of metallic circuits and rings interconnected within it. In the center was a small ring and hole from which all the circuits connected. The cradle was surrounded by five glass columns, each filled with a swirling cloud of mist of a different color—they were crimson, gold, jade, cerulean, and violet—forming a slight rainbow. In the floors, directly adjacent to the columns were glass touch controls and displays. The columns extended to the ceiling and surrounded a circular opening that continued to the height of the building.

Lukas stepped cautiously down the stairwell, which held no guard rails and was illuminated only by the white light at the center of the cradle itself and the swirling energy mists of varying colors. The room was empty and silent, with the exception of the low hums coming from the columns. The room had no air conditioning but gradually fluctuated between fifty and seventy degrees Fahrenheit. The columns emitted various levels of heat or cold. As their power levels fluctuated, the room temperature wavered. At the moment, due to the recent sequencing by the chiefs, the room was uncomfortably warm and humid.

Adjacent to the cradle assembly room was the command center. One long window next to the entry way was their vantage point. At the base of the stairwell, Lukas set the glass case down and pulled out the catalyst. He pretended to examine the catalyst closely, while shooting glances at the window. The command center was dimly lit by computer screens and light panels built into the floor instead of the ceiling. Within the room sat a crew of scientists, technicians, security staff, and, though Lukas could not see him, Senator Perkins. He knew Perkins was there. The previous week, Perkins stationed himself within an adjoining office.

Lukas hoped the Senator was distracted by surveillance and communication problems. The second prong of Lukas's Trident was activated the moment he entered the cradle assembly room. He programmed a five minute delay before all surveillance equipment and intruder alert systems shut down. Three minutes after those systems shut down, the third prong would initiate, locking all doors. At that point, Lukas would use his override code to leave the cradle assembly and disappear.

In the meantime, he would operate as though everything was going as planned and not draw any attention to himself. He would check a couple power and radiation synchronization readings, look over a few reports, and then leave, without setting the catalyst in the cradle assembly and charging it any more than it already was. He, unlike the others, knew that if he rested the catalyst in the assembly itself, the device could be activated at that moment, whether the columns were charged or not, and it would perform the function they intended. Charging the columns allowed the device to fire without the catalyst, which made him expendable.

Part of him wished there was a way he could do some damage in the cradle assembly without causing a humongous explosion or re-sequence the radiation perimeters without the additional security codes required. Unfortunately, considering he was dealing with a mixture of human and extra-terrestrial technology, the hybrid technology was extremely temperamental. And as of last week, Lukas's commands alone were not sufficient to change anything. His access was embarrassingly limited, with more administrative controls to read reports and overlook actions, than the ability to make changes. He was now in complete supervisor mode, dependent on the chiefs to follow on commands he wanted acted. To make matters worse, every action was cross-examined by the chiefs, especially Andrews and Zenji.

Nevertheless, in a last effort, Lukas leaned beside the luminous crimson column and attempted to reduce its power levels.

Access restricted.

No surprise there, but a man had to try.

He walked to the jade column and tried its controls.

Access restricted.

Perhaps, if he had more than a week, he could have programmed a glitch-free virus giving him access to the cradle system. The challenge: it would have required one of the chiefs to install it, since it was only accessible through direct interface. As much as he trusted Cartwright, he couldn't risk it. If she were read or, worse, the victim of a complete mind control, his chances of any success were miniscule.

As it stood, he only had one option remaining: Plan B, his current plan. He had to get the catalyst to Montana, where his second cradle assembly was being finished in secret, and destroy the one in front of him. It meant the possible destruction of the facility and his death.

The thought reminded him of his duties. No doubt the appropriate minutes had passed. He put the catalyst back in the glass case and carried it up the stairs.

At the door, Lukas took one more look at the cradle assembly they'd spent years working on, and suspected, the next time he saw it, he'd be annihilating it with a grenade. The energy pulsing throughout the chamber and columns would react violently, and the entire facility would be a crater the size of small town.

In the left pocket of his white lab coat was a glass flask full of chocolate milk. He tipped it back and drank its contents.

Here goes, he thought. He put the empty flask back in his pocket and reached for the heavy door.

"And where do you think you're going, Doctor Brown?" a deep, authoritative voice questioned from behind. "And with the catalyst of all things."

Turning around, Lukas saw a bald and incredibly tanned man. He had leathery skin and large, googly eyes that seemed to protrude from his head. Senator Avery Perkins stood beside the cradle assembly in his dark purple suit, silk shirt, narrow crimson tie, black vest, and well-polished crocodile skin shoes. There was a luger in his right hand. His diamond studded gold Rolex sparkled in the dim light of the columns. His big teeth gleamed as he smiled, noticing Lukas's shock at his presence.

"Surprised to see me?" Perkins teased. "Thank your daughter. Her mouth is so big; I can hear her from here."

"Perkins," Lukas said in a resigning voice. This was not part of the plan. Where did he come from? How had Lukas not seen or heard him?

"Surely, you're not going back to the lab, Doctor. Your work there is done. You and I both know it. The only thing left, so this all comes to an end, is putting her in her rightful place."

Her. Perkins called the catalyst, whose existence and science was a mystery to all men except Levi and himself (or so Lukas thought), her. How did Perkins know the catalyst was alive? How did he know that the lab work was finished? It was finished a week ago when the project was hijacked by Perkins. This man, who knew things he wasn't supposed to know, appeared out of thin air and held a pistol. Was that a scare tactic or did Perkins actually plan to shoot?

"Firearms are not allowed in the cradle chamber, Perkins," Lukas said.

Perkins unleashed a throaty laugh that echoed throughout the cradle assembly chamber. "Oh, Brown. Or, should I call you, John?"

Lukas frowned.

"John, yes, that's better," Perkins said. He smiled and crept forward. "John, we know who you are. We've been watching you for some time now. We also know what this device does. It's the world shield. It's been used against us to push us across the galaxy to our last recluse, this wretched world. Did you really think we'd let you build one and use it against us?"

"Yes," Lukas said. "No matter what you do here, you've lost. The war destroyed most of you. I hunted down all but a few. It'll take decades, if not centuries, to repopulate. You and I both know you don't have that much time. The only reason the heavens haven't rained down their fury upon the Earth is because we were given one final chance to save ourselves and renew the first world. And here you are, selfishly condemning us all."

"Oh, spare me the theatrics," Perkins sighed. He rolled his eyes. "There are more of us than you think. We are everywhere, still, lying in wait for our moment of return. We will fire the device. The beacon will sound our forces to regroup here. This will be the staging point of a new invasion. The first world will bring an end to all worlds." Perkins stopped. "OH, you got me started in a monologue. No more talk, John. Give me the catalyst."

"No."

Perkins frowned. "I have a gun in my hand, John. If you don't do what I want you to do, I will shoot you."

"And risk damaging the catalyst?" Lukas rebutted.

"I'm a marksman, John. I can shoot a flea off of a dog's dick from a hundred meters away."

"Don't hear that one every day."

"Come down the stairs," Perkins ordered. "Now."

Considering his choices, Lukas slowly began to walk down the stairs. One step per every five seconds. He knew, the closer he was to Perkins, and the further he was from the door, the slighter his chances of survival were. Once Perkins had the catalyst, and assuming it remained active, he was expendable. It didn't take a smart man to know where that left him. He still had a few tricks up his sleeve. It was time for him to take his combat skills out of retirement and become the man he used to be.

"Faster, John. I'll be dead of old age before you get down here."

"You're right about the first part, Perkins," Lukas said. "You'll be dead." He stopped and focused his mind. His head ached as he put parts of his brain to work that he hadn't practiced since training Levi.

Perkins narrowed his eyes and lifted his gun threateningly. "Go ahead, John. Try to make a move."

This remark made Lukas smile. He said, "Don't you mean, 'make my day'?" As Perkins rolled his eyes, Lukas commanded Perkins's gun from the tight grip it was held, across the divide, to his hand. He caught it and pointed it at Perkins.

First, Perkins's eyes burst open in shock, and then he

dove to the side. There was a thump as he landed and bounced on the floor. He reached for a revolver holstered at his ankle. Lukas stormed down the stairs, made sure his aim was true, and fired. Perkins's ankle exploded. He cried out in pain. He reached for the revolver again, no longer attached to his leg, but adjacent. Again the gun fired and blew away his right hand. Perkins screamed in pain, holding his wrist with his left hand. His eyes were so excited, Lukas was sure they'd fall out and roll bloodied and disused along the floor.

How they were still alive, Lukas did not know, but he thanked God none of those bullets went ricocheted and hit the cradle assembly.

Lukas, for the slightest instance, also questioned the caliber of the luger and was glad he hadn't been shot.

"Stop moving, Perkins!" Lukas said as he ran beside him, gun raised. He kicked the holstered revolver away. "You'll bleed out more." He froze.

The blood coming out of Perkins was pink. A very light pink.

"Well, you don't see that every day," Lukas added. "You're a hybrid. I thought they stopped making your kind."

"You thought wrong."

"If I remember correctly, they couldn't get their murderous rages under control and kept killing each other."

Perkins's face was twisted between an angry scowl and genuine amusement. "That's rich, coming from a filthy human being. I wonder what side of our gene pool caused that defect."

Lukas couldn't argue with that assessment. "You make a good point." He checked his watch. "Sorry about your leg and arm. I have to go. I'm on a tight deadline. No doubt, you've made arrangements to prevent my departure."

"You're not going to make it out alive," Perkins snarled. "You're dead!"

"Hmm," was all Lukas could manage as a response before he rushed and collected Perkins's revolver, just in case Perkins managed to reach it and tried to shoot Lukas in the back on his way out. He made sure a bullet wasn't in the chamber and stuck it in his belt. He did the same with the luger.

Perkins continued to spit out threats and hollered an assortment of vulgarities Lukas chose to ignore. *Hear no evil*, he thought. He looked up the stairwell and at the window adjacent to it. Half of the white coats in the command center watched the whole spectacle. The other half fought the door he knew wouldn't open. They were locked in. They couldn't communicate outside of the command center. Communications were down. However, their beating and yelling might attract the guards' interest, assuming other people weren't also beating.

Lukas let out a sigh. Had he not utilized his Trident system, he'd already be surrounded. No doubt, the security guards were too preoccupied by their own locked doors and the banging of others trapped in rooms to concern themselves with the command center or register the gunfire. Was the gunfire audible outside of the cradle assembly chamber? No one ever tested that, because to fire a gun in the cradle assembly chamber was utter suicide. Had he hit one of the glass columns or the cradle center itself, or one of the power couplings connecting to it, they would have been vaporized.

Pisces is waiting for you, he reminded himself. He looked at the door. Next on his agenda was getting to her.

If Perkins somehow knew in advance what Lukas planned, wouldn't he have informed security? Perhaps

Perkins stationed a couple of guards on the other side of the door, in case Lukas escaped through the door before Perkins had a chance to put a bullet in him.

Or worse, what if Perkins or his Red collaborators telepathically transmitting orders to security before, during, or after their struggle?

Eh. Only one way to find out.

Lukas ran up the stairs, punched his command code, and waited for the door to unlock. It answered to his command and he opened the door.

The long, white halls stretched to infinity with a locked security door between every eight rooms. As he expected, fifty meters further down the hallway, the guards at the security checkpoint were scrambling from door to door down the main drag, pulling on them, while others barked orders and struggled with their walkie-talkies. One person attempted a manual override. He slipped out of the cradle chamber, closed its door, and counted the number of access doors between him and the emergency stairwell with roof access. He counted three and rushed through the first two with ease, moving with a steady pace, not drawing any attention from the few passer-byers, and entered his command code so fast he worried the touch panel wasn't fast enough.

As Lukas punched his command into the third door, and it opened, a security guard further down the hallway, at the checkpoint, looked at him and called out, "Hey! How'd you get that door to open?"

Lukas raised his hands to his shoulders and shrugged. Then, he realized there was blood on his right hand and coat from picking up the revolver, and more than likely some on his shoes from stepping in it. Though the fresh blood stains were pink, they were noticeably out of place. He lowered his hands and bolted to the emergency stairwell access.

The guard did notice the pink stains. They did look like blood. He expertly removed his pistol from his holster and raised it at Lukas. He yelled, "Hey! Stop right there!"

That caught the attention of three other guards, who turned their attention from the doors and walkie-talkies and reached for their own sidearms.

Everyone in the hall quickly scrambled away from the scene or aligned themselves against the walls.

Lukas had no intention of being involved in a firefight, or being outgunned. He commanded the first guard's pistol out of his hand with a flick of his wrist—he always found it easier to associate his hand gestures with his telekinetic commands—and then the guns of the two guards behind him. As their guns clattered on the ground and the guards looked in confused panic, Lukas pulled out the borrowed luger from his belt, aimed, and fired a shot at the fourth guard who was rushing forward.

The fourth guard's knee exploded. He screamed, flew forward onto his face, and slid across the waxed floor. But, before he hit the ground, he got one shot off, which went straight through Lukas's left thigh and crashed into the glass case, barely missing the catalyst.

The glass case shattered and fell out of Lukas's hand. The wire frame holding the catalyst buckled.

Lukas shot the fourth guard's pistol wielding arm before hunkering down and grabbing the catalyst from its shattered case. His thigh screamed and blood trickled from the entrance and exit holes. He thanked the Lord that the bullet hit the outside of his thigh and didn't damage a major artery. He praised the Lord a second time that the bullet didn't destroy the catalyst, making all of his efforts meaningless. With the catalyst in hand, glowing and pulsing energy throughout his body, he returned his attention to the other three guards, who were already retrieving their guns.

As he was trained, and trained others, when human beings were involved, Lukas always aimed to wound or injure, but never kill. Now, outnumbered, he wondered what his odds were of successfully escaping the jaws of death without taking a life in the process. He didn't like the odds.

The catalyst spoke to Lukas, reminded him of what and who he once was, what he was capable of, and time suddenly crept in slow motion. He reached out his mind and launched two guards backward five yards. They collided with each other in the air and fell on top of one another.

That's two down, for the moment, Lukas thought and turned around to the other guard.

The guard had recovered his gun. He shot Lukas in the right shoulder, before he too was thrown back. His head hit the floor hard. He didn't stir.

Agonizing pain shot through Lukas's thigh and shoulder as he limped to the emergency stairwell access. During which, he scolded himself for being so slow to react. He spent the last few years so consumed with the advanced sciences of the other worlds, saving the world, and being a parent; he allowed himself to get rusty. His combat instincts weren't as sharp as they once were. He was sixty-three; but he was supposed to have the reflexes of Peter Parker, the strength of the Hulk, and the sharp-shooting abilities of Hawkeye. Thanks to the Lord, despite the frailties of age, he survived.

Lukas typed his command code into the emergency stairwell access. It unlocked. As he pushed it open, someone yelled, "Hey," behind him and shot his left thigh. Once more, thank the Lord, it was in the outside of the thigh, not the inside, and had only nicked his femur before passing through. He fell into the stairwell, turning on his back to avoid smashing the catalyst.

The guard ran to the emergency stair entrance. Lukas mentally pushed the guard back against the wall with a force that sent him through the wall. An echo of screams followed from wherever the guard landed before Lukas shoved the emergency door closed.

Lying on the floor, bleeding but breathing calmly, Lukas cradled the catalyst and stared up the winding stairwell. He was ten levels from the roof. He checked his watch. Five minutes to reach the top to be on schedule.

Lifting himself from the cold, blood-slicked floor, Lukas commanded his body to repair itself with haste. He was glad he drank his milk. He already felt the multiple gunshot entry and exit wounds close. Yet, the pain persisted.

At his feet, left hand on the support rail, Lukas steadied himself for the hike. The stairwell taunted him.

Time was short. Sasha would be waiting for him. There was no time for pain.

He climbed.

3

The flight up the stairwell was longer and more haggard than he'd liked it to have been. Even when Lukas temporarily deactivated his pain receptors, his movements were slowed and made healing complicated. When he made it to the roof access door, he entered his code and pushed the door open.

He was greeted by a loud, high-pitched squawk from Sasha, his messenger bird, among many other things. She was a white dove, only ten times larger and four times faster, capable of flying up to a max speed of one hundred and fifty miles per hour. She had hazel eyes, a short, narrow beak, and long, tan talons. She was one of the last of her kind outside of the western mountains, where they still held a home and where she would return when all of this was over.

"You're late," Sasha projected through their telepathic link. She squawked and rested a pouch on the ground with her talons. *"And you look like crap. What happened?"*

Lukas pressed a latch in the door to keep it open and sat down. He picked up the black pouch. Inside was a metal flask full of milk. He smiled.

"My exit strategy wasn't as discrete as I intended," Lukas said. "I had an unexpected visitor who tried to shoot me."

Sasha's head tilted to the right. *"Tried? You've been shot."* Her eyes changed from hazel to blue. *"You were shot three times. And I'm detected two different blood origins."* Her eyes changed back to hazel. *"I detect hybrid blood."*

Quickly, Lukas explained Perkins's surprise visit in the cradle assembly chamber and his firefight in the hallway. He took his lab coat off and used it to wipe some of the blood off his hands and the catalyst. He kissed the catalyst, and whispered his affections. Then, he placed the catalyst, which was glowing brighter and rhythmically humming louder than ever, in the black pouch Sasha provided.

"I'm healing," Lukas said. "I'll be just as new in ten minutes, assuming I don't decide to climb another ten stories within that time frame." He attached the pouch to Sasha's talons. Part of him worried those powerful talons would crush it.

"Why climb? Why didn't you just fly?" Sasha asked, again tilting her head to the right and then left, examining him.

Lukas smiled. It was a funny thing having a bird ask him a reasonable question and being embarrassed about the answer. "Unfortunately, I haven't been exercising that portion of my brain like I used to. I couldn't risk falling and damaging the catalyst. I made it. I'll be fine."

He sat silent for a moment. "Is Pisces in place?"

"Yes. She's in the ventilation system adjacent to the roof access of the cradle assembly."

"Good. Plans have changed. I won't make it to her and get changed before they get here."

"What are you going to do?"

"Play dead. They'll take me to the mortuary. She'll have to meet me there. It's too risky for her to go to the assembly alone. Perkins was in there. He might have armed security guarding the chamber assembly."

Sasha tilted her head to the left. *"She says 'that's a terrible idea'; but she's on her way to the mortuary."*

Lukas smiled. "Good."

"You sure that is going to work?" Sasha asked.

"It'll have to."

There was a loud explosion ten stories below. Sasha started, her eyes turning red. Lukas heard shouts and boot steps echoing up the stairwell. They were pissed off and would be there any minute.

"Looks like it's time for you to go," Lukas said and gave Sasha a hug. "Keep her safe. Go to the safe haven, give Levi my regards, and make your way to Montana, and to the second assembly. Artie will take her and get the assembly operable." He brushed her feathers. "And whatever you do, don't come back here to check on me. Not this time."

Sasha started to cry. Tears drained from her eyes and down her feathers. *"What if they kill you?"*

"I highly doubt they will, but if they do, the world will live on without me."

To live is to serve, to die is to gain, he thought.

The steps were closer. Much too close.

"Go," Lukas urged. "I'll be fine."

Sasha stepped away and spread out her wings. She

turned back to him. *"I love you."*

Lukas couldn't help but tear up. In the last hour, he said good-bye to his daughter, his protégé, the catalyst, and now, one of his closest friends. "I love you, too, Sasha. Go."

With that command, Sasha darted off into the sky. She shot away *fast*. Had she not left a trail of feathers behind, one might not believe she was there only seconds ago.

In the remaining seconds before the boots made it to the last set of stairs, Lukas grabbed the metal flask full of milk and chugged as much of the contents as he could, which was all of it.

The men, soldiers of the North American Union, instead of mere security guards, stormed the top of the stairwell in their red, white, and blues and surrounded the thirsty doctor. Their laser-sighted assault rifles were inches from his face. One man unarmed Lukas, who had his hands up.

The commander in charge was a man named Collins. He had a muscular physique, long dark hair, a thick, black beard and bright red battle scars on the right side of his face. The nostrils of his broad nose flared. He ordered all but one of the ten men to continue through the doorway to the rooftop and check for any sign of the catalyst, which they didn't find.

Collins hovered over Lukas. His face was locked in a snarl, staring without blinking like a haunted portrait. After five minutes of searching, the soldiers delivered the bad news, with the exception of one, who said he found feathers and saw a bird in the distance. It didn't register. Collins leaned in close to Lukas, his breath smelling of bad cheese, onions, and beer, and began what would be his shortest interrogation. "Where is the orb, Brown?"

"Really?" Lukas pretend coughed and shook his head.

They weren't aware of his healing abilities, and the closer to death he could make himself appear, the easier it would be to begin the next phase of his plan. "They say there are no dumb questions, but that takes the cake." Collins's eyes shot open. "I go through all of this and you think I'll just tell you where it is if you ask? It's gone. You hear me? It's gone. You're playing with technology you don't understand, but they do. They most definitely do, and they're using you. You're all puppets. You're going to kill us all with that device."

Collins didn't like being called dumb or being talked down to by a civilian scientist, let alone a filthy traitor saboteur. Being called a puppet? No, sir! Not in his house. Who's house? Collins's house. He leaned back, raised his right hand to his left shoulder, and applied a wide ranging backhanded slap to Lukas's face, making sure he put all his strength into it.

Lukas's head bounced against the stairwell wall. Blood collected in his mouth. He spat and sagged.

Collins straightened Lukas and leaned forward once more. "I can do this all day, Brown, but you've been shot three times and must be losing a lot of blood." He said *must be*, because oddly enough, he didn't see as much blood coming out of him as he thought he should and that was suspicious. Yet, he let that go. "Don't you want to live to see your dog-ugly grandchildren through prison bars?"

It was an empty remark. They both knew the powers that be wanted Lukas dead, and that was where he would be if there was no intervention.

"If you get your hands on the catalyst, there will be no grandchildren for any of us," Lukas argued.

"Lies!" Collins shot back. "We're saving our future children. That device is going to heal our planet and undo the damage of the Red."

"They're here, Collins," Brown insisted. "In this facility. They've taken over your minds. All those changes Andrews, Cartwright, Zenji, and Prost made against my recommendations changed the device against us. It's going to change the world into something else. That's why I'm doing this." He pointed at himself. "Me! I'm the guy that brought the sphere here in the first place. I started this project and hired everyone. Even you. It's mine. It's always been mine. Don't you get that? Don't you understand? The world itself is dying. It was my responsibility to save it. And once you've activated that device, with their alterations, we're goners. There will be nothing left but them."

"Enough!" Collins screamed from the top of his lungs and stomped the stair he stood on. "No more lies. Tell me where the orb is or I will end you!"

Defiantly, Lukas raised his chin and stared into Collin's fierce brown eyes, "Then it ends here, with us, but the world will live on another day."

A gust of cold air blew through the door leading to the rooftop. Collins commanded, "Shut that door! Leave us alone and find that bird, if there ever was one." They followed his orders without hesitation or question. In a minute's pass, the two were alone.

Collins leaned in close and said, "You have a tasty looking little daughter, Doctor. You're going to tell me where the device is or I'll find her. I'll get a good hold of her. Spoil her. Twist her tight little tits. Pass her around my men. We'll have her squealing like a little *pig whore*. Then, when I'm tired of her, I'll beat her to death."

That was by far the most despicable threat anyone had ever made to Lukas.

"You're a dog, Collins," he returned and spat blood into the commander's face. *Sorry, Lord.*

Collins recoiled and then swung his right fist as hard

as he could into the left side of Lukas's face, breaking his jaw and bursting his left eye socket. After doing such, Collins stomped Lukas's chest and rained down a long series of vulgarities Lukas chose to neither hear nor comprehend.

Of all the things to be grateful for, the good doctor was glad he had the ability to deactivate pain with a simple thought.

Praise the Lord our God for his many blessings, Lukas thought.

Lukas was also pleased and praising that he was able to heal rapidly. The severity of the beating he was getting was grave. His eyes were both swollen shut, his face was bruised and distorted. His ribs were cracked. His lungs would be punctured, if not for their protective layering. It was going to take a lot longer than he expected to heal from this one. *Thank God* Sasha brought milk. That wasn't part of the plan.

After a minute, Collins stopped and stared at his victim. His nostrils flared and sweat beamed off his massive forehead. He rubbed the dragon tattoo on his blood stained hand.

Sagged against the stairwell wall, Lukas thought of his daughter Abigail, his protégé Levi, and the dog, Jared. In a couple hours, their journey would begin along the same path Sasha was taking beyond the western mountains. If he didn't intervene, the restoration device, now the Red weapon, would activate and destroy millions of lives, but those three would be safe. She would be safe.

Lukas smiled as his jaw snap back into place. Phase one of his plan was complete. Now, it was time for phase two. He breathed out one hard, long breath, which Collins thought was his last; then, he willed himself into standby mode, which took the appearance of death.

As of this point, I no longer need to be Lukas Brown, and can once again become John Rider.

John lay before Collins like a possum biding its time until it struck. In his idle state, John listened to the harsh breath of his opponent, the orders he issued over his old-fashioned, multi-channeled walkie-talkie, and waited. Collins declared Lukas Brown dead and ordered men to collect the body.

There was a long pause of silence.

Collins leaned closer and pressed his fingers against John's neck. There was no pulse. He placed his hand over John's mouth. Not breathing. It was strange. The man took a serious beating. Collins felt and heard the man's jaw snap. Yet, it somehow popped itself right back into place. And, his eyes were no longer swollen. He wanted to believe that was due to the lack of blood flow; yet, something stirred in his brain and told him otherwise.

"Something's wrong about this man," Collins said, stopped. His head twisted to the left, right, upward, until he seized it. He groaned from pain. Then, his posture straightened.

"I need Lieutenant Rousseau to collect an axe, a sharpened one, and join me in the examination room with Commander Collins and Doctor Gay," Collins said in the walkie-talkie. His voice was deeper, more nasal. It was Perkins's voice. "I'm going to need to remove Doctor Brown's head immediately."

Twenty minutes later, two men raced up the stairwell with a black bag and a gurney. The first man lifted John's legs and slipped him into a black body bag. They lifted him onto the gurney, strapped him in, and lowered him down the stairwell. When they exited the stairwell, they rolled him past Cartwright and Andrews on their way to the mortuary.

Cartwright whispered to herself, "Oh no. Lukas."

Andrews, however, smiled and said, "It's about time."

She scowled, "You rancorous dog. You are foul."

Offended, Andrews frowned and pointed at the body bag. "He's a traitor, and a coward. He's jeopardized us all! It'll take us years to build another catalyst, if we can at all."

"Well, maybe you should have thought of that before you three helped Perkins highjack the project," Cartwright rebutted. "If it wasn't for Lukas, you'd probably be running tests on the radiation in the Devastation Zone avoiding God knows what kind of monsters." She sneered at him and stormed to the lab.

John, in his idle state, heard it all. He regretted having doubts about Cartwright.

As things were, she too would die.

4

Cartwright stormed into the tech center flushed and fists balled. She went to her desk chair and fell down into it, slumped. Her eyes were red. She wanted to cry, but never in her life had she cried at work. She considered herself too strong to cry, even though being able to and choosing to cry around others was an honest expression of emotion, and a strength of its own. Instead of crying, she simply forced her eyes closed and breathed. She sat that way for ten minutes, undisturbed, as everyone else in their lab was too shocked and confused to speak.

After collecting herself, she looked to Prost, sitting idly in his chair, casually looking at the cheap, two handed wall clock, and then his computer. The man was playing Solitaire. Lord of lords, a man just died, three others badly wounded, and here he was, playing Solitaire without a care in the world. Then again, she thought, perhaps this was his way of coping. She hadn't known him to take a thing seriously, but now, even Mister Chuckles was quiet. This gave her the strength to share her thoughts.

With a step to start, Cartwright slid her desk chair across the waxed floor to Prost's desk. He slid slightly to the side, but kept on playing Solitaire. He whispered, "These spades are kicking my ass."

Those were not the first words she expected to hear out of his mouth. She hesitated. Maybe he wasn't coping. Perhaps he didn't care that Brown died.

Prost frowned.

Perhaps he's really engrossed in the game? No, of course not; it's Solitaire. If he was playing Age of Nations, maybe she could believe that, but not Solitaire.

"We have to do something," Cartwright whispered.

"I am doing something," Prost replied.

"No, I mean, about the cradle assembly," Cartwright clarified.

Prost turned from the game. "Like what? The head scientist, and only reason this project existed at all, is dead. The catalyst is gone. The cradle is only at ten or fifteen percent after activation. There's nothing to do." He threw up his hands. "We've been studying the catalyst for years, and still aren't sure how it works. It disrupted our scanners, so we couldn't build schematics of it, except by visual examination. I can't even begin to tell you how many microscopic and semi-translucent circuits that thing had in its crystal shell. They almost looked like neurological circuits."

Cartwright blinked. "I'm sorry. Neurological circuits?"

"Yes," Prost said. "Neurological circuitry for an artificial brain. My father's agency has been working on a confidential project to produce artificially intelligent robots."

Cartwright's mouth dropped open.

Prost continued. "They hope, in five or so years, to

build a few hundred thousand robots and send them to clean the areas devastated by the war. They would operate more cleanly and efficiently than humans and without the need of income or medicine. Unaffected by the radiation, and only needing to recharge for a few hours, we could expect to see incredible progress in the following decade. Progress would be ten-fold."

Cartwright nodded.

"In any event," Prost went on, "because I'm a mechanical and computer engineer, and my father planned to employ me after the success of this project, he sent me details on their first prototype's brain structure. The neuro-circuitry is similar. Though, the catalyst's circuits are far more articulate. In any event, there's no success coming from the project now. I'll have to call my dad."

"Right, okay," Cartwright nodded, curious what Prost was doing playing Solitaire while his father was entrusting him with sensitive details of confidential, ground-breaking technology. Then, she decided that train of thought would take her nowhere. "I'm wondering, what if Lukas was right? I mean, you know him. In all the time he's worked with us, he's been extremely calm, sensible, caring, and completely within control."

"That describes him," Prost said, retraining his attention back to his game of Solitaire.

"Precisely," Cartwright said. "Then, Perkins comes along and takes over the project almost a week before we're ready to activate it. He changes everything, purporting they were Zenji's recommendations. However, in all the time we worked with Zenji, he never implied wanting any adjustments until that day."

"Not even once," Prost said.

"He wasn't even looking into it, according to logs,"

Cartwright continued.

"Nope."

"After that, Lukas was adamant, hysterical even, about the terrible repercussions and damage those changes would cause. He fought, hard, even threatening to pull out of the project, until they stripped him of his control over the project and claimed the catalyst as the property of the government."

"That's what happens when you work for the government," Prost replied while moving his three of clubs under the four of hearts. "You relinquish the ownership and rights of the project for which you've introduced. That's why my father is going through private investors. More money in it, too. The government will be paying him for the use of his robots."

"Okay, right," Cartwright said. "Anyway, the whole thing gave me a bad feeling. I wanted to support Lukas; so I hesitated to vote. Then, Perkins cornered me. He told me I had to vote in his favor or he'd push me out of the project. He'd put Zenji and Andrews in charge, prevent me from receiving grant money for any other projects, revoke my medical license, and effectively end my career in medicine."

This caught Prost's attention. He paused his game. "Wait, what? He threatened you?"

"Yes. He did."

"That's interesting," Prost said, rubbing his chin, then the back of his neck. "I feel a little guilty." He paused as Cartwright leaned back from him. "Perkins bribed me."

She leaned in close. "He what? But how? With what, money?"

"No, his dick," Prost snapped. "Of course with money. He said the C-S-C got wind of my father's project and, in a sign of good faith and future collaboration, would provide his project with a hefty, no strings grant, as long as I played ball and went along with him in this project. We're talking nine figures, hundreds of millions. I told my dad and he insisted. He was so excited; I thought he might cream his pants."

Cartwright frowned.

"But, I wasn't too fond of the changes either," Prost said. "Honestly, the alterations didn't make sense. The new energy matrix will apply more radical changes than we intended during the cradle's initial design."

"I know!" Cartwright was excited now, pleased with herself that she decided to talk to Prost, whose intellect, though compromised by his sense of humor and lazy attitude, closely matched hers, even at his young age. "And Lukas was actually able to prove his matrix was capable of healing, because it was directly in line with the catalyst, which can bring life from death."

Prost sat quietly, thinking about what she'd just said. If he had the catalyst with him, and it responded to his command, he could have brought Lukas back to life. Perhaps, with it, and after revealing all its secrets, he could have made himself quasi-immortal. That kind of power was highly coveted, especially by Andrews. That kind of power in the hands of anyone like Perkins, a corrupt, threatening and bribing senator, also known as a normal senator, would be a poor restart for their nation, their world. Good thing it was gone. Though, some of that power still remained in the cradle assembly.

"And neither Zenji nor Perkins have proven balls about the results of their changes," Prost said.

"Exactly!" Cartwright insisted. "How could they possibly know something will work when they haven't even tested it out?" She frowned. "Something is wrong. Something is terribly wrong." Her eyes shot to Prost. "Terribly wrong."

"So, what do you have in mind?" Prost asked.

A spark ignited in her eyes and Cartwright smiled. "We finish what he started."

Prost didn't reply.

"I discretely learned Lukas's command codes," Cartwright continued. "We can get to that assembly, realign it to the original settings, and manually fire it from the assembly access panels. But, we'll have to do it soon, while there's still confusion."

"You think they'll just let us in?"

Cartwright shrugged and stood. "We're in charge, thanks to Perkins; so, they have to. And, we'll tell them we're checking the cradle assembly for damage, which we'll have to do anyway."

She walked to the exit.

Prost followed. "Fran, if we manually activate the assembly, the radiation exposure could kill us." That didn't slow her down. "Correction, with that level of exposure, it will most definitely kill us."

"Yea, it could," Cartwright said as they strode down the hall. "I suppose it could also make us immortal."

Prost slapped his hands against the sides of his face, comically. "Or it could make us big, green, and angry."

Cartwright didn't have time for comedy and shook her head. "We'll get out of there once we've activated the cradle's initialization matrix. If we bypass the lockdown mechanism, we should have a minute or two. I think."

"Wham bam thank you ma'am."

Cartwright shook her head again. "In this instance, for your sake, I hope it doesn't take you more than a minute to finish."

They raised their chief scientist badges at the guard and mentioned checking the cradle for changes or damages. The guard knew them, but examined the badges anyway before waving them past. They walked down the hall to the cradle assembly and entered.

Further down the hall, not far from where they came, Andrews watched them. His eyes narrowed. *They're up to something*, he thought. He approached Collins, who was taking witness statements.

Andrews whispered, "I think we have a problem."

5

It took nineteen minutes to get John to the medical center. The security guards were still manually reprogramming each of the security doors to circumvent the Trident virus that was running amok with their systems. In that time, John fully healed. Though, his body warned him that he couldn't suffer any more injuries until it had sufficient time to recover, a hearty meal, and much more milk. John had the feeling he was going to disappoint his body.

In order to escape his current predicament and move on with the second phase of his plan, John had to get past the guards. If they saw his body stir in the body bag, they would want to shoot him.

Perkins was nowhere to be heard or seen since he temporarily borrowed Collins's body. Yet, John knew, once he was in the medical center, Perkins wouldn't be too far behind with an axe in his hand. He had to put his plan into motion quickly.

When the guards pushed John's gurney into the medical center, there was only one nurse to be seen. Her facial features were stiff. Her hands were shaking while she removed bloody gloves.

The nurse paced, crying, mumbling "too much blood" over and over again.

One of guards stepped in front of her and spoke, "Hey."

She jumped and shrieked.

"Calm down, geez," the first guard exasperated.

The second chimed in, "Where's the doctor?"

"He's, he's, he's in surgery," the nurse stammered. "A, umm, guard lost a lot of blood when his knee was blown to pieces. They had to stop the bleeding." She sighed. "There was, there was so much blood." She swallowed hard. "They have to repair the surrounding areas and install an artificial limb. They'll be in surgery for hours."

The guards grumbled. "Where do we put the body?"

The nurse pointed. "The mortuary."

The medical center had a small room in the back designed as a mortuary. The lights were off. The cold storage was inactive. Cobwebs stretched between file boxes full of discarded hardcopies. Damaged tablets were piled up in disarray on the floor and examination table. The men spent ten minutes moving the boxes out of the way. They grumbled and cursed about the disorganization.

John wanted to chime in, but didn't. The longer they took to unstrap him, the less likely he was to escape without another confrontation with guards and Perkins. He found humor in the reality that his plan to slow them down worked too efficiently. It slowed him down. He was behind schedule and worried they might activate the cradle assembly before he had a chance to destroy it. Even at minimal power, it would do tremendous damage to the planet and its ecosystem.

Once the examination table was cleared, the men unstrapped John from the gurney and lifted him on the table. One of the men rolled the gurney out of the mortuary and headed to the storage room adjacent to the medical center; the other stood guard at the door, grumbling about wanting a cigarette break.

As soon as the first man left, John heard a buzzing coming from the ceiling ventilation unit. It steadily grew louder, making it impossible for the guard to ignore. He looked upward at the ventilation unit and crept towards it. A small dart shot into the man's eye. He cried out in pain and reached for his face. Another dart shot into his neck. He stumbled back and fell. Not long afterward, he was unconscious.

When the guard hit the ground, John quickly unzipped himself from the body bag and jumped off the table. The ventilation vent popped open and a black book bag dropped down. John caught it, put it on the table, and quickly disrobed.

I could use a good shower right now, John thought. Because of the blood, his shirt was stuck to him. *Here goes.* He inhaled, exhaled, and then ripped the shirt off of his shoulder, pulling the hairs from his flesh and giving himself an unwanted wax job. Fortunately, his shoulder had completely healed. He felt the smooth and blushed surface of his skin, but only for a second, before he finished stripping himself down.

Pisces, a white cat, jumped down from the ventilation unit and ran, on her hind legs, to the doorway. On her strong, muscled legs, she stood four feet tall. In her paws, which were tiny hands, she held a dart gun. She wore a tight, black bodysuit of a metallic brocade fabric with randomly placed and connected silver circuits. The suit stretched along her thin tail.

John pulled out a similar outfit when the second guard stomped into the mortuary.

The guard looked at the cat on her hind legs and froze. She smiled, said "meow", and waved at him. His eyes widened, eyebrows rose, and mouth gaped. He looked at John, the guard on the floor, and reached for his gun. He had two darts in his neck before he could remove his pistol from its holster. His eyes rolled back. He fell forward.

"It's always good to see you, Pisces," John said.

"Though, you didn't have to shoot the first guy in the eye. That had to be painful."

Pisces shrugged and dragged the second guard next to the first. "He was looking at me." She reached over and plucked the needle-pointed dart out of the first guard's eye socket.

John cringed and adjusted to his bodysuit. The suit was form-fitting. Despite his age, he never let himself go. He followed the same exercise regimen for thirty years. That gave him a defined, lean, muscular build. He flexed his biceps and then moved on to the remaining contents in the bag. There were two helmets, two belts, three energy pistols, and the key component of the second phase, an antimatter grenade.

The grenade was a silver cylinder embossed with green alien symbols. It had three black touch controls.

"I appreciate you coming here and taking this risk, but now that I have the suit and the grenade, I have to ask you to go back up the ventilation shaft and head out as quickly as possible, as far away as possible," John said while reaching into the book bag again and pulling out a thin, black helmet with a crystal visor. "The chances of us getting out of this without blowing ourselves up are very slim."

"What are you talking about?" Pisces responded. She spoke with a strong French accent, as French was her first language. Jeremiah jokingly believed it would be phonetically easier for a cat. "The hardest part of the trip was getting here from Montana. Between the vicious creatures and Levi's taste in music, I'd take getting blown up by antimatter any day. At least it's quick."

"Too many lives are going to be lost. Possibly all the people here. And all the people in the surrounding area if I don't stop this. You don't have to stay. This part, I can do alone. You've done your part," John lectured. He took out a black metallic belt with an oval crystalline head and glowing dot at its center.

Pisces hopped on the examination table and pulled her own small black helmet and belt from the bag. "Are you suggesting that I follow the same advice you gave Jeremiah?"

That comment hurt, and John flinched having heard it. "I'm not going to let anyone else make this sacrifice."

"We all know the risks of saving the world," Pisces said. "Not all of us will make it, but that doesn't mean we relent from our responsibilities. You told us that on our last strike on the Red Nexus. We destroyed it. And yes, there were casualties—Jeremiah was one of them—but we wouldn't have been able to do it if every one of us was not there. So, don't beat yourself up over his death. It's been too long. If I can get over it, so can you."

Having said her piece, Pisces put on her helmet and belt. Small black fabric circuits stretched from the helmet and connected to her bodysuit. John shrugged and followed suit, putting his own helmet on and letting it link to his bodysuit. With all the parts of his suit attached, the two took the bag off the table.

"How much time do you think we have?" Pisces asked.

John lifted the first guard, put him on the examination table, and slipped him in the body bag. He closed it. "Umm, any minute. I'm surprised Perkins hasn't already stormed in here with an axe in hand, ready to take my head off like John the Baptist." He placed the second guard in a refrigeration compartment.

"Repent ye, for the kingdom of heaven is at hand," Pisces quoted. She closed the book bag, placed it on her back, and felt the bag condense to its remaining contents. The straps adjusted to her body size.

"He that cometh after me is mightier than I, whose

shoes I am not worthy to bear," John quoted in return.

There was a bang as the medical center's doors slammed open. There were low voices on the other side of the door. One of those voices was Perkins's.

"Okay," John said. "I definitely wasn't talking about him. Time to go." He hunkered down and began to shimmer, fading out of view. "We can only be out of phase for five minutes; so, we have to sprint." As he said that, he disappeared from sight.

Pisces, following his lead, disappeared too.

In stealth mode together, they adjusted their frequencies until they were synchronized and could see each other. They nodded and ran straight through the wall, and the next, and the next, on their way to the cradle assembly.

Perkins, a man who rarely quietly entered a room, burst through the door to the mortuary. He limped thanks to his last encounter with John, but other than that, he was fine, in a fresh change of clothes. Lieutenant Rousseau, a tall and lanky uniformed man, followed him with an axe in his hand.

"Where are the guards, Lieutenant?" Perkins asked. "There were two. Were they not instructed to *wait* with the body?"

"I don't know, sir," Rousseau replied. He walked to the body bag. "Are we expecting someone to steal the body?"

"No," Perkins said. His eyes narrowed, shook in their sockets, and he gasped. "Open the bag, Mister Rousseau."

As ordered, Rousseau unzipped the body bag and found the guard. He started and looked at Perkins.

Perkins lifted his walkie-talkie and said, "Initiating code Alpha-Delta-Omega-Omega-Sigma. I am taking complete control of the restoration project and initiating a full lockdown of the facility."

He waited. One by one, all of the security acknowledged.

Perkins continued, "Activate the restoration device immediately and execute kill order on anyone who attempts to circumvent the activation process."

Upon the completion of the order, Perkins put down his walkie-talkie and stared directly into Rousseau's eyes. Rousseau straightened to attention and froze. His eyes stared forward, now vacant of their own prior sentience.

"Wake up the Elders. It is time."

6

Cartwright and Prost entered the cradle assembly chamber. After a sweeping ladies first gesture from Prost, Cartwright trod down the stairs. Prost followed. They both stopped at the bottom of the stairs, where the signs of the struggle between Lukas and Collins were evident. There was a gooey pink residue smeared along the floor, as though someone tried to quickly clean it up, did a poor job, and gave up.

"I wonder what happened in here," Cartwright said.

"Looks like someone spilled some Pepto Bismol," Prost said. "I couldn't think of a worse setting to try to cure your diarrhea, cha-cha-cha."

Cartwright stepped around the pink residue and towards the cradle assembly. "It also helps with nausea, heart burn, indigestion, and upset stomach."

"Ah, so Andrews on the regular. Gotcha," Prost said. He couldn't help but linger around the residue a little bit longer, for curiosity's sake. "Though, this doesn't smell like Pepto Bismol. It has a sweet, but metallic smell to it. Also, I'm seeing." He paused and leaned closer. "Hey Cartwright, check this out."

Cartwright turned from the floor display next to the

crimson energy column and shot Prost a frown. "God, Prost. What could be more important than preventing our impending destruction?"

"I just saw movement. Very slight, but it was there," Prost said and pointed at the residue.

Cartwright sighed and stepped away from the floor display.

Prost continued, "This is biological residue. I'm thinking blood. Whatever or whoever was here bled this stuff. And unlike our blood, it seems to be capable of surviving outside of the body for minutes, perhaps even hours."

Cartwright immediately kneeled beside him. Out of her lab coat pocket, she pulled out a plastic sealed cotton swab, broke the seal, and collected a small bit of the goo.

"So, you just randomly carry cotton swabs wherever you go?" Prost asked.

"Unlike you, I'm a practicing medical doctor. There are certain things I always carry." Cartwright held up the cotton swab. They both examined it closely. "After we're finished here, and assuming we survive, I'll take this to the lab. We need to know what this is, because I'm getting a bad feeling this is something it shouldn't be."

"Something it shouldn't be?" Prost asked. "What should it be?"

"Indigenous to our planet," Cartwright answered. She plugged the cotton swab into a small test tube, sealed it, and put it back in a small kit in her pocket Prost had never taken the time to notice.

She came prepared, Prost thought. *No wonder Brown liked her so much.*

"So, what you're saying is, you suspect this pink, gooey blood is extra-terrestrial?" Prost questioned. "The only extra-terrestrials we've officially had contact with are—" He stopped and looked at the catalyst assembly.

Cartwright followed his looked and rushed to the assembly. "I hope whatever it was hasn't tampered with the device."

"No, Cartwright, listen," Prost stood frozen in place, stunned.

"We don't have time." Cartwright logged into the panel. "We have to fix this before it's too late. It might have done something. Maybe made things worse."

Prost looked at the pink blood again. "What if this is Brown's blood?"

That is preposterous, Cartwright thought, but didn't say. She turned from the panel again. "That can't be. He's spent the last seven years of his life trying to save the planet. He's used the catalyst a hundred times to restore food resources in the community, just to show the capabilities of the device. He's saving us. He can't be one of—" She stopped herself. "It can't be his."

To comfort her and deliver the message he didn't want to deliver, Prost stepped beside her, at the touch display, and sat down. "Just think about it, because now I certainly am."

Prost paused and thought about it. "He doesn't get sick. Even with all the radiation out there, not once. In the last five years I've worked with him, I have seen him sweat, but that's it."

He stopped and thought again. "He keeps to himself. Makes week long trips to the west, but won't tell anyone where he's going. He's always using weird gadgets none of us have ever seen. He won't tell us where he got them or what they do. And, a half hour ago, he was in a gun fight with our security. Whose blood could this be besides his?"

Cartwright slowly lost color in her skin as she allowed herself to consider his reasoning. She leaned back from the panel and sat silently.

"I don't want to believe this either," Prost added. "He was a standup guy. However, we have to accept the possibility that he was not who he said he was."

"Honestly, I never thought to ask him if he was human," Cartwright said.

"I wonder how many women have said that to themselves," Prost said. He pressed his tongue against the inside of his cheek and poked his cheek with his finger.

Cartwright glared at him.

"I'm getting the feeling that you two never, what's the phrase the kids are using these days, buried the one-eyed worm. Taken the skin boat to tuna town," Prost whispered.

At that, Cartwright grew red. "Sam. That's enough."

Prost shrugged, but slid a few inches from her. "I'm just saying; after seven years, a normal human male would have tried to stick his salami between your slices of bread and spread a little miracle whip."

"That's a very disturbing analogy," Cartwright said. Suddenly, she remembered she hadn't had anything to eat in hours. She shook her head, stood, and rushed to another floor display. "We've dated, sort of, but it wasn't physical. He made it very clear he doesn't mix work with romance. And I respected that decision. Lukas was a professional."

"Well, I would have professionally tapped that," Prost said.

"I said that's enough!" Cartwright insisted. She crossed her arms and shot Prost the evil eye.

Prost put a finger to his mouth.

She wiped sweat from her forehead, thought, *These columns are heating up again*, and said, "Listen, no matter what you may suspect him to be, Brown's works speak for themselves. 'Every good tree bringeth forth good fruit; but a corrupt tree bringeth forth evil fruit. A good tree cannot bring forth evil fruit, neither can a corrupt tree bring forth good fruit. Every tree that bringeth not forth good fruit is hewn down, and cast into the fire. Wherefore by their fruits ye shall know them.' That's from Matthew seven."

Prost considered that. "Wow. Quoting the King James Bible. You just had a Brown moment, and suddenly, I'm convinced. Not that he's human, mind you, but that he had good intentions with his alien technology. Perhaps he is one of them and is attempting to undo the damage done by his people. Kind of like, atonement or reparations for the crimes of his people."

That was a thought Cartwright never considered.

Again, she shook her head and tightened her hand into a fist. "He is not one of them. Now stop distracting me and help! We have to re-modulate the columns to Brown's original settings before someone interferes or tries to activate the device before we do."

"You will do no such thing!" a familiar voice yelled from the entryway of the cradle assembly chamber.

Prost and Cartwright turned sharply to see Andrews standing at the entrance with three armed guards. One of the guards was Commander Collins.

Andrews, with the biggest smile that's ever populated a human face, placed his hands on his hips, akimbo, and barked, "We have just received orders from Senator Perkins. After the actions of the late, but not late enough, Doctor Brown, Perkins has taken full authority over the restoration project. We are to activate the device immediately. He has also given us authority to kill anyone who interferes, and that includes you. So, I'm going to give you one chance to come quietly, and willingly, before we drag your dead bodies out of here."

Cartwright was the first to protest. "You're mad,

Andrews! You're really something. They can't shoot us in here. They'd hit the cradle assembly and kill us all."

"Who said anything about shooting you, Frances?" Andrews said. He'd worked with her for seven years and took pleasure in getting her name wrong every single time. "No. They're going to take their time with you two. They'll beat you two to death. That's how Brown died, right Collins? You beat him dead, and he cried like a little girl for mercy the whole time."

At that, Collins smiled, revealing his coffee stained teeth.

"Yea, that doesn't sound like an accurate depiction of what happened," Prost said.

"SHUT UP, PROST!" Andrews screamed and pointed his finger at Prost. He made his way down the stairs. The guards followed. "I personally look forward to seeing them beat that stupid mouth of yours closed."

Prost frowned. "Didn't you say you were giving us a chance to come quietly and willingly?"

"You declined that offer when you opened your big mouth!" Andrews barked back.

Prost didn't have a comeback for that one.

As they reached the bottom of the stairs, Andrews pointed at Prost. "Him first. I want her to watch. Then we can take turns on her."

The guards approached Prost, who raised his fists in a traditional boxer's position and backed away.

Cartwright screamed, "You can't do this!"

Collins smiled, showing all his teeth. "Watch us."

The first guard charged Prost. Prost threw a punch and connected with the guard's left jaw. The guard rubbed his muscular face, not phased, and shook his head. "Shouldn't have done that." He took his uniform jacket off and tossed it to the ground. In his tank top alone, the guard flexed his impressively large and toned muscles. "Now, I'm going to have to enjoy this."

Prost raised his fists again. He caught movement to his left. Two figures appeared out of thin air and approached rapidly. "Holy mother of God. Did you just see that?"

With Prost distracted, the guard threw a hard left jab. It connected against Prost's exposed right cheek. He went down after the first punch, making a pathetic thud against the cradle assembly's metal flooring. He lay unconscious.

There was a lasting silence as everyone stared downward at Prost. Then, Andrews and the guards burst out laughing. They hollered and held their guts. Cartwright rushed to Prost and checked on his vitals.

Andrews chuckled, rubbed the tears from his eyes, and said, "Finally, someone shut him up."

Collins laughed with tears streaming. He had to sit down to compose himself. Shaking his head, he turned to his right and a dart shot in his right eye. He screamed and reached for it.

The laughter immediately stopped. Hearts, in the lingering milliseconds that felt like an eternity, stopped.

In that hesitation, two streams of hot energy shot past Andrews and into the chests of the two guards standing over Cartwright and Prost. They flew back, shirts ablaze, and tumbled to the floor.

Andrews dove to the floor and put his hands over his head.

Collins held his right hand clasped against his eyes while he reached, panicked, with his left hand for his gun. An energy blast hit him square in the chest and he lay still, unconscious.

With everyone subdued, except for Andrews, who was unarmed, John took off his helmet and rushed over to Cartwright. "Is Sam okay?"

"No," Cartwright said. She hugged John. "He took that hit pretty hard. He's going to have a serious bruise. Maybe a concussion. I hope he doesn't suffer brain swelling. I'm certain he hit his head when he fell." She took a good look at him. "You're alive! How? How are you alive? How did you get in here? And, what are you wearing? And, you have a ray gun? And, you're alive?"

John smiled and assessed the situation while Cartwright rambled and pelted him with questions. "I'll explain later. Now isn't the time for explanations. It's time for action. We have to disable the device before they activate it." He looked at Pisces, who snickered. "And what are you laughing at, the fact that you shot another guy in the eye?"

"No, that was skill," Pisces said. "Practicing for the real thing." She took off her helmet, still snickering. "I'm loving the way he took the punch. He didn't see it coming. It was like the films."

John looked at Prost and shook his head. He turned to Andrews, who slithered towards Collins. "Don't even think about it, Andrews. You just sit still and stay quiet. I've had it up to here with you." He turned to Pisces. "Collect their weapons and secure the room."

Pisces nodded and got to it.

"How are you alive?" a pale Andrews asked. He blinked rapidly and licked his dry lips. His eyes darted from John to Pisces, then back to John. "You were dead. They had you in a body bag."

"What can I say? You can't keep a good man down," John answered. He turned to Cartwright. "So, what were you trying to do here?"

Cartwright raised a shaky hand to her forehead and breathed deeply, calmed herself. She then rushed to the crimson column's floor panel. "I was trying to recalibrate the cradle assembly to its original alignment before Per-

Perkins got his hands on it."

That was what he wanted to hear. He only wished he had her on his side before he finalized his plans. Things would have operated smoothly.

But what if she was always on his side and his refusal to trust others stood in his way? He spent the last few years getting closer and closer to her, falling in love but dwelling over the risks of her being read by the Red. Yet, these two were operating on their own accord against the Red. How did they get this far without being read or having their minds taken over? Were the Red unable to read them? Were they so confident of their success that they chose limited intervention?

"Do you have an implant in your head?" John asked.

"What?" Cartwright asked.

"Never mind. Maybe later," John said and rushed to a floor panel. "Enter your code, authorize my code, and we can both make the changes. Perhaps it's not too late."

The door to the cradle assembly chamber locked with a loud click and whine of mechanical bolts. A hiss followed as the sealed room pressurized. The light at the center of the cradle dimmed. The cradle assembly began to hum and rumble.

"Oh, that's not good," John said.

Andrews stood and balled his hands into fists. "It's too late! Now we're trapped. You're going to get us all killed in here. No one's supposed to be in this room when the device activates."

"I'm locked out!" Cartwright said and madly pressed the touch panel.

"Initiation protocols. Once it's been activated, all manual controls are deactivated in case of malfunctions," John said matter-of-factly and looked at Pisces. "It looks like we have to go with our original plan."

"Which is?" Cartwright asked.

"Blow it up," Pisces said and rushed to the cradle assembly. She grabbed her bag from her back and unzipped it. "With that door shut and air sealed, we'll have to phase to get out of here. How much time do we have?"

John looked at the panel, which only displayed the countdown. "Five minutes."

Pisces shook her head and pulled out the antimatter grenade. "You and your five minute windows, man."

Cartwright looked at the two. Until now, she hadn't realized John was talking to a cat. A cat spoke to her. This whole time, her vision was limited from the lighting of the cradle's columns. "What is going on? You're talking to a cat. A cat is talking to me. And, we're about to blow up the equivalent of a nuclear reactor? It's going to incinerate us."

"Well—" John started.

"AHHHHHH!"

Both John and Pisces jumped at the scream. Pisces nearly dropped the grenade. They looked at Andrews, and then turned to where he stared.

John's heart sank.

Three large, red-scaled, four-legged creatures lumbered and wavered from a large open passage in the far wall. A thick, semi-translucent pink slime covered their bodies. Their heads each had one large eye, which was still closed, no nose but two slits, and a wide mouth full of long, razor sharp teeth. The eyes were two feet round and eighty-percent of their heads. It was their most prominent feature. Their necks were long and strong. In addition to four legs, each creature had a pair of long, powerful scaly arms and hands that rubbed at the lids of the singular eyes. Those hands fought to clear the gook.

They were the *Rezarians*, nicknamed the Red.

In his heart, John knew he would see the lizard creatures, half dragon and half snake, again. He reached desperately within himself to find the person he was during the war and aimed to pull him forward.

Andrews ran up the stairwell screaming at the top of his lungs. He made it to the door and banged on it, screaming for release. The three Red turned in his direction and lumbered up the stairs after him.

The yelling woke Prost. He twitched and raised his head.

Pisces looked at Cartwright and the barely conscious Prost. "John, the grenade is set, but what about these two? They won't be able to get out. Once I activate the timer, we'll only have two minutes. And, we have less than a minute before I have to activate it."

Crap, John thought while quickly assessing an alternative exit strategy. Whatever it was, it would have to be quick. He pointed his energy pistols at the wall closest to them and furthest from any power junctions or the Red. Then, he fired both pistols, sending two energy streams into and through the wall. Both streams were four feet apart, rising from the floor and cutting through the wall in a tall arc.

Understanding his plan, Pisces turned to Cartwright and said, "If you can't wake him up, drag him to that wall. We only have seconds before I press this button. Then, we have to run like the wrath of God is falling on this place and not look back."

Nodding, Cartwright grabbed Prost, slapped him on the face, and began dragging him to his feet. "Wake up, Prost. We've gotta get outta here."

Prost struggled to his feet, with Cartwright's help, and they trudged towards the wall. Cartwright whispered in his ear, "Speed up. Come on. If we get out of here, maybe I'll show you my breasts."

Somehow, that did the trick. He found his footing, staggered; and they made their way to the wall.

John finished burning a hole into the wall, holstered his pistols, and used his mind to push the slab of wall into the other side. It crashed to the tile flooring of the bathroom on the other side. A line of ten urinals stood from the ground and connected along the left wall. Looking through the hole in the wall, John turned back and said, "If anyone has to pee, you're just gonna have to hold it."

"Ha, ha," Cartwright said sarcastically while helping Prost through the hole. "Get ready to run, Prost."

"Timer activated!" Pisces announced as she pressed the button and the timer counted down in milliseconds. Her voice trembled, John recognized.

Five more Red lumbered through the wall. Andrews was surrounded by the original three and plead for his life. They were slowly opening their eyes, which was bad news for everybody.

While putting on her helmet, Pisces ran from the cradle assembly to the wall and bolted through the hole. John picked up his helmet, put it on, and followed.

On the other side of the hole, Cartwright splashed water into Prost's face, creating a wet spot in the front of his shirt, and encouraged, "Wake up, Prost. Come on." His eyes were glazed. He wobbled.

John rushed to Prost's side and placed his head under his arm. "Prost, what's about to happen is going to make you nauseous and confused. Close your eyes." After Prost nodded and did as he was told, John looked back at Pisces and Cartwright. "Run!"

At that command, the four raced out of the bathroom and down the long, sparsely populated corridor of the research station's lower level. It was the power level. Engineers with long white coats backed out of the way as they saw the four running past. A few engineers looked from their stations and pointed. Guards turned to intercept them. Pisces fired low-powered energy blasts into their chests, knocking them backwards and unconscious.

Pisces, in the lead of the group, was glad she downloaded the facility's blueprints into her helmet. She could see the coming turns before they came and led the group to a flight of stairs fifty yards away. It was an emergency stairwell to a ground level exit. As she turned through various corridors, they followed.

Behind Pisces was Cartwright, who was shocked she kept up with the little speed devil, and was even more impressed that John hadn't skipped a step with the extra weight of Prost. She tried not to get distracted—since she would hate to miss a turn or collide into a wall—but she noticed that Prost's feet weren't touching the floor, and John's barely were. It was as though they were flying.

At the stairwell first, Pisces fought the door open and held it for Cartwright, who slipped past. Pisces shook her head when John made it up the stairs. "Something's not right. It's been two minutes and eight seconds. The grenade should have exploded. We should be dead."

"We should be *dead*?" Cartwright asked in the background.

John turned around and saw guards approaching the stairwell, pistols pointed. Not interested in being shot again, John closed the door and sealed it shut with blasts from his energy pistol at the cracks of the door and handle. "I was thinking the same thing, but we can't go back. The device is about to activate any second now."

"So, what do we do, now?" Cartwright asked. They were in a junction connecting the emergency door to the outdoors and the main hall of the facility.

Pisces shrugged and looked around, consulting the

blueprints. "You won't believe where we are, John."

"Why do you keep calling him John?" Cartwright wondered.

The lights went out. The ground shook. There were screams on the other side of the door, followed by the foot falls of scrambling people.

"Later," John snapped. He felt bad immediately. "Sorry. Looks like we're right back where we started. The medical center is next door. We have to get into the morgue and seal ourselves into the refrigeration chambers before the blast. It'll happen in the next thirty seconds."

Cartwright frowned. "What makes you think the chambers will protect us?"

John thought. "Hope. Cartwright and Prost, you go out this door and enter the medical center. Enter the morgue. We'll meet you there."

Prost was finally getting his senses back. "You aren't coming with us?"

"Yes, we are. We're just going a different route," Pisces said.

"And what route is that?" Cartwright asked.

"Through the wall," John said. At that, he and Pisces vanished before Cartwright's eyes and jumped through the wall. They saw a shimmer in the wall as matter adjusted itself to accommodate the passer-throughers.

"Where does he get all those wonderful toys?" Prost said and smiled.

The foundations of the building trembled violently. The two went through the door, into the main hall, and fumbled their way through the dark. People pushed past them. One man collided directly into Cartwright and knocked her down. Prost, still fighting his disorientation, helped her up. They kept against the wall until they found the medical center. They pushed their way through the doors and found a guard on the floor, unconscious.

John rushed to Cartwright and Prost, and led them to the morgue. In the morgue, one more guard lay unconscious on the floor.

"I see you had company," Cartwright said as John led her to one of the four open refrigeration chambers. All of them were still inactive.

Pisces climbed into a refrigeration chamber. "They didn't see us coming."

John helped Cartwright into her chamber, then Prost. After all three of them were settled, he closed them in. There was a large explosion, followed by a steady rumbling and whistling coming closer and closer. He could feel the hair on his arm rising. *The cradle assembly blast fired.* Quickly, John climbed in his own chamber, closed his eyes, and willed it shut.

In the darkness, the four waited.

The world trembled around them.

7

Seventy-five miles away was a great metallic wall. It stood five hundred feet tall and stretched fifty miles long. Along the top of the wall were automated guns powerful enough to obliterate a tank. In a tower attached to the wall, three soldiers clad in red, white, and blue, metal plated boots, and cowboy hats patrolled. One soldier who was smoking a cigar and scratching himself noticed movement in the corner of his eye. He looked up and saw a green shimmer cross beyond their authorized borderlines. It moved fast, hardly visible in the blinding light and warm colors of the sunrise. He rushed to the command console and entered his codes. There were no authorized flights this early in the day into the Quarantine Zone. Whatever it was, it didn't have a flight plan; so, it had to come down.

With a few presses on the command console, one of automated guns aligned itself, aimed at the sky, and fired a long arcing spray of propulsion-powered bullets southwest.

Miles away, a large bird fell from the sky.

CHAPTER THREE
THE FATE OF THE WORLD

THEY'RE LATE, JARED THOUGHT. He sat, legs crossed, with his long, black, hand-like paws clasped as he watched the touch-screen display in front of him. *They're all late.*

It was his job to monitor the movements and progress of all of the parties involved in their mission from the safe haven. The screen displayed a zoomed out, real-time map of Virginia. Every individual was identified by a color-coded dot. The good doctor was yellow. Pisces was orange. Levi was purple. Emma was black. Abigail was blue. Sasha was white. The catalyst was green. The screen also emphasized areas of interest with an exaggerated size scale. The research facility, Brown residence, Stockton Checkpoint, and safe haven were digitally enhanced to appear three-dimensionally and four times their size.

So far, they were more than a half hour behind schedule.

Jared knew he could expect Levi and Abbey to be late. After all, they were young; Levi was smitten; and Abbey was difficult. However, Sasha was running behind. The good doctor operated like clockwork. If he said he'd be there at six o'clock, you could expect him to be there at five forty-five with an extra latte as a courtesy. In order for him to send Sasha behind schedule, something must have gone wrong. Terribly wrong.

Fortunately, Emma was impressively fast. Watching their progress on the screen made Jared wish he had wheels. He was fast, faster than any quadruped on Earth, but never as fast as her. Then again, she had thrusters.

Sasha was remarkably fast. Though, Jared thought she had it easy. She didn't have to change paths based on terrain. There were no hills to climb or trees to avoid. She could shoot a straight path to any destination. The only thing she had to worry about was strong winds and a little wind resistance. That was why she was chosen to carry the catalyst. Her route would be the quick, easy and direct route northwest.

The white dot crossed the wall, blinked, and then disappeared. The green dot stopped and blinked. A high-pitched and repetitive beeping followed.

"No!" Jared howled and pressed numerous commands into the screen. It zoomed in on the location of the green dot. There was green land, a faint green glow, and falling white feathers.

"How?" he whined.

Retracing Sasha's route, Jared zoomed in on her flight path hoping for an explanation. After a deeper zoom, he saw the weapons mounted on the quarantine barrier wall.

"Sasha, Sasha's dead. They shot her," Jared growled, displaying his fangs. "Those animals."

The green dot continued to blink.

At least the catalyst was still in one piece.

Zooming out, Jared plotted the catalyst's location in reference to Levi's route. Too far south. Too far off of their course. If the cradle assembly wasn't destroyed, and fired on schedule, they wouldn't make it in time. So, what were their options? There were no other options. He had to get the catalyst before an animal got hold of it or some diseased mutated maniac with half of a working brain found and smashed it.

Within five minutes, Jared was dressed in his metallic, brocade fabric suit. It could absorb, disrupt, or refract light, heat, energy pulses, and harmful radiation. He hoped it wouldn't be necessary. After attaching his oblong helmet, designed to support his elongated snout, he rushed to the exit.

"Overseer, establish link with main computer," he ordered and exited. The safe haven had two entrances and exits. The primary was larger, less discreet, and opened exclusively for Emma. The secondary was a small passageway and exit point surrounded by bushes and trees. The secondary was designed for Jared to slip in and out with ease and discretion, or for others in case of emergency.

"Link established," said the computer.

At the exit point, Jared waited, "Begin transmission to Emma." There was a short pause as he waited for a beep. There was a beep. "This is Jared. Sasha has been critically injured by a ballistics assault from the quarantine barrier wall's gunnery. Her life signs no longer register. The catalyst is in the open, exposed. I am going to recover it. End transmission."

Outside, Jared activated his suit's refraction protocols and faded from sight. He raced to recover the catalyst, hoping he wouldn't get to it or return too late.

2

The first light of the day was a sight to see. Abbey loved sunrises; so, her father woke her in time to jog to the lake and watch them. They would wrap themselves in blankets, sit on damp lawn chairs, breathe in the crisp morning air, and appreciate the dawning of a new day. Afterward, they enjoyed scrambled eggs, strawberry or blueberry waffles, apple slices, and a banana-orange-peach smoothie. She took a shower, got dressed, and spent a half an hour reading the English Standard Bible. It was their daily tradition.

To her surprise, she fell asleep during the car ride. It was a sudden thing, without weariness or fatigue, and lasted for an hour and a half. It would have lasted longer, but Levi woke her. She argued until he told her the sun was about to rise. Then, instead of fighting him, she burst into tears. Was this to be her and Levi's tradition now, or would tradition die?

Turning from the sunrise, Abbey glanced at Violet and Jeremy. They were sleeping. She whispered to Levi, "Sucks being the driver. Did you sleep last night?"

Levi shrugged and said, "No. I took a nap earlier in the day, but there was too much to do. I'll take another nap when we make it to the mountain passage."

Abbey leaned forward, sticking her blond head between the driver's and passenger's seats. "You could take a break; and I could drive."

"Nah," Levi declined. "We're almost there. It would be pointless at this point. But thanks for the offer. I appreciate the gesture."

Abbey frowned and leaned back in her seat. "What? You think I can't drive? I'm a great driver. Dad said I make Tony Stewart look like a first-time driver, whomever that is."

Levi shook his head and sighed. "I don't doubt your driving skills, Abbey. At this stage of our trip, it's unnecessary."

"Uh huh," Abbey yawned and stretched out her arms. "Where are we anyway?"

"We just passed Charlottesville. We're seven minutes from the safety checkpoint. After that, we'll be ten to fifteen minutes from the mountains."

Abbey nodded, and looked out the window again. "Nothing's happened, yet. Do you think he's okay? Do you think he stopped it?"

"Your father?" Levi asked.

"No, Bono. Of course, my father."

Levi glanced back at her. His eyes narrowed. She gave him a toothy smile.

"You haven't listened to the message he left for you," Levi said.

Abbey gave out a loud sigh. "Again with the message. Can't you just give me an answer?"

"Can't you just do one simple thing without being stubborn?" Levi responded with a toothy smile of his own.

Abbey's eyes narrowed. "When we get to the stupid mountain, I'll listen to the message, okay? Now, what is he up to?"

Levi slid his finger along the touch-screen dashboard. He pulled up a screen monitoring the life signatures of everyone in the car. "In our present company, I cannot say. That is why it is important you listen to the message. Someone here is going to get very upset by what I tell you."

Frowning, Abbey looked at the screen. "Why and how are you monitoring our heart rates, and who would get upset? What's going on?"

Levi pointed to the screen. "Internal sensors are designed to monitor the health of all of the car's occupants. If someone is injured, it informs us of where and how badly. If someone has a sickness, say a fever, it detects the increased body temperature right away. It's very helpful."

"Similar to the setup my dad has in our house," Abbey said.

"Exactly," Levi replied.

"You still haven't stated who's going to be upset if you tell me what my dad's doing," Abbey said, persistent for answers. She pressed her lips together. Her eyes focused on Levi's as she stared through the rearview mirror.

Knowing she was staring at him, Levi looked back at her bright blue eyes and smiled at her. "You really do have the loveliest eyes on Earth, Abigail."

Not expecting that, Abbey looked down and blushed. "Thank you," she said. In the corner of her eye, she saw Jeremy's fist tighten for a split second. She looked at him. He sat there with his eyes closed, shoulders slumped, breathing slowed. From appearances, he was resting. She examined the monitor on Levi's dashboard and understood exactly why he was being discrete in their conversation.

What she did not understand was why Jeremy was pretending to sleep. Was he intentionally eavesdropping on their conversation? Obviously. Why was he listening? That she did not know. Was he waiting for her to say something about him? Was he listening for the same information she was trying to get from Levi? Was he simply trying to avoid being involved in the conversation? There were so many questions.

What about what Levi said? *Someone here is going to get very upset by what I tell you.* What else was there to be upset about? If that device did what her dad said it would, both of their fathers were going to die. Her father was going there to do something. The only reasonable thing to be done was to stop it from firing.

Okay. Stop it from firing. What if her father was working against Jeremy's father in order to prevent the device from firing? That would make Jeremy upset. He would be furious if he knew her father was working against his father. Considering Jeremy's father was head of security, it meant her father was working against security. That made her father and Jeremy's father enemies. She was dating the son of her father's enemy. That would explain all of his invasive questions.

Would them working against each other be enough to make Jeremy upset, or was there more to it? What was her father doing to prevent the device from firing? Was he going to reprogram or deactivate it? Was he going to destroy it? Destroying it would solve the problem of the Red using it against humanity. And even though her father would always try to avoid casualties, his actions could endanger the life of Jeremy's father.

However, how did Levi know Jeremy's father worked security? How did he know Jeremy's father?

"Levi, I understand," Abbey said.

Levi raised his eyebrow and glanced at Abbey. She darted her eyes from Levi to Jeremy and back to Levi. Levi smiled and nodded. He returned the dashboard screen to the paused road trip playlist.

"Whatever it is he was doing, do you think he succeeded?" Abbey asked and hoped for good news.

If he knew the answer, Levi didn't show it. His expressions were plain. His eyes were focused on the road. As the thick collection of trees began to dwindle, they could see a large metallic wall with spotlights, armed men, and mounted guns.

"I don't know what to think," Levi said. "If he succeeded, we'll witness an impressive nothing. If he failed, however." Levi looked at the clock. It was minutes from six. "We'll soon find out."

Abbey looked out of the window, southeast towards Richmond. "What happens if he fails? What will become of the world? Of us?"

That wasn't a conversation Levi wanted to have, either. Though the good doctor insisted he consider it, and planned for alternatives, it never crossed Levi's mind that the good doctor could or would fail. "That's a complicated question, Abigail. There are multiple phases of his mission. But he's not alone. He has an old friend from the war with him. They're both capable of amazing things. There's no doubt in my mind that, at the very least, phase one was completed. And phase one's success means there's hope for us all."

Abbey smiled, happy to hear her father wasn't taking on whatever crazy, self-sacrificing mission he was involved in alone.

"What is phase one?" Violet asked. She yawned and stretched her limbs in wild and random angles. She rubbed her tired and curious eyes and then looked at Levi. "And are we anywhere near a place to eat? I'm staaaahvin."

On that note, Abbey's stomach growled.

"Looks like you're not alone," Abbey said and laughed. "I'd kill for a smoothie and a blueberry muffin."

"Hopefully, it won't come to that," Levi said. He looked at Abbey through his rearview mirror. "We're roughly fifteen minutes from the mountain passage. There, we have plenty of food stored, including freshly frozen fruit for a nice smoothie. We also have a couple showers."

"Yes!" Violet and Abbey said in unison.

"However, be conservative with water," Levi continued. "We don't have an abundance of freshwater reserves. It stores water from rain and filters out the impurities."

"And how exactly did you and Abbey's father come about this 'mountain passage' and the food storage, this new car, and all this stuff you have?" Jeremy chimed in from the back, suspicion in his tone. He spoke out so suddenly, it gave Abbey a start.

Though Levi didn't appreciate the suspicious tone or implications of Jeremy's question, he understood why he would be suspicious. They had a lot of stuff. With strings of financial resources coming from multiple identities before, during, and after the war, it was not possible for an outsider to see the revenue stream, but only the spoils. With their access to extra-terrestrial technology, and continued impeccable health in a dying and diseased world, he'd have to be blind not to notice and suspect something. Unfortunately, Jeremy would be left with his speculations and suspicions. Levi didn't know Jeremy, but he knew enough about Jeremy's father to keep sensitive information close to his chest, and only reveal public information.

"Well," Levi started hesitantly, "my father was the good doctor's, I mean, Abbey's father's best friend. My father was loaded from medical technology research and development with Trinity Medical."

"Trinity? As in, the city of light, Trinity?" Violet interrupted.

Between her and Abbey, Levi wondered how he'd complete a thought during their trip to Montana. At least Abbey hadn't interrupted him since she woke up.

"Yes," Levi answered, "Trinity, the city of light, the city of faithful hearts. That Trinity padded my father's pockets after he and a partner laid down the foundations for breakthrough nanotechnology capable of curing cancer, repairing—"

"Oh look, we're there!" Abbey shouted and pointed.

Ahead was a sign that said, "Stockton Checkpoint". Five vehicles ahead of them were the checkpoint station and its barrier wall. The wall was five hundred feet tall and extended twenty-five miles north and south from the Stockton Creek and interstate sixty-four junction point. Interstate sixty-four was a key transport route for goods west of postwar Virginia. The Stockton Checkpoint was also a protective border post put in place to protect central and east Virginia from highly volatile, mutant animals which were populating in the western Virginia region at an alarming rate. Because of the high risk of attack and fatality, only certified and armed traders, transporters, hunters, guarded science and repair convoys, military officers, and those with a special considerations permit were authorized to pass through. The checkpoint was also put in place to keep out "the infected", mutants, non-citizens and rogues from the west and south who might attempt terrorism, weapons or drug trades, and illegal immigration. Five checkpoint guards on the incoming and outgoing lanes were moving from vehicle to vehicle performing checks on the vehicles and questioning the passengers.

Levi stopped the car behind a stopped truck and looked at Violet. "Violet, do you have your identification with you?"

"Umm," Violet reached under her seat for her purse and began to fumble through it. "I should. I don't use it for much; so, I doubt I've taken it out."

While Violet looked, Levi turned his head around to the backseat. "Jeremy, you have your identification, right?"

Jeremy reached in his pocket and pulled out a silver card with his image and a computer chip. "Don't leave home without it. It's the law."

Levi nodded, looked at Abbey, and opened his mouth, but Abbey spoke before he could. "This is bad. Dad said not to bring my I-D! He took it from me. Why would he do that if he knew I was coming through the checkpoint?" She frowned and rubbed her elbow.

"I know, and had you listened to the message your father left you," Levi paused and looked directly into Abbey's eyes, which she rolled, "you would know that I have identification documents for you, as well as another name."

"What?" Abbey asked. "Another name? Why?"

"Yea. What's going on? Why aren't you telling us anything?" Violet chimed in.

Maybe if you stopped interrupting all the time, Levi thought.

The guards stepped closer, only two trucks and an armored car away.

"I'm telling you now," Levi said to Violet before returning his attention to a flustered Abbey. "Your name is Sarah Lynn Rider."

"My aunt's name was Sarah," Abbey said with a smile.

"Yes and your grandmother's name was Lindsay," Levi snapped.

Abbey frowned. "You don't have to be snippy, prat. I'm just saying—"

"Here's your I-D," Levi interrupted. He handed her a vertically-aligned and forest green card with a gold chip from his pocket. "It's linked to your bank accounts."

Jeremy looked at her card and his. "Wait. That's not right. That's a Washington Coalition I-D card."

"Because *Sarah* was born in Montana and is, thusly, a natural-born citizen of the Washington Coalition," Levi said.

"Oh, so my history is exactly the same. It's just a name change," Abbey said.

"Something like that—" He stopped and stared out the back of the window through the rear view mirror. His features tensed. The blood rushed out of his face.

"What?" Abbey asked and turned around. She said, "Oh crap," and stared slack jawed.

Jeremy and Violet looked back.

"What is that?" Violet yelled.

A red stream of light pulsed from a great distance into the sky. The sun faded out of sight, and in its place was a growing red cloud. That stream of light stopped and in its place was a wave of energy. The cloud expanded. The wave, which stretched to the sky, moved closer and faster. They felt a rumble under their feet.

"Ei raja o dal," Levi whispered. The breath of death.

"What?" Violet responded.

"It's the end of the world as we know it," Levi said.

3

The trip look longer than Jared intended. He raced through the woods, avoided snarling and pursuant predators, and climbed up and down hills along the Appalachian trial. Jared finally saw a dim green glimmer of light and heard an endless, high-pitched humming. He rushed to the source, a small glowing sphere twenty-six feet off the ground, in a tree, tucked in the talons of a large, white dove. It lay still.

Great, Jared thought and looked up the tree with hesitation. *This will be a sight to see. A wolf climbing a tree. If bears can do it, and cats can do it, I can certainly do it.*

Jared extended the length of his sharp claws and backed up a couple meters. He measured the distance and calculated velocity versus mass and gravity. *Cats and bears don't use physics. They just climb.* Kicking himself, he raced forward, leapt, and dug his claws into the bark of the tree. Without allowing himself to second guess his approach, he quickly and frantically pushed himself into a rapid climb. His hand-like paws grappled the sides of the tree and branches as he came to them. He angled his arms and legs and used all the strength in his muscles to keep speed.

At the peak of the climb, Sasha's body lay tucked between two thick branches. He sniffed and smelled blood. It was an exciting sensation, but he settled his predator instincts. He listened. There was an extremely faint heartbeat coming from Sasha. It was so slow, it was barely notable. Jared understood what was happening. She was barely alive. Her body was near death, and all that kept her alive (if only artificially) were the little things inside of her and the power of the catalyst. They were trying to repair her. Restore her.

Assuming the predators didn't find Sasha, and she had a source of nutrition, it was possible that Sasha might heal and fully recover in a day. Unfortunately, she didn't have a day. She didn't have hours. They were in the Quarantine Zone's woodlands with highly aggressive, mutant creatures, and Jared didn't have a means of carrying her. It was a surprise to Jared that they hadn't already pounced on Sasha when she fell. It was unusually quiet, except for that humming sound.

The humming, Jared thought. It was the catalyst that kept the predators away. No doubt, it had some effect on life in this region outside of its healing properties. The tree was visibly growing small branches. In his life, he had never seen branches grow right before his eyes. The sounds of animal and insect life were vacant. Not even a cricket chirped. He didn't understand why the catalyst produced growth in plant-life but kept away animal-life, unless there was something else.

He listened. There was an approaching storm coming from a great distance.

The light of the day quickly faded. It was replaced by a deep and dark burgundy haze.

Then he felt it, a rumbling. An earthquake? Life fled because life relied on instincts. The instincts he, like the humans, had allowed to dull in place of technological advances.

The woodlands were thick, but he could still see a growing darkness. The light of the sun was replaced by a deep red. A large red cloud and energy wave was approaching from southeast. He took off his helmet and sniffed. He was overcome by the strong smell of sulfur. His eyes nearly came out of his head at the strength of it.

Jared whined, locked his helmet, and looked at his wounded friend. He had to flee. He had to take the catalyst and leave her. The fate of the world depended on it. He reached and strained against the constant pull of gravity, pressed the lower back of Sasha's skull, and held his claw there for five seconds. There was a click. He pulled out a small, wafer-like crystalline chip with luminescent circuits and stuck it into a sleeve pocket. He sealed the pocket and grabbed the thin black pouch the catalyst was in. He attached the pouch to his belt and lowered himself down the tree.

Surrounding trees swayed against strong gusts of wind. He set his course for the safe haven and tore through the woodlands.

4

Three guards pointed at the slowly approaching red energy wave, its ominous dark clouds, and rushed backwards towards the checkpoint station. They were waving the line of vehicles they'd checked through the wall frantically while another guard at the top was entering a code into a console attached to the wall. The portion of the wall connected to the incoming lanes began to blink red lights and sound an alarm. Shortly afterward was the shrieking sound of metal grinding against metal as the large wall slowly began to close. Levi knew: anyone trying to enter or exit the Quarantine Zone would be trapped.

Two guards stepped in front of Levi's car and stretched their open hands forward, signaling them to stop and stay put. Then, one of the guards came to the driver's side of the vehicle. Levi lowered the passenger window.

"I recognize this car," the guard said. He straightened his blue uniform and frowned. "Lieutenant Levi Jones of the Washington Coalition, right?"

"That is affirmative, umm, Sergeant," Levi said, acknowledging the insignia on the guard's uniform. He briefly glanced in his rearview mirror. The energy wave was slowly coming closer and closer. From its speed, he suspected they would be overcome by it in ten minutes.

Nodding, the sergeant looked to the other guard standing in front of the car and nodded to him. When the other guard spoke in his radio, the sergeant looked at Levi. "Last time I saw you, you said you were headed to Richmond. We've lost contact with Richmond. In fact, everyone has. You wouldn't know anything about that, would you?"

"I'm as curious as you are, Sergeant," Levi responded and watched the progress of the slowly closing wall. The squealing sound of metal on metal was wearing at his nerves.

The sergeant crossed his arms. "Well, I'm having trouble believing that. You've been coming in and out of the Quarantine Zone for days collecting food and supplies. I suspect you have a bunker or something out there. I also suspect you are responsible for whatever just happened in Richmond and intend on waiting it out or even fleeing."

Without a hitch, Levi raised his eyebrow. "I hear a lot of speculation, Sergeant. I've not brought anything illegal in or out of the Quarantine Zone, as you know. Simply food and survival supplies, as you've said. So, unless you have credible proof, your speculation and suspicions are irrelevant." The sergeant's eyes shot open. His mouth twisted and teeth ground. He turned a deep red. Levi continued, nevertheless, "Sergeant what's-your-name, I have special accommodations certifications, a scavenger license, and Washington credentials. You must let me through."

The sergeant clenched his fists. He looked at the other guard and shook his head. The other guard waved to six guards at the wall.

"The hell I don't, *Lieutenant*. Not until whatever that is, is answered for," the sergeant said and pointed east towards the approaching wave of destruction. He briefly glanced at Jeremy, looked right into his eyes, blinked, nodded, and then stormed away. He met up with the other guard. The two talked with their backs turned to the car while the other guards walked forward.

Levi raised his window.

"They're going to lock us in and kill us!" Abbey yelled in Levi's ear. Her voice was shaky and alarmed. "You have to do something. What are you going to do?"

Levi turned to Abbey, whose head was between the driver's and passenger's seat. His heart was racing. His adrenaline had kicked in. Their faces were only two inches apart. In another time, in another place, he would shorten that distance, inhaled her breath, and given her a kiss. He'd wanted to for years. He wanted to now. Yet, it wasn't the time. It was never the time, especially with the world coming to an end and her boyfriend in the backseat next to her.

Part of him refused to push away the thought of slowly locking his lips on her lower lip and gently sucking. His mind refused to push away the idea of leaning forward and gliding the tip of his tongue under the tip of her tongue and playfully flicking her tongue.

Kiss, suck, kiss, suck, flick. If only he could make her smile and then kiss that smile.

Get a grip, man! Now is not *the time,* a thought came to him.

"Put on your seatbelt, Abigail," Levi whispered in a voice that was barely his own. She smelled sweet, like peaches. He wanted to kiss her so much. Her stress had to be releasing pheromones. "We're going to have to rush the door before it closes."

"Are you sure that's wise?" Abbey asked, still only inches from his face. "What if it closes on us? What if they shoot us?"

"Then we get crushed or shot and we die," Levi said with a smile.

Abbey blinked. "There's got to be an alternative." She pointed at the wall, which began to close on the outgoing lanes.

"We could drive right through the wall, but we run the risk of sinking into the Earth," Levi said. "We could fly over the wall, but we might use too much battery power."

"What?" Abbey responded and scrunched her cute little nose.

Violet looked at Abbey and Levi and gripped their shirts with wide panicked eyes. "Are we going to have a conversation about this, or get out of here? Go!"

"Right! Brace yourselves," Levi said. He punched the gas, shifted to the left to avoid hitting the sergeant, and rushed past the idle truck in front of him.

The guards saw the black sedan racing forward and quickly grabbed their single-handed assault rifles from their leg holsters. The sergeant was the first to send off a spray of ammunition to the rear of the black sedan. The bullets bounced off of the sedan with a ripple effect like rain drops on a pond. The rest of the guards followed suit, sending rounds of bullets after the sedan. They, too, bounced off of the sedan.

"Thrusters on the ready, Emma," Levi announced. Emma responded with an affirmative. A small portal opened in the lower rear of the sedan. Then, a small, pulsing silver flame shot out of the car. The sedan launched forward. Levi barely slipped the sedan through the remaining eight foot gap of the wall. The guards pursued and fired rounds through the gap as the wall slowly closed.

Everyone in the car, with the exception of Jeremy, cheered as the car raced onward down the interstate. Bullets rained at them from the guns along the top of the wall.

"What? A bulletproof car, Lee?" Violet asked. Her teeth were grinding. Levi could see her blood vessels pumping out of her sweating skull. Her hands were tightly gripping the chair.

"I do work in law enforcement," Levi said to Violet with a smile.

"We, we barely got out of there," Violet gasped.

"Talk about getting through by the skin of our teeth," Abbey said. She looked at Jeremy, who stared blank, almost stunned, and gave him a hug and kiss on the lips.

"We may have been that close to the wall doors," Levi said. He was smiling. His heart was racing. Then, he saw the kiss in his rearview mirror, and the smile vanished.

"Yea, that was too close for my comfort," Violet said. "I thought we were going to slam through the wall and only the middle would make it to the other side."

"No," Levi responded, still watching Abbey and Jeremy through his rearview mirror. "If we collided with the wall, we would have been vaporized instantly and taken out everyone at the checkpoint. Probably would have left a nice crater, too."

Violet's mouth dropped open. "What? Why? We couldn't have been going that fast." Then, she looked in the rearview mirror. "Oh, Levi, it's getting closer."

"What's getting—" Levi looked in the rearview mirror, "—closer?" The massive energy wave was much closer—Levi estimated eighteen miles—and coming fast.

"It's overcome Charlottesville," Levi said. He pressed hard on the gas and began inputting commands into the touch-screen dashboard display. "Emma. Use whatever power reserves we have to maintain ion thruster pulses. We need maximum speed to make it to the mountain passage before the wave."

Emma's British voice sounded with alarm, "Levi, this request will cause critical drains in power reserves and require an extended recharge time, which may hinder the speed and urgency of our mission to Montana."

The voice startled Violet, and Abbey's head shot between the passenger and driver's seat. "Wait. Your car talks back to you?"

"I am aware," Levi growled. "No time to explain, Abigail. Emma, please proceed."

"Never is," Abbey said. She rolled her eyes and looked at Violet, who shrugged.

"Proceeding," Emma responded. The sedan once again accelerated. "I should also inform you of a pressing matter which will alter the outcome of our mission."

"Emma," said a frustrated Levi. Emma was not supposed to respond openly around the others. "What happened to our discretionary measures protocol? And what is more important than us not getting destroyed by that huge breath of death?"

"Breath of death. That's an interesting way to describe it," Violet mumbled to herself.

"Thirty minutes ago, Sasha was critically injured by a ballistics strike. She has failed to reach the safe haven,"

Emma said. Jeremy straightened in his seat, abruptly, giving Abbey a start. "Jared left the safe haven to recover the item. There is a distinct possibility that neither he nor it will reach the passage before we or the incoming energy wave do."

"Jared?" Abbey chimed in. "She's talking about our Jared?"

"Yes, Abigail, she is," Levi said.

"What's he doing out there?" Abbey asked. "Why'd you bring him along?"

Levi tightened his grip on the steering wheel. The car was going too fast to avert his attention. If he batted his eye or lost focus, he could send them off the road and into a tree. "I don't have time to discuss that either, Abbey. I have to focus on the road. Why weren't you this inquisitive when I asked you to listen to the message your dad left you?"

"Again with the message!" Abbey exasperated and leaned back into her seat. Her seat belt quickly stretched around her and connected itself without her activating it. "What the?" She grabbed at it and tried to push forward. She couldn't. "Your car just, it just trapped me in a seatbelt!"

"Good," Levi said. "Thanks, Emma. Question: if the wave overcomes us, do we have enough power to project a radiation shield strong enough to protect us from it?"

"Not at this time," Emma responded. "We are approaching exit ninety-nine. Deactivating ion thrusters now."

Violet chimed in, "What exactly is that thing coming at us?"

"If we survive it, I'll explain it," Levi said. His jaw was tightening. "If only we got here sooner."

Violet frowned. "You mean, if only you left me and Jeremy back there to die?" She scowled at him.

"Everyone back there is dead! That could have been us."

I don't have time for this, Levi thought. "I am so sorry Violet. We were so concerned with saving the planet, preventing the Red from discovering our plans, and getting Abigail to safety, that we forgot about you. Just remind yourself where you would have been and whom you would have been with had Abigail, your best friend, not come to save you."

Eyes ablaze, Violet shot Levi a death stare. Her lips trembled and pulled back from her teeth.

"I don't understand the connotations of that last part," Abigail said, noticing a growing tension from everyone in the car, including Jeremy, who was still with his eyes wide.

"Hold on," Levi said. The sign for interstate exit ninety-nine was upon them sooner than Levi had expected. He sharply guided the car on the round and winding interstate off-ramp. The unkempt woodlands that surrounded it were lush and beautiful. Old, abandoned and decrepit cars were lined along the sides of the interstate exit in ditches.

"Emma, how much longer before we reach the safe haven?" Levi asked.

"Less than two minutes at optimal speeds," Emma responded.

"Okay. How long before Jared reaches the safe haven?"

The dashboard touch-screen unit displayed an expanded satellite image of their position in relation to the safe haven. Then, it indicated a moving blue dot further south. "Considering he is traveling through woodland, I estimate an arrival time of ten minutes."

"And how long before the wave hits the safe haven?" Levi continued.

Emma hesitated. "Unfortunately, it will arrive in

approximately five minutes."

Levi nodded and undid his seatbelt. "Activate auto-pilot."

"Engaged," Emma responded. "Are you about to do what I think you're about to do?"

Violet's anger disintegrated. "What you think he's about to do? You think?"

"Of course I do," Emma responded.

Levi pulled a black, slim helmet—it was perfectly sized and contoured to his head—out of a small compartment between the driver's and passenger's seats, and unlocked the driver's side door. "Emma, maintain speed, get them to safety. I'm going after Jared."

"How are you going to do that?" Abbey asked. "You're going to jump out of the car? You'll get injured. You'll die."

"No time to explain," Levi said. He put on his helmet and opened the door.

"Wait!" Abbey yelled.

He hopped out and disappeared before their eyes.

Abigail and Violet screamed. Jeremy yelled. All three looked back at the street.

Levi was nowhere to be found.

5

The woodlands were a blur. Jared shot through the forest like a bullet; yet, he was not fast enough. He felt the rising heat, the shuddering ground, and knew the wave was about to overcome him.

The catalyst, in its pouch, attached to his belt, was humming loudly in his ear. Jared believed the catalyst would protect him from the wave. She told him that. She whispered to him, told him every tree, branch, brush, ditch, and puddle in his path before he got there. Alert of dangers, he jumped, turned left, turned right. He'd never run faster in his life. Part of him was certain he'd make it, but another part of him wondered if it was wishful thinking. He was still too far from the safe haven and the wave was less than a minute from overcoming him.

This wasn't how it was supposed to be. Sasha was supposed to live. She'd never been shot at before. In all of her trips over and beyond the barrier wall, she was never considered a threat. And if he was lost, what would become of the catalyst? What would become of Levi and Abbey?

When the good doctor asked him to monitor the mission from the safe haven, Jared felt slighted, as though he was being sidelined. Now, he was relieved he was there. No one was faster on foot. If Pisces stayed behind, instead of him, the catalyst would already have been lost. So would she. All he had to do was speed up.

A proximity alarm sounded in his ears. "I know. I know. I'm bacon," Jared barked in frustration as he continued through the deep brush and began to ascend uphill.

"I don't think you do," a familiar voice sounded in his ear. "And wouldn't you be a hot dog?"

Jared shot a glance to his left and saw a shimmer. That shimmer became a clear image of Levi flying to his left. Levi was maintaining speed with him and extending a hand.

"I'm going to grab you," Levi said.

Feeling the heat on his tail, Jared growled, "Well, get on with it!"

Levi shifted to his right, grabbed Jared, and shot into the air.

With Jared in arms, Levi pushed himself and his mind as far as he could go, flying at maximum. The wave was only seconds from overwhelming them. Their suits were sounding proximity and heat index alarms.

The wave was upon them.

There was a soothing hum from the catalyst; and then, a green glowing ball surrounded and encased them like an illuminated marble.

"Thank you, Jesus!" Levi cheered, sweating profusely. He could feel less stress on his brain, as well as acceleration towards the safe haven. They were no longer in the direct wake of the wave, but it was still within a hundred yards of them.

"I agree," Jared barked, before shifting his eyes and managing the data coming on his helmet's input screen. "Praise the Lord. With that being said, please change your vector by ten degrees to our left or we're going to crash into the mountain and die."

Levi shifted to the left. The map on his input screen showed them a minute from reaching the safe haven. The mountain passage was still open and Emma was already inside.

"Emma's inside. Abigail's safe," Levi said.

"Sasha is gone. I have no doubt she is passing the doors of the living to the light at the end of the hall."

"May the Lord's name leave her lips and open that door," Levi added.

"Amen," they said in unison. It was followed by silence.

"And what of the good doctor?" Jared questioned.

To that, Levi had no answer. The good doctor failed to destroy the cradle assembly. Was it because he was dead?

"He didn't destroy the cradle," Jared said. "Neither did Pisces. That means they're dead, doesn't it?"

"There's no other conclusion I can come to. If the good doctor was compromised, Pisces would have entered the chamber, set the grenade, and reported in.

That's just how she is. So, I can only assume she was killed first. Maybe they discovered her before he arrived. He got the catalyst out of there, and then tried to save her."

"So, what's next?" Jared asked.

"We go to Montana and save the world."

6

The steering wheel was locked in place; yet, Emma turned. She turned on her own after her operator jumped out of the car and disappeared. She turned on her own after being of sound mind to understand the decisions of her operator before the operator vocalized his intentions. She was a car capable of speech, comprehension, analysis, deduction, and independent operation. Emma was an intelligent, thinking car. Perhaps, she was alive, if such a thing was possible. That was more than Violet could accept; so she started to panic, and she wasn't alone.

When Levi jumped out of the car, Abbey, Violet, and Jeremy screamed and looked for him. He had completely vanished.

Abbey burst into tears and refused to remove her eyes from the road, hoping to see something. Some sign that he survived the fall and was running, walking, limping, or something. Why would he jump out of the car? Was it because she asked so many questions or wouldn't listen to the message her father left her?

Jeremy tried to climb into the front seat so he could take control of the wheel; but Emma was insistent that he sit tight. She tightened his seatbelt and locked it so it couldn't be unbuckled. When he attempted to break the seatbelt, she gave him a shock and politely offered to incapacitate him: "If you're feeling anxious, I would be more than pleased to place you in an unconscious state and ease your tensions for the remainder of our trip to the safe haven." He didn't accept her offer, but settled himself in his seat.

After Emma's offer, and Jeremy's submission, Violet began to search for the locks in the doors, only to find none. And when she rapidly and repetitively tried to turn the door handled, it wouldn't budge. She began to sweat, but her hands were cold as she placed them against her face. "Oh my God! Oh my God! Levi's committed suicide and we're trapped in a car that's alive. We're going to die."

At that, Emma scoffed indignantly. If she had eyes to roll, she would have rolled them. "Good grief, child. Get a grip. Levi didn't suicide, and no one's going to die. We're here."

At that, Abbey turned from the back window, eyebrows raised, "Really?"

"No, Abigail, I just said that to waste my non-existent breath," Emma said and let out a loud sigh. "Of course, we're here."

Abbey frowned and looked at the dashboard. It was the only place she could think to look to talk to a computer. "Did you just give me sass?"

There was no response from Emma.

The road wound along the side of the Blue Ridge Mountains. As the car came to a turn, a section of the mountain pushed outward and then slid to the side, leaving an open cavern projecting dim yellow lights. The cavern looked like the inside of a mouth. Sandy limestone stalactites were formed from the ridges of the roof and looked like teeth ready to bite down on the car as it endeavored into the maw. Similar stalagmites formed from the ground up. Four foot tall, glass light cylinders were placed five yards apart along the wall. They alternated between yellow and white lights.

Twenty yards into the cave, Emma stopped. She unlocked their seatbelts and opened the doors. "Please exit. You may extract any items from the trunk when Levi has arrived."

"Levi's dead," Jeremy said and stepped out of the car. He looked around at the rough, jagged interior and inhaled the smell of, was that cinnamon? It was humid, damp. He could hear drips of water and smell mildew. However, he could also smell cinnamon. It was an unexpected but welcoming aroma. "He jumped out of a car going a little less than seventy miles per hour. He's road-kill."

Abbey gasped and approached him. "How could you say such a thing, and so coldly?"

"How else should one speak the truth? What do you think happened? You think he just jumped out of the car and flew away?"

"Yes," Abbey said. She looked down and bit her lip. "Maybe. Maybe not. I don't know. I just, I can't believe he'd jump out of the car and kill himself. He's too smart for that. He didn't show any of the signs of, of, instability. It would have been a senseless, careless, ungodly act, and that's the furthest thing from what Levi is."

"So, what do you think happened to him?" Jeremy asked. He walked to the entrance and looked out at the approaching cloud. "That whatever-it-is is coming our way. We have to shut that door before it kills us all."

Abbey followed Jeremy. "But that would lock Levi out."

"Again, *he's dead*. I don't care what that psychotic car says. The guy lost it and jumped to his death. I don't know what he was planning, but he must have had something loose in his head if he thought he could jump out of a moving vehicle like that."

"And, what if he is alive?" Violet chimed in.

"Look at that," Jeremy said and pointed outside. "There's no way he is."

They looked at the approaching red wave. It was close. Too close. There was no sunlight but instead the sparkling red electric fire of the wave. The black clouds puffed bits of red lightning. Emma turned off her lights and shut down. There was a stillness and calm in the cave. They listened to the little drips of water from the stalactites, buzzing of the light cylinders, and the oncoming storm. It felt and sounded like an approaching army of trains.

Abbey ran outside and looked onward at the oncoming storm. She put her hands over her cheeks, peered at the approaching demon, and hissed at its intentions. *Are you intent on destroying everyone I love?* She challenged.

Violet and Jeremy grabbed her and pulled her back. Abbey tried to fight, but the air was thin and she was weak. The weakest she'd ever been in her life. She was ready to faint. She was ready to surrender. She was ready to die. Her father was dead. Her Levi was dead. Her Jared was dead. What did she have left but Jeremy and Violet? That felt like having nothing at all.

Jeremy pressed a big silver button on the wall, which read, "Open/Close". The mountain passage door began to screech and close. Jeremy turned away from the door, looked at Abbey in her distraught state, and couldn't help but to smirk.

She was his again. They were both his.

7

"We should be there any second now!" Levi yelled.

The safe haven was in sight. A hole in the mountain was set along an old road. It was surrounded by long grass, tall trees, and a thick patch of large purple mushrooms. Two thick lines of dead grass trailed from the road to the hole. A blond haired girl stood on the outside starring at the approaching wave of death. Two sets of hands pulled her in. Then, the door began to close.

"Oh, come on! We're here!" Levi yelled and pushed himself a little faster.

The door froze, leaving a four foot gap.

Thank you, Emma, Levi thought.

The two slipped through the gap of the safe haven's mountain passage door and it closed with a hard shudder and click. They rolled and tumbled on the hard earth and crashed into the limestone wall of the cave. There was a loud hiss coming from the door as the cave was pressurized. It drowned out the angry grumblings of Levi and Jared as they rose to their feet. Abbey, Violet, and Jeremy looked at the two with wide eyes.

Levi took off his helmet and said, "Okay. Who shut that door?"

The mountain shook violently and knocked Abbey, Violet, and Jeremy off of their feet. The dim lights of the safe haven flickered. A roaring wind beat the thick passage door repetitively with the force of a hundred men. The hairs on everyone's heads and bodies rose and made the crackling sound of static electricity.

"Emma!" Levi shouted. "Please increase radiation shielding in sector four."

"Increasing shield intensity to maximum," Emma replied from the entrance speakers.

After a minute, their hair settled and the static sensations left.

"You're alive!" Abbey yelled and stumbled her way to Levi, despite the trembling ground.

He mumbled, "Barely," under his breath before she

gave him a squeezing hug and kissed him on the cheek. He smiled. She let go of him and looked at Jared. "Is that Jared? He's bigger than he used to be."

"Yes," Levi responded. "It's Jared."

"Heck is he wearing?" Abbey asked. She took off Jared's helmet and hugged him.

"It's uh—" Levi stopped and searched for a good word to describe the suit without detailing its complete use and functionality, "—an environmental suit."

"Why is he wearing that? He's a dog." She tightened her grip. When Jared whined, she relaxed. "Sorry."

"He's more wolf than dog, remember?" Levi said and dusted the dirt off of his clothes.

"Yea yea yea, you don't see people dressing wolves either, do you?"

Levi continued, "And among other functions, the environmental suit protects him from the radiation outside."

The trembling ceased.

Violet unhooked her arms from a stalagmite and approached the two frowning. "What is wrong with you two?" She looked at Abbey. "Talking about a dog?" She looked at Levi. "Levi, you almost died out there. You almost died and, we thought you were dead. *Dead.* You jumped out of the car." She hugged him. "You jumped, *out of,* the car."

Has anyone ever told you, you repeat yourself? Levi thought to ask, but dared not.

"Explain yourself," Violet demanded. She pointed her finger at him. He didn't like it when people pointed their fingers at him. It was rude.

Levi gaped, and moved his lips to say, "I went to save Jared," but the words didn't escape. He looked at Abbey, back at Violet, then at Jeremy, who had a blank, glassy-eyed expression on his face. His vacant and trembling eyes were locked on Jared. What? Why was he staring at Jared that way? He had to have seen (and knowing his family, probably tortured or killed) a couple hundred mutant animals. So, a genetically altered wolf certainly shouldn't raise scrutiny.

Unless, no. He wasn't looking at Jared. If not Jared, what was he looking at? Maybe he was looking at something attached to Jared. The suit? Well, that suit would appear unusual, but wouldn't elicit that kind of reaction. So, what then? What else would he be looking at? What did Jared have?

Oh, the catalyst.

Jeremy looked enchanted, perhaps even hypnotized by its glow.

"Okay, Violet," Levi said. "I know you have a lot of questions. *A lot of them.* I'm sure all of you do. Just hold on a little bit longer and I'll be able to give you some answers. We have to put the, uhh, item Jared has in a safe place until we leave. We have to make sure this place is completely safe and well-contained from the radiation." He folded his hands. "Jared, please lead the way."

Jared pulled himself out of Abbey's grasp and tottered away, deeper into the cavern. Levi quickly rushed behind him. Abbey and Violet chased after the two.

Jeremy lingered behind and looked at the mountain passage door. Part of him wanted to press that button again and fill the inside of the safe haven with radiation, to hell with himself and everyone in it. He didn't know why he wanted them dead. He just wanted it with a burning passion.

"Hurt them. Kill them all, especially Levi," a hissing voice instructed.

His heart filled with hatred. He hated Levi. *Hated him*, and wished he closed the door just a few seconds sooner.

No, if he closed the door sooner, he wouldn't have

seen the item.

"Get the item."

He would get the item. That was what he had to do. He wasn't sure of what it was or what it did. He just had to get it.

"Get the item, Jeremy. Get the item. The pain will go away if you get the item."

He would get the item and everything would be all right. The pain in his head would leave him. How long had it been there? How long had his head hurt? An hour? Two hours?

Jeremy chewed on that thought for a while, and then followed the others deeper into the cave.

8

An hour passed. During that time, Levi gave a brief tour, showed everyone to their respected rooms, said he was going to meet them for a late lunch, and then snuck off for a nap. Abbey announced she was taking another nap. The girl loved to sleep. And Jeremy was, well, strangely enough, nowhere to be seen once they were shown their rooms. Violet wandered alone.

The safe haven was a massive underground bunker with thirteen rooms. There were three bedrooms: one master bedroom and bath, and two guest rooms with one guest bathroom. Levi and Jared took the master bedroom, Abbey and Violet shared a guest room, and Jeremy was left with the other guest room. There was a kitchen, lounge, library, garden, control room, small geothermal power plant, water (and wastewater) management, utility room, and two storage rooms. Each room, with the exception of the garden, had thick rubber flooring. Each door was locked by hand scanners to ensure only those authorized could enter. Violet, Abbey, and Jeremy had guest clearances, which limited their access to guest rooms, the guest bathroom, and open spaces like the kitchen, garden, and lounge, which had no security doors.

The lounge was wide, open and dark. As Violet entered, it came to life. Light shone from standing glass cylinders along the outer rims of the lounge and small, white, spherical Christmas lights which circled the limestone columns, stalactites, and reflected off of the still water that stretched from the middle to the far wall of the lounge. To the left of the entrance was a long, oval and glass dining table with a metal frame. It was circled by five chairs with rubber backing and seats and metal frames. Further to its right was a tall, enclosed, glass bookcase. Near the center was one couch and two chairs—all were plough, black leather, and covered in clear protective plastic—and a large oval glass coffee table with a metal frame. Attached to the right wall was a one-hundred and twenty inch widescreen television. Her eyes widened and stuck on the television. It was the largest television she had ever seen.

She stepped closer. The flooring of the lounge was the same as most of the cavern walkways, a gridded and black, spongy rubber that gave her steps a bounce. She nearly slipped on one of the water spots from the dew falling from stalactites. The room was cool and smelt of mold, rubber, and cinnamon. She still wasn't sure where the smell of cinnamon was coming from, but it was strong. It over-powered the wet cave smells, thank God. Was it artificially produced? She'd have to ask Levi, later.

The couch wasn't comfortable with cold plastic on it. Since the plastic didn't have any water spots, and part of her suspected the plastic was there for the dog more so than to protect the leather from water, she removed it and stretched out.

"Ahhhh. That was better. Wasn't it?" a hissing voice

spoke into the back of her mind.

Violet wasn't sure where that voice came from, but it caught her off guard. She jumped and looked around. No one was there. The lounge was as still and empty as she'd found it. So, she sat back down. She was getting a headache.

"Maybe you're tired, Vy," the voice insisted. *"You should just hop in the guest bed with Abbey and remove the tired from your eyes."*

No. If there was one thing she didn't do, Violet didn't take naps during the day. If she was tired, she stayed awake until bed time. Then, she slept a healthy, solid eight hours. No cheating. No brief slumbers to recharge. That's when she got her really bad headaches.

The headache became worse, almost insisting she take a nap. And it made her wonder something. She felt she should remember something very important about headaches. Something Levi said before she fell asleep in the car.

When Violet was younger, she had a lot of headaches. They were intense, mind-splitting. She'd be in her room crying, holding her head. Her father would come home from the pub—he worked from six o'clock to four o'clock and drank from four o'clock to eight o'clock— drunk off his pisser, yelling, "Shut her up, daggit. What are you doing just sittin there? I swear; the only time you're off your ass is when a dick's in it." (Dear old dad was a real charmer.) Her mom would come in her room upset, giving her dirty looks, frustrated about how helpless she was to fix the headaches. They were every other day and most of the people suspected it had to do with the radiation or poor food quality. "Stop cryin, Violet. Just stop cryin and take an aspirin." An aspirin a day keeps the headaches away, no one ever said.

The headaches hadn't occurred until the Browns

came into town. The first occurred when Violet met Abbey in class. Some of the other kids complained about headaches, but no one associated it with the Brown girl. The headaches were sporadic and slight, at first. Then, as she became friends and started visiting Abbey's home, they gradually became more and more intense.

On one particular evening, her headaches were so intense she blacked out. That was when the Browns took her to the hospital and paid for tests, scans, and treatment. Not too long after that, Abbey's dad gave her something and the headaches gradually marginalized to random bursts of pain every other week for five minutes.

In the last four years, she hadn't had a single headache. Why did it start again?

Perhaps a little television will help, she thought and looked around. There was no remote control on the coffee table. Nor was it on the couch. Nor was it on the chairs or dining table. Nor was it on the floor.

If she were at home, she'd have to hear about it. "Where's the remote, Violet?" they would yell. Her father never hit her, but instead made her mother the whipping boy. She was the reason Violet lost things, wasn't in bed on time, did poorly on a test at school, or made messes. "Why the hell can't you keep track of her and our shit, Margaret?" he'd yell and pop her mother in the back of the head. Her mother would bounce a couple steps forward, throw Violet a dirty look, and then search for the remote.

Her mother hated her. She could see it. Why her mother hadn't kicked her to the curb once her father died was beyond her. Though, she suspected she couldn't because of her father's will. As the lawyer read James Harrier's Last Will and Testament, her mother continually shot her dirty looks. Even in the grave, the man gave her mother a hard time. Did he leave her a dime, a single dime?

No, he didn't. Prior to reading the will, the lawyer had hesitantly handed her mother an envelope. After her mother opened the envelope and read the letter inside, she dropped it and burst into tears. While the lawyer apologized and consoled her, Violet snuck over to the envelope and letter.

James Harrier left his wife a penny, in an envelope, with a note. That note said:

"Dear Margaret,

You are a worthless, whoring snag. YOU KNOW WHAT YOU DID! I would have divorced you, but you would have got half of everything and probably Violet, too. Death was the only way I could get away from you. And now that I'm gone, I'm giving everything to Violet. The house in Richmond, the house in Washington, the two cars, her college fund, the secret savings, vacation savings, the bank bonds, the emergency savings, all of it goes to her. It's in trusts until she turns sixteen. Then she gets it all and can kick you out on your sorry fat can for all I care. You were a terrible wife, and a worse mother.

I hate you, Margaret. I'll see you and your saggy tits in Hell.

With love,
James

P.S. I couldn't leave you penniless; so I left you a penny."

Violet read it three times with wide eyes before the lawyer saw she had it and snapped it out of her hands. He shook his head, used the Lord's name as a swear word, and walked around his desk. Later, Violet hugged her crying mother and told her she loved her. She said she wouldn't ever kick her mother out of the house. She could stay there forever if she wanted. She didn't want anything but her mommy. It didn't change her mother's temperament. The woman had a shade of red in her eyes Violet had never seen before.

After that day, the two barely spoke. It wasn't as though Violet didn't try to speak to her mother—she loved her—but the woman refused to respond. And if her mother spoke to her, it was usually issuing orders and yelling when she did something wrong. Like her husband, she became well acquainted with the bottle. When she was alone, she drank for hours and then cried until she was dehydrated. After several months, she started to have strange men over. Some of them were leering at Violet more than her mother, slapping her in the butt and winking. So, she made it a mission to sleep over at Abbey's house as much as possible. Headaches be damned, there were worst things than headaches, especially since her boobs grew in.

"Of course, that wasn't the only reason why you regularly slept over at Abbey's place, was it?"

That voice, wherever it came from, popped her out of her daze. What the heck? She looked around. What was she doing anyway?

"You were looking for the remote control."

Right. She was looking for the remote control.

It took her ten minutes of searching before she gave up and walked to the television. There were no buttons to press. What if there wasn't a remote to begin with?

"So how does this thing turn on?" Violet complained.

The television turned on to a blank blue screen, then a black screen. On that screen came a message in large white letters, "This television, like everything else, is voice activated, Ms. Harrier."

She blinked at the screen.

An image of Violet standing in front of the TV

appeared on the screen. She turned around and looked for the vantage point of the camera. She wasn't aware she was being recorded or observed. Levi hadn't mentioned it. But he didn't mentioned a lot of things, even the things she demanded to know. Was he watching her now? Levi never came across as some kind of voyeuristic pervert. Then again, considering the different kinds of men she'd seen her mother with (macho men, men dressed as women, metrosexuals, sadomasochists, quiet and threatening, narcissists, and the typical, average dirty bastards), she wouldn't put anything past any man.

No. No. Not Levi. Levi was different. There wasn't a shred of deviant in him. *That* she could rely on.

"Who is that?" she asked to empty space. There was no response. She looked at the television. "Who's controlling the T-V?"

"The same person controlling the car, Miss Harrier," a familiar British woman's voice spoke from the cave walls. "My name is Emma."

"How is that possible?"

"I am connected to the safe haven's entire operations and security network as an administrator," Emma replied.

"No, no. I mean, how, you referred to yourself as a person."

"I am a person, Miss Harrier," Emma said.

"How is that possible? You're the car; but, you're alive. You, you, you make your own decisions. You understand me. You think, have forethought, and you predict. You're sentient." She let the word "sentient" linger in the air. "I didn't know such technology existed."

"Well, Miss Harrier, while I am not a product of technology, such technology exists," Emma explained. "I am capable, self-aware, and as much a person as you are because of my sentience. Was there something in particular you wanted to watch on the telly?"

"How do you exist? Did Abbey's dad create you?"

"I exist the same way you exist," Emma said. "God created me."

"Oh come on, daggit. I need some information. Levi won't tell me anything."

"He will," Emma said.

"When?"

"When it is appropriate, which I believe is soon," Emma said. "You are now part of a very important mission."

"And what mission is that?"

"Alas, *I* cannot tell you, my dear," Emma sighed. "Was there something you wanted to watch on the telly?"

"Are you serious? Ya know; I'm usually a pretty chill person; but this is bull. I need some answers."

"Want," Emma corrected.

"What?"

"You *want* some answers," Emma clarified. "What you *need* is what you currently have. You have shelter. There is food in the kitchen I am currently processing for you. You have a comfortable couch to rest yourself and a television at your disposal to distract or relax your mind. When Levi is rested, he will give you the necessary information, if it's necessary to give it. Most of what he would tell you, you are not completely prepared for."

"Like what? I'm tired of waiting."

"Patience is an absolute necessity, Miss Harrier," Emma said.

"Please don't call me that, anymore. Call me, Violet."

"Violet it shall be," Emma agreed. "Now, again, I ask you: what would you like to watch on the telly?"

Sigh. "Honestly, I don't even know. All there is is news and Link Up. You know what Link Up is, right?"

"Of course, I do," Emma said. "Link up is a complex

database of all digitally stored music, television series, and movies that streams or permits the download of selected items directly to the television. In the early twenty-tens, it was referred to as a cloud. When most of the recording and production studios in the west and in New York were destroyed, all digital content was uploaded to a public network account to preserve music, television, and movie history, thus creating 'Link Up'. It is still the primary source of entertainment material today."

"A bit of a long-winded explanation," Violet said.

"You said you needed answers."

"Right," Violet said and bit her lip. "Okay. Can you turn on the news? I want to find out what's happening out there."

"At the current moment, the wave anomaly is inhibiting my ability to receive a clear signal from outside," Emma explained. "It is highly unlikely we will have a good signal or any news of the outside world until we have passed beyond the wave barrier. It is highly disruptive to radio frequencies."

"When are we going out there?"

Emma hesitated. "We will leave in approximately five hours, which is when we expect everyone to be rested and fed, and my shell's reserves to be appropriately recharged. It is vital that we leave as soon as possible."

"Because of that wave, right? The umm, 'breathe of death' is what Levi said."

"Precisely," Emma said. "Now, if you will excuse me, I have to attend to matters within the safe haven in preparation for our departure." The television screen changed to a short listing of TV series. "These are the TV series and movies currently available in our local database."

Violet looked at the list. "Let's see. There's Star Trek,

Star Trek, Star Trek. There are like seven Star Trek series in here. These guys need variety. Um, oooh, Castle, Psych, Heroes, Hannibal. Wait, the people eating guy?" No response from Emma. "I'll watch Castle. That Nathan Fillon was hot." The series album opened and displayed the available seasons. "Why not start at the very beginning?" There was no response. Violet couldn't help but feel a little lonely. "Play episode one."

As the TV show started, the room gradually dimmed until the only light in the room came from the television. Violet said, "Ooooo, theatre mode," kicked off her shoes, and stretched out on the couch. She could feel the seats of the couch grow warmer. "Seat warmers in the couch? Oh dear God, where have you been all my life?"

Stretched out and watching Castle, Violet did the one thing she didn't want to do. She napped.

9

Abbey didn't immediately take a nap when she and Violet claimed their room. She lay in her bed, closed her eyes, and surrendered to her body's cry for rest. However, Levi's nagging voice persisted in the furthest corners of her mind to listen to the message her father left behind for her. He had insisted that he wouldn't utter another informative word until she listened. She wanted to call him stubborn, or a jerk, but something told her she should reserve those words for the mirror. It was the strangest thing; but sometimes, it felt like there was someone else inside of her head with her, setting her straight when she felt like making a left turn.

In reality, the message from her father terrified her. This whole thing terrified her. She wished she could squeeze her eyes closed hard enough, and by the great grace of God, have her father waking her up, not to flee Virginia, but to go see the sunrise, drink smoothies, and eat breakfast.

As an ongoing joke, though it wasn't a joke, Violet would say how lucky or spoiled Abbey was to have the things she possessed. She had what seemed to be an unlimited supply of money and resources, someone like Levi who watched over and loved her since she was born, and a father who gave her more love and time than she could ever hope. Compared to Violet, Abbey understood just how much more she was blessed in the father category alone. Now, she was losing him. Lost him?

On his way to take a nap, Levi slipped a dime-sized, crystalline disk in her hand and told her to listen. Was that it? Did that contain all that her father had to say to her? And after she listened to it, would that be the last she ever heard from him? Would she have to say good-bye?

In bed, Abbey shifted the disk between her index and middle finger.

Abbey didn't want to say good-bye. She refused to. He was alive, dagnabbit! Somewhere, somehow, he was alive and well. And not just well, but stronger than ever. She knew it. She could feel it. Listening to his good-bye message would only frustrate her. It would only wound her, make her doubt her instincts.

Yet, despite her doubts, her hand rose to the base of her skull. She didn't have an explanation for what she was doing or what was guiding her hand. She knew there was a small lump at the base of her skull she never had an explanation for, but what followed frightened her.

It opened.

The lump, which was not a lump, parted itself like a pair of lips and the dime-sized disk slipped in with ease. Afterward, the lump closed. She rubbed the lump. It felt as it had before, like skin over bone.

Abbey felt and scratched at the lump, not sure what it

was, but certain whatever it was had to get out of her.

Everything went black and silent. She could neither see nor hear, smell nor taste, but she could feel. It was chilly. She shivered and wrapped her arms around herself. Someone placed a blanket around her arms. She smelled rain. She could hear the rushing rain drops falling on asphalt, nearby leaves, in puddles, and on a bench. She sat on a park bench in the middle of a rainstorm.

Why wasn't she getting wet? *The bench has an overhead, silly.*

With that thought, she knew the park. She knew the setting. She definitely knew who put the blanket around her arms. As her vision cleared, she could see the sun rising over the lake, a beacon of light through the rushing rainstorm, and collections of rainbows in the sky. It was a breathtaking sight. She looked to her left and saw her father, brown-haired with slight streaks of blond and shades of gray.

Abbey smiled and hugged him. This was all she asked for. A restart of the day. She didn't want to say good-bye. She refused to. *Death be damned. You will not have a hold over my father. He's here for the long haul.*

Her father laughed and shook his head. "Why weren't you always this happy to see me in the morning?"

"I always was, dad. I was just too tired to show it."

"More on the lines of too stubborn, but I knew it. I love you, Princess."

"I love you too, daddy," she said as tears swelled in her eyes.

He pressed his lips into a line. "Do you? Do you really love me?"

"Yes, of course."

"Then follow my instructions," he said.

"Oh." She hesitated and looked down. "Oh, okay."

"Do you love me, Abigail?"

She looked back at him, cheeks burning. "I just said I did, didn't I? I'll follow your instructions."

"Abigail, you must trust me, and trust Levi. He is your protector. He was since you were born. He will be until he dies, if he dies. For his sake, as much as for yours, it is imperative that you trust his judgment and follow his instructions. Do you understand?"

"I." She looked down again and wrung her hands. "Yes. I understand."

"Do you?" he pressed. "The road ahead is extremely dangerous. You'll pass through the quarantine zones, which are full of mutants, creatures, cannibals, perverts, murderers, and thieves, and around the outer rim of a devastation zone, which has large creatures and radiation. You'll have to navigate through over-populated cities full of desperate people and criminals. This is all in the first half of your trip, before you pass over the Dead Mississippi."

"Yea, dad, I know," she said.

"From there, you'll still have to be watchful," he continued. "The rogue districts control that section. The Barren Plains is full of criminals looking to capitalize on people passing through to the Washington Coalition. There are no laws or people to enforce them. You'll see things you'd wish you hadn't seen. People will be murdered in the streets. There are scouting parties from the White Rogues District who enter the Barren Plains looking for people to forcibly recruit into their army or blatantly victimize to instill fear. If you cannot listen to instructions, you will be putting yourself, Levi, Jared, Violet, and Jeremy in danger."

She looked at him sharply. "Wait a minute. I thought you prepared this before Levi came to pick me up. How could you possibly know that Violet and Jeremy are with us?"

"Abigail, I am your *father*," he stated. "You and Violet go almost everywhere and do almost everything together. Of course you would invite her along. Part of me hoped you would listen to the audio message before going to pick her up. However, I knew that you wouldn't. I knew you would do what you wanted to do first, and consider what other people had to say later, much later. That has been your move since you were four years old."

"Well, why didn't you tell Levi to pick up Violet or have her stay over at our place?"

"Because Violet has been compromised, and it was my concern that she might have an impact on you or Levi's decisions. The two of you, alone, present the best chances of our mission succeeding. Both Jeremy and Violet are susceptible to the influences of the Red. I will not say how, but they have proven that. Jeremy, being your boyfriend, has an influence over you and may be a threat to Levi. Violet is a very attractive young woman who I am sure will have an influence over Levi. She usually did. We cannot afford to have anyone influencing Levi's judgment. His focus is essential to your safe arrival to Montana."

Abbey's eyebrows furrowed. "I, I don't understand. She's my friend. She's been our friend for years."

"Yes. Yes, she is. And if you leave her and Jeremy at the safe haven, they will be fine. They'll be fine for weeks. There's plenty of food and T-V. Once you've completed your mission, you can come back for them. Everything will be fine. Just—"

"I'm not going to leave them, dad. I'm not."

"Of course, you're not," he sighed. He ran his right hand through his hair, rubbed the back of his neck, and then below his chin. "Listen honey, there's more that I have to tell you. A lot more, actually. Some of it will come from me, and the rest will come from Levi. You're not going to take in all of the information at once, but in phases. I will start by explaining to you how the chip holding this information works and how you can utilize it for the remainder of the trip, until all the information I wanted to provide to you has been delivered. Are you ready to listen?"

"Wait. First, how was I able to put a chip in my head? That's the furthest thing from normal. Humans don't have chips in their heads." She paused and remembered her father's implants that protected their thoughts from the Red. "With the exception of the Red mind reading chip."

Her father stared at her. "Are you ready to listen?"

"You didn't answer my question."

Her father's expression and tone didn't change. He sat completely still and didn't blink. "Please say continue when you are ready to listen."

Abbey stared at him with a furrowed brow and pursed lips. What was wrong with him? "How does this work? We were having a conversation. Now, it's like, you're a machine."

Her father, or his image, sat frozen in place, waiting.

She sighed and slouched. "Okay. Continue."

The image of her father spoke, "The chip you entered into your head, with either the counsel of Levi or the nanotech within your body—"

Abigail tried to speak, interrupt, ask a question, but her vocal cords wouldn't work. Nothing came out. She could not move. She could not protest. She could only listen.

"—is called a cognitive imprint chip, C-I-C for short. A C-I-C records thoughts, memories, dreams, experiences, and stores them for sharing or memory restoration. Anyone with the required hardware can store data from their brain and share it with others. Unless a person intentionally encrypts that data, anyone with the required hardware can also read that data. This message was specifically designed to be read by you. No other person, including Levi, would have been able to access the experience of this message. A person is also capable of encrypting a chip for a particular group of individuals based on genetic markers, like family members, or memory markers if multiple people shared a specific event. An encrypted or non-encrypted C-I-C can also be read by computers with the appropriate software. If it is encrypted, and depending on the type of encryption, the person utilizing the software would have to enter a particular code established by the person or being who originally encrypted the C-I-C."

Again Abigail wanted to get a word in. Again, she could not. She fought, but found her lips trapped. She wanted to stick her lip out and pout. Even that was not within her power.

Her father paused and glared at her. She recognized the expression he always shot at her when she squirmed in their booth at church. Just like in church, after seeing that expression, she chose to be silent and listen.

He continued, "A C-I-C is created by carbon, iron, and calcium collected and crystallized by S-I nanobots. Each C-I-C has small nanobots from the host brain. If an individual attempts to use the C-I-C of an enemy to collect information, the nanobots from the host will destroy the C-I-C reader within the person making such an attempt. This could lead to significant, and sometimes fatal, brain damage.

"In order to be able to create or use a C-I-C, an individual would have to have *Ioran* or *Ioran*-sanctioned nanotech installed within their bodies. Iorans are the senior race of the fifth region star cluster. The installation of Ioran nanotech involves the injection of seven P-I nanobots. Those P-I nanobots connect themselves to the subject's digestion system and collect select elements (carbon, iron, magnesium, and calcium for example) to assemble a nanobot constructor along the digestive system. Once it is complete, the P-I nanobots collect more elements for further construction. The constructor creates thousands of P-II, S-I, S-II, T-I, T-II, F-I, F-II, M-I, and M-II nanobots. Once enough P-II nanobots are created, they take over in the collection of nutrients and elements needed for the continued operation of the nanotech network, and the P-I nanobots hide. If, for any reason, the nanotech network is damaged beyond repair or aggressively purged, the P-I nanobots re-emerge and either repair the existing nanotech network or create a new one.

"The first function of S-I nanobots is to construct a nanotech brain. The nanotech brain is usually constructed along or near the lower portion of your spine. The fully constructed brain waits until the completion of the nanotech three-brained network before issuing orders. The S-I nanobot's second function is to construct a second brain within the gray matter of the subject. The second brain is assembled along the base of the skull and near the top of the spine. After constructing the second brain and completely integrating it with the gray matter of the subject, most of the S-I nanobots return to the constructor. A few S-I nanobots remain in the second brain to produce C-I-C.

"The T-I nanobots leave the constructor with the primary function of maintaining the communication and operation of the three-brained (nanotech brains one and two, and subject brain) network. If one or both of the two nanotech brains is or are damaged, the S-I nanobots leave the constructor and repair the damage. The T-I nanobots never defer from their tasks.

"When the three-brain network is complete, the F-I nanobots leave the constructor and travel throughout the subject's body. They perform a complete and thorough examination of the subject's body and D-N-A, looking for injuries, defects, or diseases. If there are any, they use carbon elements to repair or completely reconstruct select organs or body parts. They also assemble nanotech (for instance, muscle stimulators or enhancers, lung filters, immune enhancers, skeletal armor) designed to improve the overall functionality and survivability of the body as assessed by the subject and the nanotech brains. Particular programming and enhancements can be pre-established by the individual(s) who installed the network. The F-II nanobots localize themselves throughout the body to maintain its peek functionality. When all enhancements requested by the three-brain network are completed, the F-I nanobots return to the constructor, while the F-II nanobots remain localized for any bodily repair necessary.

"The T-II nanobots leave the constructor and maintain communication between the three-brain network, the S-II nanobots' elemental supply distribution, the F-I nanobots during their construction phase, and the F-II nanobots during their constant maintenance. If there are any consistent abnormalities within the body, the F-II immediately contact the T-II, which contacts the two nanotech brains, which leads to immediate action to resolve the abnormalities."

Aww, come on!

"I'm almost finished. Listen.

"Finally, the M-I and M-II nanobots are designed to determine the efficiency of the entire nanotech network. They travel throughout the body ensuring all nanobots are operating efficiently. They ensure there are sufficient supplies for the operation of the network. If there are any failings or shortages of specific nanobot types at localized areas, they report it to the T-II or directly to the primary nanotech brain, which commits orders to fix failings or shortages. M-I nanobots can repair other nanobots, while M-II nanobots temporarily convert themselves into any other nanobot type during shortages.

"While all of these functions and actions are autonomous, the subject has the capacity to manually override and control select functions. If an individual wanted a particular enhancement to his or her functionality, the nanobots, if they are capable, would perform that enhancement. If select improvements are preprogrammed into the nanobots, certain options will be available for the person to choose in an elective database. One would simply have to think, 'Access elective enhancement database.' It would appear in the forefront of their vision. Once selected, the enhancements would begin. Since you currently have a nanotech system within your body, the remainder of the details provided will be instructive and in second person format."

Abbey's tongue was suddenly loosened.

"Wait, I'm sorry," she said. "This is too much. I have little alien robots inside my body? How did that happen?"

"I installed them."

"Why?" she asked. "And why didn't you tell me?"

"They were installed so you could survive. The world is full of dangerous radiation, diseases, and poisons. Those 'little robots' inside your body are why you're so healthy. They're why you have such a remarkable memory and great balance. They're why everything seems to come so easily to you. They've improved your brain function, given you the capacity to fully utilize your brain, even the parts others don't use."

"But, why didn't you tell me?" she persisted.

"You weren't ready for the responsibility awareness grants you. I still worry you're not; but our hands are forced. You and Levi are the fate of the world. You have to know what you're capable of, for everyone's sake. Just don't talk about this with anyone except Levi, Emma, and Jared. Not with Violet. Not with Jeremy. Not anyone else."

"What?" she spat. "Emma? The car? You don't want me talk to my best friend about this, but you want me to talk to a car?"

Her father laughed. "Oh Abbey, the things you do not know. Emma is so much more than a car, and far wiser than all of us multiplied times a thousand. She serves us willingly and humbly in the capacity of a car, at the moment. She is not a car. Not isolated to a computer. Not an entity you know or understand. She merely chooses to utilize technology as a vessel or shell for physical form and communication. Once you get to Montana, you'll have a stronger understanding of what she is."

"This is a lot to take in," Abbey said. She put her right hand on her forehead.

"That is why this will end here. I want you to think about everything that was said. Now that you understand what is inside of you, you can go to Levi. He can help you understand the possibilities the nanobots give you. However, you must be willing to *listen*."

Abbey rolled her eyes at the word "listen". "Is this it? Was that all you had to say to me? Levi said there were all these other things you were supposed to tell me. Stuff about the mission."

Her father frowned. "Seriously? Mission information was provided in the audio message stored in the car. You obviously didn't *listen.*" He sighed. "This is the C-I-C message. There is more. Come back later, when you've had time to think about what I've told you so far. You can then choose to activate the C-I-C by intentionally thinking, 'Activate C-I-C message.'"

"The, but, what if I have more questions?" Abbey pouted. "None of what you said was helpful. I have more questions."

"Not now, Abbey. Give yourself time or ask Levi, Emma, or Jared."

Abbey frowned and balled her hands into little fists. "Levi won't tell me anything. He said to listen to the message."

"Well, you should have listened to the message. Try asking Jared, instead."

"Jared's a dog. What am I going to ask him?"

"Wolf, not dog." Her father frowned. "Abigail, my precious daughter, could you at least *pretend* you know how to follow instructions and ask him?"

Everything faded into darkness and she found herself lying on the bed. She stared at the limestone ceiling and shook her head. What was going on and for how long?

10

It was four hours later that Levi awoke from his nap. He rose, yawned, and looked at the clock. He sighed. Was it Chaucer who said, "Time and tide wait for no man?" Both raced onward and it was Levi who had to catch up and surpass both time and tide to reach Montana. Since Sasha was no longer flying the catalyst to Montana, what was supposed to be a cautious but leisurely three or four day trip would now be a desperate race against time. It was imperative he got there before the wave spread too far, caused irreparable damage to the planet, and killed all of Earth's human inhabitants.

What Levi wanted to do was jump back into bed. He hadn't enjoyed a full night's sleep in a week. The week began with him driving from Washington to Virginia with Emma, Pisces, and Jared. They remained in stealth mode most of the trip, avoiding civilization as much as possible. The trip took four days, and probably could have taken less time had they gone the less scenic route. However, the less scenic route was safer. And when they ran into trouble, there weren't a lot of witnesses to see a cat and dog jump out of the car with ray guns or appear and disappear like ghosts.

Once they arrived in Virginia, the four met Sasha and the good doctor and plotted the best course of action, which was to destroy the research facility's cradle, get Abbey to Montana, and use the backup cradle they were finishing in Montana. After the meeting, they collected supplies for the safe haven and Montana trip. The good doctor gave Levi the appropriate credentials to come to and from the Quarantine Zone for supplies without hassle.

A lot of their actions had to be performed in stealth, which took planning and time. However, what took most of Levi's time was studying all of the good doctor's notes and translations. The good doctor made it abundantly clear that he might not survive the mission. He had to get the catalyst out and destroy the cradle. The most efficient option of destroying the cradle was an antimatter grenade. Once the grenade activated, they hoped it would completely annihilate the cradle and its columns without causing a chain reaction that destroyed the entire facility and everything within half a mile. If the grenade caused a chain reaction, it would probably take the good doctor and Pisces with it. And before the good doctor left the world, he wanted Levi to know everything he knew. Everything. That meant all study, and no sleep.

Now Levi wrestled with a vague fatigue on his way to the command center. The deeper he went into the cave, the cooler it became. The dips and curves of the narrow passages were programmed into his brain; so, he closed his eyes, cleared his mind, and focused on the next set of tasks to come. He had to examine the catalyst for damage. Though, he highly doubted he'd find any. The catalyst had a way of watching out for herself. After checking the catalyst, he had to transition the safe haven to stasis mode, make sure the proper rations were stored in Emma's trunk, get everyone in the car, and slice through the winds of the road.

Levi awoke from his thoughts when he heard shallow breathing and light steps behind him. He calculated perhaps ten yards away. He opened his eyes, turned slightly to the left, and focused his peripheral vision. He saw the movement of a shadow on the cave wall. Whoever it was utilized the curvature of the cave as a cover, but hadn't taken into account the direction of the light.

"Overseer, I have a shadow," Levi whispered but kept on walking. A beep acknowledged his statement was heard.

He stepped in front of the command center door. It scanned him and opened. He walked in. As the door closed, a figure rushed forward, but bounced off of an invisible energy field and fell back. Levi didn't need to turn around to know who it was. He could hear the deepness of the voice as the person released a low curse. Of course it was Jeremy. Levi knew neither Abigail nor Violet would sneak behind him. They were as blatant as an angry bull charging through a library while screaming into a megaphone. Abbey would demand to enter or else. Violet would walk forward asking questions and arguing reasonable inquires like a journalist until you caved in or fled.

The command center was a dark, open space similar to the lounge. A small stream ran below the gridded metallic floors with rubber mats. There were a total of eight, meter tall and slender metallic stands with a clear triangular glass plate top. Each stand, with the exception of one, held a small crystalline cube about the size of a toaster. Each cube, with the exception of one, displayed three high-definition holograms of events happening within and outside of the safe haven. One glass display screen stood from the ground and disclosed the current locations of all of the parties within their group. It only showed Levi, Jared, Abbey, and Emma in the safe haven. The rest of the map was distorted by various shades of blue, which Levi understood to be sensor distortion. The darker the blue meant the greater the distortion.

To Levi's immediate left, tucked into the shadows, Jared lay on a plough black bed. His yellow eyes stared at Levi. He sat in front of the eighth metallic stand. It held the catalyst, still in its pouch, and something else.

Levi walked forward. "Why didn't you sleep in the bed in our room?"

"You talk in your sleep," Jared said. "What are we going to do about him?"

Levi glanced at the holographic image. Jeremy stood at a distance from the command center door. "Haven't decided yet. With him being Abigail's boyfriend, we can't leave him here. So, we'll just have to see how it all plays out." He pointed at the item next to the catalyst. "What's that?"

Jared yawned, adjusted himself on the black bed, and telepathically said, *"Sasha."*

Not understanding, and not wanting to raise the illumination, disturbing what little rest Jared was trying to get, Levi stepped closer. He recognized the item as a

CIC.

"Oh," he said. "What are the chances she survived?"

Jared said nothing, but only stared at Levi.

Levi nodded and said, "Wishful thinking, I know." He grabbed the CIC and carried it to an inactive crystalline cube on its narrow stand. He inserted the CIC in a port on the top of the cube and stepped away. "Have you seen it?"

Jared shook his head and closed his eyes. *"No."*

The cube lit up a light blue and projected three holographic images. The first image was a time-stamped playback of what Sasha saw. The image was clear, flawless, as if they were seeing through her eyes. It immediately began playback, in reverse, of Sasha's last recorded sights, which included Jared reaching her in the tree. The second image was a three-dimensional model of her anatomy with detailed information on her physiology and nanotech network. The third image remained a blank, flat black image.

"Interface," Levi spoke at the cube. At that order, a beam of light shot from the cube and a holographic key panel appeared in front of him, two inches above his hip. There were three sets of keys, each for one of the three projections. "Let's see what happened."

"She was shot down by the barrier wall."

"I know that," Levi said as he sped the reverse playback past her death. The image was spinning from ground to air to ground to air. Then, there was an explosion. After that, the sight was a serene reverse play of flying through the open, clear sky. "I mean, before that. Way before that."

After a few commands, the image accelerated the reverse rate to five minutes per second. Ten seconds later, Levi began to slow it down, hoping not to jump past anything important. When nothing significant appeared after two minutes, he pressed in a command and the image skipped twenty minutes.

The good doctor appeared. His lab coat and clothes were covered in blood. He looked ragged and sweaty. In his right hand, he held the catalyst. Levi's heart hurt and his stomach twisted into knots.

Jared hopped from his idle state and rushed next to Levi. He stared at the image. His ears stood from his head. "What happened to him?"

"When he started the project, he removed most of his enhancements to prevent the Red from detecting him. It's made him vulnerable," Levi complained. "I pleaded with him to at least increase his molecular density."

Levi accelerated the reverse until the good doctor was near the top of the stairs and activated the audio. The two watched the interaction between Sasha and the good doctor from his entry on the facility roof until Sasha's hasty departure. Afterward, they looked at each other.

"You think his plan worked?" Levi asked.

Jared responded, "Obviously, it didn't or the cradle never would have fired. I wonder what happened to Pisces."

That was a good question.

"If the good doctor was killed, or taken elsewhere, she would have done her part with or without him," Levi said. "The mission was to destroy the cradle at all costs. Knowing Pisces as we do, if the good doctor was compromised, she would have gone to the cradle chamber, grenade in her hand, and activated it. She understood what was at stake. Something else must have happened. Maybe the Perkins guy. He must have tracked her somehow."

"We cannot be tracked in our suits. It is beyond this world's technology."

"Yea, but who's to say they're using this world's

technology," Levi argued. "What if they still have some of their old toys?"

"This technology was even superior to the Red. You know that. That's how John beat them. I highly doubt, defeated and in hiding, they'd have the resources to advance their detection technology beyond what they already possessed."

"So, what do you think happened?" Levi asked.

"I can't draw any conclusions with this limited information. I suspect they knew he wasn't working alone. They had to wonder where the catalyst went. Perhaps they had guards watching his body in the morgue and they killed her. There had to be something that prevented her from activating the antimatter grenade. I wonder if the chamber radiation affected their phasing ability as they worried."

Emma chimed. "I hate to interrupt, as I am also curious and am considering your speculations; however, the hour is turning and your guests are preparing to eat."

Levi looked at the time and grimaced. It was always on the move.

"Please tell me the food is portable," Levi said. "We have to get on the road. There's no time for sitting around and gabbing."

"They are box lunches," Emma responded.

"God bless you, Emma," Levi said. "How you do all that you do is beyond me."

"I am always happy to serve," Emma said.

Levi looked at Jared and smiled. "Was it not the Lord who said, the best of us are those who serve?"

"Sounds right," Jared agreed.

Nodding, Levi grabbed the catalyst and pulled it out of the pouch. He examined it. It brightened at his touch. He could feel its healing powers lifting his spirit and exciting his nanotech. "It's good to see you again. I had hoped to show you my place in Washington, but our good doctor was so hesitant to let anyone else hold guard over you."

"That would have been nice," Jared said.

"Right?" Levi said. "We'll have to make up for missed time on the way to Montana."

After one momentary admiration, Levi placed the catalyst back in its pouch and removed Sasha's CIC from the cube. The holographic images vanished and the cube darkened. "Let's go."

Levi and Jared exited the command center. It darkened.

11

When Levi arrived, he told them to stop eating and prepare to leave. Abbey tossed a spoon at his forehead, but he caught it. She wanted to strangle him. She wanted to stretch her hands around his neck and squeeze hard. She was hungry. Crazy hungry. She hadn't eaten a whole meal since eight the previous night, and only had a light snack before she went to bed. Her metabolism rivaled most of the other girls she knew, and it made her grouchy when she couldn't eat. It made her hangry, hungry and angry.

Still, after listening to her father through what she could only describe as an adaptation of her father's thoughts in message form, Abbey felt a self-control she hadn't known. Something had changed.

It was hard to place it. It was as though something inside of her came to life and was actively working. She suspected it was the nanotech. They were there the whole time. Until now, she'd completely disregarded the sensations. Whatever was going on inside of her, she was different. She didn't know how; but she was. After they got settled in the car, she needed to talk to Levi about it.

How would she have that dialogue? They were all headed to the car. The car didn't offer privacy. If she was going to keep everything her father said a secret (She honestly didn't want to. Part of her wanted to blurt out the details in bursts and in no particular order), they needed privacy. They had to have this conversation in a safe place, but where?

Abbey approached Levi, who argued with Violet over what was and was not essential for their trip. Since they were not initially part of the plan, Jeremy and Violet had to leave things behind to make space for food (extra food, now that there were five instead of three). She felt guilty about it; especially since she'd insisted Violet bring most of her life with her.

When the two compromised, Abbey slipped in. "Lee, can I talk to you a minute?"

"A moment," Levi said and looked at her.

"Come on, Lee," Abbey said. "I have a question."

"Yes, Abigail, I'm listening. You said, 'Can I talk to you for a minute?' The probability of your intended conversation lasting a minute is remote. It's better to say a moment, which is an undefined length of time." Abbey's eyes narrowed at him. "Now, what was it you wanted to say?"

"Sometimes, I want to punch you in the face," she replied.

Levi put his hand to his forehead and shook his head. "Was that it? Would hitting me make you feel better?"

Abbey leaned closer. "No, I was just saying that because you're a prat," Levi frowned, "sometimes. You don't have to correct me all the time. Do you know how that makes me feel?"

Levi reddened in the face. He lowered his head and looked away. He let out a deep sigh, and then looked back at her.

"I'm sorry," he sighed again and slumped. "I've been so wound up this entire week. Everything has to go right, and it's going wrong. All wrong." He hesitated. "Your dad, Pisces, Sasha. They're—" He hesitated again.

What is he not telling me? Abbey thought.

"I'm tired. I'm so tired. I've barely slept more than four hours a day this week, and I've lost so much in such a short span of time. I just need everything, including you, to be perfect. Okay? We can't afford to have anything else go wrong. Can you be perfect for me?"

Abbey smiled and said, "No. The probability of me being perfect is remote." Levi put his hands over his eyes and sighed. She stretched out her arms and hugged him. "But I'll try."

Levi hugged her back. They held each other for a moment.

Both were mourning her father, Abbey realized, but neither wanted to be vulnerable. Something had changed between them. She didn't know what. Perhaps it was the time they spent apart with Levi in Washington or something to do with what was going on. However, she could feel a strange tension between them. It frustrated her, because she didn't understand it.

How do you feel? Her father would always ask. He told her it was important to have an understanding of how she felt in any situation. He'd chatter on and on about emotional intelligence, and knowing what you feel and why you feel that way.

How did she feel? She felt like holding Levi was something she wanted for a long time. The distance kept her from what she wanted until she repressed it. Now he was back, here, and she was frustrated. She wanted to make up for all the time they missed. She wanted to hold him for a couple years. Perhaps she wanted more. But she couldn't. She had a boyfriend.

Not to mention, Violet had that look in her eyes, again. She remembered seeing it when Violet met Levi for the first time. It made Abbey uncomfortable, because Levi was hers. He was always hers, until he liked Violet. She had a little acne and was kind of frail, but she filled into her body faster than Abbey, especially her boobs, and he was hit hard by puberty. Abbey intervened, kissed him. She certainly couldn't and wouldn't do that now. Why was she thinking about that anyway?

Jared cleared his throat and the two separated. Abbey looked at Jared.

Jared. She didn't know how a dog, wolf, wolfdog, whatever he was, could clear his throat with so much purpose and attitude, but Jared pulled it off perfectly. Could wolves or dogs do that? She thought that was a human trait.

"Ask him" was what her father had said. Her father, in the message or dream, implied she should ask Jared questions. What? That still didn't make sense.

Then again, even when she was younger, Jared was a weird dog. He never needed to be walked. He walked himself. He would pee outside or actually use the toilet. He was the best trained pet she'd ever seen, though she'd never seen him trained. It wasn't as though he played normal dog games like fetching a ball, rolling over, or anything like that. He'd watched movies with the family. They all went on trips. She remembered seeing him sneak a book from the library. She told her dad, but he only chuckled. He said, "It'll be fine. Jared will take good care of that book." And that book came back in pristine condition.

So, what was the deal with Jared? What was his story?

Ask him, again came to her mind.

Jared stared at Levi, nodded, and then walked to the car. It was going to be tight in the backseat with Jared in there. She wouldn't mind, though. Oddly enough, Jared's coat was very fragrant. She assumed it was because of the animal-friendly shampoos and conditioners they used. He usually smelled of lavender, apple, cinnamon, or coconut. He smelled better than humans most of the time, even his breath. He smelled better than Jeremy.

"It's time to go," Levi said and looked back at Jeremy and Violet. Violet sat in the front seat and ate her boxed lunch. Jeremy was in the back seat giving Jared the evil eye. He was probably going to sit between Jeremy and Abbey the entire trip. "You had something you wanted to ask me."

"Yes, I," she stopped, trying to remind herself of what it was she originally intended to say. "I listened to the thing my dad left me, and I feel different now. I don't know what's going on inside my own body and it's freaking me out. I want to talk about it, but we'll be in the car for most of the trip. You'll be in the front with Violet. I'll be in the back with Jeremy. I just don't see how we can discreetly talk about all of this stuff, but I have to talk about it. What if we didn't keep this entire thing top secret, but let them in on it? Then we could talk about it openly."

Levi sighed. "We can't do that. Your father has made it absolutely clear to me that no one is to know about it. No one. I have to respect his wishes. However, I'd be happy to have you in the passenger seat."

At that, Abbey crossed her arms. "They'd still hear us." She looked at the car again. "You owe me answers. You both do. I've gone my whole life tucked under a rock. There were so many places I couldn't go or see. I was always under supervision or remote observation by my father. And now, I come to find out, there have been things in my body my whole life I had no knowledge of and no one intended on telling me until now. Do you get how terrible this is? I feel like a prisoner."

"That's one of the reasons why your father didn't tell you," Levi said. "Not knowing gave you the freedom to be yourself without feeling as though you had to hide things from everyone. Whether you realize it or not, not knowing has protected you."

"No," Abbey said. "Not knowing made me easier to control and observe. I sure as heck don't feel protected right now. I feel, I'm all stirred up inside. I need answers, Levi. So what are our options?"

"Let's get in the car, get on the road, and eat our lunches," Levi suggested. "We'll change our seats later in the trip. Then, maybe we can both sit in the back and talk. We'll have a little more privacy then. How about that?"

Abbey looked back at the car, at Jeremy. Jeremy stared at them, and did not blink.

He's reading our lips, she thought but did not say. She nodded and turned her back to the car. "Okay. He probably won't like me being in the back seat whispering to you, but he's on very thin ice right now."

Why am I still with him? Abbey thought.

"Great," Levi said, and smiled. He walked to the car. "I look forward to answering your questions. I've actually been looking forward to talking to you about this for a long time."

Abbey kept to his side and asked, "Really?"

Levi nodded and smiled. "I've wanted to talk to you ever since I first found out about it." He nodded at Jeremy and Violet. "If you're having a hard time not telling them, imagine how hard it was for me to go thirteen years without telling you, the one I love." He opened the door, picked up his boxed lunch, and sat down.

Shocked by what Levi said, for a moment, Abbey

stood there, blank.

He loved her. She always knew that. He'd said it enough when they were kids. They both did. However, the last time she heard it was when he left for Washington. It was more of a goodbye than a declaration of affection. This was a statement.

Jeremy lowered his window and asked, "You coming, or are we leaving you behind?"

Something about that was funny, because Abbey laughed and shook her head. She walked to the other side of the car, got in, and looked at Jeremy. She was glad they hadn't left him behind; but she knew, at some point in the near future, she would.

Levi said, "Overseer. You can open the pressure doors."

Overseer?

Who was this Overseer he was suddenly talking to? With talking cars, secret caves, nanotechnology in bodies, and the aliens (You can't forget the evil aliens trying to destroy the planet. Trying? Succeeding.), she decided she was done asking questions until she was fed.

The safe haven pressure doors hissed and opened. Outside, they could see nothing but a red haze.

"Emma, please activate radiation shields."

"Shields are up and operating at one-hundred percent," said Emma.

Levi smiled, "Set a course for Montana at one quarter impulse."

"One quarter, what?" Violet asked.

"Course laid in, Captain."

"Really?" Violet asked. She looked at Levi with an annoyed expression. "With everything going on, are you seriously playing Star Trek, right now?"

Abbey laughed. That was all her father and Levi did on the road. Lower the windows. Lowering the windows,

Captain. Turn left on my mark. Course plotted. Mark. Turning. It was road entertainment.

She went from laughter to tears at the thought of it.

"This family," Violet whispered. She remembered the good doctor dressed in one of those alien costumes and couldn't restrain a smirk.

The theme song played from the radio.

Levi smiled at Violet and said, "Engage."

The car thrust forward, beyond the cave entrance, and back into the world they knew.

Or used to know.

12

Out of the safe haven, the world was a wasteland. The mountain range, once full of lush green plant-life, was brown with tall sagged and fallen trees, limp bushes, dead grass and flowers, and the smell of rot was everywhere. Steam rose from the soil. There was no sign of life. Not a single bug buzzed in the air or hopped in the grass. Not a single bird flew in the sky, whistled a tune, or nested on the defunct trees. Not a single squirrel stirred in the pathetic brush. Nothing crept. Nothing crawled. There was nothing but death. The wasted land stretched for miles in all directions.

The sky and its puffy clouds were a deep blood red. Thunder rumbled like a casted and rolling bowling ball along the clouds. Waves of lightning followed in sets of threes along the stretch of clouds. The humidity was thick enough to taste, swallow, and suffocate.

Levi, Abbey, Violet, Jared, and Jeremy stared out of the windows at the decadent world in shock and awe.

Abbey cried and thought of her father.

Violet sat stone still, too distraught to appropriately respond to what she saw.

Levi closed his eyes and prayed.

As did Jared.
And Jeremy smiled.

CHAPTER FOUR
THE RED AND THE RIDER

WELL, THIS IS JUST GREAT, JOHN THOUGHT as he lay on a bed inside of a refrigeration chamber in the research facility's morgue. He failed. It was his responsibility to prevent the regeneration device turned weapon from firing, and he failed. Now the world was being ravaged by an alien radiation wave that would change the chemistry of the planet.

It was his fault. He should have sent Pisces running with Prost and Cartwright. He should have stood next to the chamber, activated the grenade, and ended it all. His sacrifice would have spared the world. But something compelled him not to sacrifice himself. Something compelled him to go with Prost and Cartwright. Secure their lives instead of end his.

In addition to his guilt was an uneasy concern for Abbey and Levi. He was sure Levi took Abbey to the safe haven. Her safety was his primary responsibility. But, he felt something was wrong. Something bad happened. He felt an emptiness, as though a connection was now lost. He needed answers. But first, he had to get himself out of the chamber.

How long was he in there? According to his internal chronometer, an hour had passed since the device was activated and launched its destruction wave. He fell asleep ten minutes afterward. He wasn't sure if it was the blast that knocked him unconscious or if he fell asleep due to exhaustion. It was a twenty hour work day.

He listened. The adjacent chambers were silent. He wondered if the others fell asleep.

John hovered over the bed and phased. He guided himself out of the chamber, hoping there was no one on the other side. They wouldn't see him; but if he passed through someone, say a guard or something worse (like the Red), that person or thing would experience the cold and numbing feeling of him passing through their body and react violently. They wouldn't be able to hurt him while he was phased. They would, however, be aware of his presence and might threaten Cartwright and Prost, assuming they were still alive.

Of course, they're alive, he told himself as he cleared the chamber. Due to his overly cautious nature, most of the people within the research facility would be alive. The facility was designed to protect its inhabitants from radiation leaks of any kind from the cradle assembly. Why he locked himself in a refrigeration chamber of the morgue was suddenly beyond him. No. Better safe than sorry.

Nerves. It was your nerves. Relax, John. You'll be your unshakable old self soon, he told himself.

No one was in the mortuary. It was silent and dark. He deactivated his phase, took off his helmet, and walked to Pisces's chamber. He opened it and found her lying there, on the bed, unconscious. He pulled out her bed. She was alive. He could see her chest rise and fall with each breathe. He removed her helmet and pressed the lower base of her skull.

Pisces's eyes shot open and locked on John's. She examined him, then groaned and held her head.

"Welcome back to the land of the living," John said and smiled.

Pisces stretched, yawned, and sat upright. She rubbed her head. "I don't know if I have a headache from the blast or from not eating for a good—" She frowned. When was the last time she ate? "Nanotech suggests resource depletion."

John's stomach growled. Both of them looked at it.

"I'm guessing both," John said.

Shaking her head, Pisces hopped off of the bed, grabbed her small energy pistol, and surveyed the room. "Any sign of hostiles?" she asked.

"Not yet."

"Okay. How are your friends?"

John closed Pisces's chamber and moved to Cartwright's. "We're about to see." He opened it and pulled Cartwright's bed out.

Cartwright was startled awake by the movement of the bed. She looked at the two and flinched at first, then blinked. "We're alive."

"I wouldn't celebrate just yet," John said. He helped her out of the bed and closed her chamber. "This is three out of four, and I'm not sure what awaits us once we leave the morgue. I didn't want to do any scouting until we were all awake and alert."

"Of course," Cartwright agreed. She rubbed her head. "Does anyone else have a headache?"

This, coming from Cartwright, concerned John. Pisces having a headache easily meant she was suffering the effects of the wave or hunger. Cartwright's headache could be caused by the wave, hunger, or Red influence. It was the last one he was concerned about, now that the Red were walking around smiling at the world like a convict on his first day out of the joint. He looked at her with narrow eyes, then at Pisces.

Pisces returned the look, understood his concern. "We should hurry."

John opened Prost's chamber. Prost lay awake with ear buds in his ear and an iPod in his hand. He looked at the three and blinked. "Finally! I thought you guys forgot about me. I was yelling for a good fifteen minutes. Then, I got tired and decided to just wait it out with some Smashing Pumpkins."

"Noise doesn't travel well outside of the chambers," John said and helped Prost out of the bed. "Are you saying you didn't go to sleep at all?"

Once on his feet, Prost rubbed his head. "No. I think it was a mix of adrenaline, medication, and my headache. I had the most agonizing headache for a while." He massaged his temples. "I've never been hit so hard. I might have a concussion. That also made me not want to go to sleep. I didn't want to make the morgue an extended stay, no matter how great the muffins are."

"Sounds about right," Pisces said and smiled.

Prost smiled back.

"Okay. We're all awake. What's next?" Cartwright asked.

That was a good question, John thought. He honestly hadn't expected to survive after the antimatter grenade activated. Since it didn't explode and the cradle fired, he was left with two mysteries. Why didn't the grenade activate? What would the next move be against the Red?

John first looked to Pisces. Was there a possibility that Pisces programmed it incorrectly? No. She'd done it fifty times and was quicker at it than he was. Smaller hands helped. Was it possible the presence of the Red impacted her performance? Hardly. She was with him and Jeremiah in the Red War. She had nerves of steel. Was there any reason why Pisces wouldn't activate the grenade? Perhaps she didn't want to die. No. She could have opted out of the mission. Jared wanted to come, but she insisted otherwise. Jared had no experience with the Red. She did. If anyone was going to bring an end to the surviving Red, it would be the veterans. She volunteered for the suicide mission. It wasn't the first one they'd been on together. He knew he could rely on her. There was no way she made a mistake with the grenade.

Was it possible the Red deactivated the grenade? Hardly. It was key locked. In order to deactivate the grenade, they would have needed an override code. Any more than two attempts to deactivate the grenade would have immediately released the antimatter into the chamber, causing instant annihilation. What about acquiring the deactivation codes from someone's mind? The only individuals who knew the deactivation codes had the nanotech network in them. They were unreadable and unfazed by the Red telepathy.

That left only one possibility: hardware malfunction. It was as improbable a cause as Pisces making a mistake programming it. It was the only remaining alternative. It never released the antimatter. The time elapsed, but the electromagnet did not disengage.

Mystery solved.

Wait, not quite yet.

Wouldn't the activation of the cradle assembly disrupt the electromagnetic shell that contained the antimatter?

Obviously, it didn't John, came a thought.

It caught him off guard. He gasped. It sounded like the voice of an old friend; but it came from within.

"John?" Pisces asked. She saw distress in his raised eyebrows and wide eyes. "Any chance you can share what's going on in your head with the rest of us?"

"Sorry. I was thinking about the antimatter grenade.

It should have activated."

"I'm sorry," Pisces apologized immediately. "I don't know what happened."

"It wasn't you," John reassured her. "I know that much. Something else is going on. I'm not sure what, but something else is going on." He could feel it. "We have to stop the Red."

Cartwright crossed her arms. "And how do you intend to do that?"

John looked at Cartwright and said, "By fighting them."

Prost laughed. "You're joking, right? You saw how big those things are. You saw how many there were. There are probably more. How do you expect to fight them?"

"With weapons and strategy," John responded as though he were explaining rudimentary math to a grown man. He didn't show the slightest trace of doubt in his abilities. His confidence was radiant.

Prost was taken aback. What was he to the Red? He was just a scientist with a couple of tricks. "You have to be kidding. I'm sure a couple of ray guns could help. And your walking-through-walls trick is pretty clever. However, you're talking about fighting the Red. I hope you have a better idea up your sleeve."

John and Pisces exchanged a look and smiled.

Cartwright and Prost looked at each other and frowned, puzzled.

"Look, kid," John said, almost smug. "It's nothing I haven't dealt with before. We'll be fine with our ray guns and clever tricks." He grabbed his helmet and passed Pisces hers. "We're going to make sure the coast is clear. You stay here."

"Wait," Cartwright said and raised her hand. "Stop." She had an instinct. She couldn't explain it; but she had one.

John and Pisces stopped and looked back at her.

"What do you mean by you've dealt with this before?" Cartwright asked. "Did you fight in the Red War?"

Pisces sighed and turned to John. "I think it's time you told them."

Reluctantly, John nodded. She was right. There was no reason to hide who he was anymore. The Red have returned. Soon all would have to know who he was. It was the only way he could get the support he needed to fight the Red or hold them off until Levi made it to Montana.

"I didn't just fight in the Red War. I was the one who ended it."

Prost blinked and said, "No. The Rider ended the war."

Cartwright gasped in realization.

John smiled, "I know. I am John Rider."

"AAAAAAAHHHH!!!" was a scream outside of the morgue. It gave everyone a start.

John grabbed his energy pistol, yelled, "Stay here; don't move," and vanished. Pisces followed. The two charged through the door, into the medical center, and then through the door leading to the hallway.

"Oh my God," Pisces whispered.

They back pedaled.

A line of twenty people—they were scientists, interns, and guards—stood hypnotized, stiff as a board, before a Rezarian. It blocked the hallway with its long, maroon, scaled body. There were olive spots on its back. *Great, it's a female,* John thought. Her singular large eye was open and wide. Two Red were in front of her. They were a tenth of her size and shared the same pattern of spots. *And she brought her babies.*

It was strange. The Red were known to have a litter

of at least eleven Redlings, not two. Those two wrestled and growled hungrily like two dogs over a kill. John couldn't see what it was they were fighting over. Neither could Pisces.

Good God, do I really have to see what it is they're fighting over? He swallowed hard with a strong inclination as to what was happening. He intentionally forgot similar scenes in the war. In each instance, a group of humans stood frozen, fully conscious of their circumstances, and helpless under the hypnotic power of the Red. It was how the Red hunted. They were pack hunters. One froze its prey while the others pounced.

John stepped closer, cautiously. In addition to having greater clarity of vision and vision at incredible distances, the Red had thermal vision. While in stealth mode, he wasn't visible, but the heat he or his suit produced was marginally visible, like a thin frame around his body. He and Pisces had to be careful not to expose themselves. Or, they had to phase periodically without draining their suits' power.

Pisces turned to him and nodded. John could only see a faint glint of Pisces, like a glass figurine. He adjusted his frequency and synchronized with hers until she came into view. They hunched down and crept closer, casually scanning the troubled faces of the crowd.

They worked their way to the front of the crowd and saw the two Redlings ripping the flesh from a woman's bones. The Redlings snarled at each other as the other tugged the body closer to itself and bit into it. John was sure she was the one that screamed. Her features were frozen, contorted in agony. Her eyes were wide, locked open. She was naked. The Redlings dug into her legs and ripped apart her arms. Blood was everywhere. And despite the gruesome nature of her appendages, she was still alive. That was also how they consumed their victims. They kept them alive as long as possible so they remained warm and gushing.

The mother Red made a sharp squawking sound which startled the Redlings. John got the strong impression she was telling them to 'hurry up' or 'stop playing with your food' like a typical mother would. They froze, looked to the mother, and then crawled to the head of the woman. They both drove their mouths into the woman's neck and held themselves there. It was then that she died. Once they were finished draining her, the two squealed loudly. It sounded like a cat clawing on a chalkboard inside of an echo chamber. Similar squeals echoed down the hall, where more victims were no doubt being eaten alive.

So that's where the rest of the Redlings are, John thought.

The witnesses watched helplessly. John turned away from the scene and saw a tear leave a woman's eye. He couldn't save the first woman—the moment their poisonous teeth pierced her skin, she was a goner—but he would save this one.

How was the question.

How would he save her?

The moment he shot the mother, the Redlings would strike. He and Pisces would kill the Redlings. What next? The rest of the Red would swarm. They would respond quickly and aggressively to the deaths of their own, especially the deaths of the females. They would swarm fast and mercilessly. That meant John and Pisces would have to get the people out of there immediately.

Where would they go?

The medical center had a secondary entrance and exit that led out of the research facility. If he led them there, they could escape the building. Where they ran off to once they left the research facility was up to them. The world outside those doors would be very different from the one they were accustomed to.

Part of him wanted to lead the people to one specific location, a place where they could raise arms and come back prepared for a fight. He would need more forces if he was going to perform a clean sweep of the facility. He had to stop the Red before they increased their numbers more than they already had. But where could they regroup? Certainly not his home. It would be surrounded not long after his escape.

Why not the church?

Why not the church? He could tell them all to go to his place of worship, Saint Luke's Church and Historical Institute. It was a spacious building with a large kitchen and cafeteria, extra rooms in the dormitory, a library, and was off the beaten path with gates. If the Red pursued them, they could seal the gates and use splendid vantage points for defending their grounds. It was an abhorrent thought to make the house of the Lord a battleground. However, wasn't it always? They were always at war with the evil spirits and god of this world. The word of God was the sword of the Spirit. Throughout the ages, it had cut down and cast away evil spirits and fallen angels in their darkened world. On sacred soil, they would be safe.

John smiled. He would send them to the church. The church would take them in. He and Pisces would go to his home, collect the necessary weapons and tools to combat the Red, and head back to the church. There, they would prepare an army (What army? *The Lord will provide*), return to the research facility, and clean house. And this time, he couldn't stop until all of the Red were gone.

"Pisces. Please, quickly, go back and inform Cartwright and Prost to exit through the back door and head for James. We won't have time to grab them, otherwise. We're going to blind the mother and blast the Redlings. The others are probably going to swarm,"

John instructed through their nanotech telepathy. He knew the Red would hear him if he spoke. They could hear a heart's beat through a brick wall.

Pisces hesitated for a moment to say something, then chose not to and jumped through the wall.

2

In seconds, Pisces was on the other side of the wall and in front of a pair of impatient and worried scientists. She half-expected to see them frozen and terrified near the plexi-glass doors of the medical center. Instead, Prost was sitting on the morgue examination table kicking his feet. Cartwright was leaned against the wall, looking at the ceiling. It was not a human custom to patiently stay put and follow instructions. Pisces was beginning to like them.

Cartwright jumped when she saw Pisces materialize out of thin air. Then she asked, "What's going on out there?"

"What she said," Prost chimed in.

Pisces established eye contact with Cartwright, then Prost, and said, "A, uh, mother Red and her children are eating lunch."

Cartwright's eyes widened. She sagged into a nearby chair.

Pisces continued, "Let's not talk about that. You have to get out of here, right now, as in, yesterday. Things are about to get bad." *Things are already bad*, she thought. "Worse."

"What?" Prost asked and shrugged his shoulders. "A couple of Reds are having a picnic. 'This sandwich is a little dry, mum. Pass the mayonnaise.' Why do you look so weird?"

Cartwright shook her head at Prost. "Sam, how could you be so daft? Don't you know what the Red eat?"

Prost shrugged, thought for a moment, and then froze. All the blood rushed from his face. He looked at Cartwright, then Pisces. "You're shittin me."

"No, but they will be if you two don't get out of here," Pisces said. "I have to go back. Leave through the medical center's exit door and run to the parking lot. Do you know what John's car looks like?"

Cartwright nodded. "Yes. It's the same blue sedan he's been driving for the last seven years."

"They're really eating people out there?" Prost asked and hopped off the examination table.

"Yes, now run. I have to get back," Pisces said and turned around.

Cartwright grabbed Pisces's shoulder. "Be safe."

Pisces shrugged Cartwright's hand off of her shoulder and said, "We'll see." Then, she vanished and ran back through the wall.

3

The two Redlings dragged the corpse to the mother Red. A long cord shot from her mouth and dug into the corpse's head. She drained the brains from the skull—her large eyeball pulsed as she did—and then pulled the rest of the corpse into her mouth.

John's stomach sank. He still felt the need for nourishment; but his appetite was gone.

When Pisces slipped through the medical center doors like an apparition, John felt relieved and pulled out his energy pistol. Hers was already out. He nodded and turned. They both aimed at the mother Red's bulbous eye. John came out of phase first, Pisces seconds after. They fired their parallel streams of hot energy into the eye. It exploded.

The mother Red body slumped instantly.

The Redlings screamed a terrible, deafening, high-pitched squeal. All of them. The screams emanated and echoed throughout multiple halls. John wasn't sure how many there were, but there were a lot more than eleven. A *lot* more. *Crap!* It occurred to him in the brief seconds after firing that he probably should have investigated how many Redlings there were in the adjacent halls before shooting their mother. But what was the point of thinking about it? It was too late to do that now.

The moment the mother Red died, the twenty people were free from their hypnosis. They were dazed, terrified, and held their hands over their ears. John and Pisces pushed past them and blasted the two Redlings before they could attack another person. They went down fast and without further complaint. Pisces took point for any new arrivals while John turned to the people.

"Run before it's too late!" John screamed. "Go through the medical center exit!" They stared at him. "Through the medical center! Now! Head to Saint Luke's Church. You'll be safe."

Six Redlings appeared over their mother's corpse and charged at Pisces and John. The people bolted down the hallway. Some followed John's instructions and went through the medical center. A few didn't, and instead, kept on running down the hallway screaming. They were caught and eaten alive minutes later.

John and Pisces fired two wide arching streams of energy blasts, cutting and torching each of the Redlings that approached. Those that were shot were followed by two more. Those were blasted. Then five more came.

"Oh yea, come on in. The water's just fine. The more the merrier," John taunted with a sarcastic undertone.

Pisces fought the urge to shake her head.

They backed towards the medical center door, but kept on firing. They shot two of the five Redlings that were approaching. The other three paused and then fled.

"That was—" Pisces started.

"No," John interrupted before she could say the word *easy*. If, in fact, that was what she was going to say, it was a terrible word. It was like poking the red button of the universe and unleashing a hell storm of *let's see how easy this is.*

"Short," Pisces said.

Heavy footsteps approached. The floor trembled. John looked past the corpse of the mother Red and saw two larger Red approaching. With them were twenty Redlings and ten soldiers armed with assault rifles. One of the Red shot a fiery plasma ball from her mouth.

"Time to go," John said and ran. Pisces followed. They dove through the doors and charged through the medical center like cats with their tails on fire. The hallway erupted in a fiery explosion. They pushed through the exit.

Though John had traveled to and through the devastation zones and seen far worse, it hurt his heart to see a lifeless, poisoned earth. The damage from the wave stretched for miles. The grass was brown and dead, except for small buds of blue grass (*It's the enemy's grass,* he thought) that were beginning to sprout from the blackened soil. Most of the trees that surrounded the research facility were collapsed, black and leaf-less. The air was thick and humid. The sky was as red as a Crayola crayon. For a moment, John wondered if the sky was on fire, until he realized it was the sun, barely visible through the red haze. He hadn't realized he was standing still, agape, in awe of what happened to his world, a living resemblance of Hell, until Pisces pulled him along. Then, they raced once more.

A plasma bolt blew the exit door from its hinges and sent it flying ten yards away. Not too long afterwards, soldiers poured through the hole, assault rifles pointing and aiming. They were followed by the twenty-something Redlings, then the two Red.

"Cloak," John yelled to Pisces as the bullets started to fly. Bulletproof suit or not, he wanted to avoid getting hit by a high caliber projectile.

The two both vanished and changed course, turning around the corner of the building towards the parking lot. What they saw on the other side was discouraging.

The guards at the main entry and exit gates were all dead. Multiple attempts were made to smash through the facility's reinforced steel, multi-layered, electrified gate. Those attempts caused two wrecks. Those wrecked cars were pushed through the passage by a heavy truck, which then fish-tailed for no observable reason and flipped on its side. People ran through the newly opened passage while cars honked horns and slammed into each other's tails to get past the pedestrians and damaged vehicles. There were a line of cars to get out of the packed exit way. One man shot into the air and pointed at the cars in front yelling for them to speed up, or else. Approaching the panicked collection of cars from the other side of the parking lot were three Red, five Redlings, and ten armed guards.

Cartwright and Prost stood next to John's sky blue sedan. Glassy-eyed and sweaty, they stared at the scene with their mouths and noses buried in their sleeves.

"I don't think any of these people are going to make it out alive," Pisces said.

John couldn't help but to agree. He looked over his shoulder. Their pursuers weren't too far behind them, searching. "I hope James can outrun plasma blasts."

The two approached the car seconds later. Without command, the car started and its front and rear doors opened. "Couldn't remember to give them the password?" James, the car, asked.

"You couldn't just let them in?" Pisces asked back.

"Right," James said as cool air began to burst from his vents. "And let them drive me into that train wreck with those panicked people. No thanks, lady."

Pisces looked at John, who shrugged at her, and jumped into the passenger seat. John got in the driver's seat.

Cartwright and Prost hopped in the back seat. Cartwright wanted to comment about the car, but couldn't take her eyes off of the approaching mob of Red enemies and the wreck that was their escape route.

"Please tell me we have another escape route," Cartwright pleaded, hoped.

A plasma bolt shot towards James. Without a hiccup, James launched forward and pushed everyone backward in their seats. The plasma ball slammed behind them and blew up the light blue truck that was parked next to James.

"Jesus!" Prost yelled as he saw and felt the shockwave from the explosion. His face was pale. "They're spitting fire. I don't remember reading about that."

"You use that name as a swear again and you're out this car," John warned. "They can personally explain it to you."

As John navigated around the clustered parking lot, and more plasma balls crashed in and out of their path, Pisces looked back at Cartwright and Prost. "Only the females can spit plasma. And you wouldn't have read about it. The males were predominately active in the ground invasion. To encounter a female during the war, you had to be on one of their ships or at their ground bases, not on the field. They were constantly mating and are highly aggressive. If you encountered one, your chances of survival were very slim. Also, a lot of information on the Red was sealed from the public."

Highly aggressive seems to be an understatement, Prost thought, but "records sealed from the public" was all he mumbled while staring at plasma balls exploding cars.

"Why would they hide this from the public?" Prost asked. He got no response.

The Red spat plasma balls at the pedestrians and their cars. Explosions erupted all over the parking lot. John counted eight cars destroyed during Pisces's explanation. He didn't want to know how many people died. The five of them, James included, weren't the target anymore. The escape route was. If they couldn't get through the crowd of people, they were stuck.

At least, that's what the Red think, John thought. They didn't know John still had a few tricks up his sleeve.

"James, as soon as we are in range, ready the anti-gravity generators and pulsing ion engines," John ordered. "I'd like to give us a good jump over the fence. Then, shut them off. I don't want to drain energy reserves for an extended flight."

"Jump over the fence?" Cartwright repeated.

"Of course," James said.

A blinking light appeared from the touch-screen dashboard.

"We are receiving a message from the research facility," Pisces said as she investigated. She glided her hands along the dashboard, inputted commands and read. "It's audio only. Would you like to listen?"

"Sure," John sighed.

The radio came to life and blared: "You're not going to escape, John. We are going to catch you. I will personally find you, and I WILL EAT YOUR BRAINS! I will rip them out of your skull, and make you watch while I—"

Pisces shut it off and apologized.

Cartwright burst into tears. "That was Perkins," she

sobbed. "Dear God. That was the chief senator of our Congress."

They made it to the gate. John told them to brace themselves and pressed a command in the blue glowing command panel on his steering wheel. The car shot from the ground like a bullet to the air as a plasma ball smashed behind them. The car shuttered.

"I think they might have given us an extra boost," Pisces said as they coasted through the air and over the facility entry and exit gate. They landed on the hard pavement with a rough bounce.

Behind them was the twisted steel of the smashed gate. Wrecked cars were turned over and on fire. Dead bodies littered the holes in the gates. Most of them were people hit by cars while trying to escape or burned from plasma fire. The panic still ensued for those who remained. Some stood out of their cars and stared back at the approaching Red. One man removed his gun from its holster and shot himself in the head. Another person, under the influence of Red hypnosis, slowly walked forward to her demise. Two white coats were trapped inside of their car and maddeningly fought their car doors as the Red stepped closer. One woman screamed for her life and cried fat globs of tears as the Redlings approached her car. Their singular eyes trained on her. Drool drained from their scaly lips. Their fangs gleamed as their lips spread.

Prost and Cartwright soberly stared back through the rear window and watched as their remaining colleagues were seized or killed. The Redlings swarmed the dead bodies and chewed on whatever flesh remained.

"Mmm, barbecued human," was a thought projected at them. Cartwright felt a cold chill throughout her body.

As the car raced away, the dead and crashed cars faded out of their field of vision. After a few minutes, the coast was clear. All they could see was dead trees and wasted land.

"James, send a message to Emma," John said. "Let her know we're okay and get a status update."

"The wave has ionized the atmosphere and the radiation is disrupting my transmission and data packet attempts," James responded. "I recommend waiting until there is less ionization in the atmosphere. I cannot access the satellite, either."

"Okay, thanks," John said having somewhat expected that answer.

"Look ahead!" Pisces called and grabbed everyone's attention. She pointed at a long-haired black woman running along the road. The woman was running for her dear life, but wobbled and shifted from left to right. John suspected she would topple over and die at any moment. He immediately slowed down and drove adjacent to her.

Cartwright lowered her window and called out. "Need a ride?"

"Oh, no thank you. I prefer passing out in the heat and dying on the side of the road like a beast," a strange thought lingered in the air between Cartwright, Prost, and the young woman's minds. "Yes!" she cried.

They stopped.

The young woman slowed and approached the car. She sweated profusely. It looked as though her face was melting. They opened the door and the hot, toxic, thick air poured into the cabin. Cartwright slid to the middle and the young woman almost fell in. Cartwright helped her in and then closed the door. John punched on the accelerator again.

"Initiate auto-pilot. Designated course is Saint Luke's Historical. Maintain optimal speed," John ordered and turned toward the back.

"As you wish, John," James replied and took control.

As you wish? John thought. He remembered the film 'Princess Bride', which Abbey loved, and wondered how his little princess was fairing. He hoped she wasn't caught in the destructive and reconstructive wave. He needed to establish contact with Emma to verify their whereabouts. He could feel a great loss; and it hurt his heart as he thought about it. He didn't know with whom to associate that loss. It terrified him to be out of control and with limited information.

Do not be anxious. Have faith.

"Is she okay?" Pisces asked as she looked back at the exhausted young woman.

Cartwright held two trembling fingers to the woman's sweaty throat. She closed her eyes and tried to calm herself first, and then nodded. "Her pulse is racing, but she's unconscious. No doubt she's exhausted from the run." She slid the woman's hair from her face. "With the heat, humidity and the strange air we were breathing, her body is struggling to adjust. We were at least two miles from the facility when we grabbed her. I'm amazed she got this far so quickly breathing that in. She must be in remarkable physical shape."

John nodded in agreement. "I'd say remarkable is the appropriate word, if not an understatement."

"Does she look familiar to any of you?" Pisces asked.

John, Cartwright, and Prost all examined her closely. John shook his head. So did Cartwright. Prost smiled and nodded. "I've seen her in the cafeteria a couple of times. She works the graveyard shift and is usually on her way out around the time you two are coming in. Can't say I know her name, though."

"One of us had to hire her," John said.

"Hmm, good point," Prost said. "Check her pockets."

Cartwright glared at Prost. "I'm not going to stick my hand in her pockets. What if she wakes up? She'll think we're trying to rob her."

Prost reached forward. "I'll do it."

Cartwright slapped his hand. "Those pockets are too small anyway. She doesn't have her purse with her. Her wallet's probably in that."

"We'll just have to wait until she wakes up," John said.

Pisces looked at the time. "How long before we reach Saint Luke's?"

"Thirty minutes."

"Why Saint Luke's of all places?" Prost asked.

John expected that question. "It's a great location. It's a good distance away from the facility. People trust the church for shelter. They have plenty of supplies and amenities, including food, housing, and a small medical office. It'll fit our needs, considering our restraints. It's also not too far from a hospital, where we could easily acquire additional medical supplies if we need them."

Prost frowned. "What makes you think it survived the blast?"

It did.

"It did," John said in response to the floating thought he'd grown accustomed to hearing. "Don't ask me how I know; but it did."

Prost wanted to comment, but chose to accept that for the moment. He heard muffled sobs and watched Cartwright's hands tremble over her eyes. He heard sniffles. He decided to give her time to recover from their situation. He accepted, honestly, that if he wasn't on medication, he'd probably be just as freaked as her, and more than likely would be later, once he came down.

"Okay, so what's the plan?" Prost asked.

"The plan is to grab some food on the way, if we can find it, and then drop you two off at the church," John shared. "Pisces and I have to get to my place and collect some necessary supplies. Then we'll return and plot out our next course of action to stop the Red."

Cartwright removed her hands from her face. Her eyes were puffy. Her face flushed a deep red. "You're going to leave us?" she asked as she wiped her face.

"Only for an hour or two, unless the Lord has other plans," John answered. "We have some important items to acquire and neither of you needs to be there for that. Plus, if there's someone waiting for us when we get there, you'll be in harm's way. I'd much rather you two stay at the church. You can rest, recuperate, and help others that come in off of the streets. No doubt, the few survivors still out there will seek out assistance. I only hope this fallen world has enough faith to hear the Lord's voice and follow his instructions to the church."

Cartwright frowned and shook her head. "No. You're not leaving us, Lukas, John, whatever. You're the only one who knows what's going on out there. You two are the only ones that can fight them. We'll be sitting ducks out there. They'll find us, and, and, they'll eat us. They might even mind control us and make us kill each other like in the war."

That reminded John of the question he wanted to ask her. "But, you don't seem to be susceptible to their mind control."

"That's because she has a rare form of A-D-H-D and is highly intelligent, like me," Prost interjected.

John glanced at Prost and raised an eyebrow.

Cartwright's head twisted to Prost so fast that she winced afterward. "How did you know I have A-D-H-D?"

"Cordrodine is listed as one of your prescribed medicines," Prost answered. "It is only prescribed for our form of A-D-H-D." He looked at a confused John. "Extreme hyper-focusing."

Cartwright went beet red. "You looked through my

medical files?" she shouted in protest.

"Yes, I did," Prost said. "I'm sorry. I'm so, so sorry. Yada yada." He waved his hand. "Point is, years ago, my father's company was researching why some people were more vulnerable to the Red telepathy than others. He discovered that people with softer, less wrinkled or articulate brains were most affected. On the other hand, the highly intelligent scholarly types were less affected."

"Go on," John said and nodded.

"The more sophisticated the brain, the less affected they were," Prost continued. "One of the things that tipped them off was book club members. Reading exercises the brain more. The regular book club members were less vulnerable. They reported hearing voices, having strange thoughts, and sometimes losing track of time. However, they never acted out or did anything abnormal, at least, outside of their normal abnormal. Also, the people being diagnosed and medicated for hyper-focus A-D-H-D rarely reported strange thoughts or weird angry voices. If they heard them, they were faint. As for the average, A-D-H-D free mouth-breathers that watched TV and drank beer, they went mad and killed themselves or others."

John didn't like how Prost chose to describe a large sum of their population, but the information was consistent with what he already knew about hyper-intellectuals. They were less vulnerable. Though, he was told humans didn't qualify. From Ioran understanding, even the most intelligent human minds would be greatly affected by the telepathy because of the youth of their species. Their brains, with the exception of an abnormal minority, hadn't developed communicative empathy, telepathy, or telepathic defenses. That's why humans needed cognitive implants. Had this human symptom ADHD been a God-blessed evolutionary gift, the beginnings of a neural redevelopment in the human brain, a subtle defense to an inevitable Red invasion? Or was it the medication?

Even in the final days of the end times, our Lord's grace never ceases, John thought. *His many gifts are still unraveled in late revelation.*

"That explains why the Red didn't or couldn't prevent you from entering the cradle chamber to tamper with the device," John said. It was all speculation, he realized. It was equally possible they were too preoccupied to consider Cartwright or Prost as a threat. Perhaps they were preparing themselves for their re-emergence into the world.

They're not all-knowing and all-powerful, John, a thought came. *There are many things they don't know and people they don't have access to.*

Cartwright blinked. "You think they would have tried to stop us? I'm still not sure where they came from."

"They came out of the walls," Pisces chimed in. "That means they had to be there during the construction. From the beginning."

John sighed.

"We need some answers," Cartwright said, eyes focused on John. "They should start with how you're John Rider, and how the Red are back when you supposedly killed them all."

John nodded and checked their estimated time of arrival to the church. They didn't have a lot of time to go over all the details, but he would tell them his story.

"Okay," John said. "We don't have a lot of time, but I'll give you a brief summary of events. Many of them you may already know."

4

"Twenty-one years ago, Jeremiah, Pisces, and I led a

team of soldiers into the Rezarian Nexus, their command base in northern Africa. We were convinced the giant pyramid was their final stronghold, since we destroyed their smaller bases in the Americas, southwestern and northeastern Europe, South Africa, and southeastern Asia. Most importantly, we believed the leader of the Red, Saratan, was hiding there. He commanded most of the war from there. Unfortunately, things didn't go as planned (and they rarely do) but we positioned ourselves near the nexus's core and planted explosives designed to completely eradicate the last of them.

"Getting into the base was challenging. Getting out of the base was nearly impossible. We were surrounded at every turn. Jones volunteered to stay behind and protect the explosives while the rest of us escaped. The explosives went off. Everything within a kilometer of the base was annihilated. All that was left was a giant crater we now refer to as the Red Crater.

"On August twenty-first of twenty twenty-three, the United States unofficially declared an end to the Red War. However, it wasn't over. Pisces and I led a task force around the world, coordinating searches behind every tree, under every rock, and in every cave. We monitored reports of attacks and missing persons. There were a couple hundred Red out there trying to regroup. Our hunting parties, in coordination with our remaining foreign allies Canada, France, Australia, India, Lian Zheng (formerly northwestern China), Shu Hua (formerly northeastern China), Tibet, and New Russia, stopped them. As was reported, and so we believed, by May fourth of twenty twenty-five, all of the Rezarians were eliminated. Then, the U.S. officially declared an end to the Rezarian Earth Invasion, better known as, the Red War.

"A month later, Pisces and I returned home. We were

celebrated as heroes. They made my birthday a holiday. Some suggested that I run for office and help lead America into a new tomorrow. However, despite my leadership in the war, I did not feel it appropriate that I become a Senator or President. 'I'm a scientist,' I said. 'I always have been, and always will be. I belong in a laboratory, not the Capitol Building or the Oval Office.' Most people disagreed, but those in power were more than happy to see me bow out of the opportunity. They smiled and shook my hand in photo-ops. They patted me on the back for my bravery. In retrospect, I realize refusing to take leadership was my greatest error. However, my wife was pregnant, and I had unofficially adopted General Jones's one-year-old son as my own. They were my priority at the time.

"Not even a year after the war's end, it occurred to me that there was something off about the newly-elected body of Congress. Their campaigns were of world peace, conserving resources, restoring America, and helping the weak and sick in a time when radiation poisoning was killing millions. Yet, most were harsh conservatives who insisted some were less deserving of help than others. They offered financial assistances to select contributors and gave them preferential treatment in moving their companies and land ownership titles to radiation-free zones. They reinforced the police and military authority to near martial law standards. They monitored election results and offered more medicine and food rations to cities and counties that voted primarily for them in federal and state elections. They passed a secret bill to de-privatize elections, so they knew who voted for whom. Most of this was done without the people knowing. They silenced journalists—as if weren't many left—and reduced transparency by cancelling C-SPAN and other programming. They claimed the public broadcasts cost valuable resources.

"Some of the privileged few who learned of these atrocities brought them to daylight. The senators and congressmen of Alaska, Washington, Oregon, and Montana specifically spoke out against these outrages, as their state resources were being pilfered and voting powers watered down by the eastern states. The northwestern states provided loads of lumber from untouched forests and core metals from mining operations in the mountains. Their lands were the richest in the nation. The Whoa Water Company, established by a Washington-Hawaii-Oregon-Alaska agreement that converted coastal salt water into highly purified freshwater (Their primary product was labeled Whoa-Whoa Water), was being taxed higher and forced to sell their water products at cheaper prices to accommodate for the desperate need of clean water. The Whoa-Yeah Gummies, which have a gummy exterior and organic fruit juice interior, was another product that was manipulated by Congress. The Whoa Water Company complained and wanted to appeal, but the Supreme Court dissolved during the Red War, when all of the justices died and no replacements were appointed. All attempted appointments were blocked by Congress.

"On September seventeen of twenty twenty-six, war-time President Green, who spoke out against Congress's actions but rarely utilized his veto power, died of radiation sickness. Vice President Reiko, who felt the legislative branch was over-reaching and threatened to veto when in office, was assassinated while being sworn into office. The interim president sworn in not long afterward was the Speaker of the House Bob Sanders. He captured the assassin responsible for the assassination of Warren and personally executed him with a gunshot to the head on live television as a message to anyone who would make the same attempt on him.

"Afterward, more bills were pushed forward to increase military presence in the four western states, suppress talks of succession, and expand U.S. military presence in the world. The interim-President spoke of spreading American interests and colonies across the world, and started by moving their military forces into Mexico and northeastern Canada. Many suspected this was the beginning of an American Empire and the first remnants of the Washington Coalition (Washington, Oregon, Montana, Hawaii, Alaska, and British Columbia) were born through secret meetings and the drafting of its own constitution.

"Not too long afterward, I was approached by the Washington delegates. They sought my endorsement of the Washington agenda. I was a highly appreciated and respected figure. Many people were still hoping I would run for office and set things on a better path. They were tired of war, greed, and hate. They sought peace in the world through the grace of God, which I had spoken of in interviews. Again, I hesitated and refused a public endorsement. I believed I had done my part for this fallen world and should focus on raising my newborn daughter and helping my sick wife. My wife, however, told me, as a man of God, I had a responsibility to persistently serve and improve the world. She insisted I get involved and reflect on the most recent events. She was rarely ever wrong. I decided I would openly support them. When I did, support flourished and the succession movement took off. Many people, supporting me, moved west.

"That was when the propaganda machine kicked into high gear. Accusations surfaced demonizing the cognitive chips we installed into the military officers and many civilians to protect them from Red telepathy.

December fourth and twentieth of twenty twenty-six and February third of twenty twenty-seven, they staged terrible massacres and framed former military officers who were under my immediate command. They built a fear campaign against Red War veterans. They first accused me of training them to be cold-blooded killers, and then blamed the implants. They additionally blamed the post-traumatic stress disorder symptoms on the implants, saying they impeded the officer's abilities to recover. Puppet scientists and newscasters said the officers' cases of P-T-S-D were worse than previous cases. Of course, in no war in our history had veterans witnessed their companions being ripped to pieces and eaten alive by vicious aliens. However, that argument went nowhere. On February nineteen of twenty twenty-seven, despite many filibuster attempts, both chambers of Congress passed a law criminalizing unauthorized cognitive implants and insisted all existing implants be removed. Moreover, anyone who had an implant, including elected officials, was considered a potential danger to humanity and could be detained and have the implants forcibly removed. If the implant could not be removed without terminating the individual's life, he or she could be indefinitely detained, and if warranted, depending on their threat level, executed.

"After the passage, all current and former military officers, including myself, were ordered to report immediately for removal of cognitive implants. Anyone who refused would be dishonorably discharged and/or forcibly detained.

"On the same day, the senators and congressmen who filibustered were harassed and detained, as they were the only officials who still had implants. Michigan, Illinois, Massachusetts, Pennsylvania, Montana, Washington, Alaska, and Oregon mandated the installation of cognitive implants during the Red War. Everyone else in the Senate and House had either removed or never had them. When Pisces brought this recent development to my attention, we put the pieces together and immediately stepped in to rescue the senators and congressmen before their implants could be removed. The capitol building became a warzone. Five senators and seven congressmen that attempted to escape were shot dead. However, the rest escaped. Hours after their escape, the president declared Pisces, myself, and all of the escaped members of Congress to be traitors who, without provocation, violently assaulted members of Congress. It was a clear sign that implanted people were damaged. If we were found, we were to be executed on the spot; and any family members still in the states were to be detained and interrogated.

"On February twenty-four of twenty twenty-seven, Washington, Oregon, Montana, Hawaii, and Alaska publically succeeded from the United States of America and the Washington Coalition held its first parliament meeting. There, we made many appointments. I was appointed Washington's Minister of Foreign Affairs and Pisces became Minister of Defense. We were first tasked with coordinating the safe removal of Coalition family members from U.S. state lines—that accounted for about fifty people, thirty of them children—and establishing relations with our world allies. We greeted the crowds on the steps of our recently built capital building in Seattle. The newly appointed Prime Minister Bedwell and Vice Minister Hurst cut off vital resources in the form of sanctions in response to the U.S.'s recent aggressions.

"The acting president refused to acknowledge the Washington Coalition's sovereignty and threatened military action if the Washington Coalition insisted on succession and enforced sanctions.

"After that threat, we held our second parliament meeting. In it, most of us understood; the only logical explanation for the U.S. government's behavior in the last three or four years was the Red. The Red infiltrated both legislative and executive branches. Our best hope of preventing similar infiltrations elsewhere was to have implants installed everywhere. So, on March second, we hosted a secret summit with the leaders of France, Australia, India, Lian Zheng, Shu Hua, Tibet, and New Russia in Hawaii. Most of them considered Pisces and me to be their closest friends since we helped them remove the Red from their homelands. We shared the details of the aggressive happenings in the U.S. Many were worried about the implications of a Red re-emergence in the west. It meant the Red War wasn't over after all. I insisted each nation install implants. Fortunately, most of them already mandated the installation of the cognitive implants during the war. The nations that didn't established mandates agreed with our terms to prevent Red infiltration, insurrection, or another war.

"Somehow, the U.S. got wind of the old Earth Alliance summit meeting and retracted its threat. Then, assassins crossed into Coalition lines and made attempts and successes on Coalition officials' lives. Some attempts where shootings. Others were explosives. They threatened Abbey and Levi's lives in three of those attempts. One of the assassins shot my wife. She barely survived. After that, I chose to change my identity to preserve their safety. We allowed the public to believe I died in a bombing. I changed my appearance and moved my wife, daughter, and Jones's son to Montana. After they were safe, I re-emerged as the new Minister of Foreign Affairs, Peter Hawk, and as a reserved and temperamental scientist in Montana named Lukas Brown. Only a select few within the Washington Parliament knew my true identity.

"In the next three years, the Coalition strengthened its relations in the world by re-establishing the Earth Alliance; and the installation of cognitive implants was mandatory in every corner of the world except the U.S. The United States took over eastern Canada, Mexico, the Caribbean Islands, and parts of Central America and became the North American Union. The constitution was dissolved and the extended-term, acting president became chancellor. Congress merged the House and Senate into one chamber and halved its members. The chancellor took over the role of the judicial branch.

"With the death of the United States as it was, most of the powers within the Earth Alliance were gearing up for what they knew would be an eventual war against the last bastion of Rezarian influence. However, they were also struggling with the complete and utter devastation that was the Red War. Most of the planet was flooded with radiation. Crops were useless. Water needed excessive purification. Resources were slim. Trade routes needed to be re-established. With the interdependency that was globalization, the destruction of that global network made all of us extremely vulnerable. In addition, mutants, monsters, and warped animal species, were surfacing and threatening human lives.

"No one considered making a move against the Union. The stakes were too high. So, we rebuilt. We let a few more years pass. In that time, I worked on multiple projects in a secret base.

"On October seventeen of twenty thirty-three, I discovered a way to restore the planet, and at the same time, eliminate the Red. It required the collection of core fragments, biomatter, and select elements from across the world. I would use them to establish an energy pattern we considered as Earth's D-N-A and produce a large enough energy matrix and pulse to restart the Earth's natural growth process. It would also destroy all nonindigenous life on Earth, the Red. The Coalition supported my international treasure hunt and clued the other Earth Alliance nations in on my efforts. They all provided endless support when I passed through looking for specific items or elements distinctive to their regions. By November of twenty thirty-five, I had collected hundreds and thousands of samples for a preliminary energy signature. When I returned to show off my results, I discovered my wife was dying from the radiation poisoning that brought her in and out of illness for years.

"My wife died on December seven of twenty thirty-five. That same day, I finished construction of the catalyst, established an energy pattern from Earth's elements, and merged the Earth's D-N-A with an energy force. The catalyst came to life, and the regeneration project had footing.

"Someone leaked the news of my success; and the Union immediately ceased all hostile behavior. Instead, they reached out to the governments for mutual cooperation. They retracted their military forces from borders. They offered to establish trade agreements between the Coalition and Union. Multiple partnerships were insisted in an effort to repair the relationship between the two nations and undo the damage in the devastation zones.

"The Coalition Parliament was hesitant but enthusiastic about the possibilities of partnership, even if Union intentions were completely selfish and the partnership was temporary. Both the Union and Coalition were beginning to suffer random attacks from the Rogue Districts, which were states abandoned during the war after crippling defeats and overwhelming radiation assaults. Prime Minister Ortega and Parliament made the regeneration project a mutual endeavor. They presented the option to the Union. The Union insisted on providing the necessary resources. They said plans were already in place to assemble an advanced sciences research facility and alternative power station in Richmond. The project could start in two years. All I had to do was apply for temporary Union citizenship.

"I did, hesitantly. The project went into motion on February eleven of twenty thirty-seven after a required, formal request before the Union's Congressional Science Committee, headed by the firebrand Senator Perkins. He tossed out a list of objections that were easy to refute. Then, he approved, slammed his gavel, and signed a thick stack of documents. From the perverse look on his face, which made my skin crawl, I should have known he knew the full potential of the regeneration device. The Parliament thought it was better to have the Red-controlled Union fund their own extinction than to stretch our already tight resources. Little did we know, they knew what we were doing.

"The Union seized control last week, and here we are now, in the present."

What he did not tell them was that, four years ago, the Coalition received funding and supplies from the Earth Alliance to begin work on its own, more sophisticated regeneration device. That device was constructed in his secret base in Montana, and that was where his daughter and Levi were headed.

5

Having listened to John's story, Cartwright leaned back and frowned. It was a fair summary of post-Red

War history. Much of it she knew, but not the details. The most harrowing part, the part that dug into her skin like an angry cat, was his description of the device. She thought it was solely a regenerative device designed to reinvigorate the planet; but John developed the device knowing it was capable of destroying an entire species nonindigenous to their planet. It concerned her that the man she'd grown to love was willfully involved in a plot to commit genocide. Moreover, he was doing so, and involved in a conspiracy full of subterfuge, while utilizing her knowledge and research. Had she not gone to the cradle assembly, she may have died like the people they left behind never knowing she was a tool of both the Red and the Coalition's plots.

Cartwright opened her mouth to share her opinion on the matter, but was cut off by the groans of their guest, whose name was still unknown. The woman shifted in Cartwright's lap and looked at her, at Prost, who was staring at her, and then straightened.

The woman had chocolate skin and long, straight black hair. Her left eye was gold and right eye apple green. Her face was oval and muscular. Her lips were full and nose sharp with flared nostrils.

"Welcome to the land of the living," Prost said and smiled at her.

The woman blinked at Prost, at Cartwright, and then to the front of the cabin. She saw John and Pisces. She looked back at John, and then did a double-take at Pisces, who stared at her.

"It's okay," Pisces said with a smile. "You're safe. The Red are miles and miles behind us." She glanced at the dashboard and slid her furry finger along the readouts of the visitor's vital signs. "Your vitals look good. Healthy heart rate. Breathing fine. No neurological damage. Looks like you're suffering from exhaustion and hunger, just like the rest of us."

The woman stared at Pisces with wide eyes and leaned back as far as she could, which pushed her against the passenger window.

Concerned she might attempt to bail, John checked the locks. They were secure. He said, "You recognize me, don't you?"

The woman nodded. Then, she looked at Prost. He smiled. She frowned and looked back at John. "You're Doctor Brown, and beside me is Doctor Cartwright."

John smiled and nodded. "Yes. What is your name?"

"Jasmine."

"Ooooh, Jasmine," Prost said. "I like that name. Mine's Aladdin, and I want to show you a whole new world."

"Seriously?" Pisces asked. "I mean, seriously."

Jasmine's eyes narrowed. "Sam Prost."

Prost displayed his pearly whites, and said, "I am. I am. Oh Sam I am. I do not like green eggs and ham."

Pisces brought both of her palms to her face and shook her head. "This is not happening," she mumbled.

"Same old Sam," said Jasmine. She shook her head. "Full of jokes, short on memory. You don't remember me, do you?"

"I know we've spoken before," Prost said and shrugged. "Should I?"

"We honestly don't have time for pleasantries, Miss Jasmine," John said to spare everyone from an uncomfortable situation. "We're only minutes away from reaching the church. There, we'll deposit you, Cartwright, and Doctor Seuss over there for some recuperation and protection while Pisces and I handle some business."

Jasmine ignored John and looked at Pisces. "You're Commandant Pisces of the Red War."

Hesitantly, Pisces nodded. "Yes. That's me."

"My father served with you in the Red War," Jasmine said.

Pisces nodded. Thousands of men served with her after she was commissioned as a commandant. "I'm sure your father was a fine soldier."

"He was, yes. His name was Corporal Phillip Davison of the United States Marine Corps. You remember him, don't you?"

John shot her a look. Pisces froze. Cartwright and Prost exchanged a look again and chimed in, "What does that mean?"

"Yea," Jasmine said. "What does that mean, April?"

"April?" Cartwright asked. "Is that your first name?"

Pisces shrunk in her chair. "Before I was known as Pisces, I was disguised as a human and lived under the alias April Miller, a close associate of John and Jeremiah. After the death of his wife, the Corporal and I had a, uh, close friendship. He sacrificed himself to save my life, as well as the rest of our squad. He left two girls without parents. I reached out to them, but—"

"Our aunt moved us," Jasmine interrupted. "We kept moving further and further east during the war. Before he died, he sent us letters. He spoke of the things he witnessed. The many atrocities and hard choices of war. He wrote about you, too, April. About how you were helping him through the loss of our mother. About how he was falling in love with you. He didn't say you were an animal. When we found out, it hurt our family that you deceived him the way you did."

"Dude had sex with a cat," Prost whispered to Cartwright.

"I'm not April anymore, and no one was deceived," Pisces said in a low voice. "He knew exactly what I was. And *nothing* inappropriate happened. I wouldn't allow that." There was a long and uncomfortable silence in the cabin of the car. "He told me about you, also. That you were different."

Jasmine shook her head and waved her hand. "No. We're not talking about that."

"That depends," John interceded and examined Jasmine. Her eyes changed color. They were brighter, almost glowing. It was a subtle trait among mutants. "Is it relevant to our current situation?"

"I'd say so," Pisces said and turned to the back of the cabin.

"I wouldn't," Jasmine argued.

The two stared at each other.

Breathing through his nose and exhaling loudly, John chose his words carefully. "Jasmine, it is not our wish to invade your privacy, which I completely respect and can relate to. There are many things about Pisces and I we prefer to keep between us and a few others. I respect your request to keep certain aspects of yourself to yourself. With that being said, it is my hope that if whatever is different about you will help us, or present a handicap in our forthcoming attempts to circumvent the Red resurgence, we will be afforded with essential information."

"Of course," Jasmine sighed. Her eyes returned to their original shades. She leaned into her seat and relaxed.

"Good," John said. "It seems you have some history with Pisces and Sam. Whatever it may be, you three have to put it behind you. Otherwise, it could get some or all of us killed."

He turned to Pisces and transmitted, *"When we are separate from the three, I would like to know what you know. Her presence is a surprise, but certainly not a coincidence. We cannot afford any more surprises."*

Pisces nodded.

"Of course," Jasmine said. She glared at Prost.

Prost shrugged. "What did I do?"

"You got drunk, slept with my roommate, and then forgot about her," Jasmine accused.

"That doesn't sound like me," Prost said. "I don't forget anything. Perhaps you have me confused with someone else."

"She called you the next day but you didn't know who she was," Jasmine said. "She confronted you in person and you didn't recognize her."

Good grief, John thought and returned his attention to the road.

Prost gaped at the accusations, speechless. He met Cartwright's gaze. She shook her head. He turned to Pisces. She stared ahead at a gated building. He returned his attention to Jasmine, who glowered with glowing, excited eyes.

"And after talking to you at that party for two hours, we thought you were a stand-up guy," Jasmine said.

"What party?" Prost asked.

"The staff Christmas party," Jasmine answered.

Prost blinked. "Oh, I thought you looked familiar. The get-together at your place after the staff Christmas party last year." He blinked rapidly. "Rachel."

"Yep," Jasmine said.

"I'm sorry, Jasmine," Prost said. She glared at him. "I really am. Really." Her glare persisted. "I'll be completely honest with you."

"Let's hear it."

"I didn't forget her; but I wanted to," Prost said. "So I pretended that I did."

"What?" Jasmine gasped. "You broke her heart! She was torn up."

"I know," Prost sighed. "I felt terrible."

"Sure you did."

"Listen," Prost said. "She called me talking about how excited she was and how much she wanted to see me again." He fiddled with his fingers. "And all I could think was that I slept with the wrong roommate."

Jasmine blinked. "That's your excuse? You mistakenly slept with her instead of me?"

Pisces put her hands over her face. *"I'm going to put my hands on him. Can we throw him out of the car?"*

"You two can finish this later," John called to the back. "We're here."

"I wanted you," Prost said, ignoring John. "But you stepped away to answer a phone call and didn't come back."

Jasmine frowned. "My aunt died. She was a second mother to me."

"Oh," Prost said. *Crap.*

"Yea," Jasmine said. "And when I came back, you two were gone."

"Honest to God, scout's honor, the moment you left, someone brought in two bottles of tequila," Prost explained. "I was so drunk that night; I would have slept with Big Bird."

Cartwright frowned at him.

"What?" Prost said. "With that weird yellow dress she had on, it felt like I did."

Jasmine's eyes shot wide open.

"I said, 'We're here!'" John called to the back as they passed the gate.

Saint Luke's Church and Historical Institute was a pocket college campus with three three-story buildings and one two-story dormitory behind them. The four buildings were aligned as a diamond. They were all tanned brick with metal frames and large paned glass windows. The three-story buildings were circular in design with pillars along the outside of the bottom floor.

The front building was twice the width of the other circular buildings, with a large marble cross on top and a statuette Christ Jesus nailed to the cross. The cross and statuette Christ were sculpted and painted in great detail, including the countless scars and open wounds from torture, and seeping blood along His abdomen, arms, in His hair, and on His face. The eyes of statuette Christ were yellow diamonds. They had a special glow in the sunlight, despite the haze.

The grounds of the church campus were full of healthy green grass, an assortment of beautiful flowers, and in the back, was the main garden, where they grew grapes, lemons, blueberries, strawberries, peas, green beans, potatoes, tomatoes, garlic, onions, and more. In the back, behind the dormitory, was a small greenhouse.

Saint Luke's was one of the few remaining churches in the country. There were only three left in the state of Virginia. Through an executive order, the high chancellor shut down the rest to be used for housing and schools.

John parked. They jettisoned the car, speechless, and strode forward to the campus's main building. Despite the destructive wave, the landscape was flawless, untouched. The grass held a green glow and Prost could have sworn he heard a hum.

John fell to his knees and praised, "Holy, holy, holy, Lord God Almighty, which was, and is, and is to come."

Pisces joined him, "Thou art worthy, O Lord, to receive glory and honor and power, for thou hast created all things, and for thy pleasure they are and were created."

The others watched in awe of the protective power God held over his temple.

As John and Pisces rose from their praises, a figure pushed through the glass, turnstile revolving doors of the church. He was a black man with a thin wrinkly frame, short strings of white hair around his head, and long white cane. He wore a crisp, black button-up shirt with a white collar, pale blue jeans, and short tan boots. He sat down his tan gloves and a small shovel. John suspected his friend was in the middle of gardening. He met the group of five at the foot of the five stairs leading to the church.

"Eddie," John said with a smile and open arms.

"Well, aren't you a sight for sore eyes," Eddie said and smiled. "When I saw that thing coming our way, I thought you were a goner." He gave John a hug and then squeezed his shoulder. He surveyed the rest of the group and looked down at Pisces, who was shorter than everyone else. "And Pisces?"

Pisces smiled and waved. "Hi, Eddie."

Eddie tried to lean down to give her a hug, then grimaced and changed his mind. "Look at you. You look exactly the same as when I last saw you. You haven't aged a day."

"I could say the same about you," Pisces said with a smile.

Eddie's head shot back and he barked a loud laugh into the hazy red sky. "You always were a flatterer, cupcake. I haven't looked young since we had a black president."

Prost laughed.

Eddie turned, squinted, and examined Prost. "Hmm. Doesn't he remind you of Oliver?" John nodded. Eddie stepped closer and examined him. "You've got to have some of his blood in you."

"Uncle Oliver?" Prost asked and stepped closer. "How did you know him?"

"Oh. When I was a hot shot lawyer, I prosecuted some of his cases while he was N-Y-P-D," Eddie said. "Boy did he make my job easy." He smiled. "Let me tell you two things about your uncle, Oliver. One, he had the most bizarre sense of humor. And two, he was an honorable man with the sharpest mind I have ever encountered. No other human being on the planet had a brain like his. Man could talk to machines. It's a shame he's not here with us now. We could have utilized his 'special gifts'."

Prost frowned and looked at John.

John whispered in Eddie's ear. "He doesn't know about those special gifts."

Eddie nodded. "I forgot how top secret everything always is with your folk. One day, it would be nice when not everything has to be buttoned up, sealed, and slipped into a hidden safe with three different passwords. I'm guessing then, they don't know about the other stuff. Trinity. The Temple. The Galactic Cooperative—"

"Galactic Cooperative?" Jasmine asked. Her eyes widened and brightened. She glanced at Pisces and John.

Eddie smiled. "Wow. My dear child, you have the most beautiful eyes. You must be one uh those mutants."

At that, Jasmine turned away from the group, blushing through her dark skin.

"Never you mind, dear," Eddie said. "After what just happened, it doesn't matter what you are. The Lord loves all His creations."

John rested his hand on Jasmine's back and said to Eddie, "Maybe we should talk about why we're here."

"Yes, yes," Eddie nodded and waved for them to follow him. He turned back to the church. "That thing you were working on didn't go as expected and those Red devils are back to bring the full blazes of Hell to our doorstep. I suspected this day would come. I had a dream that old friends would be reunited as enemies, one of them would die, and we'd be staring into one of those big ugly lizard eyes."

John wasn't sure how to respond to Eddie's remarks, so he decided not to. "The church is a safe place. No doubt the hand of God Himself rested upon this place. I believe many people will realize that and come here for aid. If you are willing, I would appreciate it if you took us in and anyone else who may come here. We'll need a base of operations to regroup for whatever comes next."

Eddie waved his hand at John as though he were speaking nonsense. "Of course! The church is always open to God's people, saints and heathens. Besides, this church is as much yours as it is mine. I stand on the pulpit and deliver God's word to the few stubborn souls who still have open ears, but through the grace of God, your donations paid for it."

John opened his mouth to respond but Eddie pushed through the revolving door. The rest of the group followed.

6

It was three hours before John and Pisces got back on the road. Eddie insisted they claim their quarters, take a shower, and have a three-course meal. The rooms were as confining as the college dorms he remembered from his twenties, a few too many decades ago. John insisted on pairing with Pisces. Cartwright paired with Jasmine. That left Prost with his own room until someone else needed a bed to lay his or her head. Prost quietly hoped whoever it might be was a she, and she wanted to lay her head on his bed or his... Cartwright slapped the back of his head.

Eddie sent robes, towels, soap, shampoo, and extra sets of clothing, all white shirts and trousers. Everyone took showers. By the time they were clean and dressed, lunch was prepared. The first course was Caesar salads and tomato soup with bread. The second course was grilled chicken over steamed rice with broccoli, onions, peppers, and mushrooms, and a side of garlic sticks. As their wastes expanded, John leaned back from the table and released a pleased sigh. The third course was apple and peach pies with ice cream.

Most of the meal, there was more consumption than conversation. When there was talking, it came from Eddie, or his wife Ruth. Eddie explained the history of the church, and there were twenty-three years of history to keep the conversation going for most of the dinner. The church opened six years into the Red War. Eddie was one of the many displaced refugees who fled the west coast when the Red arrived and destroyed thousands of cities using their destructive radiation pulse and beam weapons. Eddie, who at one time was worth two million dollars, was homeless and almost penniless. He found and moved into an abandoned house that was previously owned by a well-to-do pastor. The pastor mysteriously disappeared prior to the Red invasion like a million other people.

In the house, waiting out the war, Eddie read a decade's worth of sermon notes and Christian books left behind by the pastor and had an epiphany. After two years invested in studying the bible, he opened the house to other displaced people and reopened the pastor's abandoned church. He invited his friends to embrace a new life in Christ Jesus and worked in the community to help thousands of displaced people.

Those who were well off, despite the war, gave the church plenty of donations to restart its services and became regular attendants. The events leading up to and during the war opened many minds as to the origins and history of Christ Jesus. Eddie was more than willing to accept the donations. He used what little was necessary to maintain the church and stored the rest in church savings. As many were sure the war would not end in their favor, the church was flooded with people. Eddie feared there would not be enough space in the hallways in case of an emergency. He prayed for a larger church than the one he inherited.

During one of his services, Eddie met an engineer and owner of a construction company. They took all the money he saved and began to build a large capacity church at a discounted cost. "There we setbacks," he said. With supplies low, construction took longer than expected. Halfway through the construction, the war ended and tithes ran dry. Church attendance shrank by sixty percent. The church construction fund was in the red. Lord knew Eddie was praising God from sunrise to sunset to sunrise when the Red were reportedly defeated. Yet, Eddie felt the construction of the larger church was no longer necessary. As the days passed, he wondered if his service to God was complete.

That same day, John arrived. He stormed through the doors in a long, leather jacket, said he'd heard about the church Eddie was building and wanted to help. Most of the other churches were destroyed, used as housing for displaced Westerners and Midwesterners, or run by charlatans. John laid out his plans for the church, school, and library. They shook hands. Weeks later, hundreds of crates of books from a hundred different libraries from the western states were delivered to Eddie's construction site. They stored them in Saint Luke's Church until Saint John's Library was open. It was a major tourist attraction. The rest of the buildings, Saint Matthew's Lecture Hall and Saint Paul's Dormitory came not long afterward.

Eddie found himself in awe over his new life. He was once a cutthroat prosecuting attorney who arrogantly convicted many innocent men in his time. Now, he was a pastor, librarian, historian, law and English professor, gardener, husband, and father. It was all thanks to God. "Praise be to the Lord, who brought me from death to life even during the final conviction of the world," he said. That was the end of the story. The rest, he said, was obvious and not worth telling.

On the third course, Eddie asked what happened at the research facility. Everyone except Jasmine took their turn filling in their parts and versions of the experience. John spoke of his encounters with Perkins and Collins, but spared them many details. Cartwright mentioned seeing the body bag that held John. The memory agitated her. Prost reiterated his suspicion that John was one of km, the Red, as well as his surprise that John hadn't made a move on Cartwright in seven years. "Why hasn't he tapped that?" he reiterated. Cartwright's eyes shot out from her head. She looked down, embarrassed. Pisces shook her head and took over the story, detailed their escape.

When Pisces finished, the pie was gone and most of the group was ready to fall asleep at the table. Cartwright and Jasmine left with thanks and went to their room to rest. Prost followed behind them and went to his own. John and Pisces stayed with Eddie and Ruth.

"So, now that you're here, what's next?" Eddie asked.

John checked his internal chronometer and frowned. "We have to go to my home and collect a few things. They'll help us in our fight against the Red."

Ruth, a short, gray-streaked blonde shook her head and sighed. "You think you can still fight those things? You look good John, and you especially Pisces, but you're my age. We're thirty years beyond our prime."

John smiled. "First, thank you. Second, I'm as old as I am but not as old as I look. After a night's sleep, trust me, I'm going back to looking and feeling thirty years younger."

Eddie rubbed his chin. "That's some trick you have there. Do you think it'll be enough?"

John shrugged.

"With everything that's gone on after the war, I'm wondering what God has planned for humanity," Eddie continued. "Contrary to our expectations, it was His will for you to fail and a third of the country to be wiped away by that blasted machine. It feels to me like we were in the lull between storms, and now the final storm is coming."

There was a moment of silence.

"The storm will pass," John said. "The remaining people of the world are finally listening to reason and accepting God's testimony. In two weeks, the Alliance has planned a meeting to negotiate the terms of the first world government. They're talking about making Paris the capital, since it currently hosts most of the former world's treasures and artifacts. The only opposition to peace left is the Union and the Red."

Ruth leaned forward. "Really?"

"Yes," John said. "And, whether the Red realize it or not, they just shot themselves in the foot. The wave killed millions." John stopped and thought about that. The wave killed millions. Yet, he hadn't shed a single tear over any of them. He wondered about that. About himself. He took responsibility for building the device and failing to destroy it. Yet, he hadn't mourned for those who died in their power struggle. "They've killed millions of people in the Union, civilians and soldiers. That means: all there is left to fight is the Red."

Eddie frowned. "You say this as though it is an easy task. They're larger, stronger, and faster than all of us. They can shoot fire from their mouths."

"Only the females," Pisces corrected.

But Eddie continued, "They *eat* us, and control many with their mind powers. You had an army last time.

Without an army, how can we expect to defeat them?"

In God I will praise his word, in God I have put my trust; I will not fear what flesh can do unto me, John remembered from the King James Bible.

"Well, right now, most of them are at the research facility," John explained. "Me, Pisces, and what few remaining men we find are going to destroy the research facility. Once we do that, they'll be scattered. We can regroup and then prepare to hunt them down. That is, at least, until Levi fulfills his end of the mission. That'll be the day the music dies for the Red."

"Looks like you've got this all figured out," Ruth said. By her tone, John was sure she was being sarcastic. She picked up her plate and set it on a dish cart.

Eddie twiddled his thumbs and pouted.

Pisces stood and stretched. "We should get going. It's been about four hours since we escaped the facility. I want to get him home before the Red salvage the very things we plan on using against them." She smiled at John. "That is assuming your house is still standing."

The possibility that his home was destroyed weighed on John's mind through most of their meal. Along with the forestry, the wave destroyed most of the buildings and houses in its wake. His house was loaded with safeguards, gadgets and enhancements he hoped kept it together. Everything he wanted to find was in a sealed off oasis a hundred feet below his house, but who knew how it all responded to the destructive and transformative powers of the wave.

"Let's hope what we need is still there," John said and stood. He shook Eddie's hand, hugged Ruth, and thanked them again for hosting. Then, he and Pisces left.

7

Twenty minutes into the car ride, John was

concerned. Pisces hadn't spoken since they left Saint Luke's. He pulled himself out of his own thoughts and turned to her.

"Okay. Let's hear it. What's wrong?"

Pisces blinked. "What do you mean?"

"You're upset. I know it. Let's talk about it," John said.

"I'm fine."

It annoyed John when women said that. "I can tell when you're upset. Something is on your mind, outside of our driving into a possible ambush. I'd like to know what it is. Is it about what Jasmine said?"

Pisces crossed her arms.

John nodded. "It was Phillip's choice. We made it common knowledge within our unit that you were not human. He fell in love with you, anyway. You didn't do anything wrong."

Pisces sighed. "Then why do I feel like I broke their family?"

John sat silent for a moment, and then responded, "He made a sacrifice; and you blame yourself for it. Now, it's possible he might not have made that sacrifice if you two were not so close. It's also possible that, because he was an honorable man and a great soldier, he would have made the same sacrifice whether he had feelings for you or not. However, you were not responsible for his death or leaving those girls without a father. The Red were."

"His daughter hates me," Pisces sighed and fiddled with her fingers.

"Her father was in love with a woman other than her mother. A woman that was not human. She believes he sacrificed himself for you, not for her. She believes he left her and her sister alone, because of you. To her, you took her father away from her."

Pisces nodded and listened.

John continued, "It is worse that he didn't inform them of who you were, because she believes you deceived him. That makes his sacrifice meaningless. It means he left them for a lie. She's wrong; but she's probably felt that way for most of her life."

When phrased that way, it all makes perfect sense, Pisces thought. Sometimes, she was impressed by John's grasp of the human psyche. He would have made a great psychologist.

"What do you think I should do?" Pisces asked.

"Nothing," John said.

Pisces frowned. "Nothing?"

"Honestly, it's the least of our problems, right now."

"I know," Pisces sighed.

They sat quietly.

"James, have you been able to contact Emma?" John asked.

"Negative," James responded. "I've tried for the last three hours, but been unsuccessful in my attempts to break through the interference. When I do make contact, you or Pisces will be the first to know."

John had to accept that, he realized.

"You asked me to tell you about Jasmine when we were alone," Pisces said.

John nodded.

"Phillip told me his daughter was a mutant. His wife was infected by the radiation during her pregnancy. Jasmine was born was partially deaf. But when she was about four, they noticed a sensitivity to others thoughts and emotions."

John frowned and put his hand to his mouth. He rubbed his chin. "Did he believe she was susceptible to the influences of the Red?"

"He was worried about it; but because she was a child, she didn't show the signs. There is reason to be concerned now. Though, I wonder why or how they would have let her run away if she was susceptible."

John rubbed his chin and said, "Stranger things have happened. They were in the middle of feeding. Perhaps she slipped away without them knowing."

"Maybe she got out right after the device fired. It would have given her time. And, it would explain how she got away," Pisces said. "I can't believe this is intentional subterfuge. There was no way they could have expected us to escape, get through the gate, and pick her up. No one is that good of a chess player."

"You never played Jeremiah," John said with a smile. "So, she's a friend?"

"As far as we know, I guess, yes."

"We shall see how long that assessment holds," John said.

Five minutes later, they were close to John's house. He insisted they enter stealth mode on arrival and parked two blocks away and around the corner. They couldn't afford to be seen. No doubt, his house, or whatever was left of it, was under observation.

John told James to sit tight, but at the first sign of trouble, he was to pick them up. James agreed and interlocked communications through their helmets on an encrypted frequency. Then, they were off.

John and Pisces chose the least expected route and took to the air, hovering only inches above ground level to keep in line with the fallen and broken trees, and to avoid stepping on any sticks or branches and announcing their arrival. There were few trees still standing; and they were decayed, poisoned. The bark turned black with blue veins pulsing along the surface. John wanted to study the phenomena, having limited knowledge of alien botany.

It was the same with the grass. The ground was covered in flat brown grass. It was all dead except for a few sprouts of blue. The soil was a muddy red clay. Their feet sunk into it as they rest their feet back on the ground.

The two-story house was still standing. Half of its foundation was warped, drooping, while the other half held up strong.

As was expected, they had company. There were three army trucks sitting outside of his home. Four guards stood near the entrance, armed with scoped assault rifles. They were talking. Two men were patrolling the perimeter. They seemed to be at ease. None of them looked as though they expected any visitors. All of them looked haggard and tired. Sweat poured down their frowned faces. There were sweat spots on the armpits, fronts, and backs of their uniforms. One of the four men in the front kept wiping his face with a white washrag.

In the back of one of the army trucks was a man in a black-leather, hooded robe. *The leather man* came to John's mind. The leather man read from a tablet with his legs crossed. A mask obstructed his facial features. He wore leather gloves and metallic silver boots, which struck John as both peculiar and familiar.

In the back of another army truck was a Rezarian. It was smaller, younger. It sat, curled with its tail wrapped around itself and eye closed. John knew, of course, that at any moment, that eye could open. Since they were not completely out of phase—that required too much of a power drain from his suit—the Rezarian might be able to observe their movements with its thermal vision.

Pisces tapped John on his leg and signaled for them to keep on moving. They slipped past one of the guards doing his rotation around the house and phased right through the wall of the house.

Inside, most of his possessions were scattered. Glass bookshelves were knocked over and in pieces. Their books sprawled out. John didn't want to abandon his collection of original works and was happy ninety-five percent of his collection was donated to and stored in Saint John's Library.

As John looked over the damage, he wasn't sure how much of it was the wave damage and what was caused by the soldiers. He assumed they gave the place a good sneak peek but couldn't see any traces of entry. The front door was still locked and in one piece; but they could have entered through the damaged section of the house.

"The portal," Pisces whispered.

John entered his dining room and pulled the circular rug with a design of the solar system that hid the entrance to the secret lower level. The entrance was a crystalline glass, two-foot wide plate implanted into the floor. He waved to Pisces and said, "Ladies first."

Pisces walked to the plate, stood over it, and tapped her feet seven times. A thin white light shot from the eye of the plate, enveloped her, and then she vanished. After he counted ten seconds, John stepped to the plate and tapped his feet seven times. A similar light shot from the plate and enveloped him. He felt a warm and tingly sensation throughout his entire body as light surrounded him, then his surroundings were dark and dank. Pisces was on her knees and gagging.

"Ugh. I forgot how much I hate those things," Pisces complained.

John nodded and felt queasy. "Our bodies just aren't used to it. From what I've read, they use this all the time in Iora. Or from Iora to Diaba, Zaori Nexa, or the spaceport."

Pisces shook her head, still clutching her stomach. "Well, call me crazy, but being converted into energy and then reconverted into matter just isn't my thing, especially after eating such a big meal. Did you install that?"

John snorted and shook his head. "No. That was Emma and Artie. I studied the schematics and can humbly acknowledge that this technology is centuries beyond me. Had I installed that, we probably wouldn't be having this conversation right now."

"Lights," Pisces commanded and blue light filled the room.

Almost everything was a crystalline glass with metallic veins. Circular glass pillars of various heights and widths stretched from the floor and held displays of different pieces of technology with alien origins. In the center of the room was a thin glass stand with a small crystalline cube on top. The room was open and wide. The floor was flat glass. When she looked down, she saw nothingness. It was as though she was walking on emptiness.

"We're going to have to clear this place out," John said.

Pisces turned her attention from the floor. "Will we be able to carry this much? I have my bag. It'll hold a few energy pistols and antimatter grenades. Not much else."

John frowned. "Of course we're not carrying it. We're using the Ojiili box." He pointed.

The Ojiili box looked exactly like a giant ice cube. It was sixteen cubic meters in size and chilling to touch. It had no contents, as far as she could see, but that was one of the mysteries of the Ojiili box. No matter what was placed inside of it, it looked translucent. It had no door, and someone could reach his or her hand into it, but only if that person was the owner. Anyone else would touch a solid, cold object with no grooves or openings to pry open. It felt how it looked. If anyone held their hand on the box for longer than ten seconds, that hand froze to the box and broke off of their arm. The Ojiili box, designed by a race of traders and security experts, was one of the galaxy's finest safes. The Ojiili also designed prisons of a similar design when there was crime in the Galactic Cooperative.

Oh, that, Pisces thought. Keeping her distance, she asked, "Remind me how it works, again."

"Simple. We collect everything and place it in here. You're authorized to touch it. So, don't get skittish. I remember what happened last time," John said.

Pisces narrowed her eyes at the cube. Last time, she couldn't feel her fingers for a whole day.

"Remember not to leave your hand in there longer than thirty seconds," John said. "Authorized or not, it'll give you a sting. Once we get everything in there, we'll do a quick inventory. Then, I'll shoot it through a Koiaxan dimensional door. We just have to make sure we keep one beacon on us." He picked up two silver hand-held devices shaped like TV remotes. "And not both on the box, so we can recall it when we get back to Saint Luke's. Otherwise, it'll be frozen in-between dimensions and we'll be stuck trying to find another solution for fighting the Red."

At that, Pisces nodded. "Put stuff in box. Don't lose a hand. Send it through a door, and pray to God it works when we're back at Saint Luke's."

John stared at her. "We'll be fine, as long as I reprogram the frequency." He chuckled. "How funny would it be if I send this thing into the door, and then the past me recalls it. Or worse, what if I recall the box the past me was supposed to get, by mistake, and we incidentally pollute the timeline. We'd both be knocking on the door at the end of the hall."

Her eyes widened. "Is that possible?"

"No," he reassured her. "It used to be, though. I read in the database that the first models would vanish. They didn't understand why until it appeared in the future when they made further attempts. They realized that anything sent through the rift is displaced in time. So, you could recall the device in the future before the past if you had a stronger signal and was utilizing the same frequency and code."

"Alright, then," Pisces said, not feeling as comfortable with the plan. She adored John; but sometimes, in tight spots, he provided more information than she wanted or needed. "Let's just do this and get out of here."

The two spent the next twenty minutes going to each glass pillar, collecting the items, and carefully securing them inside of the Ojiili box. During which, John made notations of inventory: four Ioran fire igniters and converters, two matter-energy converters, six Koiaxan beacons, three Koiaxan dimensional projectors, one small canister of programmable Ioran nanobots, two holographic display cubes, twenty crystalline neuro-cables, one self-replicating matter assembly model, one android-cyborg prototype, four phasic protection suits, two shielding armor suits, two energy/plasma shields, two energy pulse rifles, two standard-stream energy rifles, two plasma pistols, six standard-stream energy pistols, one standard and two short crystalline energy swords, four crystalline energy daggers, ten antimatter grenades, twenty light burst grenades, ten plasma grenades, and fifteen miscellaneous items.

"Are we going to activate Adam?" Pisces asked and pointed at the prototype.

John thought about it and smiled, "I'm considering linking James to the Adam construct. Unlike Emma, James is stuck and can't develop beyond where he is. He was linked to the house; but that's not the same."

Pisces smiled and nodded, "I'm sure he'd love the mobility and—"

They felt a tremor.

The room lights shifted to red and a small crystalline cube in the center of the room shot three holographic displays into the air. One of the displays showed two additional army trucks parked in the front and four soldiers piling out of each. The second display shifted between different cameras, showing other soldiers surrounding multiple corners of the house with weapons raised. The third display showed the young Rezarian and the leather man walking to the front door. Two men cleared debris.

"I don't understand. How did they detect us?" Pisces asked.

John frowned at the display, said, "At this point, does it matter," and rushed to the Ojiili box. He slapped a Koiaxan beacon on the side of the box and synchronized frequencies, spatial coordinates, and encryption codes with the device in his hand. "They'll be inside any minute. The Red may be able to pinpoint our location through thermal vision."

Quickly, Pisces rushed around the room, made sure there was nothing left behind that could be used against them. When nothing remained but pillars, she grabbed an antimatter grenade.

John pointed. "What are you doing with that?"

With a sly smile, Pisces walked to the small, circular, crystalline transportation platform. "Oh, I'm going to welcome them to your home."

"What?" John breathed. "You're going to blow up my house? The blast radius of that thing will annihilate *us* too."

Pisces gave John a long hard gaze, and then set the grenade on the platform. "Where's the trust, John? Once you shoot that thing off into the gap between dimensions, we'll set the timer, phase out of here, and be out of range just in time before it annihilates everything."

Finished with the synchronization, John checked the dimensional projector on the box. "We'll be phased and flying through irradiated soil and solid rock. The radioactive properties might slow us down."

"Have faith, John," Pisces said and winked.

In the holographic display, the soldiers entered John's home single-filed. Pisces frowned at the display, programmed the antimatter grenade with a ten-second countdown sequence, but did not activate it. She rushed to John.

John inhaled at the sight of the number and activated the projector. A thin, long streaming beam of yellow energy pulsed from the projector and shot ten feet from the box. It emitted a high-pitched squeal, the kind that made glass shatter. John and Pisces lowered the volume in their helmets to a whisper. A small hole of white light emerged in the center of the room. The hole swallowed the box and closed with a loud popping noise.

John attached the beacon to his belt and looked at the display.

Through the holographic projection, the leather man examined the crystalline glass plate. The Red, on the other hand, stared directly at them through the projection. Then, it looked straight down at the ground. It found them. The leather man pointed down at the ground and then vanished from the display.

"Who was that with the Red?" Pisces asked, startled.

"I don't know, but let's go," John said. "I'll set the transportation platform to activate on a five second delay to prevent them from tampering with the grenade on the other side." His instincts told him that was what happened to the other grenade. "I'll activate the grenade. We'll get out of here. It'll blow."

John hurried to the platform and programmed the time delay. He nodded to Pisces, looked up, and saw a pair of silver, metallic boots appear. The leather man shot a foot into John's chest and kicked him back eight feet. John bounced on the floor with his hands clutching his chest. He groaned in agony.

Pisces grabbed her dart gun and shot at the leather man twice. He caught the darts and crushed them in his left hand. He looked at Pisces, shook his head, and rushed at her. She rolled into a ball and slipped between his legs. Behind him, and as he turned around, she shot him three times, two in the back, one in his jacket.

The leather man stopped, pulled the darts out of his back, and swung a low kick at Pisces. She dodged the kick by jumping over it and launched a straight fist into his groin. It didn't faze him. His next kick connected with her stomach. She tumbled to the floor and nearly tossed her lunch. Before Pisces could pick herself up, the leather man hovered over her with his fist ready to smash her into unconsciousness.

An energy beam shot into the leather man's side and he flew forward to the floor. He lay for a moment, and then sat himself up. Another energy beam followed the first and punched him in the chest. He fell back, still.

John kept his energy pistol aimed at the leather man as he rushed to Pisces and helped her up. She panted and blinked her watery and wide eyes. They were caught off guard and lost their one advantage over the Red: the element of surprise.

"You okay?" John asked.

"No," Pisces sighed. She held herself and looked at the leather man. "Who is he?"

"I don't know; but I can happily live without an introduction," John said. He rushed to the antimatter grenade. It sat on the platform, unperturbed. "On my mark, we run."

There was a groan from the leather man. He slowly

sat up.

John took that as a clear sign. He activated the transportation platform, pressed the grenade activation key, said, "Mark," and ran.

The leather man rose to follow.

Pisces and John went into phase and launched themselves at rocket speeds through the wall. They flew upward, at an angle, through soil, seed, metal, and rock. It felt like swimming through mud. For a brief instance, John wondered if the time window was too narrow. Then, they were clear. Through the heavy resistance, all the mental effort of telekinetic flight sent them shooting into the air like steam from a geyser.

There was a roaring thunder below and behind them. Everything erupted in a blinding flash of light. His home, the soldiers, and the Rezarian were gone. All that remained was a small crater.

The two came out of phase mid-air and lowered themselves to the ground ten yards from the maw of the crater. They stood in the street and stared at the crater.

"Thus is the end of the leather man," John said. He wasn't sure why he said it. And it suddenly frightened him, because he knew he was wrong. He didn't know how he knew, but he knew whoever or whatever it was they just fought was still alive and watching them.

John called James to pick them up.

A minute later, James arrived and opened his doors. John and Pisces sat in their seats and sighed.

James said, "I have the feeling I missed the first sign of trouble."

Pisces cracked a small, tired smile.

John harrumphed and said, "You can say that again."

"Shall we head back to Saint Luke's?" James asked and reversed.

Staring at the crater that used to be his, Abbey's, and

Levi's home, John nodded. He closed his eyes and reclined his chair. "Yes. There's nothing left for me here."

James drove them back to Saint Luke's.

It was high noon when John and Pisces returned to the church. Eddie looked confused when he saw John walk through the door with only a small device in hand. He asked, "That's it?" John nodded, not wishing to go into detail as to what the device did. He was exhausted. The nanotech kept him going, but human mental and physical fatigue was taking its toll. He wanted to lay his head down, collapse, but didn't like the idea of giving the Red an advantage of time.

When Pisces fell asleep in a chair ten minutes into a discussion, it gave John an excuse to go to their room. He put her in her bed and rolled into his own. He looked at the ceiling and asked God what was next. And as he asked, he knew what was next.

While he slept, he needed to change. He needed a complete transformation to become the man he used to be. He had to reactivate his old abilities and revert his facial features to what they were before he became Lukas Brown. Lukas Brown was dead. It was time for the John Rider of old to rise again and lead the people.

But he resented that old life. Decades later, he still tired of it. He could feel the sticky Rezarian blood on his skin and remember all the ugly things both sides did to win battles. The Red didn't hold back. How could he? They were vicious, intelligent, and brutal. They were calculating. He had to capitalize on any opening or weakness instantly if he expected a victory. Unfortunately, under his command, he lost many men. It wasn't by fault of training on their part, or leadership on his. It was the simple reality that humans carried the disadvantage. They were smaller, weaker, slower, dumber, and technologically primitive compared to the Red. It was a miracle their species survived.

Now, they needed that miracle again. They needed John Rider again, whether he liked it or not. But not for long, he told himself. He would fight the Red long enough to distract them, keep them busy while Levi led his daughter to Montana. There, the true victory would be won.

Reinstate John Rider bio-settings, he instructed the nanotech. After which, he closed his eyes and fell into a deep sleep.

CHAPTER FIVE
THE QUARANTINE ZONE

THE FIRST FEW HOURS OF THE ROAD TRIP were quiet. Violet wasn't in a talking mood. She was in an eating mood, as was Abbey. Both noticed, when they weren't talking, no one was talking. The car drove itself, which Violet couldn't get over, while Levi ate his food and stared off into the destroyed landscape. Jeremy was unusually quiet and peered out of the window. Of the four, he finished his food first. She hadn't seen him take a bite. The food was there, and then it was not. She half suspected that he drank his sandwiches.

Then again, Violet thought. Her eyes barely left her plate until it was empty.

She completely ignored the wolf. She always did, which was interesting in its own sense. He was the smartest animal she'd ever encountered, and certainly worth further examination. Yet, her thoughts only hovered on him for a moment before passing. She wasn't intentionally disregarding him. It just so happened that one minute she was thinking about him, and the next...

After everyone ate, Abbey pulled out a Stephen King paperback (*There went talking to her. She'll be in that book for hours*, Violet thought) while the rest stared silently out of the windows at their dead world.

Violet sighed and looked at the defunct world. What was left? How broad was the damage? Was there still a need to go to Montana if this was what remained there?

Stupid Levi, she thought. *He said he'd give me some answers. It's time for him to deliver on that promise.*

"Alright, Levi. It's time for you to start talking," Violet said. The radio was singing about an octopus's garden. She lowered the volume to a whisper.

"What?" Levi asked and turned from his window. His face was blank. She wondered: where does his mind go? He was always a mystery. In the years she'd known him, he was warm and caring; but his mind was closed off. He would let her in, but only an inch past the surface. Abbey's father was the only person he confided in. She wanted, more than anything else, to be able to get inside of his head and finally know him. Who was he behind the barriers?

"You have to tell us what's going on," Violet said.

"We're driving to Montana," Levi said with a frown on his face. He seemed confused by the question. Where were his thoughts?

"Okay, and, what will we find when we get there? Will it look anything like all of this?" she asked and pointed out of the window at their seemingly dead world. She took a quick glance and, for the first time, noticed blue sprouts of grass along the road. What were those?

Levi shook his head and looked at the clock on the dashboard. "No. It won't look like this. The initial wave had a limited range. I suspect, after another fifteen miles, we'll be clear from the affected areas and will see a lot more vegetation and people. Though, this is the Quarantine Zone. So, we'll have to be careful. They don't call it that because this is the friendliest and safest area.

There are some brutal creatures and characters out here."

"Okay," Violet said. "You didn't answer my first question. What's in Montana?"

"It's beautiful there," Levi said and forced a half smile. "It's full of lush, vibrant plant-life." He thought. "Despite its major increase in population, there's a lot of forestry, clear and clean rivers, ponds, and streams, crisp air, and cool breezes in high altitudes." He paused. "There's snow. It's still snowing in northern Montana. I wouldn't be surprised if we got to have a snowball fight. Have you ever skied? Or gone sledding?"

Violet shook her head. One of the unfortunate things about her upbringing was that her family rarely went anywhere or did anything besides drink, bicker, and putter around the house. Her mother spent a lot of time socializing, drinking, and on her back. She would usually shoo Violet off to spend time with other kids or by herself playing video games and watching old TV shows. Travel? When she was little, her father took her fishing once in the Chesapeake Bay (not by choice), camping once in Luray near the caverns, hiking once in the Blue Ridge Mountains, and to Virginia Beach twice (so he could check out the babes and get a fresh tan). She was pleased when the Browns were kind enough to take her on their summer vacations to Beaver Island and Hiawatha National Forest in Michigan. After her father died, they became her family.

"You'll like it there, and in Washington," Levi continued. "We've been proactive in preserving the beauty of the state and respecting the environment by utilizing alternative energy, and cleaning the rivers and lakes. We recycle everything and make it a mission not to create anything that is not biodegradable or easily recyclable."

Violet frowned. He didn't answer her question.

"Sounds great, Lee. You should write a brochure. What exactly and specifically are we going to Montana to do? Why Montana? What does it have to do with everything going on?"

"We're going to Montana to save the world," Levi answered. "There's a mountain passage there very similar to the one we were just in. Only, it's a lot nicer, and more spacious. There's another regeneration device there. We're going to use that to undo the damage done by the Red War and the other device."

"There's another one?" Jeremy asked, his eyes popped out of his head, which shot in-between the two front seats. "I don't understand how that's possible."

Levi inhaled and exhaled. His nose flared. Violet found it interesting how Levi responded to Jeremy. Of course, it wasn't a giant secret that Levi had a thing for Abbey. She couldn't imagine what was going through Levi's head, now that he knew Jeremy was cheating on her. What she didn't understand was why Levi hadn't said anything. It would have worked to his advantage if he did.

"Yes, there's another one. And that's where we're going. Next question," Levi said and eyed Violet.

"Where in Montana is the device?" Jeremy asked.

"We'll see when we get there," Levi said through his teeth.

Jeremy frowned and leaned back. He crossed his arms and looked at Abbey. She remained engrossed in her paperback. The only time she wasn't easily distracted or eavesdropping was when she read. Then, you had to peel her from the book with her feet kicking in order to get her attention.

Violet thought for a moment about her next question. She had a million questions earlier. Now that she had an opportunity to get answers, she felt blocked. *Stupid Levi!*

Why couldn't you answer the questions when I wanted them answered? It was always later. Later later later.

After a couple minutes, and the beginning of the radio's continual repetition of the phrase "number nine", Violet remembered. "You jumped out of the car and vanished. How is that possible? I don't understand how you survived and made it to the mountain."

Levi sighed. "You know who my father is, right?"

"Not really," Violet said. "You rarely talk about him."

Levi blinked. "Really? Abigail didn't tell you?"

Abbey pulled her head from her book when she heard her name. "Tell her what?"

"That my father was General Jeremiah Jacob Jones."

"Oh that. No," Abbey said and returned to her book.

Violet's mouth and eyes opened wide, and she asked, "Wha-what?" She leaned closer to him, very close, to examine him. "How is it I've known you for seven years and didn't know your dad was a celebrity?" She paused. "No. Not just a celebrity. A freaking war hero who died saving the planet."

"I told you my dad died in the war," Levi said and shrugged. She slugged him in the arm. Her hand ached. She shook it. He didn't flinch. For a split second, she felt weak, then, aroused.

"I wrote a ten page essay about the Red War," Violet said. "Most of it was centered on General Jones. You helped me." She pointed at Levi. "You spent two weeks tutoring me. In all that time, you didn't think to mention he was your father?"

Levi remembered and smiled. "Actually, I told you. You said, 'How do you know so much about him?' I said, 'He's my father.' You thought I was joking."

"Yea," she recollected, "because I said, 'get outta here', and you got up as though you were about to leave."

Levi laughed and remembered the expression on her

face.

"Then, you pulled me back in my seat and," Levi stopped. They had kissed. She was his first kiss, before Abigail came along and stole his heart with a kiss of her own. It was interesting to him that even with a technologically enhanced brain, such things slipped through the gaps. Once recalled, he experienced it all over again. Her soft lips were between his. He tasted her jolly rancher breath and inhaled her mango body wash. She was thin and fragile in his slim but toned arms.

Violet saw the flushed expression on Levi's face. She winked, puckered her lips, and twirled her hair around her finger. "And then Abbey's dad walked in and said it was getting late. Time for me to go home."

Abbey's father wore a concerned frown on his face as he walked her to the car. She remembered the car ride home. He asked how long she would need Levi as a tutor. Was he concerned they were fooling around at such a young age? The other kids were. Then, he asked how things were at home. How was her mother? Was he perhaps concerned that she was taking after her mother, the Henrico Harlot? After she said all was fine, he grew quiet. The rest of the drive was silent.

How different would things have been if he'd stepped in that room five minutes later? She had to wonder. After that night, Abbey's father ensured the two were never alone in Levi's room again. Every tutoring and study session was in open space, in their library, with Abbey. And occasionally, if Abbey was practicing the violin, Abbey's father would check on the two to make sure they weren't kissing. And she always wanted to. She wanted to isolate him away from Abbey and her father. How many times had they tried to sneak away and steal a kiss?

Levi, she thought with a smile.

He turned to her as though she'd said his name aloud.

His expression was blank. He was deep in thought again. What was going on in that mind of his? Was he thinking the same thing? Did he remember that longing they shared for each other? She hoped. Wasn't she asking questions? You're darn tootin.

"So, you were saying, about the jumping out of the car thing and your father," Violet prodded.

"Yes," Levi said. "My father had special technology and abilities that helped him and John Rider fight in the Red War. I have inherited those abilities and technology. It allows me to do things other people cannot do. It permits me access to things other people do not have. I cannot go into further detail than that."

"Why not?" Violet asked.

"Because it's not safe," Levi answered. "Once we reach Montana and activated the device, save the world, I will be able to tell you everything."

"Everything?" Abbey asked from the back. Her head peeked out of her book.

"Everything?" Violet repeated.

Levi nodded and smiled at both of them. "Yes. After we reach the Montana home base, the world will be reborn and everything shall come to light."

"It's only a couple days. Why can't you tell us now?" Violet asked.

Levi looked at Jared for a moment, smirked, and then turned back to Violet. She looked at the wolf confused and felt as though an unspoken dialogue was exchanged. She almost asked about it, and then decided not to. She honestly couldn't remember a time when those two didn't exchanged similar looks. He had the strangest rapport with his pet. It was as though they read each other's minds.

"Because revealing that information will threaten our safety," Levi explained. "My safety. It would put you at unsound risk. Remember: the Red are still out there. They can still read your mind. Thusly, anything I tell you is just like speaking directly to them. It's as though I'm detailing our plans and information to them. Honestly, I've already said too much."

Violet grew red in the face. "That's a cop out. There's absolutely no certainty of that. That sounds like a paranoid excuse. You just don't want to tell me."

"Of course, I want to tell you," Levi said. He shot a quick glance at Abbey, who caught his eye, then looked back at Violet. "Do you know how frustrating and lonely it is not being able to tell people stuff? Not being able to speak your mind because you might say something that exposes a weakness or threatens the life of a friend or family member. You don't know where evil is; so you have to remain vigilant and keep your mouth shut. These are hard times. Evil hides behind the faces of allies. I want to tell you. I just don't have the luxury of giving in to what I want. They'll only use you against me."

"Well, I'm not evil," Violet said.

"I'm not saying you are."

"You think I'm stupid?" Violet argued. "That they can use me against my will?"

"I am not, nor would I ever imply you are stupid; because you are not," Levi clarified. "But they have used some of the most brilliant minds in the world against their will. They're powerful."

Violet turned away and looked out of the window. She was frustrated. It all came back to those Red Zarians or whatever being in her head. He had no proof that they were in her head. It was all speculation. Speculation that couldn't be verified, but could easily be used to justify his actions. It's easy to say an invisible threat exists to avoid telling someone something important.

She sighed. Perhaps he was a victim of it all. Paranoia

was a side effect of war. Paranoia or not, she wanted to know more, especially after seeing Levi and Abbey whispering to each other about God knows what.

How was it that he had such strong feelings for Abbey? She was a blabbermouth. Why was she the one who got special treatment and hidden messages from her father when she could barely hold the spittle in her mouth, let alone a secret?

Hmm.

What if she could convince Levi to trust Abbey? Abbey would undoubtedly blab. She could tell Levi that Abbey wasn't trustworthy and then convince him to tell her things instead.

No. After what happened between Violet and Jeremy, Levi would doubt her. Question her loyalty. She had a better idea.

Like he said, he was lonely. All she had to do was get close to him. He was a boy. She was a girl. She would get close to him and lightly touch his hand or face. He would inhale her sweet perfume, shampoo, and feel the warm, soft touch of her skin. Then she would smile, giggle, and stick her chest out. He would look. Those eyes he had were men's eyes. They would move down to her protruding chest whether he liked it or not. Eyes had to see. Sometimes, men's eyes had a will of their own. She could stick her butt out too. Make him want to twist his head for a better look. She would get close. Really close. Close enough for him to want to know what it would feel like to hold her in his strong arms. She would look in his eyes. Those eyes would twinkle. She would part her lips and get on her tippy-toes. One kiss would seal the deal. One kiss would be all it took to get him hooked. You couldn't kiss someone as lovely as her once. You needed a second helping of something sweet. And she would let him have her. He could kiss her as many times as he wanted, as long as he wanted. He could completely have her if he wanted. Then, he would spill out all his secrets and choose her over Abbey.

Violet turned to Levi and touched his hand. He looked at her with a confused frown. "How can we ever be close if you can't trust me?"

"It'll only be a couple days. Can you honestly not wait a couple days?" Levi asked.

No. It would be too late then, now wouldn't it?

"Honestly, I don't think I can," Violet said and ignored the strange thought that came to her mind. "I just can't stop thinking about what I don't know. It's scary and confusing. Everyone I know, except the people in this car, is dead. Killed by some secret device I didn't know about. By aliens I didn't know were still around. You keep withholding information from me saying I don't need to know or can't know. I have to know something. This is ridiculous, Levi. I'm lost. Can't you see that? Can't you see I've lost everything and you're withholding the one little thing I ask for? Information that would clarify what is going on. You and Abbey seem to be in the center of all of this. I was dragged into it. I have a right to know these stupid secrets that might get me killed, as opposed to being a victim, again."

Please stop, Levi thought.

"What if something happened to you, Levi?" Violet asked. She rested her hand on his, again, and looked into his eyes. "We'd be completely lost."

"Like I've told you; I'm willing to answer questions. I'm just not going to answer questions about my abilities, Emma, the mountain passage, or any of the other sensitive stuff. If there is anything not of a sensitive nature you wish to know, I am happy to tell you. I could tell you plenty about the Red, the war, or something else. Just, don't push me. You know I don't like to be pushed.

We've been through this."

"Fine," Violet said and crossed her arms.

Levi sighed and turned his attention to the road.

Not long after they entered West Virginia, they passed through a lightning storm. The winds pushed the car in and out of its lane, and almost into a ditch. A thick wall of charged air stretched from the ground to the heavens like a veil. Levi requested an increase in energy shields and punched the car through the barrier. On the other side, they were saturated in sunlight. The sky was blue. The grass was green. And mountains were covered in trees. It was a refreshing sight to see.

Levi assured them the device in Richmond was not completely charged and its range was limited. Having seen the desolation, Violet struggled with doubts. Those doubts left her. She felt comfortable, if only for a while.

Violet lowered her window to breathe in the fresh, clean air. She gagged. It wasn't so fresh. It smelled of decaying meat, vomit, and vinegar. Everyone complained. She raised the window. They were still in the Quarantine Zone. It was still soiled from the poisonous radiation of the Red War, and smelled of the slow decay of human society. It looked lovelier than it was.

The following hours were spent staring at trees. She'd made it a game to spot old decadent houses, nice looking abandoned cars, and pointed out mutant animals. Levi focused on houses and less on cars. She loved cars. She didn't know how anyone could abandon a deep-sea blue BMW roadster on the side of the road, and wanted Levi to pull over so she could check it for keys. He warned her that it was idle for a reason. As odd as it was for them to hunt during the day, he was right. There were creatures lurking in the light shaded bushes waiting for someone to approach. She changed her mind about investigating when Levi pointed them out. They continued forward.

She told herself she'd come back for it.

After that, she kept a good eye out for mutant animals. The first one she found was a chanella. They looked like bears but had cheetah spots, two extra arms, and were extremely aggressive pack hunters. She remembered seeing a story about them on the news. They reproduced in the thousands. Hunters were recruited to keep their numbers in check.

The second mutant animal she spotted was a skorg. They were large skunks with a long mane, muscled body, and five eyes. They were also aggressive and mated like rabbits. They sprayed their targets with a sedative and attacked them. Unlike normal skunks, the spray had a sickly sweet smell. If the person ran, the skorg and any other skorgs in the area could track the scent and attack.

The games were boring after an hour. With the exception of Levi, no one else wanted to play the games. So Violet leaned the chair back a little and closed her eyes. She hated being trapped in the car for hours. There was nothing to do. This sucked.

"A pit stop," Levi said.

Violet opened her eyes.

They were approaching a collection of buildings adjacent to the interstate and a sign that said 'Chelyan Truck Stop'. It was a sight for sore eyes. They'd passed five truck stops since they entered the Quarantine Zone. All of those were abandoned or destroyed. Most truck stops were heavily guarded fuel depots with small diners and enclosed residential areas. Some had motels for passer-byers. Most of the men who guarded the fuel depots were mercenaries, scavengers, and hunters. The rest were former police officers or soldiers. The further a person traveled from the Washington Coalition, the more likely he or she were to find truck stops run, guarded, and operated by drug cartels. Cartels were a major problem after the war, trafficking women, weapons, and new drugs.

The newest drug smuggled was called wigglies. The cartels collected and smashed purple mutant worms and worm eggs and injected them into the blood stream. The wigglies stimulated extreme pleasure, euphoria, and hallucinations. They were also highly addictive. The many side effects of the wigglies were nosebleeds, rashes, tremors, strange cravings, paranoia, violent behavior, and fatal worm infestations in the body, if the tiny eggs weren't completely destroyed before injected.

Violet remembered her mother disappearing for a week and coming back with glassy eyes, a nosebleed, and weird purple rashes on her back. Oh, mother dearest had a case of the wigglies all right. And because class was her forte, she brought back three strange men. Men that leered over her mother like lions over a calf. It was the strangest coincidence that Abbey's father called minutes after her mother arrived. Abbey asked her to sleep over at the Brown place. Of course, her mom didn't care, "Good. Get out." The men seemed disappointed, and argued to the contrary. They wanted to get to know her better. But good ole Doctor Brown was there to pick her up before she'd made it to her room from the phone. The man drove like a beast, she'd first thought.

Later that night, Violet figured it wasn't a coincidence. The good doctor was watching them. He usually arrived or called when she needed to leave her home, pronto. Her father wasn't the nicest man in the world—no, he was a cruel, misogynistic jackass—but maybe his dying wish, outside of his wife being left broke and alone, was that someone took care of his daughter, and Doctor Brown happened to get the request in the mail. If that was so, she felt bad, really bad, because something changed. Why didn't the good doctor think about saving her from destruction? Neither did Levi. There had to be more to the story than Red telepathy paranoia.

If Abbey hadn't come knocking on Jeremy's door and my window, I would have died, she thought. In the end, the good doctor wasn't so good to her after all.

She didn't want to think about that anymore.

"Can we stop?" Jeremy called from the back. "We've been cramped in here for four hours, and I have to take a giant dump." He smiled at Abbey when she turned slowly from her book and gave him a dirty look.

Eloquently put, Violet thought.

"Honestly, I'd like to stretch my legs, too," Abbey said. "I'm surprised that I haven't had to go, even now."

"The food is artificially designed to completely metabolize and produce little waste," Emma said. It was the first thing she said since they left the mountain passage. "It has all the vitamins, minerals, and proteins needed for the body without any excess."

"Okay," Abbey said.

Levi looked at Violet. She nodded and pointed at her stomach.

"Fine. We'll take a thirty-minute break," Levi said. He turned into the rest stop and parked in front of Papa Jo's Diner.

Violet sighed. *Finally.*

2

Abbey, Violet, and Jeremy entered Papa Jo's Diner to pee and grab a couple canned sodas and snacks for the road.

Levi honestly didn't care what they did in the thirty minutes of their break, as long as they were careful, kept a low profile, and stuck together. He stuck by the car, leaned against it, and looked with surveying eyes at the small village that was the pit stop.

It was a dingy looking establishment. The front of the building was white but covered with gray grime. Its windows were smeared and stained. The wooden stairs and walkway that stretched along the front were splintered and cracked. One young black man with dreadlocks, baggy jeans, a wife-beater, an oxygen mask, and a pistol on his hip stood near the entrance. Four similarly dressed men swaggered up and around the fuel depot adjacent to the diner. One of those men carried an assault rifle hooked around his torso. Another man dressed in tattering khaki shorts sat on a bench sharpening his machete.

"Friendly looking group," Jared transmitted.

Levi nodded slowly, as not to catch anyone's attention, and continued surveying the area.

The fuel depot had ten pumps and two customers. Both customers were males with potbellies and beards long enough to get caught in the machines if they didn't pay attention. One man wore a red baseball cap, no shirt, blue jean overalls, and faded black sneakers with a white swooshing symbol. The second man wore blue jeans, also didn't have a shirt, and wore white sneakers.

Levi noticed five single-story houses fifty yards behind the diner during their approach. He suspected the young men lived in one, while the motel manager, fuel depot owner, diner manager, and whoever staffed the establishments lived in the others.

A motel was further to the left. There were four cars in the parking lot and fifteen windows and doors in the front with a main office connected on the side. A young, dark-haired woman strutted from the far end of the motel to the front desk. She wore light blue jean shorts (He'd seen panties that revealed less cheek than those shorts), a tiny yellow tank top that barely met her belly button, and sandals. There was a tattoo on her right calf.

Levi sharpened his vision. She had a narrow face and blue eyes. There were red, fresh scars on her back from a recent whipping. Yet, she smiled and laughed with the office manager. Levi wondered.

"We're not here to save her," Jared said.

"Who's to say she wants to be saved," Levi mumbled with his hand over his mouth and nose. Everything reeked. How could these people stand it? How could Jared stand it? Levi told his nanotech network to deactivate his sense of smell.

"Why not just think back to me?" Jared suggested. *"You won't have to open your mouth and take in that filthy air."*

"Sometimes I do; sometimes I don't," Levi said and smiled. "I keep thinking of the story of the Yiriini. They developed telepathic abilities and stopped speaking completely. Their vocal cords became relatively useless. And, their first contact with an alien species was the Hryakkr—"

"Who were resistant to telepathy and had an extremely complicated alphabet, sentence structure," Jared finished. *"Yea. John told me that story, too. Took them years before they could establish a comfortable line of communication. I don't think you'll have that problem with Abbey and Violet around."*

"God knows that's the truth," Levi said and laughed.

Jared scratched himself and said, *"They're watching us."* He looked at Levi and then turned his attention towards the depot.

The men glanced in their direction and then away.

Subtly at its best, Levi thought.

He said, "I saw their reactions when we drove up. They were eyeing the girls as they entered the diner." He crossed and uncrossed his legs. "We have to be ready in case they try to move on us."

The young woman walked towards Levi and the diner.

"You think they might?"

"We have to consider the possibility and have a plan in the event they do," Levi whispered.

The young woman smiled, winked at him, and entered the diner. He couldn't help but notice her defined abs and well-rounded rear. He shook his head and chastised himself for noticing.

"So, what do you have in mind? We're exposed. You can't arm yourself without raising suspicion."

"I am armed," Levi replied. He ran his hand along his bald head and leaned his back flat against the car. He peered at the diner, but couldn't see anything inside with the light reflecting off the dingy windows. "I have my crystalline sword attached to the back of my suit. It'll protract and activate on command."

"So, you brought a knife to a gunfight."

"I'm not the only one," Levi said. "That guy over there has a machete."

"We'll see," Jared said.

They waited.

Minutes later, the dark-skinned man at the entrance to the diner left his post and walked into the diner.

"That's unusual, isn't it? A guard leaving his post."

Levi frowned. "Maybe he has to pee. That's been going around."

Jared turned his head slowly and stared at Levi. If he had the capability, Levi was sure he'd see a raised eyebrow.

"Okay, fine, maybe we should go inside and check it out," Levi said and took another random glance at the four other guards. They talked amongst themselves in a huddled group. Their two customers drove away in their rusted, red pick-up truck.

"Something's up. I'm getting a feeling."

Levi knelt down and rubbed Jared's head. "Can you

hear anything?"

"Not while you're rubbing my head," Jared responded with a smile. Levi shook his head. *"I get what you're trying to do, but rub my back or something."*

They waited and listened.

"They're talking about the girls inside. How much they would charge."

Levi's balled his hands into tight fists and scowled, "They think they're prostitutes?"

"No." Jared paused. *"They're estimating how much they, the men, would charge for the girls, once they've killed you and Jeremy. They plan to sell them as sex slaves."*

"Ah," Levi said and gazed at the diner. "Emma, transmit an internal scan of the diner into my visual and auditory cortexes. I'd like to know what's going on in there. Jared, growl if anyone makes any kind of aggressive move in my direction or implies that they're about to. Oh, and Emma, please be so kind as to lower my energy pistol to the ground."

Jared nodded.

"Transmitting telemetry," Emma announced.

There was a humming sound and then his vision shimmered. Everything in front of him faded and the inside of the diner spilled into view. In the furthest distances of his mind, he heard the familiar clatter of his energy pistol dropped from the bottom of the car to the cement and waited for him.

3

When Abbey, Violet, and Jeremy entered the diner, Jeremy rushed to the bathroom. Abbey admired the interior. There were eight black booths, four red tables, and fifteen black stools arranged around the u-shaped bar in the middle of the diner. To the right of the u-shaped bar was the bathroom. To the left was the kitchen. The marble counters, tables, and floors all sparkled. The place smelled of freshly brewed coffee.

Behind the bar was a short, balding old man with a thick gray mustache and green eyes. He smiled and waved as Abbey and Violet approached the bar.

"Welcome to Papa Jo's," the man said. "New timers, right?" They nodded. "Thought so. A dirty old man like myself would remember a couple of sweet little tarts like yourselves." He smiled. "I'm Jo. Owner, manager, chef, and sometimes waiter when the girls are takin their smoke breaks. Filthy habit, but I have a few of my own, so I'm not fussin." He pointed to the booths. "Why don't we find you a seat and then I'll get you started?"

Abbey and Violet exchanged a smiled, nodded, and sat at the closest booth. Joe sat two paper menus on the table, and then walked to the back. They picked up their paper menus and perused their options. There was an impressive selection of breakfast items: pancakes, eggs, ham, bacon, sausage, biscuits, sugar biscuits, muffins, oatmeal, cream of wheat, and fruit; lunch items: turkey, chicken, steak, and roast beef sandwiches, salads, soups, mac n cheese, and fries; and dinner items: fried, grilled, and baked chicken, steak, shrimp, fish, or ham, personal pizzas, mashed potatoes, rice, and beans. There was a separate dessert menu listing apple, cherry, peach, pumpkin, lemon, and orange pies, chocolate and lemon cake, and more. Their mouths watered over the options. They were hungry again.

"It's hard to believe this little place makes all of this," Violet said.

"Mmhmm," Abbey said with eyes locked on the menu. "Oh. I haven't had a cherry pie a le mode in an age." She licked her lips and looked at Violet. "You want to split one?"

Violet peered over her menu and glared at Abbey.

"No. I'll pass. I'm watching my figure." She hid behind the menu. *You're the one who can eat everything and gain nothing.*

Abbey took a glance at Violet's body. "What are you talking about? You look like a stick wrapped in muscle."

Violet snorted.

Abbey continued, "I saw the way the guy outside was eyeing you. You're not the only one watching your figure."

At that, Violet smirked.

After a few minutes, Abbey and Violet decided to share a plate of fries.

"You think we should wait for Jeremy?" Abbey asked.

Violet shrugged. "We'll wait until the waiter gets here. It's not as if we have the luxury of time. You know Levi."

"We have time," Abbey said. "We have all the time in the world. He wouldn't leave us behind. He never has, even when we were kids. He just pouts and talks about how we had to be there a half-an-hour ago. You know him."

A young thin woman in a red plaid mini-skirt and black, button-up belly-shirt strutted from the kitchen to the table. Her green eyes sparkled in the dim light. Her short brown hair bounced with each step. Each step in her black, four-inch heels clomped and echoed. Abbey eyeballed the woman's heels, amazed anyone could walk in them. There was a tattoo of a dragon on the woman's right calf. The dragon had three heads and each head had one eye.

"You girls look nice," the waitress said. She straightened her skirt and pulled out a writing pad.

Abbey smiled. "Thanks. So do you." She hoped she looked sincere.

Violet nodded and smiled. "Yea. I like your heels… and the tattoo. What does it mean?"

The waitressed looked down at the dragon tattoo and back at her pad. She held back a frown. "It means I'm employed. What can I get for you?"

Confused by the response, Abbey peered at the dragon tattoo again. The eyes of the dragon turned and looked right back at her. She stared, blinked her eyes a couple times, and then looked at Violet.

Violet shrugged and looked at the menu. She said, "We're going to share a plate of fries and I'll have an apple soda."

Abbey barely heard her. She couldn't stop looking at that tattoo. *Those eyes did not just move. Those eyes did not look back at me,* she thought.

Another thought came to her from an outside hissing voice that gave her chills. It said, *"Oh yes. Yes. What you saw was real. Those eyes did move. They were looking right at you. You better believe it."*

"Abbey?"

Coming out of her mind, and breaking eye contact with the tattoo, Abbey looked at Violet and the waitress. "Huh?"

The waitress mumbled something under her breath and then said, "And what about you?"

Abbey nodded and smiled at the waitress. "Sorry. I think my blood sugar is low or something." She paused and took one more glance at the tattoo. "Yea. We'll share the fries and, I'll have a strawberry soda. I love sodas, but dad never let me have them. Said it wasn't good for me."

"Great," the waitress said and scribbled in her pad. "And that's it?"

Abbey thought. "Um, for now. My boyfriend might order something when he gets back from the bathroom."

The waitress froze. "Your *boyfriend* went to the bathroom?"

Violet and Abbey exchanged a confused frown.

Abbey said, "Yes. Is there something wrong with the bathroom?"

"No," the waitress said. She smirked. "Your fries shouldn't take too long. I'll be back with your drinks shortly." She strutted back to the kitchen with a coy smile on her face.

Violet watched the waitress until she was out of sight and then looked back at Abbey. "Hell is her problem?"

Abbey shook her head. "I don't know. You think they make her dress that way for work? Says something about the decorum of this place."

"Yea," Violet said. "And what was her deal with the bathroom?"

"I don't know," Abbey said. She pouted. "Maybe I should check in on him."

Violet snorted. "Right. Hey honey, you still taking that dump? You want me to hold your hand?"

Abbey burst out laughing, covered her face, and shook her head. "I wouldn't offer to hold his hand!"

"Right," Violet replied with a smile. "Offer to cup his balls, instead."

"Yea, I'm sure he'd take me up on that one," Abbey said and shook her head. "He's spent the last two weeks trying to get me to," she lowered her voice to a whisper, "rub his penis. Not saying I haven't been tempted. He's a nice looking guy and he's shown me his hardware. He has some 'impressive tools'. But unlike the other girls he's dated, I'm not ready for that kind of stuff. You're supposed to save that for the wedding night."

Violet nodded and looked around the place. With the exception of her and Abbey, the place was empty. Jo shuffled back to the kitchen, probably to make the fries. The waitress was probably in the back getting their drinks.

"I wonder what Levi's doing out there," Violet said.

"Why didn't he want to come in?"

Abbey looked outside. They could hardly see a thing through the grimy windows. The sunlight coming through made seeing anything around the grime impossible.

"Maybe he was worried those guys outside would break into the car and steal it or the stuff inside," Abbey said.

Violet snorted again and put her hand to her nose. "It's bulletproof and alive, remember?"

"Yea, but they don't know that. And once they tried to break into it and found it was bulletproof, they might want it even more."

Violet nodded and pursed her lips. "Good call."

They sat and thought.

"You have a very paranoid family," Violet added. "Have I told you that, lately?"

Abbey laughed. "Yes. You have. Dad and Levi might be the most paranoid guys I've ever seen or heard of, but they're usually right. You've seen it. It's hard to fault a guy for being paranoid when he's right most of the time."

To that, Violet reluctantly agreed. Did that mean Levi was right about her?

"Look at us now, sitting here, alive," Abbey said. "I'll take paranoid over dead any day of the week."

"I just wish we could all get past this and share things. Did your dad ever tell you how Levi got his car?" Violet asked.

Abbey thought about it and shrugged. "Honestly, I never asked. I just assumed he bought it. I didn't know he had a car until he came to pick me up. And, my dad's car never talked. Or, at least, if it did, it didn't talk when I was around."

Ten minutes later, they sat staring at the empty bar.

"Where are those drinks?" Violet asked. They were

still alone in the diner.

A young, dark-haired woman in a yellow tank top and light blue jean shorts entered Papa Jo's and walked straight to the back towards the bathrooms. She briefly glanced at Abbey and Violet on her way. Abbey couldn't help but notice the tattoo on her calf.

Abbey put her hands to her mouth and whispered, "Well, it's official. We're in Snagtown, West Virginia."

"Yea," Violet agreed. "And she just entered the men's bathroom. Is there only one working bathroom here?"

Abbey frowned. "What's taking Jeremy so long, anyway? He should have been done a long time ago."

Jo stepped from the kitchen holding a tray with fries and two tall glasses of soda. He carried it to the girls and set the tray on the table. "Two sodas and a plate of fries for the ladies."

Took you long enough, Violet thought. She collected her soda and asked, "What happened to the waitress?"

The man looked hesitant to respond. He put the plate of fries on the table and pulled the tray away. "She's helping a customer with something in the back."

Abbey looked around the place. It was empty and had been empty the entire time they were there. There were no customers. What customer was he referring to? "I'm confused. We're the only ones here. Who is she helping?"

"The young gentleman in the bathroom," Jo said. He avoided eye contact.

Abbey and Violet looked at each other. Abbey tried to jump to her feet and banged her knees against the edge of the booth table. She grimaced and shifted herself from the booth. Violet rose as well.

"*What's going on* in the bathroom?" Abbey demanded. Her voice raised to a near shout as she rubbed her knees. "Is he hurt?"

No, but he's going to be, Violet thought. She had a strong inclination as to what kind of place this was and what went on in the bathroom. She tightened her fists and frowned. She was glad Abbey didn't have a clue yet. But it wouldn't be too long before she connected the dots.

Then again, Violet started to wonder. Abbey still hadn't connected the dots between Violet and Jeremy. Perhaps Abbey was a fortunate kind of dim. She was an 'A' plus plus student, but as dumb as a doorknob when it came to deductive reasoning.

A young man with dreadlocks came through the front door and approached them. He had a three-headed dragon tattoo on his right forearm and a small tattoo of an eye in a triangle over his left eye. He pointed at the pistol on his hip and then at Abbey and Violet.

"Sup ladies," Dreadlocks said and smiled. His eyes danced up and down their bodies. "My boss wants to speak to you. So, let's take a little trip to the back door."

Abbey and Violet looked at each other, then at the pistol on Dreadlock's hip. Abbey squealed and whined, "Why? We didn't do anything. We didn't even finish our fries, yet."

Dreadlocks removed his gun from his holster and held it to his side. "To the back. Now."

Panicked, Abbey's heart raced. She turned and walked towards the back at a snail's pace. Violet followed, trembled all over.

"That's right," Dreadlocks said. His eyes wandering their bodies.

Jo looked at the abandoned fries and frowned. "Couldn't you have come in before I made my food? Now it's going to go to waste."

Dreadlocks turned to Jo, smiled, and said, "Don't worry, Jo. After we're finished with them, I'm sure they'll have an appetite."

After hearing that, Abbey felt a wave of panic and fear

overcome her. *Where is Levi? I need Levi here. He's supposed to protect me!*

Warm tears rushed down her face. She looked at Violet. Violet's face was as pale as chalk. Her eyes were wide. They locked eyes. Dreadlocks pushed them forward with his hand. Violet bumped into the back of Abbey and Abbey sprawled to the floor.

Dreadlocks pointed his gun and yelled, "Get up!"

She stood slowly, her legs wobbling as she trembled, and continued forward.

A meter from the bathroom, they could hear loud panting and breathing through the door. On the other side of the door, one woman was giggling; the other was moaning. Then, there was a man's voice.

Jeremy's voice, Abbey thought. She felt a stabbing pain in her stomach and a growing emptiness in her chest. She threw her hands to her face and cried. Violet put her hand on Abbey's back to console her.

"Shut that up and move," Dreadlocks said and dug his gun into Violet's back.

The two walked towards the closed black door in the back with a crack of light coming from the bottom. Neither wanted to know what was on the other side. Yet, the closer they came, the more curious they were of what menace awaited them.

"Was it not Levi and your father who regularly mentioned the door at the end of the hall?" said a whisper in the back of Abbey's mind. She wasn't ready for it. That was the afterlife; and she wasn't ready for it.

There was a large explosion behind them. The front window of the diner shattered into a million pieces. The ground trembled. Everyone stumbled and bounced against the wall of the hall. Five more explosions followed the first.

Jared jumped through the broken window and

charged to the back. Dreadlocks raised his pistol and aimed to shoot Jared. Violet threw a hard punch into the small of his back and he fired into the ceiling. He turned in her direction to fire a shot at her; but Jared jumped on top of him and dug his teeth into his right arm. Dreadlocks screamed and twisted his wrist towards Jared. He tried to pull the trigger, but the trigger wouldn't budge.

It was locked somehow.

Jared slashed deep gashes into Dreadlock's right hand until he let go of the gun. He balled up his left fist and swung it into Jared's muzzle. The hit connected and knocked Jared against the wall. He let go his hold on Dreadlock's arm. It was bleeding profusely.

Dreadlocks forced himself up and reached for his gun with his left hand, but Violet kicked the gun away. Jared locked on Dreadlock's leg and pulled him to the floor as he tried to stand. Dreadlock's head bounced on the hard floor. There was a loud cracking noise. He stopped moving.

Jared moved to the man's head and sighed.

Violet turned to Abbey to see if she was okay. Abbey stood frozen, pressed against the wall. Her eyes were open and wide. Violet turned back to Jared. He opened his mouth as though he were about to speak, and then shut it. As always, Jared was the most peculiar animal she'd ever seen.

Behind Jared, Jo jumped behind the counter and grabbed his long barreled pistol. He pointed it at the three and yelled, "Jesus! You killed Kanye." He looked at the window and briefly peered outside. There was nothing but pavement and a darkening sky. "And my window is broken."

A long bolt of energy shot through the window and punched directly into Jo's side. He fell back hard against the bar and tumbled to the floor. His pistol flew to the opposite side of the counter. Levi came through the front door and rushed to Jared, Violet, and Abbey.

"Everyone okay?" Levi asked.

Violet shook her head and hugged him. She cried.

Levi held Violet and looked past her to Abbey. She stood against the wall of the hall, vacant in expression. Jared walked to her and barked. It startled her.

"We have to get out of here, now," Levi warned and looked around. "Where's Jeremy?"

Abbey sobbed. She ran past Levi and through the front door to whatever awaited them on the outside. Jared looked Levi in the eye and then followed her.

Levi unclamped Violet's hold from him, held her in front of him, and asked, "Where is Jeremy?"

Violet whispered, "He's in the bathroom."

Levi frowned, "Still?"

Nothing he ate should have caused diarrhea or constipation, he thought. *Everything was carefully supplemented.*

The waitress and the yellow tank top girl stepped out of the bathroom. They saw Kanye's body, a trail of blood coming from his head, and screamed. Then, they looked around at the front of the diner, at Levi and Violet, and rushed out of the back door. It led to the houses behind the diner. Ten men with assault rifles were rushing to the diner. One of them was a black bald man with a scar over his left eye. He pointed at Levi just before the door swung shut on its own.

"Go," Levi ordered. "I'll get Jeremy."

Violet grabbed his arm, shook her head, and said, "No! Don't! He's not worth it."

Levi opened and closed his mouth and looked back at the bathroom. "I thought you and he were—"

"No, we're not!" Violet yelled.

"But this morning, you were in your panties," Levi

said.

"No! Let's go! They're coming!" Violet screamed and pushed Levi.

He didn't budge, but regarded her with furrowed eyebrows. He could see the tears in her eyes and frowned.

What happened? What did he miss?

She pushed him again, harder. He didn't want to fight her. He also didn't know why he was leaving Jeremy behind. (Truthfully, he didn't mind leaving Jeremy behind.) Perhaps he was already dead? *No. That's not it. She said he was not worth it.* That meant he did something unsavory but was still alive.

Jeremy came out of the bathroom flushed. He discovered Kanye's corpse and a pool of blood on the floor. His head shot up, his mouth wide open; and he saw the hole in the front of the diner that used to be the window. Finally, he looked at Levi and Violet, who stood near the entrance.

The two young women were in the bathroom, and Jeremy, Levi thought and frowned. *Wait. Two women? He's already dating Abbey and hooking up with Violet. For what does he need two more women? What do they see in this guy?*

Violet scowled at Jeremy and pushed Levi toward the door one more time. Angry voices yelled from the other side of the back door and Jeremy ran. He jumped over the dead body and rushed to the front. The back door opened and five men with raised guns appeared. They fired. Levi pulled Violet through the front and out of the diner. Jeremy followed.

Outside, the fuel depot was a blaze of fire. Every one of the ten pumps was gone. The front of the fuel depot was destroyed. Roaring flames expanded and consumed the right side of the diner and the left half of the motel. Four flaming bodies lay on the ground in the wake of the spreading flames. There wasn't a lot of mystery as to what happened.

Levi shot the pumps, Violet thought. *I can't believe it.*

Believe it, said a voice from nowhere in her mind.

They kept on running forward to the car. It angled straight towards the road. The back doors were open. The driver's seat was open. Abbey was in the shotgun seat.

She stole my seat, Violet thought but didn't say. She jumped into the back.

Jeremy climbed in behind her. Bullets ricocheted off the side of the car. He quickly closed the door. Levi dove into the driver's side. Before his feet were inside, the car had already started to drive off. Bullets ricocheted off the car's shields as the men chased them and fired. They raced up the road and out of weapons range.

"I can't believe you blew up the gas station!" Violet yelled at Levi.

"What happened?" Jeremy asked, confused.

"You're a dirty vop! That's what happened!" Violet fired back. Her attention returned to Levi. "Why'd you blow up the gas station?"

"Because they were talking about killing Jeremy and I, and selling the two of you off as sex slaves," Levi replied. "The four guys outside huddled up and checked their armaments."

"Oh," Violet said. She held her hands and willed herself to stop trembling.

"That talking turned into pointing a gun and abducting the two of you, while the four guys outside were just about to aim at me and blow me to pieces with their machineguns." *Or at least try,* he thought. "I grabbed my pistol first and fired at the closest pump. It caused a chain reaction."

Energy weapons, he thought. *Had I used a conventional*

weapon, it wouldn't have caused as much damage.

Levi glanced through his rearview mirror at the men. Four men had jumped into a car. They would chase him for the rest of the night, he suspected, assuming they had a full tank of gas.

I'm going to have to put some distance between them and us, he thought. *Hopefully, that will be enough.*

But it wouldn't be enough. Something told him he'd see his new friends again. He'd see them soon and when he least expected. That was how road trips operated. You met someone and, coincidentally, you saw them again and again and again, and it wasn't because you wanted to.

4

The car ride was quiet, except for Abbey's sniffling in the front seat. She cried for twenty minutes before finally letting up.

It's about time, the little brat, Jeremy thought.

It was all her fault. If she'd just given it up, he never would have had to dip his foot in someone else's pond. Though, he did a lot more than dip. He dove in, front stroked, back stroked, breast stroked, butterfly stroked, and cannonballed. He went way down deep under and came up for air only once in a while. He knew how to hold his breath and make the minutes count. He was a real deep-sea diver. Not that she'd ever know.

Violet knew; but she gave Jeremy the silent treatment. Turned her back to him and stared out at the world with narrow, hateful eyes. He wanted to talk to her, ask her what she was mad about. It's not as if they were ever a couple. She knew what they were, just a string of flings. He was dating Abbey. He didn't cheat on Violet. She honestly didn't have a right to be upset with him. Screw her. She could go on being upset because he banged another snag.

It wasn't as if he didn't know the girl. Honestly, she had more claim to his junk than either Violet or Abbey. While they swooned away at Levi, their old "friend"— and he was certain they were more than friends with Levi—he hooked up with an old flame who took her sweet show to the road.

Oh boy oh boy was he glad to see her again.

After Jeremy entered the bathroom of the diner, he was ready to walk right back out. He put his hand over his nose and wretched.

The single occupancy bathroom was filthy. There was dirt on top of grime on top of dirt on every surface of the bathroom. When he gazed into the mirror, he couldn't see his reflection past the accumulated white and black film. He didn't know what it was. He didn't want to know. Someone peed on the tile floor and in the sink. There was no evidence of soap or paper towels. The toilet seat was up and someone left a live one in the toilet. It looked like a three-foot long brown snake curled in on itself. He put his second hand up to his nose. Who left that and how long had it been there? It looked like the bathroom wasn't cleaned in weeks. Whoever used the toilet last sat on top of all that filth to drop a major load off.

Jeremy turned to leave, but noticed how clean the doorknob was. It had a shine. It was pristine. *What the hell?* The cleanest part of the bathroom was the way out.

Then a woman's voice came over the speaker in the room. "Jeremy?"

He froze. "Yea?"

"It's really you. Holy shit."

Jeremy frowned and looked into the dingy speaker on the wall. "Yea. Someone sure left one."

The woman laughed. She sounded young. Jeremy supposed she had to be to recognize him. He didn't talk to old chicks, except Violet's mom, and that was only because she kept herself tight, except for her...

The grimy wall opened and revealed a larger, fancier bathroom with marble floors, a red couch, mirrors everywhere (even on the ceiling), two large flat-screen televisions, three smaller flat-screens with video feeds of the diner, kitchen, and bathroom, and what looked like changing booths but had red, heart-shaped loveseats. The booths had multiple thin long white silk curtains that provided limited privacy. He saw a wine rack stacked from the floor to the ceiling. The smell of perfume filled the rank bathroom. Approaching him was a gorgeous, young brown-haired woman wearing a red plaid mini-skirt and black, tight, button-up belly-shirt. He recognized her immediately.

"Melody? Is that you?" Jeremy asked and approached her. When was the last time he saw her? Three years ago? Yep. Three years ago, they both graduated from the same high school and hooked up the first semester of college. He probably read the lines of her body more than any of the textbooks.

"It's me alright. I thought you were dead," Melody said. She gave him a hug and pulled him from the path of the wall. It slid to a close on its own. "I can't believe the Alliance attacked and killed all those people in Virginia. I thought you were dead."

"I almost was," Jeremy said, peering into her green eyes and breathing in her perfume. He completely disregarded her remark about an Alliance attack. He missed her perfume. She always smelled better than anyone else. "I happened to get out by the skin of my teeth. You know me. Nothing can keep me down."

Melody smiled and nodded. She wrapped her arms around him. "Yea. I remember."

A voice came over the speaker. "Melody, we have

customers at the front. Be a doll and play waitress for me."

She rolled her eyes and walked to a metal panel on the wall. She pressed it. "Jo. I'm busy. I have a guest in the back room. Can't you ask them what they want yourself?"

"Daggit! Just go up there. It's not like he won't wait for you," Jo said and closed the line.

Jeremy watched the video feed of the diner and saw Violet and Abbey sitting at the table, talking.

Melody stepped in front of Jeremy and gave him a short and soft kiss. "I'll be back. If you need to use the bathroom, use that one." She pointed at a booth. Its curtains were thick and black.

"Mel, I'm not here to rag on your place or anything, but your bathroom back there looks like someone tossed in a shit grenade and it went off, twice. Had I known what I was headed into, I would have dug a hole and took a dump outside. That's how bad it is in there. Someone should fix that."

She cocked her head back and hooted. "It's supposed to look that way to deter anyone but our regulars. We had an out of order sign on the door. It looks like someone removed it."

She left him alone.

Jeremy did his business and cleaned himself up nice before Melody came back. When she did, she wore the combination of a frown and smirk.

"So, you have a girlfriend," Melody said, her hands on her hips.

Jeremy shrugged. "Eh, not technically. We barely kiss. We haven't done anything besides lightly grope each other. She has nice tits, but it's hard to tell when limited to light petting. She's kind of a selfish, blabbermouth little prude. I'm pretty much done with her, but it's hard to dump her since her dad just died."

Melody glanced at the camera feed and nodded. "Yea. She seems like the type. The way she looked at me. Gave me this daddy's little princess, entitled rich girl, dumb-blonde vibe."

"That's a perfect description," Jeremy said.

"Why'd you date her in the first place?"

He shrugged again and said, "To hit that. You know I like a challenge. I thought: if she's as tight as she is uptight—"

Melody shook her head and walked to one of the booths. "That's all you think about, isn't it?"

Jeremy followed her to a private booth. "You never complained before."

"Who said I was complaining?" she asked before kissing him. She pulled him into the booth and undid his pants. "I have a surprise for you."

"That's supposed to be my line," Jeremy replied with a smile.

Melody snickered and slowly pulled down his boxers. "How much is it worth to you?"

Jeremy frowned. "What? No freebies for an old friend?"

"When has it ever been free, honey?" Melody asked with a smirk on her face. She slowly pulled his boxers up.

"Okay, fine," Jeremy resigned. He leaned over, reached into his pants, and pulled out his wallet. He took out a thick wad of cash. "Take what feels right."

She took all of it. "I'll give you the friends and family rate. Make it a two for one sale."

"Are, are you serious?" Jeremy stammered, his jaw slack.

"She's already on her way."

"Sweet," Jeremy said with the biggest grin on his face.

"I'm just going to get you started."

Minutes later, they had a visitor. She wore a short, yellow tank top and light blue jean shorts. Her name was Symphony. And she and Melody were ready to make some music. And music they made. They were both in prime shape. It was the best moment of Jeremy's life, up until the ground started to shake.

At first, Jeremy was sure that it was all so good that it just felt like the ground was shaking. *Two chicks, man! Two chicks!* Then, they heard a gunshot. They stopped and listened. Symphony rushed and watched the video feeds. The feed in the diner showed the blown out front window.

Show's over, Jeremy thought as Melody and Symphony decided they wanted to get dressed. He convinced Melody to at least let him finish, and he did. After he was gratified, they left.

(And took his wallet with them.)

He washed his hands, gave himself a high five, and went through the bathroom exit. He honestly didn't care how filthy the bathroom was after his recent experience. He'd stay in there an hour if it got him a second chance at two chicks at one time.

Thank God for Melody, he thought. That girl was the kind of woman a man could stick around for.

Waiting on the other side of the door was a bloody corpse, blown out windows, and a scowling Violet trying to push the nigger through the front door. Oh joy. He almost wanted to turn back around and wait inside for Melody to return until he heard the angry voices. No doubt, those men weren't going to extend him a hand of friendship because he knew Melody. No, not when he came in with the people who just killed one of their men and blew out the front of the place. What happened?

He didn't have time to ask questions. The voice told him to run. Move. Stay with Violet and the nigger. At least for a little while.

He jumped over the dead body and ran for dear life away from eager bullets and into a car with a bunch of whiny snags.

On the bright side, Melody did give him her phone number. He'd give her a phone call as soon as they stopped. At some point, they'd have to stop. He was sure her friends would be grateful if he told them where the nigger that blew up their gas station was located. Perhaps they'd even offer him a free night with the ladies. Perhaps he could trade Violet and Abbey for Melody. A two for one sale.

Oh, wouldn't that be nice?

"Your first priority is the catalyst," the hissing voice told him. *"Do what you must to eliminate Levi and acquire it. Then, you can do as you please with the women."*

Of course, Jeremy thought.

He smiled.

5

Not long after they left the fuel depot, when it was clear their new friends would pursue a lengthy chase, Levi activated Emma's cloaking shield. Emma informed him, at their rate of energy consumption, they would have to recharge in approximately three hours. If they kept on the road longer, they would have to use essential energy reserves and there would be no radiation shielding.

A half an hour passed before their pursuers slowed. It was another half hour before they completely lost visual contact. It made sense for his pursuers to slow down or even stop and reassess their situation, but Levi suspected they were still on the road in pursuit. Eventually, his group would have to get off the road and find a place to sleep for the night. They would drive through the rest of the twisty, turning mountainous paths that was the West Virginian interstate and rest before entering the Devastation Zone, which began roughly ten miles into Kentucky. Would they turn around and help put out the fire or wait for him to stop?

To his right, Abbey read her pocketbook. It still had the musty book smell of her father's library. He missed that library. It was a hobby of theirs to collect and trade books. Most of the major bookstores and franchises were hit hard by the war. Anyone with a permit could scavenge through the old cities and claim the spoils left behind. Doctor Brown and Levi collected quite a number of books from the Carolinas. He wondered what happened to all those books. Did the Brown house survive the wave?

The wave affected organic matter. Levi wondered if the wood foundations of the house splintered. The wave would have altered the genetic makeup of the wood and the paper. Whatever was in the library may have disintegrated, or would.

Levi sighed. The books were gone.

"Levi," Emma said. "Despite the atmospheric ionization and the interference from radiation in this region, I can detect and translate radio transmissions coming from Union territory and orbiting satellites. I am downloading transmissions. Would you like to hear what is being said?"

"Yes!" Violet chimed in from the back. She leaned forward and placed her head between the two front seats. Levi turned to his right and found his face inches from hers.

God, why do these girls smell so good? Levi thought. *Can just one of them be smelly and unattractive so I can think straight?*

"Levi," Emma emphasized, "would you like to hear what is being said?"

"Not really. It's just about to start playing the U2 Anthology," Levi said and pointed at the dashboard. The radio sang about a girl named Lucy in the sky and the U2 Anthology was next on the playlist.

"Why don't you want to know what's going on out there?" Violet frowned. She stuck her finger into his ear. "I'm tired of listening to the Beatles."

"Blasphemy," Abbey whispered.

Levi swatted Violet's finger from his ear. "Well, they're on their last song. Then, we can listen to the anthology. After that, we can play your two favorite bands, Coldplay and Sleeping At Last. You love both of them."

Violet's lip stuck out. "I know I do, but it might be important. What if there's something on there we need to know that might affect our trip to Montana?"

Abbey pulled her sad eyes from the paperback and said, "She's right."

Violet stared at Levi with unblinking eyes and pursed lips until Levi sighed and said, "Yea. Sure. Let's hear it."

The Beatles were cut short and radio chatter filled the cabin.

Radio: "...ranging in the tens of millions. There are few reported survivors..."

There was static.

"Clean that up, Emma?" Levi asked.

"Reception is being disrupted by ionic interference," Emma replied. "I am compensating."

Radio: "The High Chancellor strongly urges you to stay in your homes until further notice. This notice, and our entire coverage, will play and repeat every hour, on the hour, for those who may just be seeing the effects of what looks to be a large oncoming storm."

Static.

"Emma?" Levi asked.

"I'm sorry. Telemetry from Union territory is still too compromised. However, I'm receiving a clearer signal from our satellite now that we're further from the wave. It recorded the entire transmission. It appears the transmission has repeated itself for the past three hours. Playing it now."

The static ceased.

Radio/Chris: "This is Chris Hutchinson from the Union News Network reporting to you from Cleveland, Ohio, home of the wranglers. If you are just tuning in, there's been an unfathomable attack on American soil. Millions of people have been killed and thousands more are critically injured. Eric," he sounded choked up, "would you take it from here?"

Radio/Eric: "Yes, Chris. According to reports from spectators, at five fifty-two, a strange beam of light shot from the ground and went into the sky. After that, the sky around the beam became red and lightning storms rumbled in the clouds. Then, it happened. A large explosion of some unidentified force shot in every direction and consumed everything it touched. 'It was like seeing a nuclear bomb go off,' a survivor described. It grew, crossing many miles in seconds. In thirty minutes, it expanded to more than a hundred miles. Whatever it was, it created a barrier between us and everything that once was Virginia. As far as we know, the state is gone. Washington D.C. officials have been evacuated. Maryland and Delaware officials have also been evacuated. Casualties are ranging in the tens of millions. There are few reported survivors. Whatever it was, whatever it is, it appears to be expanding—"

Violet and Abbey gasped. Levi sighed.

Radio/Eric: "—but slowly. There is panic everywhere. People are abandoning their homes, looting, killing each other in the streets, and fleeing for the west. There's an average of a thousand incidents reported every hour now. The numbers are expected to increase the more it expands. The High Chancellor strongly urges you to stay in your homes until further notice. This notice and our entire coverage will play and repeat every hour, on the hour. For those who may just be seeing the effects of what looks to be a large oncoming storm, stay calm. I am going to send you to Elaine. She has some updated information from Union authorities. Elaine?"

Radio/Elaine: "Thank you, Eric. I am standing here with Richard Head. As most of you already know, he is the Secretary of Defense. Since the High Chancellor and Vice Chancellor are currently in route to a safety bunker, the director has been authorized to speak on their behalf in public channels. Sir, what are you allowed to tell us in regards to this deadly phenomena?"

Radio/Head: "I can tell you, with absolute certainty, that this is an Alliance attack. The Washington Coalition has been coordinating with the Eurasian and African Continental authorities for months on this. We weren't completely certain of the accuracy of our intelligence until now. They have been working with a Coalition-American spy in Richmond, Virginia, to circumvent the strength of the American people and force us into a world government, controlled by the French and Russians. It has also been brought to our attention that the Coalition-Alliance spy responsible for the attack is none other than the presumed dead, once hero John Rider. He operated under the alias of Lukas Brown, a well-renowned scientist we trusted to help us with a very important piece of restorative research. To enact revenge against our nation for not supporting their lust for power, it appears he succeeded in sabotaging our efforts to save the planet. He has doomed it instead. We believe he has used technology from the Red he acquired during the war to destroy years of research by our top scientists. I say this with great sadness. We all respected and loved him as a war hero. However, in his last act of hatred against American freedom, he has killed himself and millions of people."

Radio/Elaine: "Shocking, shocking revelations, sir."

There was a pause.

Radio/Elaine: "Oh. Is there more, sir?"

Radio/Head: "Yes. Intelligence suggests he was not working alone. John Rider had a daughter named Sarah, who is operating under the alias, Abigail Brown—"

"No, no, no," Abbey cried.

Levi shushed her.

"Don't you shush me, daggit."

"Abbey," Violet pleaded.

Radio/Head: "—and raised Levi Jones, the orphaned child of war hero General Jeremiah Jones. They are traitors and collaborators. If they survived the attack, they are most likely on the run on their way back to Coalition territory. We will be sending out what pictures of them we have on file to all local authorities, including those outside of the safety zones. We have also put a bounty of ten million dollars on each of their heads to all certified scavengers, head hunters, and mercenaries who can enter or live in the restricted areas. Be cautious. The two are considered extremely dangerous. They are wanted, dead or alive. If you find them, please do whatever you can to detain them. If you cannot capture them alive, you are authorized to use extreme measures to deliver their bodies to us. They will have a device with them. A green, glowing orb—"

"What?!" Levi exclaimed. His eyes were nearly out of his head from shock.

Abbey shushed him, simply for spite, even though she was curious about the orb she saw for only a glimmer of a moment as he arrived in the mountain passage and again as he snuck it into the cabin of the car.

Radio/Head: "If you find it and turn it in to us, we are willing to offer a ten million dollar reward for it. Whatever you do, do not damage or destroy the device. In total, for Sarah Rider, Levi Jones, and the device, you can achieve a total of thirty million dollars. Good hunting."

Thirty million dollars, Abbey mouthed. She watched Levi's hands tightened on the steering wheel. In the corner of her eye, Jeremy leaned in closer to hear. She could almost hear him salivating at the thought of cashing in on thirty million. Something in her, an instinct, told her to eject him from the car and keep on rolling. The sorry sucker.

Radio/Elaine: "Thank you very much for this exclusive one-on-one, sir. Tell me, what will be our response to the Alliance attack?"

Radio/Head: "You can rest assured that no one strikes the American people without full, unrelenting retaliation. You can expect a full-fledged strike by our military against the Washington Coalition. Nothing is off the table. Nothing! We will hit them with everything we have. I obviously cannot disclose timetables or specific targets. However, I assure the American people, that the blood of your family members will be paid in full."

Radio/Elaine: "Very poetic, sir. What about this growing energy cloud, sir? Can you tell us more about it?"

Radio/Head: "It was designed to heal sickness and repair the ecological damage caused by the radiation. From what I've been told, John Rider has made sure it does the exact opposite. Outside of the initial wave, and as long as it no longer expands, we do not believe it will pose any further threat to the people. You are more in danger going outside and exposing yourselves to looters. You are in greater danger if you intend to flee further west. We will be violently retaliating against our western enemies for this horrific, irreprehensible attack. People, whatever it is out there, it's getting bigger, but it'll fade out. That's how the original was designed. You can trust that the Union will survive. Your freedom is secure. We shall prevail over our attackers."

Radio/Elaine: "We are most thankful and grateful for your service and protection of us, sir. Thank you for coming on our show."

Radio/Head: "It is always a pleasure, Elaine. I wish it was under better circumstances."

Radio/Elaine: "Back to you, Chris."

Radio/Chris: "Thank you, Elaine. Please give the secretary my regards. I am a fond admirer of his work." Pause. "So, Eric, what are your thoughts on what the secretary said? It's clear we are now at war with the Coalition and Alliance. Did you see something like this occurring?"

Radio/Eric: "I am shocked, but at the same time, it doesn't surprise me. They're a nation of traitors. They turned against the will of the people when they chose to separate from the United States in our time of need. When the nation was hurting and needed their resources, they turned their back on us. They made allegiances with our known enemies. It doesn't surprise me at all that they would take such a cowardly act to prevent us from growing into the strong, powerful country that we're becoming again. We're the greatest country on Earth. No doubt, they envy us and wish they were back with us."

Radio/Chris: "I couldn't agree more, especially considering the paranoid propaganda they've been spreading about our government over the years. I can't believe we allowed ourselves to be fooled by their genuine interest in cooperation. Obviously, our nation is too kind and trusting. We should have known they might attempt to attack us in such a sensitive area. I believe Virginia has been the most stable state in our union, despite the mutants. Now, we've lost it and D-C. You think we'll recover easily from that?"

Radio/Eric: "Chris, you're talking about America. We can recover from anything, even a bullet to the head."

There was clapping, cheering, and laughter in the background.

Radio/Chris: "Right you are, Eric. I certainly hope we never have to prove that one, though." He chuckled. "We're now going to share the response we've received from Vice Minister Juliette Kelley. Cover your nose. I hear a big pile of stinky coming."

The clapping, cheering, and laughter returned. They played a sound effect featuring the long, whiny blast of a horn that sounded like a fart. The laughter was even louder.

Levi put his hands over his eyes.

Radio/Kelley: "Hello everyone. For those who are unaware of me, I am Juliette Kelley, Vice Minister of the Washington Coalition. I have two speeches today. I hope you will have patience with me." She paused. "The first is to the citizens of the North American Union, the former United States of America, from the citizens, Parliament, and Minister's office of the Coalition. We feel great remorse and outrage over what has occurred. The loss of millions of lives is tragic, unbelievable. We find any such attack to be appalling, and claim no responsibility or involvement in any willful attacks on your people. We respect you. We love you. Many of you are fathers, mothers, brothers, and sisters of our citizens. To us, even after the divisions of governments, many of you are still considered as family. We were all citizenry of a once great nation. To many of us, we are all still one. And to hurt you, is to hurt us. So, you can bet your sweet cakes we have no interest in your harm.

"Now, there are many allegations coming from select parties that we are responsible for an attack. We are not. Let me explain our part in this. We have sought to unite the world. We have sought to bring peace to a world that has been war torn for far too many millennia. Our goal is world peace; and we're one nation away from accomplishing that goal. In an effort to bring your nation aboard, we offered a peaceful exchange of information, technology, and let the Union utilize our restoration research in a joint scientific effort to restore the planet. That effort was headed by our lead scientist, Doctor Lukas Brown, who worked with them on the project for about seven years. However, recently, it was brought to our attention that what was once a joint project was taken out of our hands. Your government aggressively took sole control of the project and made alterations without our or Doctor Brown's permission. The unlawful acquisition of our joint project and the unauthorized changes to very sensitive and complex technology are the cause of this travesty. But there's more.

"It is going to be hard to hear this. Many will want to refuse to accept it. Many will deny it. However, the truth is the truth. And the truth is: the Rezarians, the Red, have returned and are in control of your government. They are the ones who intentionally tampered with our joint restoration project and changed it into a weapon against humanity. Instead of repairing and healing our planet, that coming wave out there is changing our planet into their planet. It's making our planet more hospitable for them and less hospitable for us. So I issue this warning. If you do as your high chancellor suggests, if you sit still and quiet and stay in your homes, you will be killed by the wave. We do not want this. We want you to live. We want you to prosper. So, instead of sitting in your homes and waiting for the storm to pass, we urge you to head west. Cross the Mississippi. The storm will grow thinner. It will dissipate. We can make a new home for you on the other side until we undo what they have done.

"We are not asking for your allegiance. We are not asking you to betray your country. We are asking you to protect your families. Collect your valuables or secure them until you return. Be wise. Be safe. Protect each other. Do not rush to violence when your supplies get low. Share with each other. We will happily share with you to compensate for this hard move from your homes. We just ask that you get out of the path of the wave. Remove yourselves from the control of the Red. We will make every effort we can to help you. All we ask, among the things listed, is that you trust us. We mean you no harm. We have done you no harm. We love you. You are our family. You are still our countrymen.

"The second speech is a much shorter one to the citizens of the Washington Coalition and our partners in the Earth Alliance. We have a grave, rising threat that has returned. Some of us knew it and were making great strides to prepare for or prevent it. It seems that those strides were not enough. However, we do not want you to lose faith. The Red were our enemies decades ago; and we defeated them. We shall do so again. We have improved our defenses. We have refined our weaponry. As our national standard requires cognitive implants, we are protected by their mental powers due to our implants. They know this. So, it is their intention to use humans against humans until our defenses and resources are lowered enough for their invasion. Just like last time. They want the Union forces to hit us with everything they have, so that we are no threat to them. However, humanity has now learned to co-exist. The Earth Alliance is proof of that. We are all one. We shall be a united force. We shall drive out the enemy who has distorted truth, instigated violence, and perverted our people. We will prevail, once and for all. And there will be a new era of unity, peace, and love across the world. May the loving grace of our Father in Heaven, and His Son, our Lord and Savior Jesus Christ, sustain us all in our time of adversity. Thank you."

The news correspondents played their fart-horn again, and burst into laughter.

Radio/Chris: "Well, Eric, those Coalition neighbors of ours sure know how to spin the truth."

Radio/Eric: "Yea. No kidding. I think I nodded out through half of it. Talk about long winded."

Radio/Chris: "Speaking of long winded." Chris played the fart-horn again. And again, they all laughed. "That's exactly how we feel about the Vice Minister right now. Can you believe they have the nerve to blame our government for destroying one of our most valuable states? Do they know the revenue lost? The history lost? The military bases that are gone? The lives that have perished? It wouldn't make sense."

Radio/Eric: "Yea. I think those implants in their heads have finally driven them mad."

Radio/Chris: "Exactly. They sound genuine, but don't be fooled people. All they want is to get you over there, plug those things in your heads, and control you. I bet there's no individuality over there. Everyone walks around like zombies doing their jobs and going home. From what I hear, they don't even have sex. And if they do, it's not the good sex we have over here in America. You know, the curl your toes, tongue wagging, make your knees weak kind of sex we have over here. Don't put no chip in my head. I'd rather be dead."

Radio/Eric: "Right. If you want to live a boring, adventure-less, sexless life, by all means, run over to Washington. You can read books, listen to boring music, and sleep next to each other fully clothed and quiet."

Radio/Chris: "Speaking of which, we're going to take a brief commercial break, and then we're going to talk to Doctor Jessica Charlotte, the host of our highest rated show, Sex with Jessica. I hear her next guest could be pop sensation Joel Tripleton. We'll find out after this. This is U-N-N Breaking News."

The radio went silent. Then, low, piano music began to play. A young woman's soothing voice whispered, "Enjoy the fragrance. Enjoy the soft warm touch. Enjoy the sensation of bliss. Enjoy soft skin with the newest cream from Madeline's Secret, Illusion. It warms you on a cool day, softens your skin, and makes you tingle with excitement all over your body."

"Shut that off," Levi said with disgust. His face grew hot. Instantly, the radio was silent.

Levi, Abbey, and Violet sat in a stunned silence. Violet recollected a bottle in her old bathroom and said, "My mother used that cream."

"I bet she did," Jeremy said and chuckled.

"Shut up, Jeremy!" Both Abbey and Violet yelled at him.

Jeremy shrugged, but kept a smirk on his face.

Violet tightened her fists and frowned. She resented her mother and hated who she became prior to and especially after James Harrier's death. Her mother fell apart and become a stranger. She gave herself away to alcohol and strange men. She treated Violet as though she was the enemy. Yet, even after all of that, she felt a need to defend her. She was dead after all. There was no doubt about it. And you didn't speak ill of the dead.

"They're hunting for us!" Abbey wailed and stared at

Levi with wide, panicked eyes. "I can't believe it. There's a bounty on my head. What is this, the wild west? You don't just put bounties on people. We didn't even do anything!" She stuck her hands in her hair and held them there. "You said my dad changed names. My dad is John Rider? *The* John Rider?"

Levi didn't respond but stared straight ahead at the road. His eyes were vacant and dark. His hands were tense and tightened on the wheel.

The Secretary of Defense knew too much. He knew the good doctor was John Rider. How long had they known? He knew Levi and Abbey were headed to Coalition territory. Did they capture the good doctor and somehow got information out of him before they activated the device? How did the secretary know that Levi had the catalyst? There were so many unanswered questions.

According to their plan, Levi wasn't supposed to have it. He shouldn't have it. Sasha was supposed to be more than halfway there, across the Mississippi River and flying over the Barren Plains. Even if the secretary or someone else ordered the wall guards to have Sasha shot down, there was no way the secretary could have known that Jared recovered it without having the mountain passage under surveillance. There was no way they could have accomplished that. Could they have?

What other possibility was there?

"You're missing something," Jared communicated.

And what's that? Levi thought, disregarding the fact that Abbey was calling his name.

"Besides the overseer, the only people who have seen the catalyst are in this car. The overseer was programmed to scrub telemetry files the moment the safe haven was breached, if it was breached. So, that leaves you, me, Emma, Abbey, Violet, and Jeremy."

Levi frowned. *No one here has a phone. We haven't been*

able to get in contact with the outside world until now due to the interference from the radiation and charged particles in the atmosphere.

"Yet, you and I are communicating fine."

That was because they were telepathically linked. His eyes went wide.

"That's right. Yours and the good doctor's suspicions about our guests are verified. We're not the only ones telepathically linked."

Abbey leaned in close and yelled, "LEVI!"

Levi brought the car to a halt in the middle of the mountain road at the Fifth Street East, exit eight sign. His eyes blazed at Abbey, tired of her yelling in his ear, and said, "For the life of me, Abigail, can you let a man think?"

"What is it? Why are we stopping here?" Abbey asked. "Why didn't you tell me my father was John Rider?"

"To avoid what has just happened."

Abbey frowned and looked around. "What do you mean? What just happened?"

Levi balled his fists and breathed. "Do you know how they know who you are, that we're involved and carrying sensitive cargo?"

"No," Abbey said.

"You know; I was just going to ask about that," Violet interjected. "And what is this device you have that is worth ten million dollars to them? Some kind of green orb, they said."

"Not now, Violet!" Levi barked and stared directly at Abbey, a network of veins popping out of his head.

"Don't yell at her," Abbey ordered. "Why are you being so pissy?"

"Because we had a plan," Levi argued. "Your father and I, we had a plan to get you to safety, get the device to safety; so we could save the world. But you had to be defiant. We had to bring those two along. You had to nag and complain and demand answers and answers. You wouldn't let enough alone and just trust us. And guess what, Abbey? I was right. I should not have said anything. Your father and I were right."

"What, what are you talking about?" Abbey blushed. She trembled.

"You want to know how the Secretary of Defense knows about your father, me, us, and the device? One of your friends here is connected to the Red. While you're asking questions, they're listening in, getting all the information, and passing it along to the enemy. They're the only ones who have seen me with the device. Especially Jeremy. Mister snooping in our mountain passage, Jeremy. Mister sex'em up in the bathroom, Jeremy. He's the spy. He's a Red spy. You've ruined the mission. For all we know, your stubborn mouth got your dad killed."

Abbey was as red as a ruby, but silent.

"Good grief, man, you're paranoid," Jeremy said. "In fact, you three are ridiculous. Don't blame me, and don't be pissed about those two snags I banged. It was just sex. Everyone does it, except you two." He pointed at Levi and Abbey. "Even Violet has sex. Isn't that right, pumpkin?" Abbey and Violet gasped. Violet was quick to her denials. "That's right. It's time it got out. Everyone here knows it but Abbey, anyway. I had sex with Violet."

"You did what?!" Abbey yelled in an octave that made Levi's ears ring. She quickly went to tears and looked at Violet. "This isn't true. Tell me this isn't true."

"Twice, if you don't include bee-jays," Jeremy continued with a wide, toothy smile on his face. "I'd say about four times if you do."

"SHUT UP, JEREMY!" Abbey screamed, while Violet argued about how not true what he just said was. Abbey reached for his face around the car seat and mistakenly hit Jared's nose. Jeremy leaned back, still smiling. "You betrayed me! You both did. You betrayed me!"

Violet studied and wrung her hands in her lap. Her hair fell in her face. She didn't try to adjust it. "Abbey, it's not, it's more complicated than that."

Abbey broke down into sobs. "How, can, you, do this, to me?" She breathed. "You were supposed to be my friend! How could you do such a thing?"

"I'm sorry, okay?" Violet said. "I was mad at you. I was—" She paused and gulped air. "You're always interfering with my guys. Every time a guy comes around me and shows me attention, you start batting your eyes. You instantly install yourself between us." She briefly glanced at Levi. His eyes darted away. "You have to own every guy and no other girl can have them. All the other girls hate you, Abbey. They hate you."

"I hate you!" Abbey yelled. She exited the car and stormed down the road. She fixed her hand over her nose to block out the stench of decay that lingered in the Quarantine Zone.

"Abigail!" Levi called after her. He exited the car and chased after her.

"Leave me alone, Levi!" Abbey yelled and accelerated into a fast march away. "You knew! You knew about it and you didn't tell me. You never tell me anything. I'm tired of it. Just leave me alone!"

Where does she think she's going? Levi wondered.

A car door opened and Jared jumped out. He raced to Abbey and maneuvered in front of her. He barked. She yelled, "Get out of the way, Jared."

Jared barked at her some more.

"I said move it!" She kicked at him. He didn't flinch. "Stupid dog."

Jared frowned and said, "Abigail, I am many things;

but if there is one thing I am not, it is *stupid*." His voice was clear and sophisticated.

Abbey froze and stared at him. "What?"

"You heard me," Jared said.

Abbey blinked at him. "You, you, you talked. You can talk."

"Yep," Jared said.

"This is too much. This is, this is too much." She glanced back at Levi. He shrugged. She rubbed her head and then fainted.

As she fell, Jared bore her weight. Levi rushed to Abbey and picked her up on his shoulder. When he turned around, he saw Violet standing outside of the car and Jeremy in the front seat prying his way into the compartment between the driver's and passenger seat.

"What the heck do you think you're doing?" Levi yelled and rushed forward with Abbey bouncing on his shoulder. Jeremy glanced at him but continued his attempts to pry it open.

Levi bumped Violet out of the way and laid Abbey in the back seat. Then sped around the car so fast Violet missed him between blinks. He pulled Jeremy out of the car by the back of his camouflage t-shirt and pushed him away.

Jeremy stumbled backward, nearly fell on his butt, and then stabilized. He rushed forward and swung a fist at Levi's face. Levi blocked the fist with an arching left-handed swap. He followed it with his own swift jab straight to Jeremy's chest that knocked him down. Jeremy held his chest and gasped for air, shocked by the might of the punch.

Levi checked the compartment to make sure it was still closed and secure. It was.

"Stop!" Violet screamed.

Levi turned back and found a fist connecting with his

left eye. Instantly, his vision was spotty. His eye burned. His hands shot to his face. Jeremy continued in his momentum with three arching blows to Levi's abdomen. Jeremy grunted with each punch. It was like hitting thick tires. Levi wasn't fazed. Jeremy continued his assault with two more arching punches to Levi's abdomen and threw one below the belt.

The brief, searing pain from Levi's eye faded, and he dropped his hands down to block the low blow from Jeremy. Jeremy stopped his punches. His hands ached.

Jeremy scowled at Levi's unmarred face and removed a switchblade from his pocket. He spat, "What are you?"

Levi threw a hard kick into Jeremy's stomach that knocked him to the ground. Jeremy gasped and held his stomach.

Levi said, "Stay down," in a calm voice, and walked around Jeremy to the back of the car. He pulled Jeremy's black bag out of the trunk and tossed it on the cement road.

Jeremy picked himself up into a crouch and threw the switchblade into Levi's neck. Only the tip stuck. Levi sighed, undamaged, and flicked the blade. Jeremy's mouth dropped open. Not sure what else to do, Jeremy lunged at Levi. Levi raised his palm and Jeremy hung in the air, off the ground.

"What the—?" Jeremy asked before he was slammed to the ground. All of the air came out of him and his vision became spotty. He heard a ringing in his ears.

"I said, stay down," Levi commanded.

This time, despite all of his effort, Jeremy couldn't pick himself up. An invisible weight pressed down on him.

Levi stepped past a trembling Violet and checked to make sure Abbey was secured in the back seat. She was. He walked back around, stepped over Jeremy, and got into the car.

"You're going to leave us?" Jeremy yelled at Levi in between groans. "You're going to dump us in the middle of the road in the Quarantine Zone to die?"

Levi shut his door and opened the passenger door.

Violet stood still next to the car. She held herself, shaking and crying.

Levi asked, "Are you coming or not, Violet? It's him and here, or us and redemption."

What? Violet thought.

The word "redemption" lingered in the air and echoed in her mind. Redemption? Redemption for what? Having sex with her best friend's boyfriend? Yes. That was it. That was all she did, wasn't it? That was bad; but it wasn't necessarily so bad that she needed redemption. She hadn't killed a guy like Levi and the wolf. She made a mistake. And forgiveness was all she needed. She didn't believe Abbey would forgive her. She didn't know what Levi thought of her. He knew the whole trip that she had sex with Jeremy. Not once did he treat her like a criminal, as if she needed to be redeemed. Okay, maybe once or twice, because he didn't trust her. That lack of trust was clearly deserved, wasn't it? Any trust she hoped to have from him had to be earned.

"Well?" Levi asked.

The weight lifted off Jeremy. He slowly rose and stared at Levi, Violet. Jeremy stared long and hard at her, peered into her soul with his cold eyes. Blood streamed from the corner of his mouth.

"You going with that freak nigger and the stupid little cock tease spoiled snag?" Jeremy yelled and pointed at the two. Violet gasped. "Or are you going to stay with me? We have something special, Vy. We have something extra special. We don't need them."

Violet shook her head, said, "Bye Jeremy," and got

into the passenger seat.

Levi nodded and thanked her.

"Fine!" Jeremy yelled. "Leave then, you slutty little cunt! You're just like your mother! You know that? Easy as pie and lazy in the sack."

Violet looked back, scowled. Her face was covered in tears.

"Go on. Leave!" Jeremy continued. "I'm going to find you. And I'm going to—"

Levi slammed on the gas and flew down the interstate with a vroom sound, leaving a dust trail.

Jeremy watched and screamed a long series of vulgarities until the trail was gone. He gazed at the setting sun. The sky was a dance of orange, maroon, and violet. Soon, the mutants would come out, and so would the night predators.

"Dammit!" he yelled and kicked some rocks in the road. He grabbed his bag and walked.

6

"Wake up, honey. You have to wake up, now," said her father. It was wonderful to hear his voice again, but she wasn't quite ready to cooperate with that request. Never was. Never would be.

"No. I don't wanna. I don't wanna go back," Abbey replied into her pillow. She could already feel that soothing, warm sleeping sensation fading away. With all her will, she was calling it back to her. Don't go. Stay. I don't want to wake up. I just don't want to.

There was the typical, annoyed sigh of her father at their daily routine. "We go through this every day, honey. If you want to see the sunrise, you have to rise before the sun."

Abbey whined and pouted. Then, finally, she turned over and looked at her father. The lights in the room were dim, thank God. "The sun needs to take a load off and sleep in once in a while."

"I'll take that up with God next time we talk," her father said with a smirk. "Though, I don't think that's as appealing a concept as you think."

He tossed her a sweater, jacket, and pointed out her jogging shoes were on the right side of the bed. He said she could walk or jog in her flannel pajamas today. It was warm outside. She highly doubted it. His idea of warm and her idea of warm were two very different creatures.

Once Abbey was on her feet and fully dressed, her father handed her bottled water and they started their walk to their usual spot. He kept a rolled up, extra-large and fluffy blanket under his right arm while telling her stories about courting her mother. How she was the one that started a similar tradition. She was the early riser, not him. She was always chipper and full of energy. They found a different venue each time, bundled together, and took in the sunrise.

"She was a phenomenal photographer," he said. "She found a way of catching even the most mundane spec of existence and giving it a heavenly aura."

He told Abbey that she was a miracle baby. The war took a lot away from them, including three pregnancies that ended in injuries and miscarriages. The first was a boy they wanted to name Samuel. He was lost in the second trimester during a surprise attack by the Red that destroyed all of New York City. The second was a girl they wanted to name Mary Elizabeth. She was also lost in the second trimester two years later while her mother served as an Army nurse in Paris. The third child died late in the first trimester during the fall of China. They wanted to name him Paul or her Lindsey. After the third, they were too upset to consider a fourth attempt. Even if the war ended, the world was in no condition for a child. But once the war was over, and they were met with a surprise, they moved to Montana and, heroes or not, kept to themselves until the child was born.

After that story, she and her father arrived at their spot. They sat on the bench, bundled, and silently admired the sunrise. Then, her memories of the drive to Montana, the destruction of Virginia, and the betrayal of Violet and Jeremy returned like a slap to the face. Her head cocked back. She blinked, and looked at her father.

"How is this possible?" Abbey asked.

Her father looked at her incredulously. "If you're asking me how the earth revolves around the sun—"

"No," Abbey interrupted and examined her father. "How am I here? How are you here?" She frowned and rubbed her head. It couldn't have all been a dream. There was no way it was all a dream.

"God put us here."

Abbey stared at her father with piercing eyes. "That's not what I mean."

"Do you want to know why you keep coming here?" He spread his arms out to emphasize the lake.

"No. I want to know how I come from standing in the middle of the road to talking to my father on our bench. I was angry, and hurt. I, I fainted I think. I've never fainted before. But, this can't be a dream. It feels so real. I'm cold. I'm shivering. I don't shiver in dreams."

He shrugged. "In this one you do. Is there some place you would rather be? Some place warmer?"

"No," she said. She shivered again. "Well, maybe the library."

Just like that, they were in the library. She was stretched out on the couch. He sat on his fluffy recliner sipping tea and holding a copy of the King James Version. The room was lit by candles and a fireplace. The warmth of the fireplace filled the room. She breathed in the scent of burning oak and admired the crackling sound.

Her father turned to her and said, "I concur. This is better suited for what I have to tell you next."

"And what exactly is that?"

"That we're back on track, and it's time for your training," he said. "Phase two."

"That means nothing to me. What are you talking about?"

"Have you taken the time to think about what I said?" He asked. "Have you been able to communicate with the nanotech network within your body?"

Abbey frowned. "Umm, I thought about it for a while. You pretty much just laid out details of how certain parts of the network install and operate. You didn't provide me with much instruction as to how to communicate with it."

"I did, actually. I just didn't lay it out. That is what I'm here to do today. I am here to tell you how to communicate with the nanotech network. Once you've learned, you'll be able to do amazing things."

"Yea, I'm sure," Abbey said. "I'll be able to talk to cars and wolves, and jump out of moving vehicles."

"Jump out of moving vehicles?" her father asked with raised eyebrows.

"Levi jumped out of the car while it was going about eighty miles an hour. He vanished into thin air right before our eyes."

Her father sipped his tea and nodded. "Ah, yes, of course. Levi always had a flair for the dramatic."

"So, what he did, I'll be able to do with this nanotech network."

"If you want," her father said with a shrug.

Abbey sat up from the couch. Her eyes pierced through her father in examination. "So, that's the secret behind John Rider."

He smiled. "One of very many, my dear."

"You can say that again," she mumbled under her breath.

"I'm in your head; so you might as well speak clearly," he responded.

Abbey said nothing in return.

"Before we begin, do you have something you'd like to say to me?" her father asked. He set down his cup of tea and folded his hands together on his lap.

This was a rare opportunity to ask a lot of questions she'd had on her mind. Yet, she found herself completely void of questions. It was completely unlike her. The only thing she could think of was that the dream or vision was interfering with her thought processes somehow. Perhaps they were even inhibiting her. At that thought, whatever it was that was hindering her instantly ceased, as though it had an intelligence of its own and recognized her awareness. The presence of another mind became apparent. Was that the nanotech brain at work?

"Yes. Yes it was," her father responded. She hadn't asked the question directly. Then again, like he said, he was in her head. "The nanotech brain is designed to help organize human thought processes in more efficient ways so you can retrieve information in critical moments in relation to your circumstances. It does this in a way that improves focus on a situation but does not circumvent creativity. And, it can be deactivated after an awareness or intentional thought."

"An intentional thought, opposed to an unintentional thought?" Abbey asked.

Her father smiled. "Indeed. In an intentional thought, you issue a command to begin or stop something from occurring. Stand up. Sit down. Grab this. Grab that. When you decide to reach for a cup, your consciousness sends a command from your brain to your arm and you just reach for it. Our actions are in fact intentional commands that's become so trained and practiced that they're reflexes. An intentional thought is willfully remembering something or focusing your mind. An unintentional thought is a passing contemplation."

"I didn't intentionally tell the nanotech brain to stop hindering my questions. I just recognized that this experience might be. Wasn't that unintentional?"

"Yes, it was an unintentional thought but also an awareness thought," her father said with a growing smile. "Your awareness of the problem alerted the nanotech of the problem and they instantly corrected it."

"Huh," was all she could say.

"That very system is how the nanotech network works. All you have to know is what to tell them and they are programmed to take care of the rest. In some instances, if it's a very advanced process, they may need some extra instruction or guidelines. If that is the case, they will alert you of that. The nanotech will specifically, and directly, ask you a question."

"So, what should I tell it?" Abbey asked.

Her father shrugged and lifted his cup of tea. "That depends. What do you want to do?" He sniffed, admired its aroma, and then gulped the rest down.

Abbey stared down her father. "It can't be that simple."

"Why not?" he asked.

"Because nothing ever is."

"Oh?" Her father raised an eyebrow.

"I need more instruction," Abbey said. "How do I directly talk to the nanotech to give them instructions?"

"Just think," he said. "To start, until you get comfortable, you can directly think to it. Say hello. Start a dialogue. Issue specific orders by name like, 'Nanotech, give me super strength', or, 'Nanotech, help me move items with my mind.' Those are usually one-time requests. Once those changes are made, especially alterations to your brain structure, they're made. However, when you're using equipment that interface with your nanotech network, such commands are required."

"Okay," Abbey said with her hand on her chin.

While she pondered the possibilities, her father leaned back and lifted his cup of tea. He went to take a sip, but it was empty. He frowned and it replenished itself. Pleased with the refreshed supply, he took a nice swig of the tea and started reading the book again.

"When you asked me if I had any other questions before starting, you intentionally subverted my ability to ask questions in order to teach me this lesson, didn't you?"

Her father smiled. "That's my girl." He put down the book. "You know, I'm not me, err, him. I'm not your father. This program and message has its limits, even if it mapped his personality and brain patterns to make this process easier for you and more interactive. I can't answer all your questions. I can only answer those necessary to help you reach your full potential. I am programmed to activate you, and I have. The answers you are seeking will more than likely come from Levi, Jared, and Emma, but I will answer what I can."

Abbey frowned and crossed her arms. "Levi is persistent in his refusal to tell me the important things. And, and he blew up on me because we're being hunted down like fugitives. He blames me because Jeremy is a stinking dirty cheating liar and I'm the one that invited him to come. Levi even knew he was a cheater and didn't tell me. I, I can't rely on Levi to tell me anything."

"Oh boy," her father sighed. He put down his tea, got

up from his recliner, and sat next to Abbey on the couch. She could smell the mint of the tea on his breath as he spoke. "Do you know what's most important to Levi?"

"Fulfilling the mission," Abbey said with a sigh of her own. She looked down at her hands. "He wants to get to Montana so he can prevent the end of the world. I get it. I'm wrong. I shouldn't have brought them along. All those people died and it'll be my fault if everyone else dies too."

Her father took her hands in his and shook his head. "You're wrong, Abbey, not just about Jeremy and Violet, but about Levi too. You're what's most important to him."

"Yea, right," Abbey said and shook her head. She kept her eyes on her hands. She couldn't meet her father's eyes.

"Yes, indeed. If the mission was the most important thing, he would have left you in the capable hands of Emma and Jared and flown the device to Montana. He doesn't need to be in that car with you. He doesn't need to drive at all. Emma could navigate the entire way. He's there because he wants to be there. He's there to make sure you make it to Montana. He's there to protect you from whatever is out there, and yourself."

Abbey snorted. "I don't need protection from myself."

At that, her father smiled and nodded. "Well, that's all for today." He stood and walked to the fireplace.

"What? Wait," she said and stood.

He ignored her.

"Aren't you supposed to tell me how to become Super Abbey?"

"I already did," he said and calmed the flames of the fireplace. "Just tell the nanotech what you want to do or be capable of doing. Provide it with specific guidelines, if you'd like." He killed the fire and turned around. "You want to know what helped Levi?"

"Sure."

"Comic books and super-hero movies," her father said with a smile.

"I, uhh, I don't follow," Abbey said with a blank expression on her face.

"It's simple my dear," he said. "Watch the movies. Imagine you're one of those characters. Tell the nanotech you want to do what they do, within reasonable limits. Be careful what you wish for. We don't need you controlling the weather or draining a person's life-force with a touch, assuming either is possible."

Abbey simply opened and closed her mouth. She wanted to say that was stupid, but she could imagine Levi doing it. And honestly, didn't she see him fly into the mountain passage right before it closed?

Is it that simple, nanotech? If so, I want to be as strong as Levi is. I want to be able to fly, like Levi can, Abbey thought.

"The requested changes are detailed in the cognitive implant chip and require no additional clarifications. Would you like an overview of the requested changes?" the nanotech asked. The voice was her own, but mechanical.

No thanks, she responded.

"As you wish," the nanotech said.

Her father snapped his fingers and all the candles went out. She found herself sitting in the darkness and felt her consciousness slipping. As she sank into a deep sleep, she heard her father's parting words.

"The greatest power of all is love. Learn it first, my darling angel."

7

Fifteen minutes later, and after passing a "Welcome to Kentucky, Birthplace of Abraham Lincoln" sign,

Violet finished crying and wiped her nose in the handkerchief Levi provided. She thought it was strange that he had it, since she'd never seen him use one. In fact, she'd never seen him wipe his nose or sniffle. She put the handkerchief in her pocket and stared at him. His eyes were fixed on the road but shifted in her direction after a four-minute stare-down. Neither of them had said a word after they'd left Jeremy miles behind them to fend for himself. Abbey slept in the back. The wolfdog, which she could have sworn she heard talk, but wasn't sure, sat quietly in the back seat next to Abbey.

That was another thing that bothered her. He was the best-trained animal she had ever seen. He didn't bark. He hadn't made much of any noise most of the trip. He fidgeted, but only as much as any other person would if trapped in a vehicle for hours. She was pretty sure he spoke and Abbey fainted. Levi carried her to the car, put her in, and Jared settled her on his own, without instruction. It was the oddest thing.

"What's going on Levi? What are you?" Violet asked, breaking the silence.

Levi shrugged and said, "A dude."

"You're kidding me," she said. She ran her hands through her hair and let them settled there for a moment. "Jeremy punched you and stuck you with a knife in the neck. You made him hover in the air and then slammed him on the ground. You, that wolf of yours spoke. I need some answers."

"You want some answers," Levi corrected her.

Violet's face went red. She clenched her fists and shook them. "I can't believe this! You're a prick."

"I could have left you back there with him," Levi said. His tone was calm and settled, as if they were having a casual conversation about the weather over tea.

Violet wanted to cry again, but she didn't. She turned

away from Levi and crossed her arms. She wouldn't get anything out of him. She was going to be trapped in that car for another day or two and have nothing to do, nothing to talk about.

She didn't know what happened to him, what he'd become, but she missed the old Levi. She missed the romantic boy who used to pull a cream wool blanket over them on the couch and watch a romantic comedy with her while she avoided her mother and a mystery man for the umpteenth time. She missed the musician who practiced the violin, and played *Tchaikovsky's Romeo and Juliet Fantasy Overture* to her while she studied for chemistry.

The car was silent for another ten minutes. Outside the window, the last traces of sunlight slowly crept away. There was no moon in sight. There were no stars in the sky. The moment the sunlight was gone, they were going to be driving through absolute darkness.

Levi turned his headlights on, including the high beams, and then turned off the interstate. He squinted out of the driver's side window and slammed on the accelerator. Violet wanted to ask why, but chose not to. She didn't want to talk to him. And even if she did, she couldn't expect to hear anything she wanted to hear.

"How do I know I can trust you?" Levi asked.

Violet wasn't expecting him to break the silence, but didn't have an answer for his question. She simple shook her head.

"You don't get it, Vy," Levi continued. "I shared information with all of you, and the Red were in Jeremy's head. Now they know we're going to Montana. They know I have the catalyst and that I'm going to use it there. People are looking for us. There's a bounty on our heads. The mission is in danger. Abigail is in danger. *The world* is in danger. We are all that stands between the Red and end of the human race on Earth. I can't tell you anything else, because they might be reading your mind, too. For all we know, they may have been the whole time. There's too much at stake."

Violet looked at him with fire in her eyes. "If I'm such a risk, why am I here? Why didn't you just leave me on the side of the road with Jeremy?"

Levi watched the road. His eyes darted out the driver's side window, and at the rearview mirror. After mulling it over, he said, "Because I care about you."

Violet rolled her eyes and shook her head. "All you care about is your mission and Abigail."

"Violet, I care about you, too. I don't want to see you get hurt. I," Levi stretched his hand out to Violet's. She pulled her hand away. "I want you to come with us to Montana. After this is all over, we can all go back to the way things were. You know, before I left."

That would be nice if I wanted things back the way they were, Violet thought.

"Why did you leave?" Violet asked. She wasn't expecting an answer; but she was hoping for one.

"I graduated high school," Levi answered.

"So? I graduated high school," Violet said. "I didn't leave."

"Well, as of age sixteen, I was legally an adult in the Union, and under Union law, resident males have to enlist. So, he told me he needed me back in the Coalition to help oversee a very important project. Plus, the best colleges are in Washington. The options were simple. It made sense to go and become my own man."

"That must have been nice," Violet said.

Levi smiled and rapped his fingers on the steering wheel. "It was great. I made friends. I could be myself. They all knew who my father was. Most of them were aware of his capabilities; so, I had more flexibility. I got a job in law enforcement, too. It was easier there. I think the good doctor knew how hard it was keeping to myself and having secrets all the time."

"I see," Violet said. She wondered if he met a woman in Washington. "I thought you left because of me or Abbey."

Levi frowned. "That doesn't make much sense. Why would I leave because of one of you?"

"Because," she said and grew warm in the face. "I thought her dad made you leave because he was concerned we might, you know, do what everyone else in high school was doing."

Levi blinked. "I don't follow. What was everyone else doing?"

"Having sex, Levi," Violet said. "They were having sex. Didn't you pay attention at all in high school? Everyone was pairing off. Sometimes they were doing it in groups. Hell, even the teachers were having sex with the older students."

Jared whined. Violet glanced back at him and found Jared had his paws over his ears.

"What's up with your wolf?" Violet asked.

"He umm, he's, don't worry about it," Levi said and glanced back at Jared, who simply shook his head and returned his attention to a sleeping Abigail. "You're right. The good doctor did notice a lot of sex was happening at the school. We live in a godless society, immoral times."

Violet wanted to comment on the fact that the wolf was somehow picking up on their conversation, but decided she had better not mention it. Levi might clam up and decide to uphold his code of secrecy again. "So, that is part of the reason you left, right? Because her dad didn't want you to succumb to temptation?"

"He wanted both Abigail and I to be out of that

wretched, immoral sinkhole as soon as possible, yes. You are correct, to a degree. I was becoming more hormonal and you two were very important to me. He already knew you and I had kissed plenty of times, a lot actually. I don't think he wanted us to go any further than that. Sex is not for children. It is for married adults that can handle the adult responsibilities that come along with it."

"Well, I think you're a very responsible guy, Levi," Violet said and smiled. They shared prolonged eye contact. The two leaned in closer to each other.

Jared cleared his throat and stretched his head in between the two front seats. His eyes were narrow as he glared at Violet. There was intelligence behind those eyes. She glared right back at him.

What the heck, wolf? Are you cock blocking? Violet thought.

"You're right, of course," Levi said to Jared. Violet didn't know if he was responding to her or the wolf. Levi leaned back and returned his attention to the road. "Oh, look at that. We're here."

Violet looked forward and shielded her eyes. The building was so bright with florescent light poles and spotlights that she could have sworn it was competing with the sun. It was roughly ten stories tall and had a cream brick structure and metal-plated framing on the outside. Guards armed with scoped assault rifles and laser-pointing machineguns were posted at the large brick wall perimeter. The perimeter had cameras and much larger chain guns attached to it. Four guards stood at the entrance gate. The guards wore black, rubber body armor and black helmets.

"What is this place?" Violet asked.

"It's the Alexis Hotel," Levi responded and pointed at the red letters on the front of the building.

She responded, "Oh." He flashed the headlights at

the guards. "What are you doing? Don't do that." One of the guards walked to the wall, typed a code into a panel, and the gate opened. "Oh." They drove past the gate and into the busy parking lot. There were about forty cars and ten large container trucks. "Does it have to be so bright?" She put her hands over her eyes. "Why are we stopping anyway?"

"It's bright because it's a mutant-free hotel, and they hate the light," Levi said. "We're stopping because—I'm not sure you've noticed—the light of day has passed. The mutants are out. The wild animals are loose. We need to stop and stretch our legs, get something to eat, and rest until sunrise. It'll reduce our chances of being attacked by a predator. They jump in the road and attack cars on the interstate." He parked. "Before the sun rises, we'll get back on the road and enter the Devastation Zone."

"I thought you were being dramatic when you mentioned entering the Devastation Zone," Violet said and pointed at the map on the dashboard. "We can't go in there. They have the roads blocked off. There are guns to deter scavengers. And even if we get past all of that, the roads will probably have crumbled. They haven't been serviced in a decade. You've got to be kidding."

Levi sighed. "I wish I could say I was. However, we don't have many options. I was going to drive north up route sixty to interstate fifty-two, since that's the only way across the Ohio River on this side of West Virginia, but with everyone looking for us, we'll have to challenge ourselves with tougher terrain."

"What about the radiation?"

"As long as we're in this car, we're fine. You haven't felt any ill effects so far, have you?" Levi asked.

"No."

"Once we get a little food in our stomachs, walk around, and get some rest, we'll drive straight to

Lexington, hop on seventy-five, take seventy-five to two-seventy-five to seventy-four, seventy-four to eighty, eighty to twenty-nine, twenty-nine to ninety, and follow ninety all the way to Montana. We'll be there in no time." He pointed to the map on the dashboard screen and detailed their route. She wrinkled her nose at him.

"You're saying everyone's looking for us, and yet you're driving around Cincinnati," Violet said. "It's probably the second most densely populate city of Ohio. How do you expect to meander through without being recognized? They have customs and checkpoints at the different highways we'd have to pass through just to get back into the Union to maintain this route."

Levi frowned. "You're right. East Cincinnati is the second most densely populate city of Ohio. However, we're completely circumventing Cincinnati and a corner of Ohio by taking two-seventy-five. See?" He pointed again and zoomed in.

"Oh. Gotcha. But what about Indianapolis? Won't they be looking for us there as well?" Violet asked.

"Probably, but after you get into Indiana, the checkpoints are easier to slip through, especially if they can't see you coming," he smiled, happy to have a car that could turn invisible. "Our faces will be known, but they know we know there's a bounty on our heads. Considering the sensitivity of our mission, they'll expect me to take the most conservative route."

"Not necessarily," Violet said.

"I know," Levi said. "I'm sure they're looking through all of the routes with scrutiny. We'll just have to do our best." He slapped himself in the forehead. "Darn it. Now I have to change my route."

Violet stared at him. "Why?"

"Because I just told you the route."

"Son of a," Violet bit her lip and swore silently. "You

and your trust issues again."

"It's not," Levi sighed. "They're in your head, girl. Anything I say can and will be used against me because of that."

Violet crossed her arms. "We have to do something about this, then. We can't go the whole trip without you talking to me. Wherever we go, if they really are in my head, they'll know. So, what are our options? How can we stop them from reading my mind, if they are?"

Levi rubbed his chin. "I wish I had an answer for you, but I didn't bring any implants with me. I wasn't expected any added company. There were some in the mountain passage, but it was in storage and it hadn't occurred to me to grab any. I was preoccupied with," he glanced at the compartment between them, "something else."

"So, if they'll know where we're going, and where we are, then I guess we're stuck."

"I'll just have to randomly change my route as we go without telling you. And you will have to stop looking at signs or sleep the rest of the trip."

Violet glared at him. "I think you're taking this too far. Tone down the crazy a bit Levi. Let's at least wait for proof that they're reading my mind before jumping to that conclusion. Maybe it was just Jeremy, if it was Jeremy at all."

"You don't think Jeremy was responsible for leaking information to the Red telepathically?"

"I think Jeremy was responsible for being a giant jackass, but telepathy? No. He was too thick-headed for anyone to read his mind, let alone receive anything from him."

Levi laughed. "I wish that was true."

"Levi, the fact that you have not entered the hotel is drawing attention from the guards," Emma warned. "It would be in your best interest if you two exited the car and entered the hotel together. I will keep watch over Abigail."

"We should wake her," Levi said with a wrinkled, concerned brow. "I honestly don't understand why she's been sleeping for so long. She just fainted."

"She is in phase two. She should be awake in ten minutes. Enough time for you to get a room," Emma said.

"Phase two?" Violet asked.

"Great!" Levi said and smiled. He opened his car door and breathed in the repugnant odor of rotten fish, raw sewage, and vinegar. He could almost taste it. He gagged.

Also, it was hot. According to the display on the dash, it was ninety-five degrees and with a ninety-percent relative humidity. The southern regions were usually hot, but more so in the outskirts of the Devastation Zone. In the zone, it was rarely under a hundred.

Levi reached back inside the car and put on his helmet and belt. The pair of energy pistols attached to his belt felt oddly comfortable back on his hip.

Violet got out of the car and quickly shot her right hand to her nose. She almost gagged and held her stomach with her left arm. Beads of sweat exploded from her pores. She leaned against the car and struggled with the stench and heat. Levi rushed to her, put her arm around his, and walked her to the hotel entrance.

"If you think this is bad, you never want to smell the Devastation Zone."

The entrance doors were thick, plated with iron, and had two handles. Levi pulled them open with ease and helped Violet through. Once inside, there was the sound of grinding metal and a click as the door sealed behind them. It was followed by a long hissing sound. The air freshened. Violet sighed in relief, but still held on to Levi.

Ahead of them, two tan and metal plated inner doors opened.

CHAPTER SIX
THE DOOR AT THE END OF THE HALL

CARTWRIGHT CHECKED HER WATCH and frowned. It was six o'clock. Her day had started yesterday, Sunday morning, at seven o'clock. Her elderly neighbor, Mary, had banged on the door and reminded Cartwright that she was helping Mary with some early morning grocery shopping. For the life of her, she couldn't remember agreeing to the early morning part of that arrangement, but suspected a timetable wasn't mentioned. She threw her things on and spent the next two hours pushing a cart, sorting out the bad fruit from the ripe fruit, making sure none of the genetically-modified organics came from the Dakotas or Northern Texas, where people were still trying to push out crops, even though the soil was tainted. She had to read all of the information on the milk cartons, because Mary's vision was failing, and the reading glasses were giving her headaches. "Change the prescription, Mary," Cartwright told her. Mary said she hadn't needed to change her prescription in twenty years. It didn't make sense. Her eyes weren't changing.

Sigh. Of course they weren't.

Once they were done grocery shopping, Mary wanted

to grab some yarn so she could knit her granddaughter some nice, thick pajamas. She said her daughter and son-in-law always kept the air conditioning on. It was so cold sometimes that you could see the girl's nipples pointing right through her shirt. She could put an eye out with those things. The last thing she wanted was her teenage granddaughter walking around a house full of teenage boys with hard nips. Siblings or not, the boys of this generation stuck their penises just about anywhere. Soon, she'd probably have to buy some plastic plugs so they didn't stick their little peckers in the wall sockets. Cartwright felt uncomfortable, but couldn't help but to laugh at the last part.

After helping Mary carry her groceries inside and stock them in her cupboard, she returned home. It was noon. She gave the clock a cold stare, trying to intimidate time into going backwards a couple hours. Time ticked forward, nevertheless.

Cartwright lied down to take a nap; but the moment her eyes closed, the phone rang. She ignored it. It kept on ringing. She ignored it. It went to voicemail. She sighed and relaxed. The phone rang again. She scowled at it and worried, if she answered it, her hopes of taking a nap would fail. By the time she reached it, it went to voicemail. She decided not to check the message, but entertain sleep instead. *Just for a little while.* She set the phone to 'Do Not Disturb' and pulled the blankets over her head.

Ten minutes later, she heard the doorbell. Cartwright tried to ignore it; but the person at the door was persistent. The person pressed the doorbell for five minutes with three-second pauses between presses. Finally, she rushed to the door and saw a tired looking, short, brown haired intern named Amy Bagwell. This one had a reputation. She wanted the approval of the residents so badly that she was willing to do anything. She stood at the door with an envelope in hand.

"Don't tell me you woke me up to deliver mail, because if that is why you're here, I will drag you inside and beat you with a meat tenderizer," Cartwright threatened.

Amy froze, mouth half open. She stepped back, turned to walk away, and then reversed and pulled four x-rays out of the envelope. She shuddered as she passed them to Cartwright. Her brown eyes focused on her shoes.

"It's, it's a severe gluteal nerve rupture," she said. "Apparently, the man overexerted himself at the gym. Doctors Reilly, Sanchez, and Zimmerman are all in Cleveland at a conference. That means you are the only surgeon qualified to perform the new nerve fiber growth and repair procedure." She paused, thought, and nodded. "At least, you're the only one available within the time window for a same day recovery."

Cartwright examined the x-rays, nodded, and waved Amy inside. She changed into scrubs and followed Amy to the hospital.

Four hours later, the gluteal patient was shuffling out of the hospital with a cane, and Cartwright was trying to avoid being pulled into another surgery. She wanted to do the work, but the government contract with the restoration project prohibited her from doing more than consultation or emergency work on scheduled workdays. She knew Perkins, Andrews, and Zenji wouldn't be keen on her being late, even if her involvement in the project wasn't essential anymore. So, Cartwright left the hospital and went home. She napped for an hour, changed, grabbed a bite to eat, and went to work.

The radiation tests and final alignments of the cradle assembly were scheduled to take all night. She drank coffee every chance she got and prepared a long snooze right after the device fired off and started to revive the planet. While others celebrated, she would rest peacefully. That plan flew out the window when the world spun into chaos. Alien invaders, thought dead, had returned. The man she'd grown close to for seven years had a shocking and legendary alter ego. It was as if she was working with Clark Kent for seven years.

After escaping death, and eating a full meal, she'd finally laid her head down and dozed off. Did she get the rest she was hoping for? Nope. No matter how tired she was, no matter how little sleep she'd had in the last two days, someone shook her out of her beauty sleep so she could provide medical assistance to some church visitors. That was the beautiful thing about being the only practicing medical doctor. The rest got to sleep. She had to shower, dress, and meet a few arrivals.

She sighed and put on the white tank top from the spare set of clothes she was given. She didn't hate the work. This was what she became a doctor to do. She loved helping people. It was almost exhilarating to know she'd be back in trauma and emergency care with her adrenaline rushing, instead of sitting in a laboratory comparing the effects of specific radiations on tissue samples, or in an office or operating room as a consult, with limited involvement in administering medicine and performing surgeries. Her wish was that she could do all of these things and still be able to sleep.

Who was she kidding? She barely slept in medical school. She barely slept as an intern. She barely slept as a resident. She hadn't had solid sleep until she started working on the restoration project, which took a deep cut into her schedule at the hospital.

You can't have it all, Fancy, Cartwright thought. *Either you work your butt off as a doctor and don't sleep, or you get plenty of sleep as a consult, but don't get to do what you love. It's one or the other, so suck it up.*

She blew a stray hair that fell into her face and went downstairs. Eddie stood in wait at the back entrance to the main building and hobbled over to her when he saw her. He smiled and said, "Thank you for coming down, Doctor. I'm sorry I had to disturb your sleep."

Cartwright smiled. "Of course. Don't worry about it. That's what us doctors are here for. Neither snow nor rain nor heat nor gloom of night stays these doctors from the swift completion of their appointed rounds."

Eddie laughed and nodded. "You and postal workers. Such noble, committed work." He opened the door for her and swung his hand towards the entrance. "After you."

She entered. They walked down the long hallway past classrooms and offices. It connected to the main atrium, where Prost sat at a glass table covered with radios. He had short band radios, walkie-talkies, and a ham and citizen band radio. She stopped and stared at him. "How long have you been awake?"

Prost shrugged. "I woke up about an hour or two ago. Good thing I did, too. I popped right out of sleep thinking about using radios to listen in for chatter, cries for help. Eddie pointed me to the back storage, which has loads of things for random emergencies. Some of this stuff has to be at least fifty years old, but never been opened. They work just like new. So, I plugged them in, made a few modifications, and listened in on some chatter."

Cartwright nodded, suspecting Prost was the reason for their new visitors, and the interruption of her sleep.

Prost continued. "First thing I heard was a man asking for help. Said he got his family to the nuclear shelter he built right before the wave hit, but his wife had a tumble down the stairs and broke her right arm, badly bruised her hip, and hit her head. Their daughter is suffering from a little radiation poisoning. So are two others that came in. Here, I wrote it all down." He gave her a piece of paper and thumbs up. "It's not a chart, but it's something."

"Thanks. This is very helpful."

"You bet," Prost said. "During and after the Red War, a nice amount of people built and lived out of nuclear shelters. I've heard from a few rebel friends that there's a secret underground community that refused to come back out after the war. They didn't believe the Red were all gone, just in hiding. Surprise, surprise. Some of them probably got wind of the blast and took shelter. If I could get them to come here, we might have some muscle at our disposal. A few extra men and guns."

"I'm sure John will be happy to hear that," Eddie chimed in.

Cartwright nodded in agreement. "No doubt."

"In any event, I think I'm going to be keeping you busy for a while, doc. I hope you got enough rest." She shot him a glare. He swallowed. "You know, I took a few first aid courses. I'm willing to lend a helping hand if you get overwhelmed."

"I'm going to hold you to that," Cartwright said. She and Eddie walked to the medical facility.

In the medical facility, there was a sitting area with three sand colored couches, a sectioned-off office area for a clerk, two rooms with two beds, and one room for operating. She was impressed. This was a lot more than she expected.

Eddie could tell by her facial reaction that she was impressed, and answered the question that was on her mind. "Monday through Friday, one of our junior pastors, Doctor Saxton, uses," he stopped, thought about it, and sighed, "used this space for his private practice. He believed it was our duty to walk as Christ did and that it included healing the sick. We took in people who couldn't afford hospital care. Those who could pay paid. Those who could not did not have to. Many were willing to donate to the cause. People were happy to give him business because of what he was doing, what he stood for. His service brought many people to Christ. I'm sure Christ Jesus has welcomed him with open arms at the door at the end of the hall."

Cartwright blinked. "The door at the end of the hall? You mean the gates of Heaven."

Eddie smiled. "Yeah. Something along those lines." He studied her eyes. He stopped smiling. "You aren't baptized, are you my dear?"

Cartwright instantly felt uneasy and scanned the room for others. She changed the subject. "So, where are my patients? I thought they had already arrived."

He gave her a long hard look and said, "Doctor, I'm not going to pry. I'm not going to pressure. But considering our current circumstances, I must encourage you to think about life, what it all means, and what comes next."

"Pastor," Cartwright said. "I uhh, I've talked to John about this so many times. I just, I'm undecided still."

"Okay, Fran," Eddie said. "Just, just think about this, what you have seen so far. This place. The war. Your life. If things go bad here, know that there's a place for you with the Lord, our Father in Heaven, who loves you. There's more to life than this one. But this life determines the rest of your life after this life. It's important you know that the answer to life and afterlife is our Lord and Savior, Christ Jesus. He paid for our salvation and eternal blessing with his blood."

Cartwright nodded. She was raised in a Christian

household and knew the spiel. Her mother was incessant about daily bible time and prayers, church every Sunday and Wednesday. There was something inside of her that always resisted, until she lost her family. After that, she picked up the book looking for answers. When she didn't find any, she slipped back into the mechanics of the world. While she admired men of faith, it wasn't until Lukas came along and tried for six years to evangelize her that she strongly considered the proposition of faith in a higher power. Still, she was on the fence. For some reason, even now, she was hesitant.

"Well, thank you," she said. "I'll be sure to take that under advisement. My patients?"

"Of course," Eddie sighed. His face fell, and it looked as though he aged five years before her eyes. She felt guilty. "We gave them clean clothes and sent them to the bathroom to get cleaned up."

"Great. Will you let me know when they're on their way while I start prepping the beds?"

Eddie shook his head. "Actually, no. I have other matters to attend to. My wife used to be a nurse. Sometimes still is if they need an extra hand. She's in the bathroom shower helping the lady with the broken arm. She'll be assisting you."

Cartwright nodded. "Okay."

"If you need anything else, please, don't hesitate to ask," Eddie said. He turned to the door and started to walk away, then stopped. "Oh, and you should talk to John."

"About?"

"The door," Eddie said. "Ask him about the door. And tell him I said to look into your eyes. It's very important that he look into your eyes." He walked out of the small medical office.

Cartwright watched him leave and frowned. What was

wrong with her eyes?

2

"Well lookie what we have here," Pisces said as she stood over John. "John's actually looking like John again."

John opened his eyes, looked at the feline, and smiled. She hand him a mirror. His cleft chin was longer and broader. His eyes a quarter of an inch closer together. The muscles of his face were toned. His cheekbones were more pronounced. His hair was longer, with blond highlights.

"I don't know about you," she said, "but I'm going to miss some of the gray in your hair. It was flattering, really. You looked distinguished."

"I'll slip a few strands of gray in my hair, if you do in yours."

Pisces snorted and shook her head. "Not going to happen."

John climbed out of bed and stretched. He could feel his old strength returning to him. Everything felt lighter. He stretched and then balled his fists. Part of him wondered why he'd ever parted with his stronger frame. He made himself frail and normal to avoid raising any red flags. Yet, they knew who he was all along. How long did Perkins know?

Does it matter? Can you change the past?

Not without permission, and it wouldn't come.

"I'm surprised nothing's happened in the last seven hours," John said. He walked to the window and peered out and at the main building. He saw Eddie outside filling a basket of fresh fruit and smiled. "I expected my sleep to be interrupted."

Pisces shrugged. "Well, there were things to report, but nothing that couldn't wait until you were awake."

"Okay. I'm going to take a shower. Fill me in?"

"Sure."

John walked into the bathroom, disrobed, and hopped in the shower. He closed the curtain and started the water. "Curtain's closed."

Pisces entered the bathroom. "Doctor Prost has proven to be more useful than I anticipated. He found some old radios and has been using them to contact people. In the last two hours, he's contacted over twenty people. Ten of them were pedestrians who were fortune enough to get wind of the wave and get into shelters. Others were already living in their shelters. They're rebels."

"Rebels? Really?"

"So they say. Prost had some contacts and used a few call signs to get them to start talking."

"Rebels stayed off the grid. Some of them were Red War vets who kept their implants. Though, I'd have thought they'd moved to Coalition territory by now. This is great."

"We'll see," Pisces said. "Five people arrived a little over an hour ago. They were regular pedestrians. One needed serious medical assistance and has been under Doctor Cartwright's treatment. The rest have been treated for radiation exposure. Seven more people are expected to be coming within the next hour."

"Exactly seven? Are they all together?"

"Yes."

"The veterans?"

"Yes. They were hesitant to say their names on an open channel, but they said at least two of them have worked with John Rider."

John laughed. "Yes. It wouldn't be the first time someone said that only to be lying. By not saying their names, there's no way to know otherwise until they're here. But, I do respect their hesitance. How much do you trust this approach? The radio? I'm worried the Red may utilize the radio bands to expose a weakness."

"Right now, it's what we have. I'm just happy that some of the ionic interference is fading. We can't communicate outside of the radius of the bubble, but from within, we can."

John stuck his head out. "Bubble?"

Pisces nodded. "The wave didn't fire, spread, and dissipate as projected. It's still expanding and connected. From outward looking in, it'll look like a bubble."

"Crap," John said. "Rate of expansion?"

"About ten miles per hour," she said.

"How?"

"I don't know. You said they were manipulating the radiation and matrix. Who knows what they would have done?"

"Is it accelerating or decelerating?"

"I don't know, but since it's not being powered by the catalyst, or any of her multi-dimensional energy, it can't possibly cause as much damage. It'll dissipate."

John sighed. "It'll be fine. Once Levi and Abigail make it to Montana and activate the cradle there, it'll completely undo everything the Red have done."

"Oh, about that," Pisces sighed. "Sasha's gone."

"What?" John yelled. He stuck his head out of the curtain again. "How do you know?"

"James was finally able to establish a communication link with the overseer program. He sent a packet detailing all of our movements and visual and auditory telemetry within the safe haven. Sasha was shot down by a long range rocket powered bullet from one of the turrets on the dividing wall. Jared left the safe haven to recover the catalyst. He did. Emma arrived with Abigail, Violet, and the Collins boy. Levi and Jared arrived not long after them. They slept, ate, and left for Montana."

John nodded. "Well, at least they're okay. I'm not too happy to hear that Jeremy's with them. That kid is a slime-ball." He turned off the water and dried himself with a towel.

"Perhaps Levi will have a positive influence on him," Pisces said.

No. He won't, John thought. "Levi's probably not going to respond well to him. He's a good kid, but sometimes he can be a hot head. He had a liking for Abbey and Violet. I didn't tell him Abbey was dating Jeremy. And neither Abbey nor Levi knew that Violet and Jeremy have a secret affair. It's likely to come out during their trip."

Pisces put her paws to her face. "Oh, the soap opera that is life."

"Yes." John called his suit with his mind. The black metallic garment flew over the curtain and attached to him. In seconds, the piece lined up and sealed him in. He stepped out of the shower as the soles hardened. "But the most important thing is that they are alive, safe, and on their way to Montana. Levi will do whatever it takes to get them there safely."

They exited the bathroom and collected their belts, pistols, and the Koiaxan beacon. With everything in hand, they left their room, rushed downstairs, and walked to Saint Luke's.

"Anything else I should know?" John asked.

Pisces thought about it and nodded. "Cartwright wants to talk to you as soon as you're in. She said Eddie was making her uncomfortable."

John frowned. "Did she say what he did?"

Pisces smiled. "He told her... that she should tell you... he said to look into her eyes. It's important that you look into her eyes."

"Okay, so he's a bit of a romantic," John said and shrugged. "That's it?"

"No," Pisces smiled even wider. "She's supposed to ask you about the door."

John stopped at the back door to Saint Luke's. "What door?"

"I am the way, the truth, and the life," Pisces said.

John smiled. "No man cometh unto the father, but by me." He rubbed his chin. "Looking into her eyes takes on a whole new meaning. I'll have to talk to her once we've run a partial inventory." Pisces nodded.

They entered Saint Luke's Historical and headed for the main atrium.

Prost was dipping a thick stick of bread into his soup. He bit into it and smiled, then shot a glance at John and Pisces. He blinked. His eyes were glassy. "Holy shit. It's really you."

John frowned and raised his hands. "First, we have to talk about the language. Let's tone it down, okay?"

"Okay, okay," Prost said. He stood from his chair and closely examined John's face. "You just. You look like you from the posters and history books. The way your hair is, with the streak. You look just like my John Rider action figure." He backed away and smiled. "You're a handsome man, Doctor."

Pisces laughed.

"Good grief, Prost," John said, exasperated. "I didn't know you were a closet fan. Please. You're going to make me uncomfortable. Let's just hear what we have from the radio contacts. I hear there are rebels coming to help us with the Red."

Prost nodded and stared at John a moment longer before turning back to the radios and notes he put on two separate pads. "Maybe." He shot a glance at Pisces, and then continued. "They said they were coming. But because radio transmissions can be heard by anyone, they've changed their mind about offering us a time frame. They don't want the Red to know where they are or when to expect them. They believe providing a time frame could reveal where they're hiding. They're trying to get the word out to the entire Virginian rebel network using Morse code. It'll be a coordinated effort getting people to come out of hiding, stay protected from the radiation out there, and get them here. It'll take a day at least before we can expect a larger assembly of rebels. However, if we're lucky, we could have about two hundred armed men and women by late Tuesday night or early Wednesday morning."

That was good news. They would need as many able bodied men and women as they could get to fight the Red. Though, now he was concerned about space and provisions. That would be a lot of mouths to feed, backs to clothe, and beds to fill. How many rooms were in Saint Paul's Dormitory? He couldn't remember.

"That's excellent news. Did you get any names?"

Prost shook his head and sighed. "That's another thing. They're not very comfortable with sharing their names with people. Instead, they gave us some call names they use. The leader is named 'Gray Too Young'. The second in command is called 'Curls In Ball'. Apparently, most of their group operates under subtle names along that route. Some of the other guys coming to meet us are named 'Laughing Peacock', 'Sleeps Too Slow', and 'Eats By Water'." Pisces and John exchanged a glance. "No, actually I think I confused those last two names." Prost laughed.

"They've chosen an interesting style for code names," John said. "What ever happened to Red Dog and Blue Ocean? Something simple and less cute."

"Considering their lifestyle, and the fact that they've

stayed under the radar for twenty years, I can respect these names. It shows they have a sense of humor, despite a life of constant discretion and paranoia."

Pisces looked at John and smiled. "Sound familiar?" He rolled his eyes.

"So, what's the plan until they arrive?" Prost asked, looking at the two.

John smiled. "Sam, you've done a nice job here. I've decided I'm going to promote you to chief communications officer of our resistance."

Prost smiled. "Thanks."

"Since we're pretty much starting an army, I'm going to return to the rank of General. Pisces, how do you feel about being a Commandant, again?"

She shrugged. "It beats the crap out of being called Madam Minister."

Prost laughed.

John chuckled, "Okay. Commandant Pisces it is." He looked at Prost. "There are a few things we have to do in the library. I'd like you to join us. Take a load off of your communications duties. I'm assigning you the rank of Lieutenant."

"Doctor, Lieutenant Prost," Prost said to himself. "I never thought I'd be commissioned in the military, especially with an officer's rank. Thanks. I won't let you down." He extended his hand. John shook it.

The three of them walked to the second building, Saint John's Library, and headed for the main room. Prost admired the solar glass exterior walls and the multitude of glass cases they passed that held first editions and final copies worth tens of thousands of dollars. The main room was circular in design, just like the building. It held thousands of shelves of books on three floors. At the center of the room were ten glass tables and a circular counter for the staff librarian. The chair was empty.

"Did Eddie ever say how many of his staff are still alive? I've only seen about five," Prost asked.

"He had five full-time staff," John said. He pulled two glass tables on wheels aside while Pisces rolled the chairs. "The rest were students who worked part-time shifts for free room and board. It's spring break. So, seven of the fifty students who lived on campus stayed. The rest went home." He sighed.

"Too bad," Prost said.

There was an open space on the floor where the tables and chairs used to be. John pulled the Koiaxan beacon from his belt and pointed it towards the floor. A thin, long beam of yellow energy fired from the beacon and created a small white hole six feet above the floor. The hole rippled and squealed as it grew wider. Prost put his hands over his ears. John pressed a code into the beacon and the yellow beam became blue. The hole in space expanded, and a large ice cube stretched out of it like a baby through a birth canal. When it was completely out, the beam died and the hole sealed with a loud popping noise.

"Why didn't we bring our helmets?" John complained while rubbing his ears. "We knew what we came here to do."

"We were distracted," Pisces said. "I'll have the nanotech remind me, if there is ever a next time." She glanced at Prost. "At least we have the ability to deactivate our auditory receptors."

Prost pointed at the Ojiili box, his mouth agape. "That was amazing. Where did it come from?" He pointed at the beacon. "You created some kind of portal."

"Yep," John said. He walked to the box and leaned in. He pulled out an injection device with three short needles connected to a small canister. "Now, before I answer any more questions, we have to tie up loose ends."

Prost stepped back with his hands up. "That doesn't sound good. You mind clarifying?"

John smiled and pointed at the device. His breath was visible. "It's a cognitive implant installer. It installs small nanobots into your blood stream. They meet in your brain, and install the necessary implant to disrupt unwanted telepathic communications. Call it, a telepathic firewall."

"Oh," Prost said. He lowered his hands. "But I don't need one. They can't read me."

John and Pisces exchanged a look. John said, "You see. I've been thinking about that. And something someone said encouraged me to look into your eyes."

Prost shrugged. "Okay. I have beautiful brown eyes."

"Yes. However, there's something dark deep down behind those eyes. I saw, for a brief moment, that your eyes changed. They trembled. Nystagmus is a byproduct of Red invasive telepathy as they temporarily highjack and stress your optical nerves and muscles. When it happens, you don't even realize it. Their eyes are obviously bigger and more powerful. So, looking through human eyes, they put more strain on yours."

Prost became pale. He sat down in a chair and closed his eyes. "I thought, I thought they couldn't read us, because of our A-D-H-D." He swallowed. "How much do you think they've seen or heard?"

"Probably enough to know we're building a resistance with the rebels, and that I'm utilizing technology from the Galactic Cooperative," John said. "However, they're already aware of the latter."

"Galactic Cooperative?" Prost asked.

"It's a long story," John said. "A story I'm soon to

tell. First, I'll install an implant in you. Second, we'll do inventory. Third, I'll pull Cartwright in here for an implant. And finally, I'll tell you the story of the Rezarians, the Galactic Cooperative, the door at the end of the hall, and how we came about this technology. Okay?"

"Okay," Prost said.

John jabbed the installer into Prost's neck. There was a sharp hiss from it as Prost yelled "Ow", and then John pulled it away.

"You could have at least warned me," Prost said.

"I said, 'Okay,' and you said, 'Okay,'" John said. He put the installer back into the box. "It was the first thing on the list."

Prost put his hands to his ears. "Why are my ears ringing?"

"It's part of the process," John said. "Just close your eyes for a minute. That won't be the only side effect."

"Wait, what other side effects?" Prost asked while rubbing behind his ears. "We probably should have gone through the whole list. Diarrhea, nausea, headaches, heart attack, erectile dysfunction…"

John smiled. "Not even close to the actual side effects."

Pisces shook her head and tapped a command into the touch interface along the side of the box. "If you don't mind, I'm going to make it easier to see inside."

John shrugged.

"Thank you," she said and pressed a command. The box appeared as a glass cube. The objects inside hung in the air, free of gravity.

Prost pointed at the Ojiili box and said, "They're not affected by gravity. Whoa! Hey, is that a body in there?" He stepped closer and reached his hand to touch the box. Pisces slapped his hand. "Ow."

"If you like your hand, you won't touch that box," Pisces warned.

He frowned. "Oh come on. You guys just injected me with that implant thing. We're on the same team. Why can't I touch it?"

"Well, if your bio-signature isn't recognized as an owner of the box, your hand will be frozen to it, and then break off from your arm," Pisces said. She smiled as Prost put his hand in his pocket. "I think the surface temperature of the device is about minus one-hundred degrees Celsius."

"How can that be? John leaned his body right through it. It wasn't even a pause."

"I can't explain the science to you," Pisces responded. Prost raised an eyebrow and crossed his arms. "Honestly, this technology is beyond us by about a thousand years, and the box is created of a mysterious substance indigenous to only one planet in the galaxy."

"At least, as far as they know," John chimed in as he reached inside and started pulling out various items and placing them on the table. "You're not missing out on anything, Sam. It feels a lot like sticking your hand in cold pudding."

Pisces joined in, keeping an eye on Prost to make sure he didn't touch anything.

"You know," John said. "In a worst case scenario, this box makes a great hiding spot."

Pisces regarded John with narrow, golden eyes. "In the absolute worst of worst cases, perhaps."

"You can access the settings from inside and make the internal temperature twenty-five degrees Celsius," John convinced. "The external temp would still make it impossible for an unauthorized entry. They couldn't see inside. The substance is impervious to most hand-held blaster fire. If there was a hole I needed to climb into to recharge, this would be it. My own personal ice cube sanctuary. My fortress of solitude."

"Yea, you have fun with that," Pisces said.

Prost crossed his arms and leaned over the table covered with alien technology. "So, are you going to tell me what all of these things are?"

"Hold your horses. We're almost finished," John said. They pulled out a few more items, pressed a few commands on its side, and then the Ojiili box went back to looking like an over-sized ice cube. "The rest can stay in there. I love how much fits in there." He looked at Prost. "The spatial dimensions of the cube are adjustable. It's a safe, but it's one of the most advanced pieces of tech we have."

"I bet," Prost said. "I'd love to see some of the world's greatest safe crackers try to get into this."

Pisces laughed. "Yea, only if you want to see them getting hurt."

Prost thought about that and nodded with a cheesy, toothy smile. "Blooper real. When safe crackers get cracked." He mimed sticking his hand inside the cube and then held it up, frozen in a gnarled twist. "Ah, my hand!" The two chuckled.

John shook his head and examined a data tablet. "Well, that'll be that for now."

"Are we setting up Adam tomorrow?" Pisces asked. "We could use an android against the Red, or even as part of a search party for survivors."

"That was an android?" Prost chimed in.

"I was thinking late tonight or early tomorrow," John said, ignoring Prost. "He'll need time to adjust and charge before we strike. I think he'll be very helpful watching guard here if we head west to assist any rebels that need to get here."

Pisces nodded. "So, he'll be with us on the frontal

assault."

"Yes, why do you ask?"

"Well, the great thing about Jeremiah was that he was very direct and aggressive in his approach. Sometimes, he was so precise and focused; it was almost as though he were a robot. He was a good balance in the group dynamic. I'd like to think James might supplement that loss in our attack dynamic."

"Agreed," John said, remembering his best friend. Jeremiah came from a family of military men, with the exception of his father. His grandfather, Isaiah, was an Army Colonel. His uncle, Jacob, was an Army Major. His other uncle, Samuel, was a Navy Captain. Even though his father Joseph hadn't pursued that career, but fell on hard times, mental illness, and eventually died of mysterious causes, Jeremiah's extended family raised him with strict, military discipline. Upon war times, he was the first up, last to sleep, and always on guard. John missed Jeremiah, and tried to raise his son as he would. "You know. It probably wouldn't require much modification to make Adam look a little more like Jeremiah."

"There's no replacing him," Pisces said, "but it might instill an emotional reaction from the Red. We should do it."

"Are you two going to keep on talking as though I'm not here?" Prost asked. He was leaned against the table with his arms crossed. "I know you two are used to being in each other's heads, but I'd like to be clued in."

John turned to Prost. "I'm sorry. You're right. James is our artificially intelligent counterpart who navigated the car. We have a fully-functional android prototype in there. All he needs is activation of his cyborg, organic components with human DNA. We're considering utilizing a small sample of Jeremiah's DNA and using that for the final initialization of his construct."

Prost nodded. "Okay." He thought for a moment and smiled. "While we're talking about initializing, what if we made the android a, umm, fully functional female?"

John and Pisces stared at him for a moment, eyed each other, and then turned to the items on the table. Pisces said, "Let's go back to talking as though he's not here."

"Good call," John said. "Let's get started." He went through each of the items on the table and matched them with what was on his tablet. Prost leaned in closer as they went through the items. "Ioran fire igniters and converters. Will definitely need those." Mark. "Matter-energy converters. Left one inside. We'll need this one to produce a few more pulse rifles." Mark.

"You left the projectors and beacons inside, right?" Pisces asked, looking at a copy of the inventory on her tablet.

"Yep." Mark. "Have you performed a diagnostic? Will you need any replacement core nanobots?" She shook her head. "Good. I kept them in the cube as well." Mark. "Holographic cubes are still in the cube." Mark. "I pulled out five crystalline neuro-cables to be duplicated. I'm thinking we should have at least one room in this building that's completely realigned with a crystalline shell."

"I don't know. I think the conversion could cause structural damage. Why not place it underground like the last?" Pisces asked.

"That's fine. Entry will probably be between the dormitories and the main building. Anywhere else would compromise Eddie's garden and crops." Mark. "Ah. This is the matter assembly model. Once we're finished, you should sit this one outside with the converters and let it get started with its self-replication process." Mark.

"Already discussed Adam." Mark. "Our backup suits are in the box. Do you need a replacement?"

Pisces stretched and hopped. "Nope." Both marked their tablets.

"This is torture," Prost said. "What is all of this stuff?"

John frowned. "Haven't you been paying attention?"

"Yes," Prost said. "You point, ask her a question, and then move on. I don't know what any of this stuff does. Well, except matter-energy converter. That sounds pretty self-explanatory. That small device converts matter into energy and then what, back to matter or is it used as a power source?"

"It usually operates as both depending on what it's connected to and programmed for. I usually use it to convert matter into other types of matter. You know, turn a pile of dirt into a chair or crystalline glass or something like that. The closer an item is to the desired outcome, the less power the conversion consumes. It will usually absorb more matter than it produces, with the excess being converted to energy to power the conversion."

"Interesting," Prost said. He rubbed his chin. "And, what about this cylinder looking thing you first pointed to? It looks similar to the catalyst orb." He pointed at a cylinder made of crystalline glass and metallic circuits interweaving through the exterior. At its ends were black stones incased in a metal plate. The top had a small spiral and metallic opening. Inside was a blue flame. The cylinder was covered in frosting dew.

Pisces smiled. "It's an Ioran fire cage. It ignites and stores Ioran fires."

"Ioran? What's that?"

"They're one of the oldest and major species of the Galactic Cooperative and on the counsel of the seven chief worlds. Their planet is a lot like Earth. Full of vegetation and made mostly of water. One of the major differences is select elements like illordium," Pisces pointed at the black stone, "atmospheric particles, and temperatures. Temperatures don't fluctuate for them as much as they do for us in our seasons. It's usually around ten degrees Celsius in what we would consider fall and spring. It'll get to twenty degrees Celsius around summer time. And, during their winters, it'll be negative ten."

Prost leaned closer to the cage and shook his head. "You said it ignites fire. What's that inside? It moves like a flame, but this is frosting over."

John and Pisces smiled. Pisces said, "That is one of the mysteries of the Ioran flame. It absorbs heat and converts it into electricity."

"Really?" Prost examined it closely. "That's unbelievable. With something like this in the south, we'd have limitless supplies of energy." He stopped and frowned. "Wait. The Trinity Towers."

John laughed. "Let's just take this one step at a time. No point in jumping ahead of ourselves. That's a story for another day. Perhaps we should get back to inventory. Once we've finished, I'll grab Cartwright and we'll explain to you how all of this got here."

Prost nodded, curious to hear what other extra-terrestrial technology they had.

"I'm placing our combat armor on standby. I left it in there, but if we get hit by a sneak attack, you know."

Pisces shrugged. "Would be nice to know I could survive if I was hit by one of those plasma balls."

"Exactly," John said. "Once we put everything back inside, we'll move the armor suits to the front. It'll make the emergency in and out a grab and go."

"Cool," said Pisces. Mark.

"I'll take a moment to attach the shielding units to the

suits." Mark. "Ahh, weapons time." He opened a five foot long, stainless steel case. Inside were four silver rifles with cylindrical shafts and thin, arched handles. The grips were a black, rubbery material. Two of the four rifles had red symbols on it. The other two had blue symbols. "One of these fires energy pulses like a semi-automatic assault rifle." He pointed at the red symbols. John looked Prost straight in the eye, "The blue symbols represent standard energy stream, or beam, rifles. Assuming you ever have to carry one of these, grab a blue one. Beam weapons are easier to control for someone unaccustomed to weapons fire."

Prost nodded.

"They're also tactically different. The pulse weapons can strike multiple targets in a spray assault. The beam weapon directly focuses on one target but inflicts greater damage. The only disadvantage is that it's slightly slower. More powerful. Slightly slower."

Prost nodded. He held out his hand to hold one.

John shut the case. "We'll start target practice and training tomorrow, after we've talked to you and Cartwright about the other things." Mark.

He turned to another case and opened it. It held pistols, also with cylindrical shafts and thin, arched handles. Two had yellow symbols, four red, and six blue.

"I've already detailed what the red and blue symbols stand for," John said. "The same rules apply for the pistols. The yellow symbols are for plasma pistols. These things get hot, but they will burn a hole through anything you point at and shoot, even a Red. They are highly resistant to heat, but not to these bad boys. I might construct a rifle version of these. Just be extra careful. They use more energy, fire in streams, and sometimes overheat if you fire too quickly between bursts. That means: they could blow up in your face if you get too excited. Plasma rifles are better for short-range snipers. Plasma pistols are better as a sidearm. If you double-wield pistols, as I do," he stopped and thought of Levi, who also double-wielded pistols, carried a plasma sidearm, and was probably going to blow up something serious sooner or later (like a gas station), "it would be good to have one for bursts and another for beams. One for speed and another for the punch."

"That makes sense," Prost said, trying to remember all of that.

John nodded to Pisces. She marked it off the list and opened another case. It was full of silver cylinders, each ten inches long. They each had green, white, and yellow symbols on them.

"By the way," Pisces said, "these are Ioran weapons. They believe in uniformity, which will also explain why most of our stuff is made of crystal or crystal-like composites. Unfortunately, because they make their devices so similar, they can be confused. Fortunately, with grenades, they don't have crystalline casing, so you wouldn't confuse a grenade with a fire starter and blow yourself to Jesus."

Prost snorted.

"Each of these is different," she continued. "I hope you never have to touch them. Fools have a tendency to get their hands on grenades and throw them just about anywhere as a quick solution to killing a group. They inflict serious damage on everything, not just those they're trying to hit. If you throw a grenade in the wrong spot, at the wrong time, it could harm you more than those you're trying to take out. The green are antimatter grenades. Never touch the green. Never." She gave Prost a hard look. "I need you to understand me. These are only for John and I to use. No one else can touch these, ever. They would vaporize us all in an instant. Say,

'Never'."

Prost nodded and repeated the word "never".

She smiled. "The white symbols are for the photon slash light burst grenades. They burn and blind. These things release pure energy in a blinding flash. They're wonderful against the Red, because they are the only tools in our entire arsenal that can incapacitate a Red without killing it. They also have the ability to blow out energy weapons. With that being said, if you drop or misthrow a photon grenade, you may kill most of those in your party, including yourself, and disable the weapons of those that survived." She gave Prost another hard look before continuing. "The yellow symbols, just like for the rifles and pistols, are for plasma. As I've made it clear, most of these grenades are very dangerous. These grenades will burn through anything. That includes walls, doors, armor, anything. They don't have the same range as the other grenades, but if you see a pack of Red huddled together, you'll definitely take out the pack or at least wound them. They'll be easy to pick off."

It was strange hearing them talk this way. Prost always saw Brown as a peaceful man. He thought the same thing of John. He knew John Rider was a war hero, and a highly religious man. What he didn't know was what people had to know and do in order to come out of war as living heroes instead of bodies in coffins. You were either one or the other. He wasn't sure he was ready to flip the coin and discover the outcome.

"Gotcha," Prost said. He looked at the two, glanced at the door, and asked, "Hey. I'm curious, why don't you have Cartwright here to listen to all of this stuff?"

John smiled. "She's a medical doctor, Prost. She took an oath to do no harm. If anything happens to anyone, she'll be the person to mend them. Besides, if ever the point comes when she has to pick up a weapon, I worry it will be of no use to her."

Pisces closed the case, marked it on her tablet, and opened the last. Inside it was one long sword, two short swords, and four daggers. Each had crystalline blades and black, cylindrical and arched handles. Written along the sides of the crystalline blades were purple symbols. "These crystalline blades emit and cycle heavy particles to produce laser swords and laser daggers. You don't have to worry about these. They're for melee combat. If you're close enough to where you have to use these against the Red, you might as well throw a grenade into its mouth, close your eyes, and think about what you're going to say to the Lord."

"Thanks," Prost said. "But I was a fencing champion five years in a row. I could handle myself with one of those."

Pisces glanced at John. He nodded. She smiled. "Okay, Sam I am. We'll have to test your skills on that."

Prost said, "Bring it."

Pisces rubbed her hands together. "Oh, I will. It will be brought. It's been a while since I've had a solid opponent."

"Hey!" John said. "I beat you the last time."

"Yea, but that was before you literally got soft and became the world renowned Doctor Brown."

Prost smiled.

John blinked. "Okay you two. I think we're done." He closed the last case and marked it off on the tablet. "Let's put everything back in the cube for now. Then, I'll grab Cartwright."

They slowly put items back into the cube.

3

"Finally," Cartwright mumbled as she made her way to the resident doctor's office. Their guests had all left.

Broken arms were mended. Radiation inoculations were administered. All worries were set aside. Questions were answered. Now, she would claim the couch in the doctor's office. He wouldn't need it anymore, God rest his soul. Now, it was time for her to rest hers for a little while.

She stepped to the black satin couch, fell into it, and adjusted herself until she was comfortable. The cushions formed to her frame. She smiled. There was a half-folded blanket on the back of the couch. She pulled it on top of her. Toasty. It was one of those heating blankets. The previous doctor must have left it plugged in. It was a poor waste of power and fire hazard. She didn't care. It was instantly pleasing. She began to doze.

There was a knock at the door.

She wanted to cry.

"Go away!" she yelled.

"Okay," a man's voice said through the door. "But, you're going to miss one heck of a story."

An alarm sounded in the back of her mind. The voice sounded familiar, yet it didn't. It was a voice she heard when she was younger, much younger, and in college. Her roommate burst in and told her to turn on the TV. What was left of TV, anyway, were public news broadcasts. She turned it on and flipped through the static until she got to the news. A tall man with long, dark brown hair and blond highlights stood at a podium. He spoke of change. He spoke of rebuilding a new world on the wisdom learned from lessons of the old. He spoke of peace, love, and turning away from petty bickering, lust, slander, theft, anger, and greed. He'd said, "If we rebuild ourselves, but go back to the way we were, we would have been better off victims of invasion, than victims of ourselves." He'd said it was time for them to work for each other, instead of themselves. It was time for them

to give more than take. It was time for them to honor
and love each other, and still their tongues of
uncleanliness. Her roommate shook her head and called
him another super Christian quack trying to manipulate
the world. "Great. Another Bible thumper. Guess things
are pretty much going back to the way they were. How
much do you want to bet he runs for office?"

She never believed that. This man was sincere,
because in everything he said, he didn't want anything in
return. He wasn't running for office. He didn't need or
ask for any money. From what little they knew of him,
he was superior to them in every way. Yet he helped and
served them. He built houses in Montana for the poor
on Sunday evenings. Some made comments that he was
Christ returned. He nearly toppled over in disbelief and
disapproval. He said, "I am not worthy to wash the
sandals on Jesus's feet, let alone be compared to Him."
Still, the man cropped up out of thin air, saved the world,
and then chose to slip back out of view. Any money
people threw his way for endorsements in campaigns or
employment was put in the hands of the needy. She
respected that man. She fell in love with him. They never
met, and probably wouldn't, but she wished they had.

When she heard on the news that he died, a part of
her died. When she met Brown, a voice in the back of
her mind told her he was different from other men. He
reminded her of the great John Rider. It was the subtle
things. It was the humility, how he spoke, how he
walked. She started to fall in love with him, too. Only
secretly, of course. The man was married to his work and
focused on raising his daughter and adopted son. He'd
hardly ever made time for personal conversation. But
when he did, a year into the project, he was charming,
funny. They would laugh their heads off over silly things,
pop culture references of the old world, music, and other

people. They ate with each other every day they worked together. They had an unbreakable bond, and a stockpile of sexual frustration. She'd suspected, hoped, that after the project was over, they would be together.

Her mother would say it was a long time coming. She was forty. What was she waiting for? At this point in her life, she'd be lucky to find a man. They were all going for younger women. No, not women, girls. Teenagers. Everyone was trying to look younger, be younger, act younger, and have younger, pubescent. But not Lukas. He kept gray in his hair, even though most guys were coloring to compensate. He admired her over the young, pretty interns who wore their clothes extra tight, sometimes revealing little poking nipples at the front of their shirts. Some of the guys stared. Prost even had the nerve to pinch one or two.

No, not Lukas. Not Doctor Brown. Not John Rider. He was a standup man.

The man she secretly fallen in love with turned out to be the man she admired like a goofy fan girl when she was younger. And now, through the door, he sounded like the man he used to be.

How long was she thinking, anyway?

"Are you still there?" Cartwright called out. She wasn't going to leave the warm blanket until she was sure he hadn't left. Whether she loved the man or not, she was tired and the blanket felt comfy.

"Yep, still here," John said. "I'm sorry to wake you. If you want, I can come back later."

She closed her eyes. Did she want to get up? No. Did she want to see him? Yes. Was the door locked? No. "You can come in. It's not locked." Compromise!

John entered. The light from the hallway filled the room and hurt her eyes. She shielded them and waited until he closed the door again. Right away, she could see he had changed. He seemed taller. His hair was longer. It wasn't just his voice that had changed. His steps were heavier. His stride was off.

"John?" she asked.

"Yes?" he responded.

"What's going on? You've changed," she said.

"Yes," John confirmed. "Yes I have. In order to defeat the Red, I had to become the man I used to be." He stepped closer to her. Very close. He knelt down to her so they were face to face. "This is the face of John Rider."

At that, she smiled. "I know. I used to—" She used to kiss his poster on her wall before she went to sleep at night. It was a silly thing. All of his face was marked with sparkly lip gloss. "I used to see you on the news a lot."

John shrugged and waved his hand. "Eh. They had to find something to talk about." He smiled. He was exactly as she remembered him. She leaned in closer to kiss him, and then she remembered something else.

Millions of people had just died. Millions that wouldn't have died had they not built that stupid machine, had he clued them in on what they were making. It was capable of bringing life to the world or ending life as they knew it. They made a gamble. They lost the bet. The lives of millions were at stake. Those lives were vanquished.

She leaned back into the cushion and sighed. She wanted him, but not now. Now, she felt used and hurt. She felt deceived and betrayed.

"Are you here to talk to me about Eddie?" Cartwright asked. "He said some things earlier. He wanted you to look in my eyes."

John smiled and nodded. "That's one of the reasons I'm here."

Her eyebrow rose. "Oh? What other reason do you

have for being here?" He leaned forward and kissed her. This caught her by surprise, but she went with it.

I'll be mad at him later, she thought, her mouth open and accepting his. She adjusted herself on the couch and he sat next to her. Their lips never stopped touching. Their tongues played on each other in a dance. He smiled. She smiled. He wrapped his arms around her. She climbed on his lap. They kissed, trading turns sucking and lightly nibbling on each other's lips. One of his hands cupped her butt. The other held firm the back of her neck. Cartwright pulled her lips away from his and laughed at the ceiling.

John watched her.

She looked down at him. "I've wanted this for years. Why now?"

He gazed into her eyes and said, "I've wanted this, too. I've wanted this for quite some time, but I was committed elsewhere. Now, that commitment is gone. It's honestly been gone for quite some time. I just. Anyway, time is short. We could have died today. We could die tomorrow. I don't want things to end without me telling you how much I've cared for you. How much I love you."

"I love you, too," she said and smiled. They kissed again.

"There's a lot I haven't told you. A world of knowledge I've kept. It's time I told you about how I am the way I am and what's going on out there in this world. You should know what's coming next."

"Okay," Cartwright said. She didn't know what else to say. *It's about time? Finally? What took you so long?* She wouldn't say those things. She wasn't in the mood. She was pent up. He was as well. They needed to unload. "But not right now. We have some unfinished business to settle." She undid her shirt, revealing her freckled chest and red laced bra.

They kissed. He sucked on her chin, nibbled it, and kissed her softly and slowly from her chin to her neck, her neck to her collarbone. He sucked her collarbone. She gasped. He kissed back to her neck and something cold and metal slipped into her bra.

Cartwright pressed one hand on his chest, and lightly pushed herself away. With one quick pinch of her fingers, she recovered the object lost in her bra. It was a yellow gold ring with three round cut stones: a sapphire, diamond, and ruby. She looked at it and her eyes bulged from her sockets.

"It's, it's a ring," she said. She held it up to her face. "It's an engagement ring." She blinked and looked into his eyes, while he admired hers. "You're asking me to marry you?"

"Fran," John said, "the moment I met you, I was blown away by how beautiful you are. You're intelligent, funny, charming, strong, moral, and full of my favorite personality quirks." She smiled. "I hesitated because I had just lost a wife. I wasn't ready to move on. After being around you for a year, almost two, denying myself, a voice kept screaming in my head that it was time for me to move on, that we were meant to be together. We were destined."

He kissed her, and then continued, "So, I made it a point to spend as much time with you as was allowed. I scheduled our lunches together and called you over the smallest, most insignificant work-related thing until we were friends and it wasn't work-related anymore. Eventually, we talked to each other every day, even on our off days. And, I couldn't go a day without talking to you. Over time, I could see something else, too.

"I've noticed how you've looked at me for the last five years. That you, an incredibly beautiful woman, haven't dated or slept with anyone else in the last six. I knew you loved me. I wanted to act on it. I wanted to say something. But I couldn't let what we had get in the way of what we were trying to do. I couldn't let the idea of us put either of us in danger of the Red if they took control of you or saw through you. You were so patient with me. I love that about you."

Cartwright smiled, blushed. "I never thought it would take six years of patience for a proposal."

"I wish it hadn't," John said. "And as long as it is within my power, I will make sure there is nothing else you have to wait for. All boundaries have been lifted. In this new life with me, new possibilities await us. A new world awaits you."

Cartwright liked the sound of that; but the words felt heavy on her ears. Beginning a new life with him meant more than she could imagine. New possibilities? The man could fly and walk through walls. What did he have in mind for her? She peered deep into his eyes searching for answers. A new world was awaiting her, indeed. She hoped she was ready for it.

"I want to spend the rest of my days with you. So, marry me," John said. He grabbed her hand and held it to his lips. He kissed her left ring finger.

She had to think about it. It was sudden. She loved him, but...

But what? It wasn't as though she was getting any younger and a line of suitors were waiting on the other side of that door. As was noted, they could be dead tomorrow. Wasn't it better to be with the man of her dreams, even if it was just for a day? Wasn't it better to be with a man who had proven to be strong, brave, wise, and capable of supporting and protecting her? Wasn't it better to be with a man who was compassionate, loving, sensitive, funny, empathetic, and sensible? Hadn't she loved him for almost six years? If she didn't take this man as her husband right now, she would be a fool, right?

She nodded and held the ring in front of her ring finger. "Yes. I'll marry you."

John cheered, "Yes!" and they kissed. They hugged. They kissed again. "Good. For a moment there, I thought I was going to walk through that door a very disappointed man." He pointed at the ring and asked, "May I do the honors?"

Cartwright handed him the ring. She couldn't stop smiling. "Yes, of course."

John slid the ring on her left ring finger. It fit perfectly. She didn't know how. They never mentioned rings or ring sizes. She didn't wear jewelry; so he couldn't have measured anything she owned.

"It's perfect," she said, admiring the three stones. Ruby was her birthstone. Sapphire was her gem of choice, but exceptionally rare these days. Diamonds were traditional, and a girl's best friend. Only a man like John would get her all three. "When did you get it?"

"Two weeks ago. I bought it three days before they took the project away from me. You have no idea how I felt when I saw your signature on the paperwork."

Cartwright froze, lowered her head, and sighed. "They threatened to lock me out and revoke my medical license. My life is medicine. I don't know what else I'd do if I wasn't a doctor. It was the hardest choice I've ever had to make."

John nodded. "I suspected it had to take some coercion. I thought maybe the Red used their telepathic powers against you. Part of me questioned—"

"You wondered if what we had was real," Cartwright said.

"Yea," he agreed.

"It was real." She kissed him. "It was all real."

They kissed, held each other, and made plans.

A half hour later, John and Cartwright smiled at each other on the way to Saint John's Library. They held hands like a couple of kids discovering love for the first time. John's expression changed to a frown when he reached the door. His gaze turned upward at the sky. He paused and arched his head, listened.

Cartwright wondered what was going through his mind, but hesitated to ask. John opened the door and waved Cartwright in. "Ladies first."

She winked. "Why thank you, future husband."

John laughed. "My pleasure, future wife."

They entered the library and walked down the hall to the main room. They could hear clinks, clanks, clinks, and zaps.

"Ow!" Prost yelled.

John accelerated and rounded the corner.

Pisces and Prost stood two yards apart. Prost held a standard energy sword, Pisces a short energy sword. Their blades were surrounded by humming yellow and white energy.

John spread his arms. "What's going on?" He looked at Pisces. "I can't believe you two are sparring."

"You took too long," Pisces said. She waved at Cartwright. "Hey Doc, how are your patients?"

Cartwright cleared her throat and nodded. "They're fine. Are those swords?"

"Yep!" Prost yipped with a smile. "These are crystal laser swords. Cool right?"

"Laser swords capable of cutting off a limb with great ease, I might add," John said as he approached. He extended his hand and the sword flew from Prost's grip. It landed in John's hand, handle first, and he powered it off.

"How did you?" Prost gaped. "What the hell?"

"These are dangerous, Prost," John lectured. "You could kill yourself with one of these. I said we'd train you tomorrow," John said. He walked to the Ojiili box and gently placed it inside.

Pisces deactivated her sword and attached it to the slim black holder on her back. "I was watching him, John. I wasn't going to let anything happen to him. Besides, you were gone for an hour. What took you two so long?"

John and Cartwright glanced at each other for a moment. Cartwright blushed. John smiled. He said, "We have exciting news."

"You two boned," Prost said and smiled. "Congratulations. It's about time."

Cartwright side-glanced John.

John said, "Thank you for that, Sam."

"So, you two are official now?" Prost asked.

"Yes," John and Cartwright said at the same time. They looked at each other and laughed.

"John," Pisces said. She pointed at the implant installation device on the table.

"Of course," John said. Without another word, he walked over to the table, picked up the device, and rushed to Cartwright.

She pointed her finger and said, "What's that?"

"It's a cognitive implant installation device," John replied. "It'll protect you from Red or any other invasive telepathy." John stuck it to the back of her neck and injected her. She cringed. "There. In a couple minutes, we can get started."

"Get started with what exactly?" Cartwright asked. She pointed at the Ojiili box. "And what is that?"

John briefly explained what an Ojiili box was. When he was finished, Cartwright was astounded. She examined it but at a distance and said, "It's unbelievable.

Our species may not have this kind of technology for centuries or a millennium."

John nodded. "That's how I felt when I first encountered it and some of the other items. I was excited, but also disappointed knowing how far we humans have to go as a species. Intergalactic space travel, inter-dimensional gateways, there's so much to the universe. It's all a part of *His* plan. It's all beautiful. Oh, there's so much we have yet to see. So much awaits us on the other side of the door."

Cartwright frowned. "Eddie said something similar. He wanted me to ask you about this door. What is this door?" She put her hand to her right ear. "And what is that ringing sound?"

Prost laughed.

"It's one of the side effects of the implant," John said. In a comforting, softer voice, he whispered. "It'll subside very soon."

"Good," Cartwright said, trusting him.

"You want to know about the door, and I brought you two here to talk about it," John said. He pulled a chair from under a table and rested. He patted his thigh and smiled at Cartwright. She sat on his thigh, wrapped her arms around his neck, and gave him a peck on the cheek. He looked at Prost.

"The other thigh? Nah. I think I'll pass," Prost said with a smile. "I'll take a kiss, though."

John chuckled. "Just pull up a chair and get comfortable. This might take a while to explain."

Prost pulled up a chair. Pisces settled next to Prost.

John smiled and said, "I'll start with time."

4

"Time is not equal throughout the universe, nor is it consistently linear. There are regional fluctuations and barriers established between different realms, dimensions, star systems, and worlds. It is best to call them temporal disparities. In some regions of the heavens, five seconds for us could be five minutes or hours for them. In others, one day for us could be only seconds for them. Our disparity with the other worlds has fluctuated and significantly increased. Our temporal disparities are linked to our development and or God's will.

"In the beginning, God created the heavens and the earth, and time crept. The heavens by His design were vast, far greater than any of us could imagine. There were temporal, spatial, elemental, and dimensional barriers established for different types of beings and purposes. Each type of being was created in its own time to interact with each other at separate times. Most of these barriers are temporary. Some barriers are thin and easy to pass as a species develops. Others are massive and difficult by design. A species would have to evolve spiritually, emotionally, intellectually, and technologically in order to breach different barriers. For example: we have not developed intellectually or technologically to traverse space, time, or other dimensions.

"The angels were the first beings created by God. They were His first children, extensions of Himself, and had no boundaries. They could travel to all reaches of the heavens and were not limited by any of the barriers put in place for other beings. The heavens were and are created, populated, and governed by God. The angels were and are His knights.

"As time passed, according to His will, select species eventually developed so that they were worthy of greater responsibility in the heavens. As they proved themselves, they were offered self-governance and then governance over particular regions of space. While they were still accountable to God and His angels, they were given liberties. Thus is when the first Galactic Cooperative Council was established. It was an assembly of seven of the oldest, most advanced species. They came together utilizing technology we haven't even considered to resolve natural issues of resources and expansion.

"Unfortunately, the youngest of the seven, the I'ari, were influenced by a dark angel who sought to destabilize the harmonics of the heavens. He was the same one who brought disruption to the First World. The I'ari sought more power. They became proud, certain that they had developed further than they were recognized. They questioned God and the counsel as to why they were not given greater governance and flexibility than some of the other species. They were told that they had not yet developed enough to afford them the governance or flexibilities they desired. Their own hunger for power would limit their development and potential.

"When the I'ari were denied, despite their persistence, their hunger for power led to poor judgment. They threatened the counsel and their sister race, the Iorans, and then isolated themselves from the council in pursuit of their own goals. They worshiped a dark angel who sought to use them as a means to strike at and possibly take over the entire Galactic Cooperative. Since the cooperative had never seen war outside of stories of the First World, the I'ari were deceived into believing they could accomplish a swift and easy victory. Utilizing genetic manipulations to make themselves stronger, better, and resilient to the harshest environments, the I'ari perverted their original and beautiful design to become monsters, a completely new species called Rezarians. They multiplied quickly and amassed a great army.

"Concerned, the Iorans sought out the council's

assistance with assembling a defense and evacuation of their world. They reached out to the Rezarians over the span of years compelling them to embrace wisdom, peace, and patience. The Rezarians did not listen. They were warned that any hostile behavior would result in losing their seat on the council. They did not care. Not long afterward, they were excluded from the council meetings and denied their previous governances.

"Eventually, having amassed a great army of starships and soldiers, and with the help of a handful of dark angels, the Rezarians began an assault on the Ioran world. It was a futile attempt. The Iorans were one of the wisest and most advanced species. They discovered the infinite power source and learned how to tap into it. With this technology, they created a world shield that protected their planet from the Rezarian strike forces. Unfortunately, one of the disadvantages of the world shield was that, while it protected the planet, it also prevented their ships from returning home or leaving orbit. This left the Iorans isolated from the intergalactic community.

"When the Rezarian's continued efforts against the Ioran world shield proved useless, the Rezarians split their forces and began to invade other worlds within the council's governance. In surprise assaults, they took ten different regions. That infuriated the galactic council. They assembled an army of ships and, in the midst of battled, created spatial vortexes that swallowed and crushed half of the Rezarian's forces. The remaining ships retreated and regrouped in an orbit over I'ara.

"The Iorans were still under attack by some of the Rezarian forces and cut off from the rest of the heavens. Aware they couldn't stay behind the world shield forever, they decided to realign the power of their world shield to create a powerful energy wave. They lowered their energy shield. When the Rezarians noticed this, their whole army rushed forward in a frontal assault.

"The energy wave was massive. When it was fired, it destroyed all of the Rezarian ships in orbit of Iora, but it kept on going and growing. The wave disabled all of the Rezarian ships that did not retreat, and caused extreme atmospheric and physical damage to I'ara, their sister planet. The wave destabilized the planet's core. Within a short time, the planet died.

"Broken and splintered, the Rezarian survivors went into hiding, plotting their revenge against Iora. They attempted multiple times to acquire the technology the Iorans used against them and failed.

"Many years later, the Iorans reached out in compassion. They discovered new technology that allowed them to reshape worlds from fragments of others. In exchange for recreating I'ara, there would be a treaty of peace between the worlds. The Rezarians accepted the fragments and demanded the terraforming technology so they could utilize it themselves. The Iorans offered to create a New I'ara, but would not provide the Rezarians with the technology. It was too dangerous. They feared it would be weaponized.

"The Rezarians accepted the offer, but attempted subterfuge to achieve the technology. They succeeded in breaking into an encrypted database and stealing information involving terraforming and radiation engineering, but failed to accomplish the protected schematics of the terraforming device and its power source. They modified their ship systems with the new radiation engineering technology. It was used for medical purposes, and for weapons.

"After the betrayal, the Iorans refused any further dealings with Rezarians. The council deemed them untrustworthy and dangerous. The Rezarians were exiled. Whenever they entered any star system under council governance, they were fired upon.

"Many, many years passed. The Rezarians returned as a much more dangerous creature with a new leader. They were strong, volatile, and had once again amassed an army with newer weapons. Though the Galactic Cooperative had grown as well, the Rezarians somehow infiltrated multiple planets and regions with spies. When the Rezarians returned, they caused a great civil war within the Galactic Cooperative.

"Infuriated, the seven key council worlds decided the only solution for the Rezarian problem was to completely wipe out the entire Rezarian species. So, they systematically eradicated Rezarians utilizing the weaponized radiation technology being used against them. Connected to the infinite power supply, all of the key worlds within the Galactic Cooperative used newer planet shielding technology that immediately disabled all non-indigenous forces in orbit.

"The Rezarians were defeated at every turn. The Cooperative showed no mercy. They destroyed the Rezarian's secret base and new world. They searched for years, wiping them from the face of the galaxy. The last surviving warships of the Rezarian Army turned their eyes to the First World, the only place the Cooperative was not allowed to go. It was also the last place the dark angels resided. It was their only hope.

"The Lord lowered the barriers that separated the First World from the rest of the heavens so the Rezarians would bring judgment upon the First People. It would be a message to all who went down the path of the dark angels, First People, or Rezarians. Once the Rezarians were within the barrier, the barriers rose again. They were trapped inside.

"Throughout all the stretches of the heavens, all walks

of life have watched the final fight. The extinguishing of the last remnants of evil.

"That fight is here. We are the First People. God created us first with the intention that we, the first mortals created in His image, would be at the head of the Galactic Cooperative. The Lord illuminated and enlarged the First World in perspective so that all the planets, in all the realms, and all the people would be able to look upon it. We would spread peace, love, knowledge, and growth throughout the universe. We would mentor younger species in their development. It was a beautiful vision of an advanced human society, far grander than we could possibly imagine. We would eventually evolve to a state where we were not bound to technology and physical form. We would move freely through the galaxy like the angels do. We would travel between time, dimensions, and different forms of space.

"The First People were to be different from angels. We would have more flexibility in choosing our own destiny. God knew the benefits and setbacks of such liberty. He saw all that was to be, all that could be, and knew that with choice came chaos and death. He knew the nature of all of His angels. God knew the darkest angel and his followers would act against Him for their own interests; so he defined the rules of existence, life and death, to compensate for chaos.

"For one thing, you should know that, outside of His will, there is no death. Our mortal forms are three dimensional forms; but we have immortal souls. The Lord has touched all living matter with His essence. The physical form may perish, but through Him we have our fifth dimensional forms. All the pain and chaos of our third dimensional life is small and temporary. The growth and love of our third dimensional life sustains and enlarges our fifth dimensional essences. (This is why the elements of darkness intercede in our lives and try to weaken our souls, so that our souls cannot overcome them.) People must come to understand that through God we are larger than our third dimensional selves. We can become larger than our fifth dimensional selves. We can become seventh-dimensional. The highest of highest, the Kingdom, the Throne of God is in the seventh dimension. All other dimensions, be them the third, fifth, sixth, eighth, ninth, and so on, all connect to and are governed by the seventh dimension.

"Back to the story, the First People were interfered with by the dark angel as the Lord knew they would be. And as they went through their life trials, all of the cosmos saw by example the consequences of sin. The dark angel's plan to pervert the cosmos had backfired. Instead of sabotaging the Lord's first people and embarrassing the Heavenly Father on a grand stage, his actions deterred other future developing worlds and people from defying the Lord's commands. For who would want to live out life as the First People did? They fought and killed amongst each other for petty, trifling things. They lied, stole, and lusted. Their darkness came with the consequences of famines, diseases, hunger, isolation, and death in the flesh. And after their third-dimensional forms were vanquished, what became of their fifth-dimensional forms? Those forms had not grown and matured as they could have in the graces of God. They were smaller, weaker, and were limited by the pre-established barriers our God created in the universe's infancy. They could not even leave the world.

"Despite these lessons, not all were dissuaded from the ways of the First People. There were minor crimes that took place across the cosmos. Once in a while, a newly developed world would be diverted in its path. However, they were corrected. None were as severe and constant as the First People until the Rezarians.

"After the initial defeat of the Rezarians, when they went into hiding, God saw it time to show the people who He was by living on the First World in the flesh. The Word of God was spoken into the flesh and birthed as a human child, Jesus. You know this story. His life was a testament to God's glory, grace, love, compassion, mercy, and vision. The cosmos watched in awe of the new King of the Heavens who would govern the cosmos.

"After Jesus's sacrifice of blood for our sins, in His death and resurrection, His essence created an opening between the First World and the seventh dimension. That opening became a gateway, a doorway. Upon His command, the angels built a fifth-dimensional temple at the doorway. That temple, the Temple of Spirits, became a link between our physical forms and the doorway. Once a man falls to sleep, his third-dimensional frame and fifth-dimensional essence separate. The essence goes to that temple. In the temple lies a door at the end of the hall.

"Now, when one sees the door, one immediately believes that the door itself is the source of the light. No. It is not. The source of the light is beyond the door, but the light is so powerful that the door itself is illuminated. On the door is text scribed in the language of the Most High, a language only our souls can read. The text says, 'I am the way, the truth, and the life. No man cometh unto the father, but by me.'

"You must understand the connotations of that text, for it does not speak merely of the door itself, but the lifestyle, the heart, our choices. You must follow the way of Jesus, peace and love. You must accept, believe, and speak the truth of Jesus. And you must embrace Jesus as your life. He is not simply the answer to a riddle at the door. Your essence must resonate Jesus to open the door. Your hand does not open the door as much as your faith in Jesus opens the door. The Spirit of Jesus within you opens the door.

"Remember, it is written, 'Behold, I stand at the door, and knock: if any man hear my voice, and open the door, I will come in to him, and will sup with him, and he with me.' He stands at the door of our lives; and if we open our door for Him, so will we open the door to Him.

"Now, to that temple no Rezarian can travel. Through that passage no dark angel can pass. The temple and door are designed only for the shepherd's sheep. A great barrier was placed between this world and the heavens with only one way out. That is through Jesus.

"And now that you have a simplified history of things, I'll tell you how I know about the door at the end of the hall and how I came to be John Rider.

"About thirty years ago, Jeremiah and I were fresh faced doctors with genius ideas. Jeremiah was bouncing between internal medicine and oncology residencies. I was working on a nanotechnology engineering project in conjunction with the hospital and a medical technology firm that was funding my research. Jeremiah and I had known each other since our sophomore year of college. We supported each other in our individual career pursuits. He was more helpful for me at times, since I was a paraplegic and needed special accommodations everywhere I went. It only fueled my drive to complete my research.

"My research involved utilizing nanotechnology to repair and rebuild organs, tissue, nerve fibers, you name it. My goal was to either have the nanotech do it or have the nanotech transmit commands to the cells, telling them to initiate specific repairs. I spent all of my days for years studying the signals between the brain, neurons, and cells and trying to duplicate them. I designed the nanotech cells to be almost exact duplicates of cells and neurons. It was a remarkable and exciting process. It was also important that I study fetal development. The idea was for the nanotech to imitate or initiate the cell behavior during our initial development process. I wanted to use the nanotech to stimulate nerve cells and tissue repair in my spinal column. I was determined to be my own guinea pig, despite the dangers. Jeremiah called me Doctor Frankenstein.

"Jeremiah saw other uses for my research. He wanted to utilize the technology to remove tumors and seek out mutant or cancer cells. He was hoping the nanotech would revolutionize medicine. The processes would put most of the healthcare industry out of work. I was more than happy to have a second opinion and an extra hand in my research if we could accomplish such. I didn't trust others with my research. You'd be amazed how many selfish and greedy vultures there were in the medical industry. I was this close to electrocuting a guy—Doctor Avery Yarborough was his name—with my defense taser when I caught him digging through my research without my permission. I would have loved to have had an Ojiili box then. Bye-bye, hand! Anyway...

"While we were working on that research, Jeremiah had a cancer patient named Alan. Alan was a stubborn man dedicated to his work. He'd made his own condition worse by working too hard. But he wasn't doing it for himself. He had a sister, Juliana, and a niece, Emilie. He spent more time working and killing himself to build a life for Jules and Emilie, and less time settling down and healing. In fact, for the first year, he hid it from them.

"It was Alan's car accident that changed things for him and us. He had just left the hospital when he was stopped by a well-dressed man in a black suit with a forest green silk shirt and light gold tie. He wore gold cufflinks shaped like sevens with tiny diamonds embedded in them. Alan told me it was the strangest thing, because he couldn't remember the man's face. He could remember what he was wearing, but not who he was. The man handed him a crystal keycard with gold trim. The moment Alan touched it his name was inscribed in gold lettering on the blank crystal. He was told not to let anyone else touch it. If it left his hands and entered someone else's, he'd be a lost duck. Alan agreed to hold on to it. The man told him to get going. He didn't want to be late. Only minutes after that conversation, Jules was driving Alan home when they were struck by a car that ran a red light. Alan was knocked into a coma.

"A woman named Skye was a passenger in the other car and wasn't wearing a seatbelt. She also entered a coma. Comas are not common occurrences. You don't just hit your head or get into a car accident and find yourself in a coma. You can be unconscious. You can be difficult to revive. You can be dead. Comas are a special case. This was an especially unique case.

"Prior to the accident, Skye and her fiancé stopped at a stop light. The same gentleman Alan had encountered knocked on her window, the passenger window, and handed her a crystal keycard with gold trim. When she touched it, her name was inscribed in gold lettering. He said it was nice to see her again, gave her the same instructions—do not let anyone else touch it—and told her she'd better hurry. Minutes later, Skye and her fiancé crashed into Juliana's car.

"After the crash, Alan and Skye both found themselves standing outside of a door in the Temple of Spirits. Neither saw each other. Even though they both fell into a coma around the same time, they didn't arrived at the same time. Alan arrived first, standing in front of a crystal door with gold trim. His name was inscribed in gold letters. The door was almost an exact replica of the key he was given. The door was semi-translucent, but there was only darkness on the other side. There were no handles for which to open the door. It was non-responsive to his touch and efforts to pull it open. The door was cold, lifeless.

"After struggling with his door to no avail, Alan looked around. He was in a hall that stretched for miles. It was full of doors similar to his. On one end of the hall, the furthest end, there was darkness. The darkness wrought a cold so ominous he could feel it building in his chest as he pondered it. On the other end of the hall, closer to him, was a door so bright he initially had to shield his eyes. Then it changed. His eyes either adjusted to the light or the light adjusted to his eyes. He was filled with a hope and peace he'd never felt before. He had no anxieties. His mind was clear. He was overcome with a desire to go through that door and walked for miles to reach it. He said it felt like an hour walk and yet only felt like a few minutes. Time is funny in the temple. It both exists and doesn't exist. I cannot elaborate.

"When he finally made it to the door, he found the light faded just enough so that he could read the inscription. As I have said, the inscription said, 'I am the way, the truth, and the life. No man cometh unto the father, but by me.' Below that inscription was another, it said, 'I am the door. By me, if any man enter in, he shall be saved, and shall go in and out, and find pasture.' Below that inscription, one more manifested itself in gold lettering, it said, 'My sheep hear my voice, and I know them, and they follow me.'

"The very instant his eye passed the final word, Alan heard a voice beyond the door. He could not tell me what the voice said. Every time his mouth opened, the words refused to part from his lips. He said the voice was as clear as the light. It resonated throughout his fifth dimensional essence. The voice and its word defined his very being. At that moment, he knew."

"He knew what?" Prost asked.

"He just knew. When the time comes, you will know what it is to know and what it is that is to be known. He knew what it was he needed to know, and he knew that it wasn't his time. He turned around, not necessarily of his own accord, and walked. He walked for miles, many miles in the opposite direction of the light, past many doors towards the darkness. It grew colder.

"Eventually, he made it to an opening. There was a wide lobby like a hotel. There was a concierge, the same man that gave him the key. The man greeted him with a smile and handshake. He said he'd been expecting him. Alan wanted to know what he was doing there. The man told him he couldn't tell him. Not yet. But once they were finished, there were a few things that needed to be done and a couple messages he wanted Alan to deliver. In the meantime, Alan was to enjoy the temple. Later, Alan met Skye. The circumstance of their meeting is another story for a later time.

"While Alan and Skye's spirits were in the temple, their bodies were still on Earth, still alive. Jeremiah was doing his best for Alan, but comas weren't his territory. They brought in a rising star neurologist from Chicago. Her name was Doctor Kennedy Trout. Everyone teased her because of her name and the fact that she had a Jesus fish as a necklace. Years later, she married Jeremiah. Assisting her was the woman that would later become my wife, an intern named Doctor Faith Gibbs. She was also from Chicago. She is the doctor who, a couple days after this accident happened, helped a young Francine Cartwright with a sprained wrist after a regional youth tennis tournament. If I remember correctly, she's who inspired you to become a doctor. Right?" Francine nodded. Her eyes were wide. "This one accident put a variety of pieces together for future events.

"Jeremiah called in Doctor Trout because Alan and Skye's brainwaves were linked and operating on the same frequency. Their heart rates were the same. In the history of medicine, this had never happened, especially to two complete strangers. But heck, I'm getting off track.

"The message the concierge intended to be delivered was for Jeremiah and I. It was delivered through one of the crystal keycards. I touched it with my finger and a Koiaxan transceiver and beacon materialized above it with a shrill sound not too different from metal grinding against metal. Jeremiah and I were terrified and in awe. The transceiver told us to go somewhere private and distant. Under no circumstances were we to be anywhere public or accessible to anyone other than the two of us when activating the beacon. We went to my place. It was the only place women never went, neighbors rarely knocked, and pets sniffed and walked past in haste. The transceiver told me to clear out as much space in my living room as possible, sarcastically. I say that because it was a spacious and relatively empty apartment. I activated the Koiaxan beacon and the Ojiili box over there appeared through an inter-dimensional vortex. It was twice the size it is now. From what I'm told, it was originally designed to be sixty-four cubic meters.

"You can suspect, after having heard the account of Alan's experience in the temple and witnessing a vortex open before our eyes, Jeremiah and I were overwhelmed. Nevertheless, we could feel God's presence in that moment. We were stronger, braver than we should have been. I could personally feel His will in play. It felt heavy, like the whole world was coming down and we were the only ones in on the secret. He had a plan for us. The plan was for us to make the fight between us, the First People, and them, the Rezarians, a fair one. Without His involvement, we wouldn't have stood a chance against such a formidable foe. How we did so anyway, being such a primitive race with a few toys from an advanced species is beyond me. But nothing is beyond Him. I was the first one to brave the Ojiili box. I figured: I had no working legs. So I lost a hand, what was it? Either I had faith or I didn't.

"When I reached in, the box became transparent. Its contents exposed. The transceiver told me to find an injector. It hung in the air not far from the entrance. I was told to inject myself.

"Now, I'll be honest with you. I hesitated. Lord, forgive me. Despite all the things I heard and saw, part of me hesitated. It was a couple seconds of hesitation, but it felt like an hour. I mean, we were diving into the unknown blind, armed with trust and faith. The unknown is terrifying. Even when it's a good thing, even when it's an eternity of peace and love, you'd be amazed how frightened you are at the edge of it all. I injected myself in the base of my spine, as I was instructed.

"At first, I felt no change, just a pinch in my lower back. Minutes passed. The transceiver said to wait for it. Jeremiah was told to inject himself. He gave me a look. I thought the man was going to croak. We'd been to a few wild parties in our college years. I knew that face. A few too many shots of tequila and he'd make that face. He'd run to the bathroom, and you'd hear at least three flushes within the span of ten minutes. When he came back, he was glassy-eyed and quiet with a glass of water. Party's over, kids. Jeremiah's passed his limit.

"About twenty minutes after my injection, I felt my legs. I hadn't felt my legs in nineteen years. I looked down and wiggled my toes. Jeremiah watched my feet.

He pointed and said, 'Did you just wiggle your toes?' I said, 'Yea. By God, Jerry. I just wiggled my toes.' 'You wiggled your toes,' he repeated, astonished. I wiggled them again and laughed, 'I'm wiggling my toes.' After that, we were running on high. We were laughing and cheering. I was standing within a minute. We turned on the music and started dancing. I couldn't believe I could wiggle my toes. I couldn't believe I was standing. I definitely couldn't believe I was dancing. We were celebrating my legs so much, we forgot about the transceiver and the cube. Eventually, we remembered how it came about and got scared again. We knew this was serious. We knew this cube didn't come here just to give me legs. We knew God didn't pull a man to the stretches of death, have him stand a few feet from Christ himself, deliver a box from another dimension, all just to see a paraplegic dance to Justin Timberlake."

"Who's Justin Timberlake?" Prost asked.

"Oh never you mind. The transceiver told us to come closer. We did. And it showed us the universe. Oh, if only I had the time to tell you what we saw. We saw it through our eyes as though we were there. There was a woman there. Her name was, well, we couldn't understand it so we called her Emma. She told us the history of the universe, the Galactic Cooperative, Iora, the I'ara slash Rezarians, all of it. I saw it all so vividly I could have sworn I was there. I could touch the council members' chairs with my hands. The different species were all unique, beautiful, vastly different and yet similar to us. It was profound.

"Again, time is a funny thing. The experience felt as though we were gone for a week, but it was only for an hour. When we woke up, we knew what had to be done. In the box were the tools necessary to fight the Red. We understood the tactics that needed to be used. We knew their strengths and weaknesses. As time passed, as we prepared for the war coming, we became different people. We told our friends at the hospital about what was to come. They joined us. Because I was a man that could not walk, but then could, I had to be discreet. In the hospital, in my known forums, I was myself, stuck in a wheelchair. Outside of the hospital, when I needed to be on foot, I had to be someone else. I created a new identity for myself, John Rider.

"After a year of preparation, the world began to change. The remaining dark angels fought the Trinitan Champions. And once the dark angels fell, and the entire city of Trinity vanished, the Rezarians revealed themselves to us. Some worshipped them as gods. Others fought. Jeremiah and I led the fight, and we prevailed.

5

John smiled at Cartwright and Prost, his eyes a little brighter. He patted Cartwright lightly on the butt and she got off his thigh. He stood and stretched. "Well, that was story time. Anyone have questions?"

"Only about a million," Prost said with a frown. He looked as though he was contemplating the mysteries of his own existence. "Have you been to this temple?"

"When I was shown the many things, I was given a glimpse of the temple, and the door. Have I been there? Have I walked down the longest hall to the door itself? No. I have not."

Prost nodded, slowly. "And yet, you're absolutely certain it's real."

Cartwright laughed. John did not.

"Have you been to Tibet, Sam?"

Prost shrugged. "I see where you're going to go with that. I just, I'm having a hard time with this. God created a barrier between us and the heavens, and all the heavens have been watching us this whole time? How? Through what technology?"

"Through the Spirit, Sam. It's the same way the old prophets of Earth learned of things. God spoke to them. They saw visions. In the stars, there is one planet visible everywhere in the universe. It is us. God tells them all our stories. Some species have the ability not just to operate in multiple dimensions simultaneously, but to see multiple dimensions simultaneously. They have seen us. And even though the barrier rose so that they could not pass into our world, as technology developed, others could see and hear us, too."

"I've never believed in a God," Prost said. "I'm not sure I can start now."

"So, you're calling me a liar, then," John said.

"No, not exactly," Prost said, defensively.

"Well, I have told you my experience. Before your eyes walks a man that used to be a paraplegic. Before your eyes stands a man that has fought an evil alien species from another world. Behind you is a box transported from another region of space, through a seventh dimensional portal. The truth stands before you. It is all because of God, Sam. And I hope you'll believe that someday soon. His hour is approaching."

Prost frowned. John looked at Pisces and Cartwright.

Cartwright shrugged. "I believe you."

"Do you?" John asked, uncertain.

"Yes, because I remember that day," Cartwright said. "I wasn't supposed to play that day, but I did. We drove from Portland to play and my stupid brother tripped me on my way to the elevator at the sports center. I caught myself and felt pain in my wrist." She felt her wrist. "It throbbed. My mom didn't want me to play on it and was pissed at my brother." She smiled. "I pretended it wasn't as bad as it was so I could play. I would have felt guilty if she drove us all the way there and I didn't play. Before I started, a man, just as you described him, but with a navy blue suit, the seven-shaped cufflinks, and gold tie stopped me on my way to the match. He rubbed my wrist and said, 'You should go to the doctor after the match, but this will do until then.' My wrist felt perfectly fine after that. I thanked him, not thinking much of it, and won the match.

"The pain returned immediately after the match was over. I told my coach and mom about my wrist and they took me to the hospital. They admitted me almost immediately, but when I got in, the doctor that was supposed to examine me got called away. Then, Doctor Gibbs came along with her blond hair and red highlights. She had such a warm and cheerful attitude. I felt comfortable right away. She helped me with my x-rays and pointed out which bones and muscles were which. It was all fascinating. I knew then that I wanted to be a doctor. I wanted to be just like her." She looked at John. "That man that rubbed my wrist, he was an angel, wasn't he?"

John nodded hesitantly. "That's one of my theories. I'm not very clear on his history. I was never told."

"How long have you known?" she asked. "How long have you known that I was that girl?"

John scratched the back of his neck. "Well, I didn't know. Faith did. She told me to hire you. She said I should trust you, even when I didn't."

Prost and Cartwright frowned and exchanged a look. Cartwright said, "I thought you said your wife died before this experiment. How could she tell you to hire me if she was dead?"

Pisces stepped in. "It's complicated. Just like everything else. Remember, just because your physical body dies, it doesn't mean your fifth or seventh-dimensional spirit is dead as well."

Prost threw his hand to his head. "Okay. I'm done. This is too much. Intergalactic wars, evil aliens, angels, a temple with Jesus waiting with open arms, and people talking to people beyond the grave. I'm a scientist, but even this is too much for me." He stood and walked to the door. "I'm going to find out what's going on with our friends. They haven't arrived, yet. I'm kind of curious what's taking them so long." He left.

It was quiet in the library for a moment. Pisces pointed at the door and said, "He's right. Something feels funny. I'm going to head out and see if I can spot them on their way here." John nodded. She left.

Alone stood John and Cartwright. She shook her head at him. "Why didn't you tell me that you were still communicating with your dead wife?"

John smiled. "Do I really need to answer that question?"

She stared at him for a moment, and then shook her head. "It sounds crazy, yes. However, it wouldn't be any crazier than what we've been through." She paused. "It just, it feels weird knowing she's still out there. She's still communicating with you. We're engaged. We, we were kissing. We, I took my shirt off." She paused. "Was she watching us?"

John laughed and shot a hand to his mouth. "It's not like that, just, don't worry about it. She wanted me to start dating other people six years ago. She suggested you. We communicated for quite some time. However, she's, she's gone now." He collected Cartwright's hands. "She's somewhere else now."

"Oh," Cartwright said. She wanted to ask where this somewhere else was located. However, after his explanation of the framework of the universe, she could only imagine where the spirit of his wife ventured. She could be halfway across the galaxy or in another dimension. She hugged him. "Well, enough about her. You have me now." She kissed him.

"You might want to get out here," Pisces transmitted to John.

John separated from Cartwright, extended his hand, and the crystalline sword from the Ojiili box flew to his hand. Its black holder followed. It magnetically attached to his back and he said, "We have to go." Cartwright opened her mouth to ask why but he had already grabbed her hand. They rushed out the main room, down the hall, and to the back door.

Outside and to the west, they could hear explosions and gun fire coming from a distance. John and Pisces exchanged a look and came to the same conclusion. "The cavalry."

Prost said, "Dag. If the Red kill our guests, the other rebels might think this was a trap. They won't send anyone else and certainly won't tell us where they are. This resistance will be squashed."

"Not if I have anything to say about it," John said. He shot into the air and flew to Saint Paul's Dormitory. Pisces flew after him. He opened the window of his room and summoned their two helmets with his mind. The two then flew west towards the rapid weapons fire.

"I wish I could do that," Prost said. He blinked, looked back at the library, and rushed in.

Cartwright said, "Oh no. Don't you go doing what I think you're thinking of doing." She followed.

6

The battle was in a small suburban neighborhood. Beautiful, multi-story houses on both sides of a two-lane road had sunk into their infrastructure. Where there had been freshly cut and tamed green grass, there were fresh crops of blue grass growing rapidly. The once lush and trimmed bushes were brown and decayed bark, but brilliant, florescent orange flowers flourished from the dead roots. Black fuzzy creatures with four big red eyes, eight legs, and big bushy tails scurried throughout lawns, feeding on whatever small animal and human remains there were from the previous tenants.

In the road, the fight continued. Cars were tilted over. Shattered glass surrounded the cars and reflected the flashes of weapons fire. On one side, bearded men in flannel shirts and camouflage pants cursed and fired assault rifles behind overturned cars. Each of them wore oxygen masks with antennas. They yelled old Army commands back and forth to each other and gradually adjusted their positions closer to their targets. One man charged to his left, rolled, got behind a car, and tossed a grenade a clean thirty yards. It exploded on the other side.

On the other side were ten uniformed men positioned behind Union armored trucks. The truck itself had two giant, laser focused and armor-piercing Gatling guns. There was a man at each gun aiming and firing. When the grenade came down, one of the Gatling guns blew. The flannelled men cheered and kept on firing. Two large Rezarians stood in the back with their single eyes open. The veins in their eyes pulsed as they issued telepathic commands. Two Union officers ran from behind their trucks to the right side of the road towards the houses. Two others ran to the left. The remaining six lay on heavy weapons fire.

One of the flannelled men yelled, "They're going to try to flank us! Keep sharp."

"I can't track them. It's too dark," another man yelled.

"Keep sharp and trust your instincts. If God is with

us, He's with us," the senior flannelled man ordered back.

The weapons fire continued. The Gatling gun ripped one of the overturned cars apart and a flannelled man fell to the ground, clutching his stomach.

"Sleeps is down!" a flannelled man yelled.

"Daggit! We gotta take out the other gun," the senior flannelled man yelled while pulling a grenade from a pouch connected to his belt. He flung it in the air and a bullet blew his hand clean off his forearm. He screamed in agony and fell to the ground.

The grenade was caught in the wind and exploded left of the truck. It knocked the uniformed man at the gun off the truck and head-first on to the cement road, but left the gun intact. Another uniformed man ran up to take the gun.

"I'm hit!" the senior flannelled man yelled when he could finally speak through the pain. A flannelled man ran beside him, ripped off his shirt, and wrapped it around the senior man's stub. Seconds later, the shirtless man was gunned down from behind. The senior flannelled man yelled, "We've been flanked!"

Some of the flannelled men turned around and then dove to avoid bullets from both directions. The uniformed men rushed forward from both sides to advance on the opportunity.

The senior flannelled man yelled for the retreat. The weapons fired drowned him out.

John appeared beside him and fired a stream of blue energy from one pistol and rapid red pulses from the other. He hit two men. The others dodged. Pisces appeared to his right and fired a yellow plasma stream that blew the Gatling gun to pieces.

The Red stepped back, aware of the changing dynamics of the battled. Their heads turned right and left, pulsing veins with each new command. The uniformed officers all pulled out grenades and lobbed them at John, Pisces, and the flannelled men.

A flannelled man yelled, "Grenades!" He dove under a car.

John and Pisces raised their hands and the grenades hung in the air. They launched them back towards the uniformed men. The men turned tail and ran, but got caught in the explosions of their own grenades. The flannelled men cheered.

Pisces said, "Freakin stupid guys and grenades. What did I say about grenades?"

John nodded, said, "Yep, I know," and surveyed the battlefield. There were four flannelled men left. One was badly wounded. There were two uniformed men left. They were advancing with weapons raised.

Pisces aimed and shot plasma streams through their chests. They fell flat. There were no more uniformed men remaining. She hissed, connected the plasma pistol to her belt, and shook her hand. "It usually takes more than two rapid blasts for these things to get hot. We're going to have to make some adjustments when we get back."

"We both know you have to fire that in five second increments."

One of the Red launched a plasma ball in their direction. The two saw it and dove right. The plasma ball exploded the overturned car next to them. The senior flannelled man was charred.

The Red charged forward. The ground trembled at their heavy feet. Each Rezarian was twenty feet long, muscular, and wore a green metallic armor John hadn't seen since the war.

"They're soldiers," John said as they approached. "I never thought I'd see soldiers again. Never saw a female one." In the corner of his eye, he saw the flannelled men fleeing. "We might need your plasma pistol."

"Okay, but you're a bit more patient and resistant to plasma burns than I am," Pisces said and traded him the plasma pistol for a standard energy pistol. She reached for the short sword on her back and said, "I'm going to cut through their armor the old-fashioned way."

John frowned. "Careful, love. Don't underestimate them, and don't get cocky. We haven't fought them in years." She nodded and vanished. He peered over his shoulder and saw the Red bearing down on his position. Crystalline visors lowered in front of their eyes, protecting them from weapons fire. "Crap. Eyewear."

The flannelled men hopped from behind a car and laid on solid gunfire on the Red, diverting their attention long enough for John to career around the exploded wreck that was his cover and to their right. He fired a plasma blast to the Rezarian furthest away, aiming for a known weakness in its armor in the joints of the knees. The Rezarian's armor popped open and its knee sizzled. It fell. The other turned sharply and charged at John. It punched him with an arching fist that knocked him twenty yards backward. He hit the ground hard and groaned.

Yellow energy pulses fired rapidly at John from turrets attached to the Rezarian's visor. John rolled to avoid the blasts and hopped to his feet. He fired a return blast that missed wide left and hit the other Rezarian in the visor.

"Oops, darn it," he said while running. "Well, at least I hit somebody." He activated his phase and jumped into the air.

The Rezarian's visor turrets pointed up and fired aimlessly into the air. Pisces appeared behind it, dropped on its back with a glowing white sword in hand, and plunged it into the back of Rezarian's head. Its eye exploded into the visor.

The other Rezarian wailed. It fired energy pulses from its visor turrets and blasted Pisces. She fell back and to the ground.

"Pisces!" John screamed.

The Rezarian turned in his direction and fired a volley of pulses from its turrets. John dodged them and landed a couple yards away. He focused his mind, tightened his fists, and the turrets were ripped from the visor. The crystalline visor fell to the ground. The Rezarian charged at him, its knee restored. John charged forward and removed his blade from its holder. In arm's length, he slid under the Rezarian's swinging fists and plunged the glowing crystalline blade into the bottom of the Rezarian's body, through its armor. He twisted and pushed it into its heart, burning it from the inside.

At first, the Rezarian staggered and attempted one more swiped. John dodged. Then, it sagged and sank.

"Oh, crap," John said and retracted his sword.

It collapsed on top of him.

"Ugh," John moaned. He crawled from under the corpse, got to his feet, and ran to Pisces. The front of her suit had a burning glow from the energy blast. "Pisces," he said. He dropped down and lifted her on his knees. He removed her helmet. She laid peacefully, her eyes shut. He frowned. "Analysis."

His suit displayed: *Subject is undergoing extensive internal organ repair and has initiated auto-standby. Estimated time of revival is one hour.*

John released a sigh of relief and shook his head. He put her helmet back on and lifted her over his shoulder.

The flannelled men approached with their guns to their sides. "It's you. It's really you. Freaking John 'I Believe I Can Fly' Rider," one of them said.

Another flannelled man carried their senior officer. He said, "Man is as tough as an ox. He's still alive, but we have to get him treated as soon as possible."

"We have a medical facility in the church," John said. He scanned the man. "How is this possible? He was hit by a plasma ball."

"Heck if I know," the flannelled man said. "Man's got more cyborg implants than original body parts, though. If Darth Vader, Frankenstein's monster, and Robocop had a freak love child addicted to yogurt, it would be him."

Without any further need for explanation, the three moved as one to a beat-up, bullet hole riddled pick-up truck. It was blue with a lightning bolt painted on each side. They put their injured senior officer in the back with one man. The other two hopped in the front. They zoomed off down the street and to the church.

John collected Pisces' sword and flew behind them.

7

Only seconds after Prost re-entered the library, he froze in place. Cartwright bumped into him and wondered why he'd stopped. Further explanation was unnecessary when she saw what strode further down the hall. It was a man clad in full leather with a long jacket. His face was concealed. Beside him was Jasmine. She wore a tight, pink lace slip and pink slippers. The two entered the main room.

Prost shook his head and whined, "I've got a very bad feeling about this."

"Who was that?" Cartwright asked. "Was it one of our guests?"

"No," Prost said. "I haven't seen him before. But he gives me a bad vibe." He paused. "Jasmine was killing it with that tight slip though, right? Think he brought it?"

Cartwright frowned and jabbed him in the arm. "Can you stop being a perv for one minute? They just went in there where the alien box is located."

"I'm going to investigate," Prost said. He walked the opposite direction of the leather man and towards the secondary entrance to the main room. Cartwright followed. When they made it to the door, Prost barely opened it, leaving a crack for them to look through.

The leather man and Jasmine stood in front of the box talking.

"I've never seen someone's hand freeze and break off of their arm," Prost whispered. "I guess I'm about to."

The leather man stuck his right hand into the box. As expected, it froze mid-way inside. He tugged and tugged, but it wouldn't come out. Jasmine watched with wide eyes. She reached forward to help, but he shook his head. Finally, he shrugged and pressed his wrist. His wrist separated from his hand.

"Well, that was anticlimactic," Prost whispered. "Shouldn't he have screamed or something?" He glanced at Cartwright. She didn't respond. She simply watched.

The leather man reached into his left jacket pocket and pulled out a hand. He attached it to his wrist, waited a minute, and then flexed his fingers.

"What the hell?" Prost whispered. "He has a spare right hand? Who carries around a spare right hand?"

"Jealous?" Cartwright asked with a straight face.

Prost glared at her. "I'll have you know—" He stopped and smirked. "Okay, a little. But it would come in handy in more ways than you'd think."

She thought about it. "I don't even want to know where you're going with that." She pointed at the leather man and whispered, "What's that?"

Prost narrowed his eyes. He saw a small silver cylinder. A grenade? Why? He examined it closer. It had green symbols on it. *The green are antimatter grenades. Never touch the green. Never. They would vaporize us all in an instant,* he remembered. His eyes widened.

"Good God! That's an antimatter grenade," Prost said.

Cartwright shushed him. They listened to the low voices.

"It's a dead man switch," the leather man said with a deep voice that sent chills down their spines.

"What does that mean?" Jasmine asked, emotionless, lifeless.

"It means, as soon as John gets close enough, you let go of this button and he's a dead man," the leather man explained.

She frowned, confused. "Won't I die as well?"

"Of course you will," he said with a smile. "Two birds with one stone. Maybe three if Pisces is with him." He thought about it. "Hell, if you can manage it, take the whole party with you."

Jasmine didn't respond. She simply looked down at the device in her hand, confused.

"Just stay right here," the leather man ordered. "Don't go anywhere and don't get closer than a meter to the Ojiili box." She nodded, slowly. He pointed to a spot on the floor. "Don't pass that spot. You hear me?"

"Yes," she responded.

"Good," the leather man said. He left the main room.

Prost and Cartwright slowly tip-toed down the hall to see if the leather man was leaving. He went through the front entrance and flew away.

"He can fly," Prost whispered.

"Oh really? I just thought he jumped really high," Cartwright said.

Prost glared at Cartwright. "I was just thinking out loud."

"Well, try to keep your private thoughts to yourself," she responded. "Especially the very private ones, Mister Tight Slip."

He flushed. "Hey, it's not my fault she has a banging body. I'm just acknowledging the artistry of her curves."

Cartwright stared at him for a moment and then walked away, back to the secondary entrance of the main room. Prost followed.

When they entered the room, Jasmine turned to them. Her face was void of expression. Her eyes were black, empty, and trembled in her head. Prost never witnessed eye movement like that before. They were vibrating.

Cartwright saw it at the hospital more times in the last year than she felt comfortable acknowledging. The people didn't realize it was happening. It was a phenomena no one had an answer for, but it was affecting more and more patients. Now she had her answer. Eddie had mentioned her eyes. How long was she suffering the same symptom without realizing it?

They drew closer.

Jasmine stiffened. "Don't come any closer," she said. Her voice remained lifeless.

"Hypnosis?" Cartwright asked.

"Worse," Prost said. "Well, maybe part hypnosis and part mind control. Probably by our leather clad friend." He stepped just a bit closer.

Jasmine raised the grenade with her finger tightly clinched on the dead man button, and said, "I said, 'don't come any closer.'"

Cartwright stopped. Prost stepped a few steps closer. "Sam."

"Okay," Prost said. He stopped. "But I don't think that was meant for me. Was it?"

"No," Jasmine responded. She lowered the grenade. "Not yet."

"Yet, okay, I can live with that," Prost said. "While we're waiting, mind if I ask you a few questions?" He didn't get a response. He nodded. "I'll take that as a yes. Are you Jasmine? Is that Jasmine in there?"

"I am Jasmine," she responded.

"And who was that man?" Prost asked. "The man in the leather. What's his name?"

Jasmine shrugged.

Prost nodded. "It was probably 'need to know', right? He needed you, and you didn't need to know why or who he was." She didn't respond. "Where'd you get that pink slip? You're looking sexy."

"Sam, what is wrong with you?" Cartwright asked and frowned. "She's hypnotized."

"I can't think of a better time to ask a woman an honest question."

Jasmine cracked the slightest smile.

"Look at that, she smiled," Prost said. He grinned. "My dad did a study on involuntary mind control. The person is still in there. If you can illicit the right emotions or thoughts, or even the right state of mind, they can take control."

"Well, just, don't illicit the wrong emotions, or you might get us blown up," Cartwright said.

Prost looked at Cartwright. "Oh, we wouldn't get blown up. That's an antimatter grenade. We'd be vaporized instantly, annihilated."

Cartwright backed away and bumped against the table. "Oh yes, that would be so much better." She turned around and noticed an injector on the table. John used it to install the cognitive implant devices. She got an idea.

"So, Jasmine," Prost said while reaching into his left pocket. "Do you like weed?"

Cartwright's head shot up in time to see him pull out

a plastic bag a quarter full of dark leaves. "What the, Sam, how long have you had that?"

"Wouldn't you like to know," Prost said. "I'm not sharing with you."

She flushed. "I wouldn't dream of it. Did you take that to work with you? I've been trying to figure out for weeks which person was smoking with the staff in the morning. It's not permitted on work premises."

"Really, Fran?" Prost asked. "You're giving me a lecture on my work ethic right now?"

Cartwright nibbled her lip and reluctantly returned her attention to the injector.

Believe it or not, Jasmine's smile widened.

"Oh look at that," Prost said. "Unlike somebody, she likes weed." Prost reached in his pocket again and pulled out a couple rollers. He took his time wrapping the leaves, making sure it was extra stuffed and fat. Then, he sealed two joints and held them in front of Jasmine. "Look at that. It's time for sunshine."

Jasmine's eyes vibrated rapidly. Her eyes changed colors, excited.

"That's my girl," Prost said. "Can we keep her this way?" Cartwright refused to acknowledge that question with an answer. He shrugged. "Okay." He pulled out a lighter, sparked a flame, and puffed on one of the joints until it was lit. He blew out a plume of smoke and released a sigh of relief. "Baby, are you ready for this?"

Jasmine didn't respond. She simply watched him. Her eyes were focused and brighter, trained on him. Prost slowly stepped closer to her with the joint stretched out. She didn't flinch as he tucked it into her mouth. His eyes and hands never moved to the grenade. She puffed.

"I'm terrified as to the outcome of this endeavor," Cartwright chimed in from the back. Her hands trembled. She held the injector with both hands.

Prost turned around. "You need to trust my delinquency. There's a method to my madness."

Jasmine puffed a few more times and released plumes of smoke through her teeth. Prost watched her eyes. Saw them gradually vibrate less and less. "Just keep on puffing, darling," he whispered.

Twenty minutes and four joints later, Jasmine's eyes no longer vibrated. They were glassed over. She swayed.

"She's going to let go of the grenade, you idiot!" Cartwright cried out. "We're about to die!"

"Crap," Prost said. He reached out and placed his finger over Jasmine's finger.

The moment he did that, something inside her came to life again. Her eyes were red. Her face contorted into anger. Cartwright ran forward and punched the injector into the back of Jasmine's neck. There was a sharp hiss. Jasmine grimaced and tried to pull her hand from the grenade. Both Cartwright and Prost's hands mashed on her hand and kept her fingers locked on the dead man switch.

Jasmine launched her free fist into Prost's groin. He screamed and grappled for his crotch, but Cartwright's hands locked on both his and Jasmine's. He held himself with one hand. Jasmine swung a fist at Cartwright. Cartwright dodged and threw her head forward into Jasmine's face. Blood poured from Jasmine's nose. She fell back.

Both Cartwright and Prost kept her from falling, but instead pulled her back up. Cartwright eyed the Ojiili box and cried out, "The box, Sam! Push her to the box!" He nodded and the two used their weight to force Jasmine towards the box.

Jasmine struggled to pull all her weight away from them, twisted, and then swung a fist to the side of Cartwright's head. Stars exploded in Cartwright's vision and she faltered, releasing her grip. Another fist flew into Prost's jaw. He cried out and fell with a twist, pulling Jasmine down with him.

The two fell with their limbs tangled. The grenade popped out of Jasmine's hand and bounced in front of the Ojiili box.

Prost closed his eyes and braced himself for the inevitable vaporization. Part of him wondered if he'd be standing outside of a door, just as John implied he might. Would he be accepted? Hell, no. Where did that leave him? The dark end of the hall?

"Perhaps, but you still have time," a whisper implied. He had never heard that voice before.

Wait. He still had time? Prost looked up. Nothing happened. He turned to Cartwright. She gawped at the grenade. He said, "Well, she smoked my entire bag of weed and it was a dud."

"No," John said as he rushed down to the Ojiili box. "It wasn't a dud."

Prost and Cartwright spun around in surprise. How long had he been there?

"The box disables all explosive devices armed within a two meter radius, even antimatter grenades," John said. He noticed the dark-skinned hand stuck inside the box. "Good thing for us I extended the range after we did inventory. I just had a feeling."

Prost stood and looked down at Jasmine. She was unconscious.

Cartwright staggered to John and hugged him. He hugged her back, kissed her, and then released her. He removed the hand from the Ojiili box, examined it, and sighed.

"You recognize that hand, don't you?" Prost asked. He had a feeling as to whose it might be, but he didn't want to say it. He needed to hear it from John.

John nodded. "Yes. It's the hand of an old friend. Looks like he's not dead after all."

Prost scratched his head and pointed at the grenade on the floor. "Where'd he get the grenade?"

"That grenade is from the catalyst chamber," John said. "It's the one Pisces set to explode before we ran. He was the one who stopped it. He brought it here." He sighed and looked at Prost and Cartwright. "This is bad. This is very bad."

8

Pisces woke up and saw John sitting at the foot of her bed. She was in the medical center, as if it was of much use to her. She clutched her chest for a moment and sighed.

"Yep. You took a blast straight to the chest, love," John said while pointing to her chest. "That was too close."

She nodded in agreement. "I'm not arguing with you there. Why didn't we grab our armored suits first?"

John smiled. "Instinct, I suppose. We're jumping in right where we left off, but forgetting the important things. We can't be reckless anymore. We have to get ourselves together." He sighed and looked down.

Pisces watched him. "What is it?"

"The man in the leather was here, at the library," John explained.

Pisces leaned forward. "What? Is everyone okay?"

John nodded. "Yes, surprisingly. The moment we left, he went in with Jasmine. She was being controlled by a very strong mental link. I'm guessing she was more vulnerable than the others because she's a mutant and not on medication."

"It works one way or the other," Pisces said, aware of some that were resistant and others who weren't.

Opposite of their expectations, Jasmine was clearly the latter.

"He gave her an antimatter grenade to destroy the box and us when we returned."

Pisces frowned. "I don't understand. How did he get an antimatter grenade? Surely he didn't get one from the box."

John shook his head. "He got it from us, when we were in the catalyst chamber."

"Oh," Pisces said. It clicked. "That's why it didn't go off. He disabled it. How'd he get the override code?"

John rubbed his face and established eye contact. "Because it's Jeremiah."

"What?!" Pisces blurted. She hopped out of bed, staggered, and then straightened. "I don't believe it. Where is he? I have to see it for myself."

"He's gone," John said. He hadn't moved from his spot at the end of her bed. "Once he gave her the antimatter grenade, he left. No doubt, he watched from a distance, waiting for the building to tremble."

Pisces grabbed her belt and connected it around her hip. "We're not safe here, are we? No doubt he's going to bring the Red here. He must have followed us after we left your place."

John nodded. "No doubt." He reached behind him and came back with a thawing, disembodied right hand. "This is his."

"What the!?" Pisces yelled. She backed away and stared at the hand. "Why do you have his hand?"

John stood and lay the hand down on a metal tray. "He left it in the Ojiili box. Apparently, he brought a backup hand. My immediate conclusion is that he was testing to see if he was still an owner. If he was, we probably would have come back to squat. He would have taken everything and left us a big surprise when we came to investigate."

Pisces nodded. "Wasn't it Levi who suggested you remove his father from the list?"

John nodded back. "Yes. He said, 'I see no logical reason to keep my father registered. He's not coming back.'"

"Right," Pisces scoffed. "The kid jinxed us."

John laughed. "If that existed, yes, we could claim that. He also saved our lives." He looked at the hand and thought. "If we ever get in contact with Levi and Abbey, I can't tell him about this. It would be too much for him."

"For once, when it comes to secrecy, we agree unanimously," Pisces said.

Two bearded men in flannel walked past her room talking, wishing they brought a few patties and their grill.

"Those are some brave men," John said.

Pisces nodded. "How many survived?"

"Four," John said. "More are coming. They sent some pretty elaborate coded messages to their compatriots. We can expect about a hundred armed men and women when they're all here."

"Think it'll be enough," Pisces asked. She walked to the door and waved him on.

John shrugged. "I don't know." He followed her out the door. "I guess we'll see. We have a lot of work ahead of us."

The two exited the medical center. They peered outside the far back glass door and into the darkness. John wondered if his friend Jeremiah was out there. How was he alive? What was his state of mind? Why was he working for the enemy? What was he planning next?

Leaving the antimatter grenade was a clear message. Jeremiah was coming for him, and John couldn't use his old tricks. Not this time. He had to think outside of the box. Jeremiah was formidable. He was a great ally and terrible enemy. Was John going to be able to pull back the fog of years and beat his old friend?

He repeated himself. "I guess we'll see."

They stood silently, thinking.

"It's going to be fine, John."

"Is it?"

Pisces saw the worry in his eyes and quoted, "Fear thou not; for I am with thee. Be not dismayed; for I am thy God."

John smiled, joined in, and together they said, "I will strengthen thee. I will help thee. I will uphold thee with the right hand of my righteousness. Behold, all they that were incensed against thee shall be ashamed and confounded. They shall be as nothing; and they that strive with thee shall perish. Thou shalt seek them, and shalt not find them, even them that contended with thee: they that war against thee shall be as nothing, and as a thing of nought. For I, the Lord thy God, will hold thy right hand, saying unto thee: 'Fear not; I will help thee.'"

CHAPTER SEVEN
THE ALEXIS

THE ALEXIS WAS IMPECCABLY CLEAN and contemporary. It was lit with bright, round Japanese lanterns that hung on purple flecked decorative string from tall cream ceilings. There wasn't a trace of dust or dirt in the place. It had polished, dark chocolate wood flooring, cream walls and marble countertops. There were tall, potted plants at every corner. On the floor, at the entrance, was a cream welcome mat with purple lettering that said "Welcome to Alexis". Straight ahead was a rectangular sign that said the same thing in smaller letters and included arrowed directions to the lobby, bar/restaurant, elevator/stairs, restrooms, and the front office. To the left was the bar/restaurant. To the right were the lobby, restrooms, and front office. Straight ahead was the elevator and stairs.

To the immediate right was the front desk counter. Behind the marble was a brown eyed man with a streak of gray in his slick black hair. He wore a black suit, skinny cream tie, and crimson shirt with sparkling gold cufflinks. He was pale. White copy paper pale. Levi's first thought was that the man was anemic until he remembered seeing the small green veins in the man's neck. He was infected by one of the mutants and required regular injections to prevent his blood from turning pure green.

At the sight of his new guests, the man revealed a set of large, perfect sparkling teeth in his narrow lipped mouth. His mouth was strangely wide for his thin, narrow face. He opened his arms and said, "Welcome to the Alexis. I am Alexis." He fluttered his eyes and pointed his small hands at himself. "I'm happy to have you, especially considering the news. I won't share it if you haven't heard it. And if you've heard it, I highly doubt you want to hear it again. Come on over. Come, come my darlings." He waved Levi and Violet over to his counter with both hands. "Let's get you settled in, yes?"

"Yes," Levi said and reached for Violet's hand. She froze and stared at the hand as though she'd never held one before. Then she smiled and latched on. He had to admit, it felt good holding her hand, even if he was wearing gloves. "You should have my name and the payment type on file. I've been in and out of this hotel on and off traveling to and from. It's under Malachi Hiatt."

Violet shot a glance at Levi.

"Oh, I know who you are," Alexis said and smiled. "You're the darling man who always keeps his helmet on. I remember." He looked down at his computer and started to type. He typed for a full two minutes before sneaking a quick look at Levi. He smiled again and looked down.

It took every ounce of effort to not cringe at that smile. The man was a creep. He felt it in his bones, always felt that way. He knew what went on in the hotel. It was a hub for drug manufacturing and distribution, prostitution, sex slavery, and weapons smuggling. This man was in the thick of it. Levi wanted to avoid the place like a bullet, but a man had to set his head down somewhere when he got off of the road. This was the only lodging in Kentucky. (Actually, it was the only lodging in the Quarantine Zone, since Levi took it upon himself to burn down the motel in West Virginia.)

Alexis looked up again, smiled at Violet (She shot a side-glance to Levi and tightened her grip on his hand), and looked back down at the screen. When he was finished, he said, "Voila. What I have here will definitely please the two of you, yes?"

Levi and Violet glanced at each other and shrugged.

"Yes, good," Alexis said. "I have the deluxe honeymoon suite with romantic, cherry-scented candles, a bottle of wine, and of course, as you seem to request quite often Mister Hiatt, an especially large cushioned chair for your canine companion. Though, for her sake, I hope you didn't bring him this time. A wagging dog in the corner sure takes away the mood of the moment, unless it's me of course." He giggled. He put the tip of his hand to his mouth and said, "Oh dear me."

Levi pressed his hand against the front of his helmet and shook his head.

Violet hugged Levi's arm and said, "That sounds perfect. We'll take it." He glared at her and she glared right back. "It's fine."

"Tell me something," Alexis said. "Is he as pretty under that helmet as I've imagined him to be?"

Violet looked at Levi, smiled, and nodded. "Yes. He's gorgeous."

Alexis tittered and clapped his hands. "Fantastic! I knew it." He smiled at Levi.

At that, Levi extended his hand, palm up, and cleared his throat. "The keys, sir?"

"Of course, of course," Alexis said and pouted his lips. He grabbed two thin metal cards and waved them in front of the computer. Then, he handed the cards, one each, to Levi and Violet. "Impatient as always, Mister Hiatt; but in this case, I can see why. You're both very delectable. I'm quite certain you're ready to get upstairs and, well, don't let me stop you." He winked at Violet and waved. "Room seven-thirteen. Off you go."

The two walked away to the elevator trading glances at each other. As they reached the elevator and called it to the main floor, Levi looked back at the front desk. Alexis stared, watched them with a wide smile on his face. His expression didn't change. He didn't blink. He just watched them.

As they entered the elevator, and the elevator doors closed, Levi released a sigh and pressed the number seven. The elevator started its ascent. Violet asked. "What was with that guy?"

"A great multitude of things, so stay away from him if you can," Levi said. Violet rapidly nodded her head. "He doesn't look like it, but he's actually a very dangerous man."

Violet laughed. "Doesn't look like it? He looks pretty dangerous, alright. I haven't seen a mouth like that since that evil clown, Happy the Destroyer. His mouth is so big; he could probably fit my entire head in it."

Levi snickered and shook his head. "He called us *delectable*. I'd be afraid he'd try."

"Yes. The way he was smiling at us, I'm sure he would," she cringed. "What's with the alias, Malachi? It seems like you guys have more names than I do panties."

"I suppose that depends on how many panties you brought with you," Levi said with a smile.

Violet's jaw dropped. She gawked at him. "Was that a joke or an inquiry? Because, if you really want to know." She bumped him with her elbow and winked.

Levi opened and closed his mouth, but no words

came out. He was glad she couldn't see his expression through his helmet. There was a ding as they reached the seventh floor.

"Saved by the bell," Violet flirted. "You going to take that helmet off at some point?"

"Yes, I will. When we're in the room," Levi said and pointed at the top of the elevator. "They have cameras in the elevator and hallways."

The elevator door opened. Levi leaned his head out and checked both ends of the lantern lit hall for people. They were empty, with the exception of a maid collecting dirty towels off the purple and cream carpeted floor outside of two rooms. A sign ahead said rooms seven-hundred through seven-ten were to the left, rooms seven-eleven through seven-twenty to the right. He reached for Violet's hand and led her to the right. "There are a few cameras in the room, too. However, I'll deactivate those."

Violet gasped. "What?" Levi nodded. "Really?" Levi nodded again. "I just, no. They do not record people in their rooms."

"They sure do. I'm sure they record a lot of nefarious and salacious activity, too."

Violet frowned. "Well that explains why he was smiling at us so much. Perhaps he was hoping to get a little show. The little pecker was probably getting a little hard on behind the counter just thinking about it. What a creep."

Levi nodded. "Yep."

"He seemed more interested in looking at you than me, Levi."

Levi didn't say anything. He walked to the room, lifted his key to the door slot, and watched it work its magic. The door clicked. He pushed it open.

"Wow!" Violet exclaimed as she entered and explored

the suite. "I love it."

It was a modest sized room, Levi agreed. To the left of the entrance was a full bathroom with marble counters, a bathtub and shower, and toilet with a bidet. To the right were a living and dining room, and full kitchen, with a refrigerator, microwave, and stove. The living room space had a plough cream couch—it was long and deep enough to fit four people comfortably and work as a second bed—coffee table, flat-screen television, and two cream fluffy side chairs. The dining room space had a long, cherry oak table and six chairs. Straight ahead was the bedroom. It had a heart-shaped king size bed, cherry oak television stand with a fifty-inch flat-screen television, walk-in closet, and two cherry oak three-drawer dressers.

"Creepy as he may be, that guy hooked us up. It's almost like an apartment," Violet continued. She moved from room to room, gawking. Levi scanned the room with indicators from his helmet and located three well-hidden listening devices and four cameras. He covered the cameras and removed the listening devices from their power sources. He put them in the ice bucket and set it outside of the door. "Isn't it like an apartment?"

It took one more scan of the suite before Levi took off his helmet and acknowledged her. "These used to be apartments."

She responded with a curious "Oh?" while looking through the restaurant's menu she'd pulled from the dining table. She could feel an appetite coming and didn't want to eat another boxed lunch they'd need later on in their trip.

Levi nodded. "Mister Blake converted the building into a hotel about fourteen years ago. Said he was taking a risk, but considering the complete lack of options for lodging in the trade and transport routes, he was looking to have a major payoff. Looks like he was right."

"Mister Blake? Is that Alexis?"

"Umm. Yes and no. Calvin Blake was the original owner. Alexis Blake was his," he used air quotes, "partner. Calvin died from radiation exposure, and Alexis inherited the business."

There was a moment of silence. They looked at each other. This was the first time they were alone together since Levi left Virginia.

"His partner?" Violet asked while setting the menu on the fluffy chair. "Not business partner, but partner-partner."

"That is correct."

Violet nodded and stepped to within a few inches of Levi. "Ah. I see." She smiled. "Explains why he was watching you so closely. He's searching for someone to pass the business on to."

Levi rolled his eyes. "Please."

Violet reached up and wrapped her arms around Levi's neck. She pressed herself against him and leaned in for a kiss with pleading eyes. He didn't deny her. Their lips met. He wrapped his arms around her and pulled her in. They held in a long embrace. His full lips wrapped around hers. He sucked on her lower lip. Their tongues lightly sparred and flicked at each other. His hands slid down to her butt and gave her a light squeeze. She smiled in between kisses, flushed. He kissed her cheek, her jaw, her neck, and then kiss back to her lips.

They adjusted themselves around the fluffy chair and shuffled as one unit to the couch. Levi removed his belt and sat on the deep seated couch. Violet mounted his lap. His hands came up to the back of her head, and he pulled her in for more kisses.

"Yes," Violet whispered. She playfully nibbled on his upper lip and smiled. Then, she leaned back and lost her small, blue jean jacket. She reached to pull off her black studded tank top, (*"Stop, Levi,"* a whisper came) but Levi moved his hands to hers and said, "Wait."

Violet kissed him again, and whispered, "Why?"

"Don't do it," the whisper warned. *"Not with her."*

"We can't," Levi whispered back.

They continued to kiss, and in-between kisses, Violet whispered, "Yes we can." She pressed herself against him. Both of them could feel how excited the other was.

"We shouldn't."

"Why not?" Violet asked and kissed him again. She massaged his chest with her stimulating fingertips.

"Deny the flesh," the whisper continued.

Levi broke the kiss and said, "We're not married, Vy." He closed his eyes and exhaled as she continued to rub his chest. "We're not even an item."

Violet pressed her chest against him, her lips against his. She said, "We should be an item, Levi. It's the only thing I've wanted since before our first kiss. When I came to visit you, and the Browns, I wanted to see you more than anyone else. I dreamed about you. You dreamed about us running away together. Remember?" She kissed his lower lip. "We would have been a couple if you hadn't moved away. You and I both know that. There's nothing stopping us now."

She's right, Levi thought. He looked back on how divided he was about Abbey, the person he loved and protected since he could remember, and Violet, the new girl who, despite her acne and braces, was beautiful, funny, and strong. Violet swept him away. Her family was dysfunctional; but she was uncomplicated. Things were always fun with her. He didn't have to compromise and argue with her on the simplest issues like he had to with Abbey. Things were easier with Violet. She went along with whatever he wanted to do, and if she wanted to do something, he didn't have a problem doing it. They were great friends. He'd come to appreciate her. How had he forgotten how close they were? How had he forgotten her once he moved to Washington?

Oh, he thought as he remembered.

After the move, he became terribly homesick and ordered the nanotech to suppress his memories of Violet.

Nanotech, restore my memories of Violet, he thought.

"Upon your request, select memories and their attached emotions will resurface," Levi's nanotech responded to his request. *"Warning. Restoring repressed memories may cause temporary confusion and emotional instability. Are you certain you would like to restore them?"*

Yes, yes, I am certain, he thought. He was instantly overwhelmed with a rush of memories and emotions.

While Levi stared off into space, Violet took that opportunity to remove her tank top, revealing her pert breasts tucked in a lightly lined black and pink bra, and her abs.

Levi's train of thought returned to Violet and her body. He whispered, "Wow."

She smiled, blushed, and said, "Thanks." She reached down to undo his pants. She stopped. There was no lining separating shirt from pants. It was a one-piece. "Umm, there's no, is this a jumpsuit?"

"It's so much more than a jumpsuit, Vy," Levi said and spread out his arms. The black suit opened as if it had a seamless, wireless zipper from his neck to his waist, and chest to his hands, and peeled away from him. It fell behind him, on its own, revealing his toned, muscled physique. Violet gaped at his suit for a moment, frozen. He said, "It's my favorite outfit. It's the only one that takes itself off with a thought."

"Stop," the whisper urged.

Violet rested her hands on his chest. Levi exhaled at the feel of her hand on his skin. They kissed and pressed their bodies against each other, enjoying the feel of the other's skin. Violet pulled away and smiled. "So, we're an item, right? You and me? Lee and Vy? Boyfriend and girlfriend?"

"No," the whisper said.

Levi weighed on that, and realized, if they weren't an item, they would have to stop immediately. He didn't want to stop. Violet felt good. She tasted good. She looked good. And she wanted him. She cared for him. He cared for her. (*"No,"* the whisper repeated.) Did he care for her more than Abbey? He didn't know. He honestly loved both of them. He had in the past and remembered the suffering of uncertainty after Abbey kissed him. But he wasn't Jeremy. He wasn't going to try to have both of them. Once he chose one, that would be it. There was no going from one to the other. If he said yes to Violet, it meant no to Abbey. If he said no to Violet (*"Say 'no',"* the whisper insisted), it would hurt her, and might mean yes to Abbey. That was assuming Abbey wanted to be with him. The only time she ever seemed to want him was when he was around Violet. That wasn't enough. But what if she did love him?

You have a beautiful, young woman on top of you who loves you and has wanted to be with you for years. Ever since this trip has started, she's done nothing but seek out your trust. What more could you ask for? Levi questioned himself.

"Well?" Violet asked and kissed his neck.

"No, Levi, no," the whisper demanded.

"Yes," Levi said reluctantly. Having said it, and heard the word leave his lips, he smiled. He cupped her face and gently kissed her. "We're an item."

"We shall see," the whisper resigned.

Violet brightened. Her eyes had a light he hadn't seen

in years. Her smile was so wide she could have rivaled the lunatic at the front desk. "You and me. Lee and Vy?" she confirmed. When they first met, Violet pointed out that Levi's name was the combination of their nicknames. Lee-Vy.

"You and me, Lee and Vy," Levi repeated.

At that, Violet plucked away her bra and revealed herself. Levi reached to touch her and there was a knock at the door. The two froze. Their eyes widened with shock. They heard Abbey's voice, and Violet scrambled to put her clothes back on.

2

Two minutes after Levi left, Abbey opened her eyes and stared at the interior lining of the car. While the seats were the softest black leather she'd ever felt in her life (Part of her wondered if it was real leather), the rest of the interior lining was smooth black metal, with black carpeted mats on the floor. It was all black. Drab. It had no color. No personality. Of all the things to think about, why that came to her mind, she did not know. However, now it bugged her.

"You're awake. Good," Jared said to her. He hovered over her. His hot breath smelled of its usual strong mint. She'd always appreciated her father for training Jared to eat natural mint and chew on breath mints. Apparently, he'd also trained him to talk.

Not trained. He learned how to talk, a thought came to her. *Just like you.*

"So, you can talk." It was a statement. Not a question. "Somehow, part of me always suspected it. Your interactions with my father and Levi were too easy. You didn't bark or howl. You just walked up and they knew exactly what you wanted. I never understood; but I always felt left out. A girl among boys, and even the wolf was in on the inside jokes. For a while, I thought it was just a guy thing."

Jared nodded and smiled. "You don't know how long I've been waiting to have a conversation with you, or to ask you to be quiet and let me sleep." He laughed. She did as well and remembered the days she used to catch him sleeping and hop or stomp at him in an effort to startle him. She thought his statement and her memory were great precursors to the series of questions she wanted to ask him.

"Jared, how are you capable of speaking?"

"I have the same nanotech that you do. They were installed not long after my birth and preprogrammed to stimulate higher brain functions, among other improvements. Speech came naturally after spending time with our family. Your father made it very clear to me from the beginning that I was unique, capable of doing more than any other within my species, and that it had to remain a secret."

"Of course. All of these secrets. This secret life you, my father, and Levi had. I surmise that this is just the beginning of my tumble down the rabbit hole." She sighed. "How deep does it go? How far beyond the surface is reality?"

It took a moment for Jared to think about her response, and then he said, "Deep." He turned his attention to the wall that barricaded the parking lot. She looked around and straightened herself. "Where are we anyway? Where is everyone?"

His eyes fixed on the wall, Jared said, "You've missed a lot. After you stormed off and then fell unconscious, for which I am truly sorry, as that was my doing, Levi and Jeremy had a physical altercation."

Abbey gasped. "What? What happened?"

"Jeremy was trying to steal our special item while Levi

and I were distracted by your storming away. Once you were incapacitated—"

"Wait! How did you knock me unconscious? We weren't even close enough for you to touch me."

Jared sighed. "I suppose I'll have to grow accustomed to you interrupting me." Abbey nodded and mimed zipping her mouth shut and putting the key in her pocket. He nodded and continued. "I have the ability to put people to sleep with my mind. It's a very passive, non-aggressive ability to avoid direct confrontation, since the alternative for a wolf would be to slash them with my claws and cause bleeding and possibly death. It's primarily focused on canines and human beings, since I'm more familiar with their brain chemistry. It would be a little more complicated against a Rezarian or mutant. Mutant brain abnormalities make some immune."

When she was sure he was finished, Abbey said, "That's pretty cool. Maybe I should add that to my list of super powers I want the nanotech to install." Jared chuckled at that and repeated the word "super powers". That was what Levi called it when he was a kid. She smiled and said, "Well, that's what they are. You guys are mock super heroes. You even have matching costumes. Though, your taste is questionable. I could help with that."

"No, thank you. We prefer discretion."

"Right. Sneaking around. Hopping out of moving vehicles. Saving the world in the shadows." She smiled. They looked at each other. "So, you were saying that Levi and Jeremy fought."

"Yes. Once you were incapacitated, Levi saw that Jeremy was trying to pry open the storage unit in-between the driver's and passenger seats. It was, of course, a pointless endeavor. Levi pulled him away from the car. There was a very brief scuffle between the two."

Jared smiled at that. "Levi won, of course. It was honestly an unfair fight. It was like the last scene of *Superman Two* when Clark Kent walked into the bar and beat up the bully who beat him up while he had no powers." Abbey nodded and said she remembered that scene. She loved how lively a conversationalist Jared was and regretted missing out on years of his companionship. "Anyway, we left Jeremy in the middle of the interstate with his bag and drove into the sunset. Eventually, it became pitch dark and we stopped here, at the Alexis Hotel." He pointed at the building.

"I see," Abbey said. She felt deep sorrow that she hadn't had a chance to say goodbye to Jeremy. Even though he was a sorry sack of crap for cheating on her with her friend and two random girls in a public bathroom, she cared for him. The two secretly dated for three months. She needed some kind of closure, an official breakup. "And where are Levi and Violet?"

Jared nodded towards the hotel. "They went inside to get a room for us."

"Or for them, if Violet has her way," Abbey said. "You should have gone with them."

"Interesting," Jared said. He turned his attention back to the wall, again. She wondered what he meant by "interesting". And what was he looking at? "I stayed behind to keep an eye on you. I suspected you would wake up with a number of questions, especially after what I did to you and after your father gave you instructions in your sleep."

"How did you know about my dream?" She stopped. Of course, he knew. They knew everything. "Whatever it was he wanted me to learn, I don't think it worked. I asked the nanotech to make me strong like Levi. I wanted it to make me capable of flying. But I don't feel any differently." She thought about that for a moment and balled and un-balled her fists. "Well, I do feel rested. I have a lot more energy. Though, I'm sure that's because of the nap I had. I think I've had a good six hours of sleep today."

Jared shot a look at Abbey. "Did you ask your father what made Levi stronger or how he was capable of flying?"

Ding dong, dummy, Abbey scolded herself. That would have helped. Then again, her father was vague. Once she asked for what she wanted, he didn't offer any explanations. He just sent her off on her way to stumble in the dark.

"Correction," her nanotech said. *"You were asked if you wanted an overview of the changes and you declined. The overview was the offered explanation."*

Abbey frowned.

"I'll take that as a no," Jared said. He sighed. "While my first bit of advice would be to ask questions, I realize that you've been shot down every time you asked them."

"You speak the truth," Abbey said.

Jared stared her straight in the eyes. "Listen, Abigail. On behalf of myself, your father, and Levi, I apologize for the way you have been treated. Your father raised you to always ask questions and seek out knowledge. Yet, you've been asking a lot of questions and not getting many answers. We've kept too much from you. We didn't think you were mature enough for the responsibility that comes with this knowledge. You listened when you wanted to listen. You acted when you wanted to act. You didn't follow instructions well. That is why your father wanted you to speak to me. He told me he'd tell you to speak to me. Once you spoke to me, you would be activated. Since you did not speak to me, I had to speak to you."

There was a silence as Abbey digested *some* of what he

said. She remembered the question Levi asked her father in the beginning of their crazy adventure. When he arrived to take her to Montana, he'd asked if she was active. That was what he was talking about. He wanted to know if she was aware of their secret life and capable of doing the wonderful things their nanotech allowed them. Her father said no. She only wished her father trusted her. Did she deserve that trust? Yes. Did he trust her? No. How would he know until he gave her a chance?

What if he did?

"I am going to answer the two questions you didn't ask."

Abbey nodded. "Okay."

"Levi is stronger because his molecular density has increased by a significant percentage. Because of your request, yours has as well. Though, not to his degree until you've had something substantial to eat. Levi can fly thanks to telekinesis. The nanotech have mapped and modified his brain to utilize that and other uncharted human potential. Soon, with mental discipline and practice, you'll be able to do the same, and many other things.

"I recognized that you were changing when the nanotech in your body created an electromagnetic shell around your body and absorbed photons. I could feel the vibrations of their collective energy at work. I witnessed alterations in your body chemistry. You need more energy to complete the process."

Abbey shrugged. "Like I said, I honestly don't feel that different. A little rested. Mostly hungry. I could eat a horse." She remembered the fries from the deli and wished she'd grabbed them on her way out.

"You're sitting inside the car, Abbey. Once we get moving, you'll feel the difference. In fact, let's get going. I should have heard from Levi by now."

Jared reached below the back seat, opened a compartment she wasn't aware existed, and grabbed his helmet. It always struck her as odd that her wolfdog had paws that expanded on command and looked like little padded monkey hands. They said he was genetically enhanced, but now it all made more sense. It also made sense how and why he was borrowing books from her father's library. Her father said Jared liked them, and wouldn't damage them. She'd just shrugged it off and thought he liked the smell of them. Perhaps she was exercising willful ignorance to all of the blatantly obvious signs of abnormality in her pet's behavior. On the other hand, there weren't too many dogs or wolves around for comparison.

In the days to come, Abbey suspected she'd recognize a lot of oddities she should have noticed.

"Here, take this," Jared said before passing her folded black clothing sealed in plastic. It looked factory sealed.

"What is this?" Abbey asked.

Jared looked at it, smiled, and said. "The last suit you'll ever wear."

At first, Abbey frowned, not liking the connotations. Then, she thought she'd heard that line before. She searched her memory, shook her head, and smiled. Trading movie lines was probably a regular thing for him and Levi. "Okay, Agent K."

"This too." Jared reached down again and pulled out a plastic sealed black helmet. On its top was the letter 'A' painted in three slim streaks of pink. Abbey smiled, ripped through the package, and held the helmet up for examination. Black glass front. She tried it on. The helmet was thin, but its frame perfectly contoured to her head.

"Get dressed, and be quick," Jared said and hopped in the front seat. There was a roughness and sense of urgency in his voice. For a moment, he sounded like her father. He said the same words in the same way. She felt annoyed, nostalgic, and bereaved simultaneously. She took off the helmet and ripped open the plastic seal of the clothing. In the fold of the one-piece was a thin, black metallic belt with an oval crystalline head and glowing dot at its center.

The folded clothing was a one-piece similar to what Levi and Jared wore. It was an interesting material. It was a thin metallic material, yet soft as silk. Just from observation, she knew it was exactly her size. Only, there was no sign of a zipper.

As if it read Abbey's mind, it opened in the back, down the middle, and separated from the lower half. She gasped. There were no zipper teeth. The fabric simply separated on its own.

"Be quick, Abbey," Jared shot back again, staring intently at the wall. "I'll explain the suit on the way. We have to get moving, now."

It was a curious remark. Abbey wanted to know why he was suddenly in a hurry *(And what was he looking at?)*, but for once, she was sure she'd get answers whether or not she asked for them. She stripped down to her bra and panties and slipped into the suit. It fit like a glove from neck to toe and felt as smooth as Egyptian cotton against her skin. The back sealed on its own. The top connected to the bottom. She felt the material harden and contour to the base of her feet.

The belt was self-explanatory. She pressed the blowing dot and the belt unlocked. She wrapped it around her waist and it locked. She felt a tingly, warm sensation spread from the belt to her body in a wave. The suit became warmer. She suspected it was a power source.

Finally, she slipped on the helmet. The suit connected

to the internal lining of the helmet and the black glass became transparent. She could see numbers on the top right corner of the glass indicating her body temperature and the temperature of the room. On the top left corner were Jared, Emma, and Levi's names and their distances in centimeters. She smiled at that. Now, she could keep tabs on them like they kept tabs on her.

"Okay. Let's go," Jared said. The passenger doors opened and he hopped out. Abbey followed him, feeling out of sorts in the new gear. She was warm, but the material felt too thin. She almost felt naked. It contoured so well to her body that it was almost too revealing, especially in the chest area. At the same time, it felt loose and free.

On her feet, following Jared to the hotel, Abbey wondered why everything felt lighter, like someone grabbed a nob and reduced gravity with a turn by two or three notches. She suspected that was what Jared meant when he said she'd notice the difference once they were moving. It was an improvement she appreciated. Jared rushed to the door at near full sprint. Without any effort, she caught up with him.

They went through the front door, waited for the room to pressurize, and entered the lobby. Abbey admired the view until Jared cleared his throat and pointed his paw at the front desk.

A well-dressed man with the smile of a stalking predator stood behind the marble desk. "Oh, look at you. I can tell right away who you're here to see. Not often you see more than one person wearing an outfit like that. You look magnificent. Can I say that? You look absolutely ravishing. I could just eat you up." His smile grew wider. "Welcome to the Alexis. I am your host, Alexis." He extended his hand.

"Oh, well, thank you," Abbey said, ignoring his hand.

Little did she know, had she shook his hand, he would have stabbed her with the syringe he held under the counter. It was full of a horse tranquilizer.

"Honestly, my dear, you look sensational, to die for. You make that outfit, not the other way around."

"You're making me blush," Abbey said, unaware that he couldn't see her face through his end of the glass. "It's new. I just got it today."

Words appeared at the bottom right of her screen: *"Ask the clerk for the room of Malachi Hiatt."*

Abbey frowned, leaned down, and whispered. "Who's that? We're looking for Levi's room."

More words appeared on the screen: *"That is Levi's alias. He uses that name whenever he's in unpleasant or dangerous territory and doesn't want his actions traced back to him or the Washington Coalition. Malachi, the alias, is a scavenger, hunter, and bodyguard for hire."*

One day, Abbey knew she'd have to ask them how they came up with all of these aliases. She wondered if she should have one of her own. Well, another one in addition to the one she had and didn't realize. It was all getting too complicated. Why couldn't they just have one name and stick with it?

"Umm, would you direct me to Malachi Hiatt's room? He's expecting me," Abbey said. Jared touched her leg. She looked down, then back at Alexis. "He's expecting us."

Alexis took a long hard look at Jared, narrowed his eyes, and said, "That's a very smart dog you have there. Malachi's in fact, right? I've never seen a dog listen in on a conversation and make sure it's recognized. That's a human trait. It's about our egos. We like to be included. Very interesting." He rubbed his chin with his hand and checked the registry. "He's in room seven-thirteen, with a female guest." His narrow, curious eyes scrutinized

Abbey and waited to see what her reaction would be to the news.

His look gave Abbey a cold chill. She nodded, said, "Thanks," and rushed to the elevator.

"Have a great day! Come back and see me if you have any questions," Alexis said. He went back to smiling. He stared at her intently as she walked away. She wondered if he was checking out her butt. The suit was tight enough to reveal every detail of her figure. She suspected it would be a pervert magnet.

The elevator landed on the first floor. She got in— Jared followed—and pressed level seven.

"That guy gives me the creeps," Abbey said. "He was flattering and welcoming, but he gives me the vibe that if I was in here alone, he'd lock me up and make me a sex slave or something."

Jared looked at her and flatly stated, "You're right. He would."

Abbey's eyes shot wide open and her hands spread. "What?! What kind of place is this? Why would you bring me here?"

"It's a very luxurious hotel, and honestly, the only decent place in the quarantine and devastation zones to eat and lay your head. Unfortunately, it's also a criminal hub for weapons sales, drug manufacturing and distribution, prostitution, sex slavery, theft, murder, and more. People come here and go missing, especially young women."

"And they're still open?" Abbey asked.

"The Washington Coalition has labeled this place off limits to travelers. The North American Union doesn't care. It's off the beaten path. They consider this area to be out of their jurisdiction simply because they don't want to put resources in place to maintain the area or do anything about the mutant population."

Abbey balled and raised her fists. "How could they let this go on?"

"You're kidding, right? The government is corrupt. Your father has told you that for years. Five senators have even been spotted buying sex slaves: four boys, seven girls, all between the ranges of ten and fourteen years old. They took them to D.C. The other senators probably refuse to travel this far."

That was enough to break Abbey's heart. She wanted Jared to stop talking. She'd had enough truth for the day.

The elevator stopped. They traveled down the hall as the sign suggested and stopped at room seven-thirteen. They noticed the ice bucket sitting outside the door.

"It's quiet in there," Abbey said and leaned her helmet against the door.

Jared frowned at her and then padded his paw against the door. "Waiting."

Abbey rolled her eyes and knocked at the door. There was silence. She knocked again. "Hey Levi! Open up!"

Jared placed his paw on his helmet. "No, no, no! It's Malachi."

"Oh, yea. Oops! Sorry," Abbey apologized. "Good thing no one's around."

Jared pointed his paw at the ice bucket. "The rooms are illegally bugged with video equipment and listening devices so they can monitor the people in the rooms, record their activity. Malachi sweeps the room and puts them in the bucket."

Abbey blinked and gaped at the bucket. "What? We were better off just sleeping in the car. This sounds like the perfect place to go if you want to be killed."

Jared remained silent, certain no honest response would bring her any comfort. He instead walked to the door.

It opened.

3

As soon as they heard Abbey's voice, Violet leapt off of Levi's lap and shot for the bra she flung away. Levi leaned back with his arms spread. His two-piece attached, stretched, and sealed itself to him and became a one-piece. It was a sight to see, and Violet was sure she'd ask him questions about his apparel later. He stood, still erect, and put on his belt. Afterward, he put on his helmet.

"You might want to do something about your umm," Violet said while slipping on her tank top. She pointed at his crotch. "Your," she sighed and mumbled under her breath on the way to the bathroom. "Daggit. She's cramping my style. That would have been nice."

Cramping her style? Levi wondered. He cringed. In the early morning, she was with Jeremy. Now, she was with him. In the heat of the moment, he had allowed himself to forget Violet's intimate side-relationship with Jeremy. How intimate was it? He didn't trust Jeremy's testimony. He had to ask her.

The thought of Violet with Jeremy murdered any excitement that existed in Levi's body and he opened the front door. Jared was in midstride before the door was completely open. He searched the room as many canines do when they enter a new habitat. In Jared's case, Levi wondered if Jared did this as his standard security procedure or was it animal instinct.

In the doorway stood Abbey. Levi admired her in the suit her father and he had prepared for her. It was perhaps a little too tight to her figure, he realized. Her father would strongly disapprove. "It's good to see you dressed up. Part of me wondered if I'd ever see you in that." He stepped back and extended his hand towards the suite. "Quickly, come in. It seems we can finally have that necessary discussion."

Abbey walked in and looked around. First thing she did was enter the bedroom. She noted the bed in the room was king sized, shaped like a heart, and draped with pink and red linen. "Just one bed?" she accused and checked the lounge and kitchen. She narrowed her eyes. "Where's Violet? We have to talk." Her fists were clenched.

Oh great. She's in a fighting mood, Levi thought. Abbey had acquired new abilities that could easily put Violet in the hospital, or worse. They were a hundred miles from a hospital.

"She's in the bathroom," Levi said. He softly grabbed Abbey's shoulder as she turned in the direction of the bathroom. She stopped. "Come, take a seat. We can all sit down, talk, and look over the menu. There aren't a lot of options, but they make some decent burgers and chicken sandwiches. They have fish, too. From what I'm told, a refrigerated truck drops off a freezer full of fish and they keep the fish on ice until they're needed."

That diverted Abbey's attention. "Fine. Where's the menu? I'm starving."

The menu was on the coffee table. Abbey snatched it. It was a tri-folded, white menu with basic selections, including peanut butter and jelly sandwiches, macaroni and cheese, chili, and burgers. The prices ranged from five dollars to forty. The fish were the most expensive. They had to be shipped from the southern coastal states.

"Is it safe to order food from here?" Abbey asked and sat on the couch. She took off her helmet and set it on the coffee table beside Levi's. "From what Jared's told me, this isn't the safest place. Would they poison us?"

Jared took off his helmet, set it on the coffee table next to Abbey's, and hopped on the couch next to Abbey. He laid his head in her lap. Both Abbey and Levi smiled. Despite everything they'd been through in the last sixteen hours, some things hadn't changed.

Levi sat beside them and patted Jared's back. "The food is fine. I've been here a number of times investigating a few disappearances, undercover work. I haven't been poisoned, yet."

"Yet," Abbey said and put down the menu. "You had to say, 'yet'."

"Well, the first time I arrived, I removed all of the bugging devices in the room and refused to show my face or expose any skin, preventing him from identifying me. So, right away, he knew I wasn't your average shmuck and suspected I was law enforcement. Poisoning me would have been too risky, especially if they were under investigation. When he got the word that I was a bounty hunter working with scavengers as protection, he acted like he was my best friend. He offered me drugs and women, very beautiful women." Abbey frowned. "I rejected them, of course."

"Of course," she said.

Levi smiled. "I discovered a lot of things about this hotel. It's easy to learn things you're not supposed to know when you can turn invisible and pass through walls. One thing I learned was that they weren't responsible for the disappearances I was investigating, but were involved in much worse. They won't poison us, but I wouldn't suggest anyone come here unless they're desperate, armed, and not alone."

Abbey thought on that, and then said, "Is it possible they poisoned you, but you were immune because of the nanotech?"

"I considered that. I suppose the only way we'll know is when we start eating the food. We're all pretty safe. The only person we'd have to worry about is Violet."

As her name was spoken, Violet came out of the

bathroom. Everyone's eyes shot in her direction. She blushed and tried to avoid Abbey's penetrating and accusing glare. She walked around the chair and coffee table, and sat next to Levi on the couch, out of Abbey's line of sight.

"I'm guessing you were all talking about me while I was in the bathroom," Violet said. "Let's hear it. I'm pretty sure it involves leaving me here."

"Sounds like a great idea," Abbey said, thinking there was no greater punishment for Violet than leaving her in a place like the Alexis Hotel.

Levi shook his head in disagreement. "No, it doesn't," he said while looking at Abbey. "And no, we were not," he clarified with Violet. "We were discussing the menu and whether or not it was safe to eat the food. It is and we should order soon, before other people get the same idea and the wait is long. They have a small kitchen staff."

They mulled over the menu and selected their items. Levi called in the order. For himself, he ordered two grilled chicken sandwiches, fries with extra ketchup, and orange juice. For Abbey, he ordered four spicy chicken sandwiches with extra mayo and tomatoes, a side salad, and strawberry lemonade. For Jared, he ordered chicken and rice with mushrooms, a side salad, and bottled water. For Violet, he ordered the salmon and shrimp platter with green peppers, red peppers, onions, broccoli, a side salad, and sweet iced tea.

Violet glanced at the final cost as Levi wrote it down and grimaced. Her platter alone was more expensive than both Levi and Jared's orders combined. She whispered an apology in his ear. He shrugged and said, "As long as you enjoy it, it's worth it." She smiled and snuck a peck on his cheek.

Abbey noticed and spoke up, "So, what? You're trying to get in Lee's pants now? Jeremy wasn't enough for you and your craven desires?" She didn't get a response from Violet, who merely shook her head and watched the television. A new film titled 'Earth Resurrected' was on and streaming from the Coalition Cinemas Network. Abbey huffed. "So, we're not even going to talk about what you did? You're just going to ignore me?"

Jared and Levi exchanged a look. Jared transmitted, *"I knew this was coming. I don't want to talk about what happened in here between you two, but it honestly could have waited a couple of days. What were you thinking?"*

Levi shrugged and shared his memories and thoughts from check-in until just before he and Violet began to undress.

The memories played across Jared's mind in seconds. He put his paws on his head. *"Of course, you weren't thinking. I know. She's very pretty."* He glanced at Violet, who had her arms crossed. She ignored Abbey, who was still asking her questions. Abbey hated to be ignored. They both knew that. *"You're back to where you were just before we left Virginia, trying to decide between the two. This can't end well, especially considering the scope of the mission."*

I've decided to try things out with Violet, Levi thought.

"Oh," Jared closed his eyes. *"Abigail is not going to take that well, especially after the affair. Why, might I ask, have you chosen Violet? Please don't tell me it's a hormonal thing."*

"Stop ignoring me!" Abbey screamed. Jared's head shot off of her lap. He glowered at her. "Sorry, Jared."

Levi sighed. "Let's just settle down. Once we've all had a bite to eat, we can discuss this with clear heads," Levi said to Abbey. "And please, conserve your energy. You're still not at one hundred percent."

"You're on her side," Abbey said. She pointed at Levi. He didn't like pointing. It was rude. "You were once on mine. Now you're on hers. I don't understand. What happened? Did you sleep with her, too?"

There was a burning in Levi's cheeks. Violet's jaw was tight, face beet red, when he glanced at her. She stared into her lap, fists in balls. He said, "No. I did not sleep with her. And if I had, it would be between the two of us, her and me, Lee and Vy." At that, Violet looked up, surprised. "I'm not choosing sides on this issue. I understand why you're upset with her, Abigail. You have very justified reasons to be angry. I just want peace." *God, I need peace.* "We've had a long day. A very, very long day. Can we sit, unwind, and not yell? You two can discuss this somewhere else if you want. Jared and I need some quiet time."

"Hey. Don't drag me into this," Jared transmitted. Levi shrugged. *"But we do have to discuss a growing problem outside, on the other side of the wall."*

Abbey balled her hands into fists. "She won't discuss it with me."

"Then, at this point, a discussion won't be had. There will be no forced conversations here. You know how I feel about pestering people to talk. Let's just sit, watch the telly, and relax until the food arrives."

Frustrated, Abbey stood, huffed, and stormed into the single bedroom. She slammed the door. There was a loud click. Levi's head hung for a moment. "Vy, you're going to have to talk to her about this."

"I know, I, I," Violet said and sighed. "There's just, sometimes, there's no talking to her." She hugged his right arm and leaned in close. "Thanks for defending me."

Levi looked into her eyes. She peered into his. He felt energy building between them, pulling them closer. He chose to break that energy. "We have to discuss Jeremy. How far did things go between the two of you?"

Violet turned away. "Do we have to talk about that?"

"If we're going to, umm," Levi started. He glanced at Jared, then her, and continued, "Be an item, I'd like to know how far things went between the two of you. You know how I feel about these things, where I stand. I just, I'd like to know."

Jared hopped off the couch and puttered over to the kitchen to give them privacy, even if he could hear everything being said. He started to look through the empty cabinets.

With the two alone, Violet leaned closer and whispered, "We, Jeremy and I, we." She sighed and covered her face. "Lee, we finally have our chance to be together. I'm afraid that, once I tell you, you'll leave me. I've wanted to be with you for so long, and I did something stupid. I loved you for years, and, are you going to leave me? If I tell you the truth, are you going to end things with me and be with Abbey?"

Things were not as black and white as Levi wanted them to be, and he didn't know what to tell her. He had always hoped and believed, if he married and had sex with someone, she would be his first and he would be hers. With Abbey, having the same upbringing, that was almost a certainty. Violet, however, had a very different upbringing. Her father was an abusive, vulgar drunk. Her mother lived up to a terrible reputation. Though Levi wanted to believe Violet's time with his adopted family was well spent in altering her choices, he wondered now if Jeremy was her first. But here she was again, loving him and pleading for him to not give up on her. Things weren't painted in the perfect picture he'd always hoped for. He had to accept that.

"No, Vy," Levi said. He kissed her gently on her lower lip. "I love you. Things aren't necessarily how I planned them, but you made a mistake. We all make mistakes. I made a mistake in allowing myself to forget everything we had and not reaching out. Had I reached out to you while I was away, or when I came in town for the holidays, you probably never would have done this in the first place."

Violet exhaled in shock. He transferred responsibility on to himself. She shook her head and kissed him. "I'm not going to let you take credit for my mistake. I've resented Abbey ever since she kissed you. She saw that you liked me, loved me, and she kissed you." She kissed him.

"Then, there was Edward. It was a year after you left. I was having a hard time accepting you were gone. And I was frustrated. I thought you may have found someone else when I hadn't heard from you. So, I made a new friend, Edward. She didn't like that I was spending more time with him than her, because she didn't have any other friends. She started flirting with him. And, because she has that special charm, he dumped me and just went nuts over her. She, of course, said she was just joking around. But, it became a thing. Every time a guy showed interest in me, she had to have his attention, and I just kind of became fed up with it." Her fists tightened. "I met Jeremy first. He's my neighbor. He and I were flirting with each other in the library. Then, here comes miss high and mighty telling me I got a B in advanced biochemistry and didn't have time for fraternizing. He saw her and, one moment he was interested in me, the next, he was getting her phone number. They ended up being a couple. He was slimy enough to date a girl on the side, and I was angry enough to be that girl."

She sighed and shook her head. "Abbey said she was saving herself for marriage. She wanted to be with the right guy, not any guy. He told me she was a teasing, tight-kneed daddy's little girl. He was happier when he was with me, he said. He considered leaving her if I had a better offer. This is after years of being looked over for Abbey. I don't know. It wasn't that she was any prettier than me. There was just something about her."

"Pheromones," Levi chimed in.

Violet nodded. "Yeah. It was nice to know that, for once, a guy would leave her for me instead of the other way around. So, we had sex. I didn't feel good about it afterward. I felt dirty. I felt like I lost something I'd never get back. And, it dawned on me that he didn't give a crap about me. It was all about him. He just wanted to empty his balls. And, I think I resented her just a little bit more because of what I did. I blamed her. And, it made me want to do it more just to get back at her for giving myself up so easily in the first place. I had become desperate for affection and given myself away to someone else." She gazed into Levi's eyes. "Someone other than you."

Levi listened and somehow understood. He nodded, cued her to continue.

She did. "Yesterday, my mom pissed me off so bad; I wanted to kick her out. I could have done it. Per my dad's will, I technically owned the house two years ago, when I turned sixteen. But I couldn't kick my drunk, slutty mother out on the streets. She'd end up dead in a ditch or get passed around some drug den. I'd feel guilty about that." She balled up her fists and sighed. Levi gave her a hug. She rested her head on his shoulder. "I felt trapped. I was stuck with her, and I wanted to run away. I couldn't go to Abbey's place. Honestly, since you weren't there, it wasn't the same. So, I went over to Jeremy's place to do it again. I was fed up with everything. School, my mom, Abbey, and honestly, I was fed up with Jeremy, too. But, I just wanted to escape it all, and the way it felt, sex felt good. It cleared my head. And, I just wanted to clear my head again. Even if it meant being with a guy like

Jeremy." She pulled her head away from his shoulder and looked him in the eyes. "It only happened once, though. I swear. We were about to do it when Abbey came knocking at his door. And, well, here we are now."

That was it. Levi didn't doubt her. He could sense that all that she said was the truth, and even though he wasn't happy that she'd given herself away to Jeremy, he understood why she did it. It was enough.

Looking into Violet's eyes, Levi could see that she regretted everything that happened. There was a pain deep down inside of her that had accumulated from dysfunction in her family and social life. He wanted to be there for her. He wanted to take that pain away and let her enjoy true love and friendship. He kissed her, and they held each other.

An hour later, Levi sat unconscious with Violet snuggled under an arm. Jared barked. They separated quickly. Levi blinked, not sure when they fell asleep. Jared pointed his head towards the door and there was a knock.

"It's peanut butter jelly time," Violet mumbled while rubbing her eyes.

Jared frowned and rushed to the door.

"What were you dreaming about?" Levi asked with a smirk on his face. He put on his helmet, and followed Jared. Through the peephole was a man in all white, wearing a mock chef's hat, with a cart full of food. Levi opened the door. The man entered and rolled the cart to the dining table, casually scanning the room with eager eyes. His eyes locked on Levi's energy pistols on the coffee table, then Violet, before stopping the cart. He smiled and showed Levi the bill.

"I won't find any surveillance equipment on the food cart, will I?" Levi scanned the man's name tag. His name was Landon. "Landon?"

Landon smiled and shook his head. "Of course not, sir. We value your privacy."

Levi nodded, disbelieving, wrote in a tip, and sent Landon on his way. Landon responded with a thank you and scurried out the door, but not before taking a final look around, tallying how many people were in the room and where. The door closed.

"Is everyone that works here creepy?" Violet asked. She approached the cart and reached for the food.

Levi grabbed her hand and held it away. He said, "Yes." He stretched his gloved hand over the food and held it over the food for a solid minute. She squint her eyes, staring at his hand, and noticed the fabric itself was shimmering. The ball of his hand had a bluish glow. He sighed.

"The next time I come to this place, I hope I'll be driving a bulldozer," Levi grumbled. He reached under the cart and ripped a small microphone attached to a long wire from the bottom. He crushed it in his hand.

Violet lightly bit her lip, said, "Okay, then," and reached for the food. "Are we good to eat now? I'm craving that fish."

"As far as I know, sure," Levi said after hesitating.

Violet's hand flew to her hip. "What? What is it?"

"If there was something wrong with the food, you would be the first to know. Abbey, Jared, and I are immune to most poisons and sedatives. Our bodies immediately isolate and remove them. Of course, our bodies would let us know which poison or sedative was in the food after processing it. But, if you ate first, you would already be affected."

"Seriously," Violet spat and checked the covered plates for her fish. She found it and took a seat. "You guys are too freaking paranoid. You're going to drive me crazy. There's no way they would keep clientele if they poisoned everyone. They're creeps." She pointed at the crushed listening device on the carpeted floor. "They obviously like to snoop. But I doubt they're going to poison us. It wouldn't make sense."

Levi and Jared looked at each other. Levi said, "I guess we'll see."

Jared walked to the bedroom, tapped on the door, and informed Abbey the food had arrived. Levi set the plates on the table and distributed the stainless steel, decorative silverware and napkins accordingly.

Violet smiled. "This almost feels like old times, but without the old doctor." She lowered her head and sighed. "It's weird. I feel saddened about him more so than my own mother. He was like a second father to me. A sober, considerate, educated father. He protected me. I can't imagine what my life would have been had he not been in it." She locked eyes with Levi. "Honestly, I don't want to imagine it. It's a grisly concept."

"That's the great thing about what ifs and would have been," Levi said with a smile. He sat down beside Violet. "They didn't happen. God brought him into your life. He brought you into ours. I don't want to think about what life would have been if you weren't there, because you brought me happiness." He kissed her.

Abbey walked into the room and froze. Her balled fists tightened at her waist. Levi and Violet separated quickly when they saw her. Jared walked forward, shook his head, and hopped on to the chair in front of the chicken and rice.

"It couldn't wait until after dinner, could it?" Jared transmitted to Levi.

Levi put his face in his hands before looking back at Abbey. "Please join us. We have things to discuss."

"No, we don't," Abbey said. She stepped forward and collected her plate. "I heard you two talking earlier. I heard every last word." She focused on Violet. "It's not all my fault. Did it ever occur to you that I was doing you a favor with those other guys?"

Violet opened her mouth, but Abbey continued, "All those guys were interested in was getting into your pants, because they thought you were like your mother. They wanted the same thing from me, but I wouldn't go for it, because that's not how things are supposed to be done, and I'm not that kind of girl. Obviously, Jeremy was just like all the other guys, sex hungry. But, I didn't steal Levi from you."

Abbey stared at Levi for a full six seconds and said, "When Levi left for Washington, I cried for days. My dad told me he had a feeling about the two of us many years ago. He saw the way Levi watched over and protected me. He saw the love. He said we were destined to be together. In some way, he knew that earlier in life and wanted to raise Levi into the right kind of man for his daughter." Levi glanced at Jared. Jared looked back. "You're an interloper, Vy. You always have been. Levi and I have a destiny together. You've just been along for the ride." She stared at Violet long and hard, and then looked back at Levi. "And you know that." She picked up her plate, glass of strawberry lemonade, and marched back to the bedroom. The door slammed shut.

4

Dinner was quiet. Violet wasn't in a talking mood. Levi and Jared ate and watched Star Trek. They asked Emma to upload two movies, *Star Trek: First Contact* and *Star Trek: Insurrection*, into the hotel database. She saw both of those movies about twenty times at the Brown residence. With Levi as her boyfriend, she knew there would be no escape from Star Trek. And frighteningly, she was starting to enjoy it. She liked seeing Captain

Picard turn into a badass and fight off a Borg invasion over pre-warp Earth. She liked seeing Captain Picard as a romantic on a paradise planet, the Ba'ku planet, where you could live relatively young and peaceful for centuries, if not forever. She wanted to go there. It sounded like a great place to escape with a lover and discover and rediscover every inch of each other for decades. But as was the case, when someone saw something beautiful, they had to try to steal it away. She thought Abbey was a great example of the Son'a. They had an opportunity to enjoy that beauty and eternal youth, but were immature and blew it. Now, they were coming back to claim something they felt was rightfully theirs. You snooze; you lose. Move your feet, you lose your seat. Finders are keepers; losers are weepers. Daddy doesn't define your destiny, sweetheart. God does.

Between showings of the movies, they moved the furniture and stretched out the large couch, which was a pull-out couch, into a bed. Levi grabbed extra pillows and blankets from a cupboard and set the bed. He asked if she needed him to go to the car and grab her luggage. She said, "No, we can grab it in the morning," but admired Levi's domestic side. Once the pull-out was set, Violet and Levi cuddled on the bed, with Jared on the far end, and watched the second movie.

Violet began to doze off until Levi started to sing 'A British Tar' along with the movie. She grabbed a pillow and hit him in the face. He laughed. So, did Jared. She meant to ask about Jared and how he was capable of picking up on their conversations, jokes, and other human nuances. Jared seemed just as human as the rest of them. She decided otherwise. A lot of her questions went out of the window when she looked at Levi, saw his smile. She was happy to finally have his love again. She trusted that he'd tell her more when the time came.

She could settle for a little less information if it meant kisses, cuddling, and the warm affection that went beyond the physical stuff.

She loved cuddling with him. He felt as warm as freshly baked bread right out of the oven. Having his arms wrapped around her, she didn't need a blanket. She wondered if she'd get spoiled by it, if she'd ever be able to sleep outside of his embrace again.

Just soak it all in while you can, she thought. *You never know what tomorrow will bring or take away.*

Halfway into the movie, they were resting peacefully. And then, they weren't.

Hushed whispers conspired at the door. Jared's head shot up like a rocket headed for space. *"LEVI!"* Seconds later, so did Levi's. There was a click at the door as it unlocked and a slim stream of light filled the room from an open crack in the doorway. Jared hopped off the bed. Levi shielded his eyes. A hand appeared in the doorway holding a small, round object. The hand tossed the object into the room.

A grenade! Levi thought. He quickly called on his abilities and redirected the object out the window. The crash of the glass echoed through the room. Seconds later, there was a large explosion. The building trembled. The television died. The lights in the hallway went out.

"Jesus, Roy Halladay!" a man yelled outside of the door. "You tossed it out the window."

"I barely tossed it," a man responded in a panic.

"Inside! Get inside!" the first man yelled back.

Jared commanded the door shut. The men tried to reopen it. It unlocked, but didn't budge. They cursed.

Levi hopped off of the sofa-bed and grabbed his belt and energy pistols. "Get behind the couch, Vy," he urged while his suit wrapped itself around him. She ducked behind the sofa-bed. He turned to Jared. "Thanks for waking me."

"You're kidding, right?" Jared said out loud. Levi smirked.

Abbey burst out of her room and looked around the corner. "What's going on out here?"

"Over here, Abbey!" Levi rushed forward to claim her arm. "There are men behind that door. They tossed a grenade in. I deflected it out of the window."

"A grenade?!" she yelled back. "Someone's trying to kill us with grenades?"

"Yes," Levi confirmed. He pointed towards Violet. "Please, go behind the couch."

Abbey put her hands over her nose and glanced at the broken window. The rancid smell of the outdoors was unbearable. She looked back at the sofa-bed and shook her head. "I'm not going over there with her."

Levi bit his lip and shrugged. "Suit yourself." He grabbed his helmet and put it on. He tossed Jared his.

Jared backed away from the door and put on his helmet. *"They're setting charges. They're going to blow the door."*

Idiots, Levi thought. He backed two meters from the door and stretched out his hand. He scanned the area with his helmet and waited for the sign that they were about to activated it. He heard the whisper, "Clear," and focused his mind.

The door exploded off its hinges, but hung inches in the air from its spot. The explosion itself travelled back into the hallway. The building buckled around them. They heard screams and expletives. After five seconds, the door sagged at its entrance.

Levi said, "I'm going out there. Abbey, helmet. Violet, put your shoes and jacket on."

"You're going out there?" Abbey asked. Levi nodded, turned to the door, and vanished before their eyes.

5

The hallway walls were ablaze. The dancing flames offered the only light. There was a hole in the wall where the door of room seven-twelve used to be. The room and its contents were on fire. The explosion wasn't just isolated away from Levi's room. It was redirected. Three men in black armor—they wore the same armor as those at the Alexis Hotel's outer wall—were picking themselves up. Two others rushed around the corner from the stairwell with weapons raised.

"The hell happened up here, Landon?" the first of the two men asked. He was bald, with a goatee and small dragon tattoo under his left eye. "Alexis is going to kill you. We've lost power, everywhere, even at the perimeter. The lights are all out, and there's a swarm of mutants out there."

"Alexis told me to wreck them and take their heads for the bounty. So, I tossed a grenade in there," Landon said. He raised his gun and pointed it at room seven-thirteen.

"A grenade? You used a grenade?" The bald man put a hand to his head. "Are you out of your mind? Why are you carrying a gun like that if you're going to use grenades? This is a business! You can't throw a grenade inside a hotel room."

"Sorry." Landon shrugged. "They're still in there, though."

"You mean they're not dead?" The bald man spread his arms around. "The place is a shambles and you haven't even killed them yet? How many grenades did you use?"

"One," Landon said, looking down. "It was dark in there, but they must uh been awake and tossed it out the window before it exploded. Frank barely tossed the thing." He pointed at the battered door of room seven-thirteen. "Then, they barracked the door. So I pulled out my plastique and used it on the door."

"What?! You used plastique?" The bald man turned around, kicked the floor, and then raised his gun at Landon. "Son of a—dammit, Landon! Your sister's going to hate me for this." He shot Landon in the head as he raised his hands to protest. Landon's body crumbled to the floor. The other men shifted their eyes and cursed.

The bald man said, "The dumbass used plastique on a hotel door. Brother-in-law or not, that don't fly." He turned to the other guys. "A horde of mutants are breaking through the barricade, so we have to be quick. Follow me. Let's go get that twenty-million dollar bounty. Not that we'll see a penny of it after this mess."

The three men's guns pointed at the bald man. Their eyes shot open. They stared at their guns, hands stuck to the handles.

The bald man looked at them. "We have a problem, gentlemen? Because if you don't like what I did to Landon, you're gonna hate what I'll do to you if you don't aim those guns somewhere else."

Their guns fired away. One of the bullets struck the bald man straight through the right eye. The bald man went down without protest. After which, the three men dropped their guns and stepped away.

"What the hell? I didn't have control of my gun," the first man said.

"Me neither," the second man said.

"Yea. It just acted on its own," the third man said.

"Karma is a snag, though, right guys?" the second man said and raised his hands and shoulders in a comic shrug.

The first man laughed.

Levi suddenly materialized with his energy pistol

raised. The three gawped at him with wide eyes. One by one, he shot them as they reached for their weapons. When they were all down, he went back to room seven-thirteen.

6

"I heard gunfire," Abbey said. She put on her helmet and was relieved to have one. A hazy fog from the outdoors filled the room. It smelled of rotten sewage, fish, and egg. She was pleased Violet didn't have one, and instead held a towel over her mouth and nose. She was trying not to gag.

Serves her right, Abbey thought and smirked.

Jared watched her, intently. She could feel his eyes on her. When she turned to him, he shook his head and pointed upward. She looked to the ceiling and didn't see anything. She shrugged, not understanding what he was implying; so he moved closer and whispered to her, "Bitterness will get you nowhere. Forgive, as the Lord has forgiven you."

She frowned.

Who was he to tell her that? How had he gone from being a quiet, well-trained wolf to her handler in a few hours? Was he not her pet? Was she not his master? The lines that defined their relationship were different now that he spoke and actively protected her. How was she to see him in their social hierarchy, as an equal, as a superior?

There was more gunfire. She hopped back from the door. "They shot Levi." She trembled. "What do we do if Levi's dead?" It wasn't as though she had time to learn the powers she acquired. If Levi couldn't stop them, what good was she?

Jared ignored her and walked to the window. Without the lights, and with a thick looming fog, it was complete darkness. Humidity was one-hundred percent and fogging his helmet. He could hear gunfire and screams below. He shifted the helmet input to thermal vision and scanned below. Hundreds of warm bodies below tussled with each other and racing towards the building. Some were climbing over the barricaded wall and others were fighting their way through.

Abbey rushed beside Jared and asked, "What's going on down there?" He looked back at her.

Part of Jared wanted to openly reassure both of them that Levi was fine. He was tired of concealing his intelligence and vocal abilities from Violet, and felt, under the circumstances, that perhaps it was time for flexibility. She knew about Levi. Who would it hurt to speak up and be known? What would it hurt to no longer be treated as a pet, but as an intelligent being with more to contribute?

No, Jared thought. There was a reason for discretion. He would remain quiet and humble until the time came for him to express himself openly.

"Well?" Abbey asked.

Violet frowned at her. "Are you asking me or the wolf? Because I don't know." Abbey glared at her. "I'm sure we're sitting ducks. We're too high to go out the window. We can't go out the door. They have guns. We don't have kitchen knives. All we have is a wolf in a space suit and us. The best choice is to hide or surrender and hope for the best."

As Abbey was about to protest, Levi appeared in the darkness. "Looks like it's time for us to go. I hope you're both rested, because this is going to be a rough escape."

Abbey rushed forward and gave him a hug. She whined, "I thought they killed you."

"Oh ye of little faith," Levi said. He hugged Abbey and then let go. He went to Violet, who stood alone in the dark, and gave her a hug as well. "We have to get out of here. The mutants don't like the light. It's painful and blinding. With the radiation fog and no light, they're going to roll over those guards and take the hotel in a matter of minutes. We have to find our way through the horde and to Emma as soon as possible."

Violet frowned. "Are they really that dangerous? I've heard mutants can be very peaceful, almost normal, as long as they're not threatened or provoked."

"You're right," Levi said. "But they're the type that won't be out there trying to rip our heads off." He looked out of the shattered window and stretched out his hand. "A lot of them have suffered severe brain damage from growths or serious genetic mutations which stimulate violent emotions and heightened adrenaline and hormones. Many have resorted to cannibalism for survival. What drives them to greater violence is desperation and justified anger because of how we've treated them. Mercenaries and hunters abuse, enslave, or kill them. If they're normal enough looking females, well, umm, they're uh, kidnapped and then, you know. Mutant girls are highly requested in some trades."

"Ugh, men will stick their things in anything, won't they?" Abbey said and glanced at Violet. Violet rolled her eyes.

"And on that note," Levi said, he collected Violet's hand. "Let's go." He rushed to the door, tossed it aside, and led them through the hall.

The fire spread to other rooms. The sound of breaking glass and crackling fire hurried their race to the stairwell.

Emergency lighting from Chinese lanterns filled the stairwell. Always first, with energy pistols raised, Levi took them flight by flight. They could hear screaming and banging from the lower floors. Other people, hotel guests, were scrambling to escape, pushing their way past others. There were bearded men in flannel and jeans with trucker hats and pistols in hands. Behind them were flustered men in unbuttoned white shirts, black slacks, and expensive alligator skin shoes. They were followed by five scantily clad women with dragon tattoos on their calves. Three of those women wore leashes. Levi suspected they were in the middle of a transaction when the power went out.

Screams escalated from the bottom floor. Abbey looked over the railing and saw two figures punching and beating on a red-haired woman in a nightgown and one slipper. They were pale, frail, and bald. Their skin was wrinkled and covered in sores and bumps. Their eyes were mostly whites with small pupils. *Mutants,* she thought. Six more hopped through the first floor stairwell exit, blocking off the escape. One of them bit into the woman's arm. She screamed and writhed from the pain.

Levi stretched his hand out, focused his mind, and seven of the mutants flew backward, slamming hard against each other and the wall. The eighth unlocked his teeth from the woman and looked around. Levi fired an energy beam. It fell back, a scorch mark on its chest. The other guests scrambled past the wounded woman and mutants and out of the stairwell. The sound of rapid gunfire and screams commenced not long afterward.

At the base of the stairs, Abbey checked on the woman. The woman shook and cried. She was losing a lot of blood. The bite was deep and took a chunk of her flesh. "She needs a doctor."

"Yea. No shit, Sherlock," Violet snapped at her. "She just got bit by a rabid mutant. She's bleeding out. Who knows what she's got."

"No worse than whatever S-T-D you and Jeremy

have," Abbey responded.

Violet's eyes narrowed.

"Shhh, no," Levi shushed with a frown. "Are you kidding me? We're not having that right now." He lifted the woman on to his shoulder. Her remaining slipper fell from her foot. The handle of her leash dangled in front of Jared's face.

The seven mutants began to stir and pick themselves up. Levi knocked them out with another telekinetic thrust against the stairwell wall. He ushered the others through the stairwell.

The lobby was a warzone.

Bodies from mutants and guests to armed men were sprawled across the floor and bloodied. Many more mutants were charging through the entrance. Guards were aimlessly shooting at the entrance. Alexis held a pistol on his side of a metal gate that protected the back office. He was reloading and cursing, dripping with sweat. The bullets slipped out of his fingers as he tried to fit them in the six-shooter. His face twisted into a scowl. A female mutant slammed against the metal gate and squealed. He fired off a shot that launched her against the wall. She lifted herself, spit green, murky blood, and collapsed.

Alexis trembled violently. He took a swig of an open bottle of whiskey and sighed. Out of the corner of his eye, he saw Levi, Violet, Abbey, and Jared standing at the stairwell. His faced contorted with contempt as soon as he saw them. He raised his pistol to shoot at them but another mutant slammed against the gate. This one was holding one of the guard's pistols. The mutant pointed it at Alexis and pulled the trigger. There was a click, a second click, a third click, but it was enough to drive Alexis into retreat further into his secure office.

"How are we going to get out?" Abbey asked,

watching the unending approach of the mutants through the doorway. The three remaining guards shot them down as they enter. The guards were so preoccupied by the mutants that they either didn't notice Levi and the group or didn't care. None of them knew how many mutants remained. Abbey wondered how many bullets the guards had left, considering their haphazard use of ammunition.

Levi scanned for exits and saw mutants breaking their way through the back door. "Certainly not that way." He lowered the woman off of his shoulder and set her on the floor against the wall. "Hold on," he said to her and fired off a couple shots at the mutants. They scattered. He pointed towards the front door and fired streaming plasma blasts that punched through five mutants. The guards turned to him and gave him two thumbs up.

A grenade bounced at the entryway of the hotel and unleashed a blinding flash and deafening bang. Violet and the guards screamed and fell back, clutching their eyes. Levi, Abbey, and Jared flinched and stumbled.

Thank God for these helmets, Levi thought.

Five dark-skinned men holding large assault rifles walked in. They wore white tank tops and jeans. Their gold chains swayed as they walked. They were followed by a dark-skinned muscular man wearing a nineteen seventies U.S. Army infantry uniform, and Jeremy.

Abbey gasped.

"Cleaned up your mess outside," the uniformed man said to the guards. "You three should make a run for it before they overtake the place. Leave us to handle our business."

The three guards shrugged and quickly rushed out the front. Two of them rubbed their watering eyes and staggered, their equilibrium off from the ringing in their ears. The uniformed man pointed at Levi and turned to

Jeremy. In a deep voice, he asked, "This them?"

Jeremy nodded and smiled. He looked Violet directly in the eye and said, "Yep. That's them all right. They're the ones that blew up your fine establishment. From the looks of this place, it looks like you aren't the only victim of our firebug here." He pointed at Levi.

Levi said nothing.

"You're a piece of—, crap, Jeremy!" Abbey yelled with her tight little fists raised.

The uniformed man and his men laughed. "That's cute. That's real cute. It's not often you come across a woman that doesn't have a filthy mouth. I look forward to making it dirty."

Jeremy laughed and nodded. "She's a virgin, too. No doubt, she'll be as tight as a keyhole." Then he pointed at Violet, who held her head, still recovering from the flash grenade. "Not her, though. I busted that wide open."

"Shut up, Jeremy," Levi said.

The smile immediately fell from Jeremy's face. He scowled, "Don't talk to me like that, you freak nig—!" He stopped himself short. The dark-skinned men all shot angry glares at him. He balled his fists and glared at the uniformed man. "Well, here they are as I promised! You kill him and that dog. I'll take the brunette. You can have the blonde. All is settled."

The uniformed man removed his pistol and pointed it at Jeremy's face. He said, "Shut up, Jeremy," and pulled the trigger. Jeremy's brains blew out the back of his head. Violet and Abbey screamed and turned away. The uniformed man blew the smoke coming out of the barrel of his gun and let out a sigh of relief. "Some people don't know how to keep their mouths shut."

He returned his attention back to Levi and said, "As for you. You have single-handedly crippled my business.

You destroyed my gas station, restaurant, motel, and now—" He pointed at the ceiling. "—my trafficking business. I had girls coming in and out of here on a weekly basis. I'm talking top dollar tricks. That's gone. It's all gone."

Levi shrugged and said, "With all due respect, sir, I was only acting in self-defense. Your guys were going to come after me and my friends, and these guys threw a grenade into my hotel room. Trust me; I'm just trying to pass through the Quarantine Zone as quickly and quietly as possible."

The uniformed man raised an eyebrow. "They threw a grenade into your hotel room? Why would they do that? And if they did, how did you survive?"

"You'll have to ask Alexis why they wanted me dead, but I was fast enough to get the grenade out of the window."

The sound of gunfire and squeals grew closer from outside. The uniformed man nodded twice to his men and two rushed outside to investigate. He returned his attention back to Levi. "Let's get this over with." He raised his pistol.

"You don't want to do this," Levi said. "If you leave now, no one will get hurt."

The uniformed man laughed and pulled the trigger. The pistol exploded in his hand. He screamed and dropped it to the ground. His men raised their weapons and tried to fire. Their guns exploded in their hands as well. They dropped them.

"Impossible!" the uniformed man yelled while holding his burned hand. He pointed his hand at Levi and the three men rushed forward with their fists.

Jared shot forward like a bullet straight for one of the men. His helmet opened. He bared his teeth and dove on top. His claws slashed into the man's eyes. The man tried to fend Jared off with fists to his ribs, but he only met hard, impenetrable muscle.

Levi rushed at the two men and vanished. The two stopped, confused, and then their heads were slammed against each other. They crumbled to the floor, one on top of the other. Levi reappeared.

There was a gunshot.

Levi checked himself and turned to the uniformed man. The man held his backup pistol. The gun was flung from his hand and into the far reaches of the lobby.

"How are you doing this?" the man yelled. "What are you?"

Levi approached the man, lifted him off the ground and above his head, and slammed him back down. The uniformed man groaned and closed his eyes. His head tilted to the side.

"Levi!" Violet cried.

Levi turned around and saw her. Blood stained her tank top and jacket. He rushed to her. Abbey stood still and watched with wide eyes. She said, "She, she jumped right in front of me." He pulled back Violet's jacket and pulled up her tank top. Blood streamed from her abdomen. He scanned her body. The bullet was still lodged in there. He closed his eyes and sighed.

"I, I don't know how to fix this," Levi cried to Violet. He took off his helmet and leaned in close. "I'm not familiar with how to remove bullets. We have to get out of here. Emma can help."

"I'll get the car," Abbey said.

"You're not going anywhere," a voice said.

They turned around. Alexis stood over them, pistol in hand. His hair was matted. His face covered in sweat. His hands were trembling. "Don't move a muscle, Malachi, or I'll blow your head off," he threatened. "Or should I say, Levi?"

Levi frowned and yelled, "I don't have time for this, Alexis! I have to get her some help."

"I'll give her all the help she needs," Alexis said and pulled the trigger.

"NO!" Levi yelled and reached out his hand and mind to stop the bullet. But it already shot through Violet's chest. She went still.

Jared raced out of the hotel at a lightning speed.

Levi fumed at Alexis with red eyes and yelled loud. Alexis's arms contorted back into an impossible twist and snapped. They were then stretched apart until they ripped off his body. Alexis screamed and fell to the ground. Levi stood over him and raised his foot over his chest. Abbey yelled for Levi to stop. His foot slammed down hard and cracked Alexis's ribs. Alexis whined, hissed, and then went still.

Abbey looked away, covered her eyes, and burst into tears again.

Levi sank to the floor and turned to Violet's limp body. He sat there, frozen. The world came to a complete stop. All was still and silent.

There was a screeching of tires and Jared shot back into the hotel with a black pouch in his mouth. It was the same black pouch that held the catalyst. Its green glow and hum awoke Levi from his daze. He sullenly stared at Jared and asked, "Why'd you bring that in here?"

Jared gave him a dirty look and moved to Violet. He removed the catalyst from the pouch and held it over her. He said, "Talitha cumi."

The catalyst hummed and gradually brightened. Its light swelled and expanded until it beamed as bright and blinding as a star. They turned away. A surge of energy pulsed and streamed from the catalyst and into Violet. Then, it dimmed and quieted.

Jared whispered a thank you and put the catalyst back

into the pouch.

There was a wheeze and cough. Violet shuddered. She opened her eyes, looked up at Levi, smiled, and then fell asleep. Her chest rose and fell in deep breaths.

Levi exhaled a sigh of relief, and then he cried.

7

They narrowly escaped the hotel before another swarm of mutants arrived to finish what the others started. Levi sat in the front seat, his eyes closed, and face streaked with fresh tears. Abbey sat in the passenger seat silent and haunted by the brutal deaths of Jeremy and Alexis, and the near death or death and resurrection of Violet. She was also stunned by the device that was in her lap.

Her father brought it home many times, but never allowed her to touch it. Now it was in her lap. She was tempted to reach in the pouch and test out the power of the device, which seemed capable of healing impossible wounds and reviving people from death. It was the tool they would use to revive the world once they made it to Montana, she surmised, assuming they made it.

They had a long way to go and a huge bull's-eye on their back. The bounty on their heads demanded the discretion her father insisted, Levi practiced, and she hadn't taken seriously. She felt saddened by that. She felt guilty.

Abbey watched Violet, asleep in the backseat, and wondered if she'd ever be able to forgive her friend for what she had done. Violet slept with Jeremy, blamed Abbey for it, and then took away the one man that truly loved her. Because of that, Abbey called her friend an interloper, diseased, and unwanted. But Violet took a bullet for her. It was hard to stay angry with her after something like that. She was shot, twice. She died.

Life was too short.

It could end too suddenly and tragically for hard feelings, justified or not. When Violet awoke, Abbey decided she'd have to have a healthy heart to heart with her. It wouldn't be easy, but there was hope for them. They'd had plenty of good times to look back on. And hopefully, better times to come.

With a deep exhale, Abbey closed her eyes and willed herself to shut out the last hour of her life.

The catalyst began to hum and glow. She looked down at it, curious. She reached her hand inside the pouch and touched the crystalline shell. A warm energy filled her body. A low voice whispered in the back of her mind. It was the voice of a woman. It sounded familiar.

The voice said, *"Oh my darling, Abigail. You're a beautiful young woman, now. You're so grown up."*

Abbey's eyes widened. "Mother?"

THE WAY, THE TRUTH, THE LIFE

MY LOVES, AND OTHERS,

Today, I want to talk to you about the truth. I have written many things in my time, and made reference to this, but have not written solely, and specifically, about it.

The truth is that, two millennia ago, in His infinite love and grace, God put His essence, His Word, inside of a young virgin woman, impregnating her with a child, a child to be known as Jesus, Yeshua, Immanuel, Christ. Jesus was born to a virgin mother and lived from a child to a man sinless, perfect, obedient. Jesus went to John the Baptist, was baptized in water, and the Spirit of God came upon Him.

In His life as both God and man, Jesus performed a great multitude of marvelous and wondrous miracles from healing the sick and casting out demons to returning people to life from what we call death. He taught the Word of God and brought clarification to inconsistent or inaccurate teachings. He showed constant compassion and love, and lived by a great example to those who would follow Him. And after He did all that was predestined and planned, when His hour had arrived, He was arrested in spite of His innocence, judged by man, tortured/flogged, and crucified. He lived a perfect, blameless life. Days later, Jesus rose from death, appeared before many, and sent His apostles on a mission to spread what they had seen and experienced across many nations, that people may know Jesus is the Son and embodiment of God in the flesh. That they may know Him, love Him, and live a free life. He ascended to the heavens and gifted His apostles with the Holy Spirit, that they may too perform many wonders upon men, speak in many tongues, and spread the message far and wide. It was a perfect plan, a perfect life, for our salvation.

Jesus lived a perfect, blameless life because we could not, because we are sinners. We are tainted by the sin of our forebears, when Adam and Eve chose disobedience over God's instruction. Jesus died innocent, as a sacrifice, as a price, so that we may be blameless before God. That we could walk comfortably before Him, and live contently for Him, knowing we are no longer condemned by our sin. Jesus died for us so that we may live and die free. And all we have to do to be free of condemnation is to accept His sacrifice. Accept Jesus as our Savior and Lord.

One can look back on his or her life, and the number of sins committed cannot be counted if one had the rest of his or her life to do it. It would be easier to count each grain of rice in a ten pound bag, than one person's sins. We are flawed, imperfect, and helpless in spite of our own efforts. Through Christ Jesus, we are free. We can look back, wave good-bye to our sin, and start fresh, blameless. Live life, blameless. We can take that mountain of guilt off of our shoulders and live fearless.

Jesus carried the burden of our sins and it was all washed away by His blood. The way to life is through Jesus.

In accepting Jesus as our Lord and Savior, we put aside our old life (old ways) of sin, and embrace a new life in Christ. And while we are still imperfect in the flesh, unwise and subjected to sin, the Lord redeems us so that we can pursue cleaner lives. He speaks to us, helps us with His in-dwelling Spirit, refining us daily into better people. We are not so easily seduced by the temptations of the world, but have a resistance through the Spirit. We deny ourselves of the world. He grows us in our trials and offers us peace in spite of what the sinful world brings.

Of course, accepting Jesus as your Lord and Savior is not a halfhearted gesture. When you accept Him, you have to believe it. You must have faith in Him, trust Him, and accept Him. You pray to the Lord that you want Him in your life. You reach out to Him. It's one thing to say you're free and still be a slave. It's a completely different thing to have the shackles removed and dance to the rhythm of a content heart. It's one thing to say you're a Christian. It's a completely different thing to be a Christian.

Being a Christian is not simply believing in God. Some people attribute being a Christian to believing in God. A lot of people believe in God. Anyone can believe in God. Most people believe in a divine force or being. Even demons believe in God. Being a Christian is not simply going to church. Some people attribute being a Christian to going to church. Anybody can go to church. Building inspectors go to church. Auditors go to church. People invite people to church quite often. The person goes, sits there, listens or doesn't, and leaves. Being dragged to church does not make you a Christian. You can go to church for twenty straight years. In your heart, if you do not have faith in Jesus, if you did not accept Jesus as your Lord and Savior, you are not a Christian. Being a Christian is not simply reading the bible. Anybody can read the bible. Religious study students have read the bible. Some Buddhists have read the bible. Some evolutionists and humanists have read the bible. Some atheists have read the bible. No doubt even Satan has read the bible. Saying you've read the bible means nothing. And having said all of this, if you believe you believe in God, go to church, and have read the bible, but you do not believe in Jesus, nor accept Him as your Lord and Savior, you are not a Christian.

The way to salvation is through Christ and that begins through prayer. To know Christ is to take the time to convene with Him and the Father, and read the Word (the bible). Through the bible, we see the journey of man in our relationship with God. The bible is a history of our relationship with God. The bible is about God, and about us, but foremost about God and His Son, Jesus. And our relationship with God and Jesus is essential. He loves us, and wants the best for us. Through prayer, you may speak to God, and Christ, and build a relationship. If you do not have a relationship, but seek one, and seek peace, freedom, contentment, in spite of the travesties of the world, go to God and ask for peace, ask for freedom, ask for contentment, and most importantly, ask for that relationship with Him. Seek out His Spirit, that it will move you in your daily life closer to Him, along the narrow path that leads to life. Join the body of Christ and get baptized.

I share this with love, because I want the best for you, each and every one of you, even the most corrupt of you, and even the petty ones who have annoyed me with high school shenanigans. We are all God's creation. I share this because there is another truth that needs to be shared. And that is that Jesus is returning, and when He returns, the world as we know it will no longer be. The world will be punished and washed of sin, the sinners and the saints will be collected and divided. Those who have wholeheartedly accepted Jesus Christ as their Lord and Savior will be pardoned, for their price has been paid. But those who have not accepted Jesus, those who are not in the Book of Life, those who have hardened their hearts, those who have chosen disobedience, debauchery, destruction, and death will stand before the Lord God Almighty. They will stand under judgment for their sins. The price of sin is death. And they will be cast into the fire. There will be a great gnashing of teeth. That will be their end. That will be their fate. There is nothing worse than this.

And even the best of us, even us saints deserve this, but we are spared by the grace and mercy of God through Jesus Christ. It is a matter of choice. Choose life. Choose love. Choose peace. Choose freedom. Choose Jesus.

I pray that all who may read this will be touched by the Spirit of the Lord, and will pursue the love, grace, and mercy of God, will pursue Jesus, and have salvation, in Jesus's name. Amen.